Quick as a hawk Ralgon's blade flashed forward, catching an enemy in the neck. Blood burst out the wound, showering the dying man's companions and, much to their disadvantage, also Drangar's face. The disturbing image was reinforced; a stubbly head caked in fresh blood. Ralgon bellowed another challenge, tried to force his way into the breach, but the Chanastardhians closed the line almost at once. It was a maneuver executed with perfection; the Chosen applauded the enemy's morale and discipline.

I0641255

# SHATTERED FEARS

-Light in the Dark Book 3-

by ULFF LEHMANN

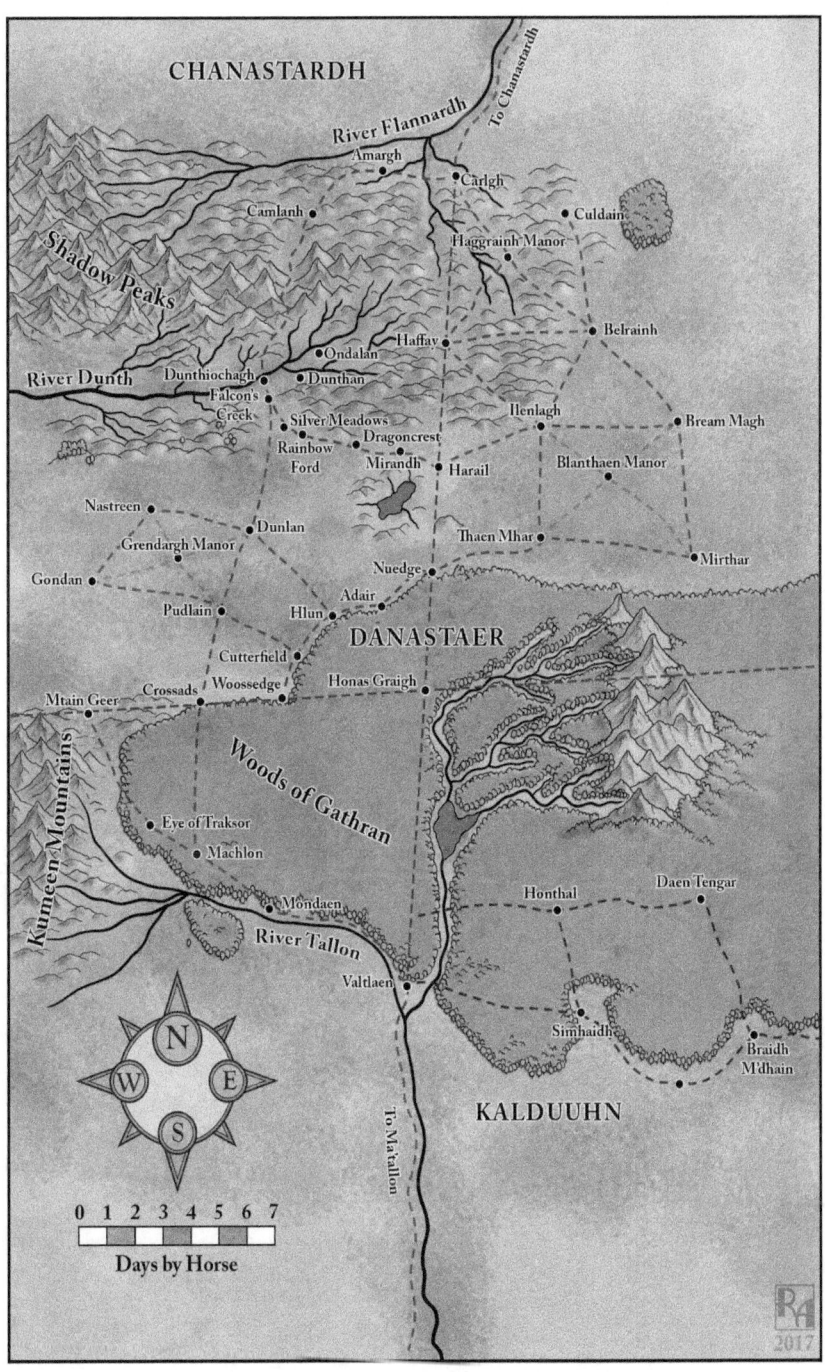

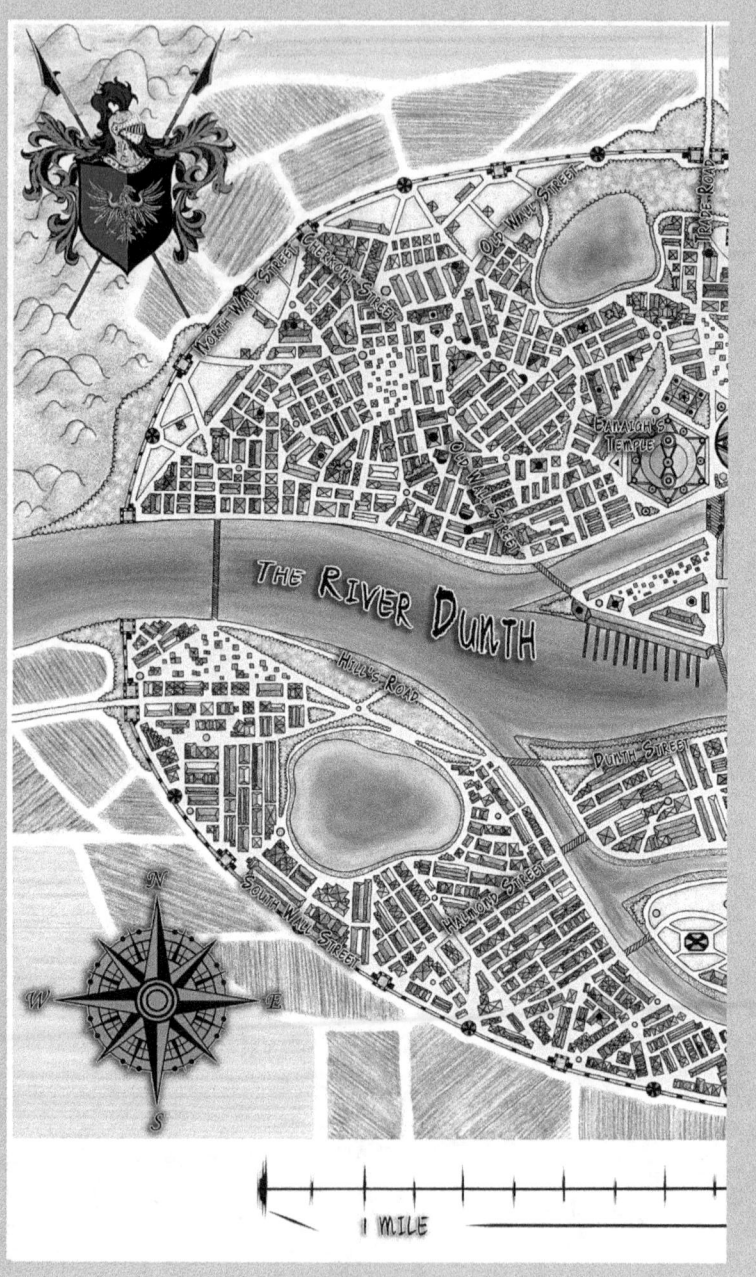

THE RIVER DUNTH

CAHILL MANOR

NORTH WALL STREET

LESGAIVAGH'S TEMPLE

THE PALACE

MILLER'S STRIP

HILLS ROAD

DUNTH STREET

TOWE ROAD

TRAIN STREET

SOUTH WALL STREET

HILLY'S ROAD

RADE ROAD

176 YARDS

# DEDICATION

*For my little monster, Charlotte, who is far too young to read any of this, for the time when she can.*

# ACKNOWLEDGMENTS

As with SHATTERED DREAMS and SHATTERED HOPES, I thank Katti Mattern who helped me hammer out the kinks, and Kathy Freuden, my friend and editor, for supporting me beyond my wildest; KathleenStammers, who gave me moral and artistic support from the get go; Anneke van Heusden and Ryan Ryker Lazslo for the inspiration, and David Dodd for giving the covers THE LOOK; Faith McKee for bringing Dunthiochagh to life; Riza Türker, for the first map; Sayan Mukherjee for the second map and for helping me flesh out the Woods of Gathran; and Robert Altbauer for taking all the stuff I, Riza, and Sayan had come up with and perfecting it. Rebekah Teller for emergency surgery on the blurb. Timy Takács for the last minute typo finding. My deepest gratitude, however, goes out to Daniela Bockhorst, without whom I never would have discovered who I really am; and Susanne Fritsch, who never gave up and kicked me until I went and got better.

I would also like to thank Charles Phipps, for believing in me, and David Niall Wilson for giving me this chance.

Without any and all of these wonderful people, this book would not be what it is!

# Dramatis Personae Shattered Fears

Anneijhan Cirrain—Chanastardhian noble
Arawn—a Son of Traksor
Baron Cumaill Duasonh—lord of the city of Dunthiochagh
Braigh—a Caretaker
Coimharrin—an Upholder
Dalgor—a Son of Traksor
Darlontor—Priest High of the Sons of Traksor
Drangar Ralgon—a mercenary
Ealisaid—a wizardess
Gail Caslin—a Caretaker
Gryffor—a Son of Traksor
Gwennaith Keelan—a squire
Jesgar Garinad—a thief
Kerral—Danastaerian General
Kildanor—a Chosen of Lesganagh
Lightbringer—a mysterious entity
Lloreanthoran—an elven mage
Nerran—friend and advisor to Baron Duasonh
Rheanna—an Upholder
Úistan Cahill–a nobleman
Urgraith Mireynh—High General of Chanastardh

# Pronunciation:

Some names, be it cities or persons, lean heavily on sounds not usually found in English.

For instance, ch and gh in Dunthiochagh sound similar to the Welch consonant ch, think Johann Sebastian Bach; same goes for Carlgh, for example.

# CHAPTER 1

## Thirtieth of Chill, 1475 K.C.

Lord Commander Noel Trileigh's return was happy news for Urgraith Mireynh. But instead of first reporting to the High General's tent, Trileigh paid wounded Callan Farlin a lengthy visit. Finally, when Mireynh was about to storm out his tent and disrupt the meeting, the Lord Commander entered.

"Good day, sir," Trileigh said, saluting. When his hand left the chest, the nobleman briefly grasped a pouch tied to his belt, as if finding reassurance in its presence.

"Why this visiting the sick business before coming to me?" Mireynh growled. "I'm about to begin bombarding the city, and any news that can help us is bloody welcome! Why did you dawdle, wasting your time with the cripple Farlin?" He didn't care if the scholarly noble or the Black Guards detected his anxiety. Damn them all, he thought. The assault had to happen now, or they would be forced to retreat to Harail, an act akin to failure in the High Advisor's eyes. And failure meant death to his family.

"I apologize, sir, for the delay. It was necessary." Trileigh looked calmer and less out of place than he had a few weeks earlier. Initially the noble had been nothing more than a fop, his pretentious affectations, the order to lay siege to impenetrable Dragoncrest, all of that had certainly left its mark on Mireynh and the others, not to mention the ridicule of the veterans.

"Necessary?" he asked, letting irritation seep into his voice. "Unless what you have to tell me is really a new divine manifest, I shall judge what is and is not important."

The time in Harail's Library had really changed the man. Trileigh closed his eyes, took a deep breath and then said, "Sir, with all due respect, it was you who sent me to find out how to battle wizardry. And judging from what occurred here a few days ago, we truly are dealing with magic." The Lord Commander's voice remained even, although he thought he detected the slightest hint of resentment.

"Well then, speak on," he said.

Trileigh remained silent, standing erect. What was the fool's problem now? Mireynh stared daggers at the noble. "Spill it, man; I have no patience for games!"

The noble's gaze met his, and for the first time he detected some fire inside. "You will address me by my name and title, High General, or at the very least my rank, sir."

"Are you mad?" he sputtered.

"Quite the opposite, sir. I am of House Trileigh, a cousin to King Drammoch, and part of the Royal Family. You, not taking into account your experience, are nothing more than a freeborn upstart. Despite this, I have given you the respect you deserve as leader of my cousin's troops. You, however, have not returned the favor. I am neither daft, nor some jester sent here for your amusement." There was nothing Mireynh would have liked better than to beat the man's superiority from his face. He held back, sensing, for the first time that maybe, despite Trileigh's lack of experience in anything battle-related, there was more to the man.

"I admit, High General, that your knowledge of warfare and combat are superior to mine, and I value your advice," the Lord Commander continued. "But your blatant disregard of my status and my expertise ends here, now."

For a moment Mireynh remained silent, stunned by the noble's vehemence. Had he treated Chanastardh's aristocracy like idiots? Sure he had. With a few notable exceptions they were a bunch of bickering sycophants unworthy of their titles. Still, when Drammoch had made Noel Trileigh Lord Commander and thus second only to himself, he had thought it a joke. Now, considering the steel in the man's voice, he wondered if he had underestimated the nobleman. House Trileigh was closely allied with the Royal House, but he had been disturbingly unaware of the nature of the relationship.

Finally, realizing he was staring, Mireynh averted his eyes and said, "I admit my mistake in underestimating you, milord." Summoning all his resolve, he added, "Still, I am your superior, and will not be intimidated by your standing at court. No matter how much you think it wise to proceed otherwise, you will inform me of your intentions, provided, of course, the situation allows it. Next time you decide to take a detour, keep me informed. Do we have an understanding, milord?"

Trileigh snapped a hand to his chest, saluting. "Yes, sir!" he replied.

Mireynh thanked the gods for being able to rein in his temper, and then returned to his chair and sat. "Have a seat, Lord Commander." He gestured to one of the other chairs that surrounded the table. For an instant he was tempted to offer the nobleman a drink, but then thought better of it. They were not on such friendly terms just yet. When Trileigh was seated, he asked, "All right then, what can you tell me? How can we defeat a wizard?"

"So now you believe me?" Trileigh asked, a slight smile playing about his lips.

"Can't be another explanation to what happened with our timber," he replied, fighting to keep his resentment down. Now that they had established a new set of rules, he already felt as if Noel Trileigh, like the Chanastardhian noble he was, would use the situation to his advantage.

The Lord Commander surprised him by spreading his hands and bowing his head. "I take no comfort in knowing I was right, sir."

Had he not known how treacherous nobles could be, he would have believed the apology. "Well then, what have you found out? How can we beat a wizard?"

"One moment," Trileigh said before he began to rummage in the pouch Mireynh had noticed earlier. The nobleman retrieved a sheaf of papers that were wound together. He untied the string and the mass of documents unfurled, revealing tightly scribbled notes in what had to be the Lord Commander's handwriting.

"Well?" Mireynh asked when the man had leafed through the pages a few times.

"You have to understand, sir, that there are some things one cannot easily solve within a Library as young as that in Harail," Trileigh said, looking at the first page.

"I thought they record all history."

"That is true. However, a Librarian starts penning history as it unfolds from the moment the last acolyte has entered the building, so to speak."

He arched an eyebrow, staring at the noble. "Are you saying that what we need is not in Harail since the city was founded after the Heir-War?"

"In a way, yes." Trileigh's eyes darted to a cluster of bottles that were accompanied by several mugs on another, smaller table. "Do you mind?"

A noncommittal shrug was Mireynh's reply, as he pondered what this revelation could mean for a defense against magic. The visit to Harail's Library could not have been a complete failure since the notes from the Lord Commander's pouch were certainly more than a quick reminder that nothing much had been found. Also, Trileigh had lingered in Harail for quite a while, which made him suspect the noble had indeed unearthed something.

Equipped with a filled mug, the King's cousin returned to his seat. He took a sip, and then set the container aside, retrieving the papers once more. "I found no direct references to how Halmond, your esteemed predecessor, managed to defeat Wizards. Those records can most likely be found either here in Dunthiochagh, or back home in Herascor."

"Here?" Mireynh echoed, regretting his lack of knowledge regarding the area.

"Certainly, sir," Trileigh said. "Dunthiochagh once was the capital of Dargh, a kingdom of minor influence, but still a kingdom; as such, it had its own Library. Everything east of the Elven Road up to where the Flannardh flows was the kingdom of Janagast, while everything west of it was Dargh. Well, not everything, the nations beyond retained their borders."

He grew impatient, already considering Trileigh a fool once

more. History lessons were not what he needed. "I need tactics on how to beat Duasonh's wizard," Mireynh snapped.

Just as the Lord Commander was about to respond, the tent's flap was lifted aside and Killoy's head poked inside. "The two 'throwers are ready now, sir."

"Start sending the packages," he replied.

"Yes, sir!" Killoy grinned, saluted and left. A few moments later, Mireynh heard the distinct creaking of slingthrowers being made ready to shoot. Duasonh would not be all that pleased with half-frozen body parts showering down on the southern end of his city.

To Trileigh he said, "Thank you for the arms, milord. Please continue."

Shaking his head, probably to rid himself of the gruesome image, the Lord Commander said, "Certainly, sir. As I was saying, there were no true historical records of the Heir-War in the Library's inner chambers. Those still rest in Dunthiochagh. In the archives open to the public, however, I hit gold, so to speak." The noble visibly became excited. "Several fighters, and no fewer than three Chosen, veterans of the Heir-War all, did pen their own memories of what had happened. Some of the texts are heavily edited, and I was unable to force my way to the originals. The Chief Librarian explained that the source-texts were never entrusted to the Library. It wasn't as if the actual battles had been omitted, rather that some passages had been blacked before the papers actually reached Harail."

"Yes, yes, enough chitchat," Mireynh said impatiently, waving his hands in circles to urge the nobleman on. "Get to the good stuff, will you?"

"As you wish, sir," Trileigh said, seeming slightly crestfallen, but right now there was no time for hurt egos. He had an escalade to win.

The slingthrowers had stopped lobbing sacks filled with body parts into Dunthiochagh by mid-afternoon, and were now pounding the city with stones. At the range the big engines were dug in, it was impossible to accurately aim for the walls, not that they needed a breach for the escalade. The return shots from the enemy artillery were as poorly aimed as theirs, and only a few actually caused damage.

Thankful for the trenches in which many of his warriors huddled, the only thing that bothered Urgraith Mireynh was his insane order to build siege castles when they had first come here. In hindsight it was always easy to analyze one's mistakes; that sort of armchair tactician thinking might have been good for drunken veterans reliving their glory days; it didn't help improve their odds now.

Someone on the defenders' side was paying attention. A barrage of stones fired from the city's eastern wall plowed into the troops assembling near the proposed siege castle construction site. Why had he relied so much on the promise of the High Advisor that traitors would open the gates for an easy invasion? Yes, it had worked with Harail, had promised easy victory with Dunthiochagh. It had also caused him to not prepare for a direct assault. Two slingthrowers were hardly enough to suppress the defender's activities, and the Danastaerians grew more daring.

The effective range of a siege engine was some four hundred yards; any precise aiming beyond that distance was impossible. But the artillerists on the city walls were adjusting. They had the high ground and were less prone to run out of ammunition. With every shot, the impact came closer to his positions. They sure couldn't aim properly, but were able to adjust their angles.

A succession of boulders hit the ground near the pits, skipped over the dug-up earthwork and continued to tumble on through the row of carts assembled beyond. Wood splintered, oxen howled in pain. Mireynh even heard some of the drovers scream. He glanced in the direction of the noise.

The boulders had cut a swath of bloodied, splintered wood through the depot that had stored his ammunition. Why the Scales had it been this important to attack at the onset of winter? He closed his eyes and turned away from the carnage.

Again, missiles from Dunthiochagh bounced across the field, this time tearing down a few of the horses tethered off to the side, beyond the pits. If this went on, the Danastaerians would beat his army by mere chance. "Drummers." Mireynh turned to the lads standing to his left. Their faces were ashen.

"Signal the advance." Best to face the enemy head on, otherwise those bastards would, by luck, eventually manage to beat the army's confidence.

Now, as the drums rang across the field, Duasonh and his band of bastards would have to quickly adjust their artillery if they wanted to slow them down. Mireynh allowed a grim smile to cross his lips when he saw clusters of soldiers rise in the trenches. Some heaved up planks that lay hidden in the holes, creating makeshift bridges across the ditches. From behind the tor, on either side, veritable streams of wooden barricades were pushed to the front. As each of the contraptions reached the timber crossings, double lines of thirty warriors stood and joined the men already pushing the shelters. Their pace increased.

Every second fighter pushed a handle that was attached on one side to a long pole fastened to a thick, uninterrupted, wooden roof, and on the other to a wheel taken from the disassembled wagons. Crossbars running from pole to pole gave the construction a minimum of stability, but it was enough. A third of the warriors carried between them ladders long enough to reach the merlons on top of the wall. Nailed to each side were shields to protect against missiles. Behind this vanguard came smaller bands of thirty each, again with a roof shared between them. If he hadn't miscounted some of the artillery, they were facing a half-dozen 'throwers, far too few to stop all the advancing columns.

And should Duasonh's pet wizard join the fray, the woman—Farlin had confirmed seeing a woman above the timber before it exploded—was in for a surprise; those pushing the wheels were equipped with bows. If the woman showed herself, she would be greeted with arrows. History had its uses, and if Trileigh's research was correct, a wizard could not concentrate on too many things at once. The assault was unusual, but so was the situation. He felt confident that southern Dunthiochagh would fall at dusk.

One of the wooden roofs splintered as a boulder struck, spilling mangled corpses left and right. A lucky hit, for his army was too quick a target for the enemy to effectively strike from afar.

"Distance?" he asked Trileigh who stood to his right.

The scholarly Lord Commander looked at the leading column and then at a chart in his hand. A moment later, he said, "Hundred and fifty yards left, sir."

The Danastaerians knew the distance as well, because as the slowing companies crossed that invisible line, arrows flew from Dunthiochagh. The missiles swarmed at a high angle across the sky, lodging themselves in roofs and shields. Some even slipped through the defenses. Mireynh saw a few groups falter then resume their advance, picking up speed once more. It was grueling work, but it had to be done.

Another roof caved, sending splinters and people flying as an enemy stone smashed through. Thankfully it wasn't one of the ladder carriers. The groups behind the shattered shelter veered off and closed ranks, just like he had ordered. Mireynh looked at Noel Trileigh. "Thank you for your assistance, milord."

"You already had the plan well in hand, sir, I only made a few suggestions," the nobleman replied. It was obvious Trileigh was grateful for the compliment. The Lord Commander looked at his chart and back to the advancing columns. "Less than a hundred yards now, sir."

The enemy's fire increased. Another line faltered. This time it was a ladder warband that stopped, but only briefly. In a matter of anxious heartbeats, they resumed their advance, leaving behind a few dead or wounded. And still the enemy fire came. Joining the mostly ineffective barrage of arrows were the tower-based ballistae. The shields and roofs offered little protection against those, and it was only thanks to the long reloading time that the damage wasn't as devastating as it could have been.

With a twang the engines on top South Gate began to fire, and the missiles went through the shields as if they were paper. Again, the advance paused, if only for a moment. With spears still embedded in walls and, most likely, people, the survivors pushed on. His warriors were determined to take the city, and angry with the arrogant defenders who hadn't had the decency to surrender beforehand. Mireynh smirked.

He would show the bastard Duasonh what it meant to fight.

The first ladder-bearers had reached the wall and were immediately greeted by oil raining down on them. Unperturbed, the mobile roof behind halted, opened the front shields, and released a group of archers. The Bows took aim and fired before the torch-wielding defenders could throw. They had only been able to practice the maneuver in theory, and he was amazed to see it executed to perfection. Now the shields would close again, and the soldiers pushing the cart would lift the contraption and rotate it until it stood perpendicular to the wall. At the same time the next unit in the column would take their place, again opening the front shields and shooting at Danastaerians who dared to throw either oil or torches. He had expected some of the movable roofs to go up in flames despite the tactic, and was, in a way, not disappointed. It seemed, however, that Duasonh's troops had not prepared enough oil to douse every ladder-band, or maybe there wasn't that much oil to keep the walls supplied. Either way, now that the second wave had established their parallel position, they would open the shields facing the wall and begin to return selective fire, whereas the subsequent units would attach to the lead roofs.

The first ladders were pushed up under cover of the archers. Now that the corridor had been established, the remaining companies pushed their shield-wagons up to the leading, perpendicular carts and set up a good score of yards behind them. Then they began to shoot as well.

In addition to a few blazing shield-wagons, it seemed as if the Danastaerians had managed to pour oil down a couple of ladders, for now there were also human torches falling to the ground. Still, his troops were scaling the walls.

Mireynh turned to Trileigh. "Nothing will go wrong now."

The noble shrugged noncommittally.

The sun was setting slowly and his soldiers were on Dunthiochagh's walls. Lesganagh was with them, the invasion of Danastaer would come to an end tonight, he was sure of it. Allowing himself a moment of self-indulgence, Urgraith Mireynh grabbed the skin of mead tied to his saddle and took a long pull. He felt good about himself and the world. Dunthiochagh would fall, his family would be safe, and his troops would be able to billet in the city's houses by midnight. Life, he felt, was good to him once more.

The escalade had not stopped by nightfall, but the fighting atop the walls hadn't subsided either. Mireynh dismissed another of Sir Duncan's messengers, turned to a runner, saying, "Relay this to Killoy: send in five hundred of the reserves, they're to bolster the center."

The young man gave a brief salute and departed. The High General was now less pleased with the day than he had been when the attack had started. It was almost evening and still Duasonh defied him. What was worse was that the escalades planned for the eastern and western parts of the wall had been repelled numerous times, and now the main attack had to do without the additional support from the flanks.

Pulling his cloak tight, he stared at the city's stony silhouette. The wall was packed with combatants. From a distance, even with fires burning within and without town, it was impossible to make out whose troops were whose. "Damn those Danastaerians," he grumbled.

"Sir?" Trileigh asked.

"Bastard Duasonh's good."

"Aye, sir, so it seems. But we can count ourselves lucky," the Lord Commander added.

"Why's that?" His eyes were back on the battle.

"The Baron's Wizard hasn't acted, yet."

He glared at the nobleman. "Don't you dare fucking jinx it!" He wasn't superstitious, but his initial confidence had soured while the escalade dragged on. "Don't fucking jinx it!"

Trileigh was about to reply when two things happened at once: the first was that an entire section of Dunthiochagh's wall, the part where his troops were thickest, or so he had hoped, was wiped clean as if someone had taken a broom and swept away dirt. And the second was the arrival of a blood-covered rider on a tired looking horse coming up their hill.

Mireynh didn't know where to look. Openmouthed

he stared at the empty portion of the battlement, and then glanced back at the rider who barely managed to leap free of his collapsing steed. It was Braddan Kirrich, leader of the force meant to take the crossing at Ondalan.

# CHAPTER 2

"Rise and shine, Princess." Briog's voice sounded louder inside the Palace's chamber. Rhea yawned, and stretched, blinking away last night's sleep.

"What?" she asked, not hiding the second, longer yawn, as she twisted her head toward the voice. Her sight fell upon him and in a heartbeat she was wide-awake.

Her fellow Rider stood beside her bed, wearing his plate-reinforced chain armor, the half helmet in the crook of his arm. His sword was already belted and his left hand rested comfortably on its pommel. "Nerran's called a meeting," he replied. "Get your ass out of bed, we're going to battle." Having said his piece, Briog headed back out.

She sat up, the pile of warm blankets slid into her lap and immediately the chill greeted her. "The Chanastardhians are moving?"

Inside the door her friend turned and shrugged. "No idea, but I doubt he wants to hold a prayer session for all of us."

"Where?" she asked, stifling another yawn.

"In Lesganagh's temple, where else?" He stepped out, adding, "Get ready and be there soon."

"Battle-ready?" Gods, she still was tired and her brain hadn't caught up with her wakening.

"No, Princess, wear your best gown," Briog retorted, winked at her, and then he closed the door.

"Bloody Scales," Rhea swore, then reminded herself which deity she served and added, looking to the hidden sky, "Sorry." The instant her feet touched the cold floor the last traces of sleep were purged from her body. She had to remember to wear socks even if her nights were not spent in the countryside. She doubted the Palace's staff would appreciate her wearing boots in bed. The rushes strewn about hardly kept the cold at bay, and this chamber was sparsely furnished, as were those of her fellow Riders—with the exception of Nerran's, of course. Maybe, she told herself, having cold feet kept the mind alert. At the very least it made waking up very easy.

A few hops later—she didn't dare to slowly walk to the sideboard—she stood before the basin and pitcher. Thankfully a servant had replaced last night's ice with something that actually resembled water. The rationing of firewood compelled most people to rely on fewer and fewer commodities that were essential to everyday life. Washing was one of those things people could very well do without for a while. The fires that still burned were mostly used for cooking, although rumor had it that Baron Duasonh's study, at least, was still well heated. No one really begrudged Lord Duasonh this small luxury, and considering that his own bedchamber was also freezing, it was a small enough exception. Hopefully other nobles were following his example. Rhea poured water into the basin and dipped her face in.

Spraying droplets of ice water, her head lashed back up. "Damnation! That wakes you up in the morning," she hissed. As if the cold tiles hadn't already done that. She washed hands and arms, and then she toweled herself dry. Would the servants heat water for her to wash her hair? No, this sort of thinking had been appropriate for little Princess Rhea, not for the woman she had become. Sometimes she could go days without reminiscing about the past; at other times, like now, the old reflex to ring for a servant when anything was amiss returned almost instantly.

Scowling and berating herself, she tied her hair into a knot, slipped into her stockings, and began to don her armor. "You've been a Rider for almost twenty years," Rhea said as she plunged her legs into the quilted hose. "An Upholder for even longer!" Next on came the chain leggings. "You haven't been the little, spoiled brat for a long, bloody time." Each of the last three words was accompanied by either a tug or a jump to make the armor fit snugly but comfortably about her legs.

"Don't complain, Priestess!" She let the quilted tunic slide down her head and chest, wriggled her arms inside. By now the knot had come undone and strands of hair tangled with the tunic's strings. "Bloody Scales!" she hissed again, this time not apologizing. If Lliania didn't understand the need for venting one's anger, so be it. Careful not to tear any hair out, Rheanna freed her head from the tunic and removed the underwear from the chainmail. Maybe she was still not as awake as she had thought, despite the cold water.

Or maybe her fumbling hands were due to the lack of morning conversation between herself and the other Riders. The meaningless banter, the snide remarks, she missed it.

Determined not to be the victim of her hair's betrayal again, she first retied her blonde mane and then pulled on the cloth cap that went underneath the chain coif. Then, finally, she slipped into the quilted tunic with far less bother than before. Her struggle into the mail shirt reminded her of another reason why she missed camping with the Riders. Here, in this chamber, there was nobody to help her get into the damned thing, and she was too stubborn to shout for assistance.

Finally, after a much longer time than anticipated, Rhea was fully suited up for war. If Briog had played her for a fool and the Chanastardhians were digging as happily as they had the past week or so, the bastard would pay. Shouldering her shield, she extinguished the lamp, and left the room.

The news of a coming battle hadn't been a joke. Throughout the Palace she encountered armed men and women, Swords, Pikes, Bows, troops of every denomination seemed busy on one errand or another. It wasn't only warleaders hurrying to and fro, but also wardens requisitioning additional supplies from the master-at-arms. No one paid attention to her, which was just the way she liked it. She had left behind the tabard identifying her as an Upholder on purpose; the last thing she wanted was to be asked to settle some dispute while her friends were fighting.

"Looks like they'll try an escalade," someone said.

"First, they invade in late autumn and now they try to take our wall?" another replied, snorting with derision.

"An escalade," scoffed a third, a woman. "Bloody likely. We'll mow down every bastard that gets within a hundred fifty yards."

"You Bows always bite off more than you can chew," the first speaker chuckled.

"You watch..." Rhea passed out of earshot into the inner bailey.

Today all the gates were open, even the drawbridge was down, the Baron and his staff obviously more concerned with a steady flow of traffic than security. She couldn't blame them. The password nonsense had taken up more time than anything else when entering the Palace.

A few moments later she was on Trade Road, dodging a cart laden with bushels of arrows speeding southward. Maneuvering through the rest of the traffic was easy, as it was almost non-existent, with the exception of columns of warriors marching toward Old Bridge. Most of the troops were billeted south of the Dunth, but things had gotten so crowded down there that the warleaders had finally been forced to requisition chambers, even entire buildings, from the people in the old part of town. Some of the richer citizens, she knew, had complained about the military taking over their property, and it had taken respectable nobles, like Úistan Cahill, to convince the others that this was indeed in their best interest.

Rhea chuckled, shaking her head. Some people would never know what was good for them, even if it whacked them in the face.

Lesganagh's Temple was still little more than an empty husk. In times of war the pragmatic followers of the Lord of Sun and War knew very well where to focus their energies, and, unlike certain Eanaighists, maintaining or restoring the crumbling façade was of no importance. The doors stood open, and echoing from the interior she heard Nerran's voice, distinctive and commanding as usual, talking, no preaching, in a way she had last heard him speak when addressing the fool Danaissan and his gang.

"... we will not yield, none of us. Lesganagh is with us, standing tall, burning strong, strengthening our shields and swords.

You…"—Rhea entered and saw the Paladin standing before not only the Riders but a host of people—"… you all know that He is Lifegiver and taker, He shines upon our fields, makes our crops grow. He protected this city…"—not only warriors were listening, she saw craftsmen, dockworkers, housewives, freeborn and villeins—"… and He has not turned His eye away from us. As long as we people of Dunthiochagh are strong and firm in our belief that it is us, not them, who deserve to be here as we have for generations, who will do everything we can do to keep the enemy out, He stands behind us, guiding our hands, searing those who stand in our way!"

Rhea found herself as entranced by the speech as the others. She saw a carter share a solemn nod with a richly dressed merchant. The pair weren't alone in this, all over the place, men and women of disparate backgrounds locked steely, determined gazes onto each other. Somebody placed a firm hand on her shoulder, squeezing it. Surprised, she turned her head and saw the toothless smile of an old man, a beggar most like, his walking staff held like a lance. "We'll get them, lassie, eh?" he said, and despite the gummy mumble she heard the man's resolve. A resolve she shared.

"Aye," she replied, returning his smile. "We'll get them." Whether the old beggar would be of use on the wall or not, she could hardly tell, but she was certain he would do something to harass the Chanastardhians.

Never before had she heard Nerran speak with such conviction, such force. He had always been mouthy, arrogant, a sarcastic remark never far from his lips. Sure, she knew about his faith and calling, every Rider knew, though their loyalty had never been based on his eloquence.

"Now, my fellow warriors, go out and gather those who can wield arms! Tell them those who do not fight do not deserve to live! We all shall fight for our homes! And remember, as long as a single soul remains, Dunthiochagh cannot fall!"

Instead of the expected shout, the people filed out in silence. Their eyes, however, showed the storm roaring inside of them. The old beggar patted her shoulder, saying, "See you on the field, lassie." Then he was gone. It was unlikely she would see the man again, but whether she did or not, she knew he would spread Nerran's message.

Another man, brawny with blond hair, passed her, nodded, and said, "Good luck, Princess." She blinked, trying to remember who he was. Then she knew. He had been one of the refugees from Camlanh who had helped them to block Shadowpass. She wanted to return the favor, wish him good fortune as well, but the mason had already left the temple. Again, like the beggar's, a face she might never see again.

When the procession had ended, the only people left inside were the Riders and, to Rhea's surprise, General Kerral. She headed for the cluster of armored warriors. Fynbar slapped her shoulder affectionately; Gail nodded in greeting, and her fellow priest Kyleigh saluted. The others noted her approach and welcomed her grimly. This was no gathering of friends as much as it was a farewell. She had no doubt that some of them would fall; even she wasn't invulnerable.

"You'll see to it that those who need weapons receive them?" General Kerral asked.

"Damn right," Nerran replied. "The master-warden already emptied out the armory. The only reserves we have are arrows, but once they take the walls those'll be useless anyway." The Paladin looked her way. "Ah, Upholder, ready for the killing?"

"To defend the innocent? Always," she replied.

"Not sure we got many of those here," Nerran grunted.

"There's nothing just about this war; I am committed." To the Danastaerian general she said, "What makes you so sure the attack comes today?"

"They had a healthy breakfast," Kerral replied. He must have seen her questioning look, and added, "Mireynh always hands out extra rations before a fight; bastard claims it brings luck."

"An escalade?" Nerran asked.

"Aye, he only has two slingthrowers, not enough to bring down the wall," the soldier answered. "Only thing we have to worry about is the bastards on the battlements." He paused then said, "I need to prepare." The general seemed not to be one for idle chat or courtesies, for he simply turned and marched away.

Nerran turned to them. "You heard the man, an escalade. Bloody business that, as some of you know. Get spears to stab the enemy while he's on the ladders. Those of you who can effectively use a bow, take it with you as well."

"Where'll we be?" Briog asked.

"Where we're needed," the Paladin said.

"So, you yielded command to General Kerral?" Gail said, frowning. "Ain't he too much of a hothead?" Rhea shared the Caretaker's sentiment, even if her assessment was purely based on secondhand information.

"Fuck no!" Nerran spat. "Cumaill and I have final say over things, Kerral will be part of the defense, yes, he'll command his own, but he will not be in command of anything else. He knows that, and even though his feathers are ruffled he will obey. Anything else?" He waited a moment and, when none of them had further questions, said, "You'll be doing what you do best, lads and lasses. Go to where you can do some good. Well, not good, but... well, you know what I mean." He chuckled. "Now, go out and kill the bastards!"

At noon the Chanastardhian slingthrowers began firing. Rhea and Briog were on the southern wall, their horses in Kyleigh and Fynbar's care below, while they observed events from atop the battlement.

"That's no stone," Briog muttered, scowling. "What the Scales are they doing?"

A moment later, when the missile landed somewhere beyond and shouts of panic could be heard, they were none the wiser. "Horse shit?" Rhea suggested.

"Packed horse shit, that's good." The reply sounded light-hearted, but she had known the man for such a long time to know he was not speaking in jest. "Now we wait."

The enemy's artillerists were good; she had to admit that much. Instead of the rather long wait she expected, the slingthrowers tweaked into action once more only a good two score of breaths later. The missile tumbled through the air, lacking the power of a properly thrown rock. Now that Rhea knew what to look for, she saw, in the blink of an eye, what the projectile was.

"That's a sack," she and Briog said in unison.

The Caretaker snorted. "Maybe you're right about the dung," he said.

Of the next pair of shots, one sack was not as tightly closed as its twin. It opened in midflight, right above their spot of the wall, and spilled its contents.

At first, Rhea was unsure what it was that splattered down. There were irregular bits of some sort of material, small and thick, brown and tan. In between these chunks of whatever it was, she saw the occasional spot of white.

Briog must have recognized what it was, for he only said "Gods!" then shook a piece off his shoulder, his face white with disgust.

Nearby she heard something clatter on the wall's granite. She turned, more out of instinct than curiosity. The horses below on New Wall Street grew restless, whinnied in fright. Then she saw what had hit the stone: part of a severed human skull. The raising of the dead enemies a few nights back had already been disrespectful of the departed, even if Deathmasks had performed the ceremony, but the Chanastardhians had done what she had thought impossible. Desecrate the corpses even further.

Rhea knew that the souls were already in the Bailey Majestic; some of them might have already been weighed in Lliania's Scales. Yes, she knew it was commonplace to lob the occasional corpse or two into a besieged city or fortress, but even the Deathmasks would not dare chop the remains of a human into hand-sized chunks.

Beside her, Briog knelt down, staring at the fragmented pieces. "Gods," he whispered.

"The gods only help on rare occasions," a warrior woman near them said. Rhea looked at her face, a hardened mask caught in a perpetual scowl. "They let things proceed, because in the end only we can shape our futures." The woman spat on the partial skull and kicked it off the wall. She knew how this gruff person felt and could guess why she felt the way she did; Rhea had experienced the same sort of anger when she had fled her father's palace.

"Whom did you lose?" she asked.

"What's it to you?" came the reply.

"Just wondering how your heart turned to stone?"

The warrior scoffed derisively. "Steel more like."

"Well?" Briog asked, the revulsion had fled his face and he looked at the Chanastardhian embrasures once more.

"They butchered my family," replied the soldier. "Was with General Kerral, joined his army at Haffay. When they had beaten us at Carlgh, we dispersed, I tracked my way home. Was easy, they don't care about people in threadbare clothes. Tossed my gear in a ditch. Came home and found my family dead. Husband strung up in the common room. My eldest, Banya,"— Rhea thought she saw the soldier's eyes watering—"the bastards used her. She must have fought them; they overpowered her. Lass was only twelve." After a brief pause, she added in a grim voice, "They'll pay!"

The image of the raped daughter invoked anger so powerful that Rhea had to turn away, clenching her sword's hilt. She had seen corpses of defiled women before, recalled the terror in their eyes, and knew it was best to speed the perpetrators onto Lliania's Scales, though sometimes she thought death was too merciful for these beings. "Who?" she asked, already knowing what the answer would be.

"Them," the warrior replied. "They'll pay."

No doubt there were many people with similar experiences inside Dunthiochagh. There might even be some children who had either survived the same ordeal as young Banya, or had seen the same dreadful deed done to their relatives.

"Any evidence on what faction of Chanastardhians was responsible?" Briog added. Rhea nodded her thanks for the clarification. "Surely not all of them are such animals."

"Found this," replied the stone-faced soldier, retrieving a bit of torn cloth from her belt. "In Banya's hand."

Her fellow rider looked at the shred and shook his head.

"May I?" she asked, holding her hand out. Reluctantly the warrior handed her this sign of her grief. Embroidered onto the sliver of green silk was a golden hawk, wielding a silver lance, definitely not the garb of a common foot soldier. Silk, too expensive for any but the wealthiest to buy, much less flaunt. One of Banya's tormentors was of noble blood. Rhea turned north, walked to the edge of the battlement, and looked for Diorbail in the cluster of riders below. If anyone knew Chanastardhian heraldry it was she.

She spotted the Caretaker next to Fynbar, sharing a strip of jerky with her fellow priest. "Diorbail, get your ass up here, need to show you something!" she hollered down. Off to the north, maybe fifty yards from where she stood, another sack of human flesh splattered onto Dunthiochagh. Just how many bodies had the Chanastardhians butchered? She finally asked the woman for a name.

"Genny of Haffay, daughter of Boann."

Rhea introduced herself and Briog, the said, "Diorbail hails from Chanastardh; she'll probably know whose crest this is."

Genny's lips became a firm line. "Not all people from there are butchers, same as not all Caretakers," she grinned at Briog, "are idiots."

Their fellow Rider arrived as another pair gruesome missiles struck somewhere behind, saying, "I hope the people won't panic too much." Then, looking Genny over, "What gives?"

Rhea answered, "Know whose coat of arms this is?" She held out the piece of silk. Diorbail took one look at the thing, her face twisted in disgust.

"House Argram," she replied. "House of butchers and rapists."

The Chanastardhian woman cocked an eyebrow and asked, "What's it to you?" Her gaze wandered from Rhea to Genny and held the woman's glare.

"Her daughter," Briog began the explanation, but Diorbail held up her hand, interrupting him.

"No need to say more." To Genny she said, "I'm truly sorry for your loss. House Argram is a bunch of mercenary cutthroats. Even the decent scions of the House are seen as weak if they do not participate in the rape and plunder that their sires subscribe to."

That caught Rhea's attention. "Are you saying that this might well have been a rite of passage for one of the sons?" The brief nod her companion gave was all the answer she needed. "Gods! Genny, find your vengeance, Lliania's blessing go with you."

"Not all my countrymen are bastards," Diorbail added, returning the sliver of cloth to Rhea. "Despite this obvious display of cruelty, many are quite decent. Good hunting." She turned and stalked off.

Another missile struck a nearby roof, showering them in half-frozen, half-rotted remains. A stout man retched up the remains of his breakfast.

# CHAPTER 3

D ressed in armor that was far too uncomfortable for his liking, Jesgar rode down Trade Road across Old Bridge. The Baron had permitted him to visit his family one last time before he would join the defenders atop the wall.

"I know the thick of battle is not the best place for a spy, but frankly if the city falls, I really won't have much use for you as it is," Baron Duasonh had said.

Now he wore chain, had a shield on his back, and an assortment of weaponry attached to belt and saddle. His reflection in one of the not-nailed-shut windows showed what many of his drinking buddies had always hinted at, what many a wench had found so attractive about him. He didn't share their sentiment. Had he wanted to join a warband, he would have done so. "I'm no warrior," he muttered, regarding his image one more time, before giving his mare the heels.

At the intersection to Dunth Street, a Sword-Warden called out. "Oi! You!"

Jesgar reined his mare in. "Yes?"

"Your name and warleader!" the man barked.

"None of your business, and none of your concern," he replied calmly, fishing a piece of parchment from his cloak. "Read this and let me pass."

The Warden flushed scarlet, was about to start screaming in his best drill instructor's manner when he took the paper and read the few lines written there. He cast a dubious glance at Jesgar, looked at the parchment once more, and then handed it back. "I beg your pardon; good hunting, sir."

He had never been called "sir" before, and truth be told

Jesgar didn't like it. Being addressed thus on the street was a sure invitation for all sorts of scum to come crawling out of their holes. He knew. Certainly, he had never been an ordinary robber or mugger, but he had far more in common with the criminal element than with even the lowest part of nobility.

The buildings he passed on his way toward Halmond were boarded up: little fortresses the owners hoped would keep invaders at bay. Some people had gathered where Trade Road led across the first canal. They were armed and surprisingly well armored. "Young Garinad?" one of them said. Jesgar halted his ride and scrutinized the throng. Many familiar faces looked up at him; some wore steel-caps, others leather. He made out the butcher Gabhan whose knives he had sharpened several times. There were the coal trading brothers Kester and Llud of Hill's Road, Jard Junath of Trann Street. They all stared at him, most likely astonished about the quality of his gear, not to mention his riding a mare branded with the Baron's seal.

"What are you doing here?" the same voice asked and now he discovered the speaker. It was Reghed, one of Ben's oldest friends. "Your brother said you made a run for it."

"Obviously not," Jesgar replied. "Isn't he with you?"

A chuckle coursed through the group. "Nah, mate," Jard answered. "Still busy trying to convince Maire she's better off across the river, away from all this fighting business."

He snorted, remembering all too well how headstrong Maire was when she set her mind to something. "You be patrolling the streets then?"

"Aye," Kester, the older of the two brothers said. "Someone has to be, don't want that thieving scum taking advantage of the chaos. The constables are on the wall, we was charged with playing watch." He doubted the Warden of the Watch had asked them to "play" patrolmen; it was Kester's way of making a task look easier than it actually was. "How about you, mate?"

Looking as he did, Jesgar saw no point in denying where he was headed. "I'll be on the wall, fighting."

"Big Ben won't like that one bit," Reghed remarked. "But then again, he'll probably be busy keeping Maire from the wall. That lass is intent on defending her home. Can't say I blame her. Would be on the wall myself, might still go there once we bashed some looting lowlifes." He didn't doubt the man's claim. Though his chainmail looked much repaired and was in sore need of an oiling, the wine-merchant and his group looked quite capable of dealing with a gang of thugs.

His fist tapped his chest in salute. "Good hunting." Then he was off again, heading home.

Halmond Street was much busier than anything north of Dunth Street. Warriors were milling about, organizing where carts laden with sheaves of arrows were supposed to go, and directing the final assembly of one of the big slingthrowers in the middle of the street. To one side of the massive weapon there was still enough space for carts to pass, but half of the road's breadth was occupied by the 'thrower. Jesgar noted the engine sat in front of merchant Wannad's house, its ammunition dumped right on the front lawn. He had always thought of Wannad as a temperamental man—almost Ben's equal when it came to shouting to get his way—and was astounded to see the middle-aged, pot-bellied merchant actually helping the engineers set up the slingthrower.

Looking around, Jesgar wondered how the engineers would be able to adjust the weapon, and then saw the lookout posted on top of the next building to the south. At the end of Halmond Street, where it met Hill's Road, another 'thrower was in the final stages of assembly. To his surprise both Bennath and Maire were busily pulling tight winches at the engine's bottom, their backs turned toward him.

"For the last time," he heard Ben grunt, "you will not be going anywhere near the battlements, understood?"

"Oh, so you really expect me to wait at home and invite the next best Chanastardhian bastard in to ravage me? Where will you be, defending my honor in a melee on the wall?" Maire retorted. "Shall I wear the mail you helped me make on the next festival instead of a proper gown? Is that it?" Jesgar saw a couple of engineers smirk, and his sister-in-law turned on them with the same viciousness. "What are you laughing at?" she snarled them into silence.

"Gods, woman, I don't want you facing danger," Ben said.

"By turning my back on it, it won't go away! I can handle a blade and a bow, you know."

"So can others, real warriors, ain't that right, boys?"

The engineers wisely remained quiet. "There are fighting women as well, you know," Maire reminded him. She turned to glare at Ben and stopped, scrutinizing Jesgar as he reined his horse to a stop. "Would you look at this!" she exclaimed, dropping the winch to face him.

Ben, confused, glanced over his shoulder and muttered, "I'll be damned." He also let go of the winch. "The Baron's drafted you, eh?"

Gods, he hoped this would not turn into yet another argument. He had had enough of those after being drugged and used for someone else's purpose. "No, I volunteered," he said. "Best thing I could do after the mess I made."

"Well, be that as it may, please tell my wife she is not to fight," Ben ordered, much to Maire's obvious anger.

He prevented her rising outbreak by saying, "She has a right to defend her home, same as everyone."

"But…" Ben sputtered.

How he did not want to get involved in his sibling's marital dispute. Sooner or later they would surely reconcile, with Bennath giving in to his wife's demands, though he doubted it would be before the enemy was near. By then it would be too late. "No buts," he interrupted. "You can't keep her out of harm's way, because, even if you send her to the Palace, the Chanastardhians might get there as well and then she'd be fighting for her life just the same, brother. At least this way she can choose where to make her stand."

"What do you know of such things?" Ben roared, and Jesgar saw how distressed he really was. His older brother had tried and failed to control every issue in their lives, and now, when reason was against him, he used force of will.

To him it was becoming a tired game. He had endured more than enough warfare to last several lifetimes already, had seen things Ben would hopefully never see, and for the first time realized just how small his brother's world was. The memory of his flight back to Dunthiochagh during the attack of the walking dead brought a shudder he could barely suppress. Instead of reacting the way he had always done, by telling his older sibling just how much he knew better, Jesgar merely said, "Enough to know she has a right to defend herself."

Maire nodded in gratitude and Ben just stared at him. Into the ensuing silence he said, "I'd like to share what might well be the last time, with people I love. I am going to the wall and the next time we see each other may well be on the Bailey Majestic, or in the Halls, so are we going to spend this time arguing about nonsense you already know is decided, or are we going to sit together like a family?" He focused his attention on Ben, saw how the realization that this might well be the last time the brothers saw each other sank in, and for a brief moment caught a glimpse of the affection Ben had so rarely shown him.

The promise to look after Maire had come lightly, but now, as the first real missiles thundered overhead in both directions, Jesgar wasn't so sure he could keep it. They stood on the strip of wall east, near South Gate, and watched the approaching columns of the enemy's wooden shelters close in.

"Bastards'll try an escalade," a gruff Warden to their left muttered and spat. "Watch your faces, ladies!"

Maire cast a questioning glance his way. He shrugged. "No idea what he means," he whispered.

The Warden must have heard him for he turned their way, spitting once more. "They'll bring 'em up close, put up a bunch broadside facing us, and then shoot up at any bugger silly enough to take decent aim. We'll send oil down, and then it's gonna be sheer luck if our torches ignite the bastards, cuz we can't aim the fires either. So, watch your faces, ladies." The veteran was loud enough to be overheard by everyone around, and those who had been as much in the dark about this tactic as Jesgar and Maire acknowledged his advice. "Bows!" the Warden added. "Aim for the feets; that don't kill 'em, but it'll slow 'em!" Thankfully the Bow-Warden nearby took no offense at having another warband's member give her troops such an order.

The wagon-like constructions advanced steadily, at intervals the Chanastardhian slingthrowers sent rocks crashing into the city beyond, and the weapons—he saw two smaller 'throwers mounted on towers left and right—responded in kind. The look-outs, people with keen eyes, shouted directions and distance of the enemy, and again stones flew across the plain, arching toward the advancing foe. Several of the steadily approaching roofs shattered when boulders plunged into them, scattering wood and bones. Jesgar tried not to think of the mothers, fathers, brothers, and sisters who would never again see their children or siblings. It all felt so stupid. Why were those people dying out there here? Did they even know the reason? If not, what had they been told by their lords when the muster came?

Those wagon-shelters unhurt by the slingthrowers moved on steadily, leaving behind the smudges of blood from the fallen. Behind him he heard a woman—or was it a man? He couldn't tell—lament the loss of somebody or something. Briefly he won-dered why he didn't hear more shouts of grief; the enemy's stones had hit more than merely one house, he was certain of it. Then he realized that this one voice was the only one to be heard amidst the din of whirring boulders, creaking wood and leather, and the jingling of chain as the warriors atop the wall stepped uneas-ily from one foot to the other, waiting for the storm that was to come.

"One fifty!" a lookout shouted. Gods, they were fast! "Artillery, keep your distance!" the woman added.

All along the battlement Bow-Wardens shouted their com-mands. "String bows! Nock arrows!"

"Aim for the feet!" the gruff Sword-Warden added.

"Release and shoot the bastards!" a thunderous voice added. "Send the bastards into Jainagath's care!" It sounded familiar, and Jesgar turned west to make out who had given the order. Beside him, Maire had strung a longbow he hadn't known she possessed. She, and a few others he saw, heeded the Warden's suggestion, taking careful aim. For an instant he wondered how such a lithe person as Maire could pull the string to her ear with-out breaking a sweat. She didn't even notice his stare. He knew next to nothing about archery, only that one had to be raised on shooting a longbow to actually manage to fire off arrow after arrow, and now, for the first time, he saw how strong his sister-in-law's shoulders were. Under a shawl, which she always wore inside the house, she seemed so small. If truth were told, he had never really seen her work with iron, and now that he knew, he wondered why Ben had been so angry with her. Another arrow sped toward the advancing Chanastardhians. Maire followed its path, smiled in satisfaction, and drew the next missile from her quiver.

Jesgar shook his head and looked once again to the west, to South Gate, and saw that the Baron's standard was raised atop the barbican. Now he knew. It was clear that the Baron was cheering his troops on.

"Gotcha," Maire breathed as she retrieved another arrow.

A huge armored figure rose behind her, she didn't even notice the newcomer. Her right hand released the feathered shaft and without bothering to search for the next shot, her hand drifted to the quiver. Jesgar now realized who stood at her back, halting her searching hand with his own: Ben. "Cheeky bastard, stop that funny business," Maire grumbled at the intercepting hand. Viciously she tried to shake off her husband's grip.

"I'm sorry, dove," grumbled Bennath Garinad. That stopped her, and she whirled around. "You're right."

Both Maire and Jesgar raised their eyes, astonished. As long as he had known his brother, he had never witnessed him apologizing for anything in public. They both got a better look at Ben, which Maire broke off immediately, saying "Busy shooting, will admire you later." She turned back to the advancing enemy and resumed firing. Runners along the wall replaced depleted quivers with filled ones while the Swords and Pikes waited for the inevitable assault.

"Fifty!" the lookout shouted.

Jesgar glanced back at the field, saw more smudges of blood and scattered wood, but also a whole lot more of the wagon-roofs. He looked back at his brother who, much like the smith he was, wielded a heavy maul. "Let's fight together, little brother," Ben said, slapping his shoulder. "Let the Chanastardhians know what the Garinad brothers can do!" In a whisper, he added, "Forgive me for doubting you; I never should have said the things I said."

He was about to reply, when the Sword-Warden near them shouted, "Get ready!" The call echoed from both sides, and a pair of nearby warriors hoisted several skins, presumably filled with oil. Briog had spoken about them on their way to Dragoncrest. One oilskin was thrust into his still empty hands.

"Aim low," Maire hissed, "in the direction I'm shooting."

"Throw!" As the flammable material left his hand, Jesgar realized he was not the only one who had heard her. Those nearby who were armed with skins had lobbed theirs in the same direction. Multiple splashes and frightened Chanastardhian voices showed they had hit their target. "Torches!" the wardens shouted.

"I'll get that, lad!" he heard Ben's voice rumbling from behind. There was a muttered assent, and then his older brother stepped forward.

"Get back, Ben!" Maire and Jesgar hissed in unison.

He turned to them, smiling. "Trust me; I know what I'm doing."

"Ben!" Maire's voice was part plea, part command, and fully concerned. "Step back!"

"Gods, woman, this is simple."

Jesgar leaped forward, hoping to catch his brother before he poked his head above the battlement, the gruff Sword-Warden hollered at Ben to stay back, but his brother did not listen. He threw a contemptuous glance at the warrior, and then looked down at the attackers, arm and torch poised to throw.

The ensuing twang of released strings and the immediate thud of missiles striking home rang like thunder in Jesgar's ears. For a brief moment he hoped it had been arrows shot from the Bows atop the wall—he prayed it was Danastaerian missiles—but when Ben reeled back and sank to the ground, one arrow lodged in his forehead underneath the helmet, and another sticking out of his chest, it felt as if time and life itself had halted. He saw his brother's descent to the stonework like he would have seen a feather tossed out a window slowly gliding to the ground below. Ben! He wanted to scream. His voice refused to obey. He wanted to rush to his brother's side. His legs denied him service. He wanted to jump back in time to prevent his brother from going to the merlons. The gods did not grant his wish.

For a moment it seemed as if Ben waved for him, but it was only his left hand flopping onto the floor and coming back up. All sound ceased to exist. His knees buckled. He dropped to the ground, clawed air to reach his brother. His brother, who had been more like a father to him. His brother, who had taught him how to measure horseshoes and how to nail them to hooves. His brother, who had always yelled at him for missing out on his chores. His brother, the only link to a mother and father he had never known.

Dead.

He heard the sharp intake of breath, a gasp, a stifled wail, and then a determined grunt. Maire stepped into his field of vision, bent down, and retrieved the torch. Through the blur of tears in his eyes Jesgar saw how she tossed the burning wood, sending it in a high, spinning arc across the battlement.

Ben was dead.

Too stunned to comprehend what had happened, he stared at the lifeless shell that had been his brother. Despite the cold, Ben hadn't put on gloves, just like he did... had done when working anywhere. Hands as big as plates, callused from all the hard labor with hammer and kiln, were just as limp as those of the walking dead.

No! He forced his thoughts away from that image. How could he compare his brother to one of those? Ben was... was...

Dead.

"Get on your feet!" someone snarled at him. Jesgar looked about. Smoke stung his already weeping eyes.

Big Bennath Garinad was dead. How was that possible? Just a moment ago he had been the same thickheaded brother he had loved to hate as a child. Ben had cuffed him more times than he could count, usually for the mischief he had been responsible for. Now Ben was dead.

"On your feet!" the voice repeated. Through the blur of smoke and tears Jesgar saw an armored figure looking his way. "Gods, you're as daft as your brother at times!" Maire—was this really his sister-in-law?—snapped.

"They're coming!" someone yelled.

He didn't see the swing, but he felt the sting of the slap. Combined with the chilly air, that was enough to make him realize where he was. It wasn't the rumbling reminder of Ben's death that echoed through his brain anymore. Now the only thing he heard was "they killed him" reverberating again and again through his mind.

The backs of his gloves were covered in chain, so he wiped his eyes clear with the inside of his left hand while his right grasped his brother's maul. Wordlessly he stood just as a Chanastardhian ladder smacked against the merlons. They would pay, he told himself, and at the same time some part of his mind reminded him of the danger of stepping too close to the battlement. He would not suffer the same fate as his brother.

More arrows whistled over his head into the city. Their Bows couldn't even return fire. Off to his right someone shouted for the archers to retreat. He felt a weight settle on his shoulder, glanced aside, and saw Maire, her face betraying her grief despite the fierceness in her eyes. He didn't hear her, blood and shouts roaring through his ears. Finally, she leaned over and kissed his cheek. Another barely felt squeeze on his shoulder; and then she hurried down, carrying her bow and two quivers.

Jesgar knew there was something he was supposed to be doing; he just couldn't remember what it was. Blood, rage, shouts, grief, everything he heard within and without joined into a cacophony he finally released in a scream as the first enemy hand showed itself on the battlement. A swing that bore the same pent up emotions accompanied the maul's head as it came down, smashing the attackers' fingers to bloody pulp.

Moments later a head poked up. He drove the weapon into the woman's skull, still keeping his distance. The handle was, thankfully, long enough. "Get the ladder, boy!" someone next to him hollered into his ear, but he waited. Ladders could be replaced; every shattered corpse flopping down into the waiting enemy would tell the Chanastardhians what awaited them when they faced Jesgar Garinad, brother to Bennath Garinad.

The force of his next strike was so hard that the glove casing the hand split at the seams, splattering gore and bone across the stonework. His ears registered the pained howl for the first time. He didn't care. Ben was dead and he would make them pay. All he saw was the twin pieces of wood poking over his section of the wall. An arrow whistled past and he jumped back. Almost too close to the killing zone the enemy archers had set up! Jesgar waited.

Next was a foe smart enough to hold his shield above his head before he ascended. Wood and steel shattered like cheap pottery under the force of his maul. That Chanastardhian too tumbled down, screaming.

Evening came, fast in his opinion. He was tired, of killing, of wielding this maul, of having screamed his voice raw. And still the enemy came.

Jesgar could barely lift the blood-smeared hammer above his head to deliver the next blow. Instead, he saw a spear dart past him, straight into the face of the bastard trying his luck here. Exhausted, he glanced to the right and saw a young woman, a Pike if he remembered his heraldry, giving him a grim nod. "You've done quite enough," she said. "Get down and find a healer to look at your wounds."

He stared at her. She was the most beautiful thing he had ever seen, but she didn't even notice. Instead she pushed past him, her spear flashing forward once more. "Get off this wall," she repeated, pushing him away.

How he got down to the street, he couldn't remember. When his feet hit cobblestone, he almost stumbled, the fall reminding him of something he had forgotten up there, on the battlement. "Ben," Jesgar groaned, staggering back to his feet. "Can't leave him there." He wheeled about, determined to make his way back up the stairs. "Ben," he muttered, putting one weak leg before the other.

He had to get his brother away from there; it was the least he could do for... Gods!

"Maire!" he tried to shout. His promise to Ben to look

after her! He hadn't kept it, had forgotten he'd given his word. "Maire!" Jesgar muttered again.

A hand halted his ascent. He turned to face the person stopping him, repeating his brother's wife's name through torn lips. Then he saw her; she was unhurt. "Let's find you a healer," Maire said, draping his limp arm over her shoulder.

# CHAPTER 4

Drangar's inarticulate howl echoed through Ondalan's alleys as Úistan Cahill's small warband hurried to catch up. Breathing came hard to Kildanor. Not only because the air around them felt suffused with forced magic, no, he still had trouble coming to terms with the fact that the demon within Drangar had obeyed him. This obedience baffled, shocked, and above all worried him. During the Demon War none of them had ever been able to stop one of them with anything but steel.

Blood and magic, the relationship that now was obvious, should have been obvious from the beginning. Ealisaid had drawn on her own life force, same as Drangar breaking out of the cage, but one could also use other people to feed one's spell-work. The demon drew power from his victims. Images of torn bodies and copious amounts of blood that had been spilled by the first casualties flashed before his eyes; he was certain this was how the monster within replenished its strength. A blood-soaked demon had been a dreadful sight a century ago, and the ghastly crimson shape they had glimpsed rushing out of the building roused the same horror.

Lord Cahill had slung his shield once more to his back and held up his hand, halting their advance. Cahill was in command, and Kildanor had no doubt he'd brook disobeying orders as much as Cumaill Duasonh. The two, Kildanor had noted over the past day, were too much alike. "I be damned," Cahill whispered, prompting the Chosen to step up to the corner the nobleman was glancing around. He poked his head forward. The scene unfolding before him, he knew, would remain with him until it was his turn to die.

Some thirty yards down the alley an enraged demon wearing Drangar Ralgon's body was trying in vain to break through a wall of shields set up by the Chanastardhians. From their elevated vantage he saw four lines of enemies, each one behind the other. The first line held their huge, locked shields, keeping the mercenary at bay. The warriors behind them held their comrades standing, their left hands steadying the shield-bearers, while their swords lashed out whenever Ralgon threw himself at the barrier. Those in the third rank, in turn, steadied their companions in front, jabbing spears at their foe whenever the opportunity arose.

The demon did not seem to care at all, his guttural challenges went unanswered, and by now the Chanastardhians had timed their stabs with his assaults. Whenever he bounded against the shield wall, at least one sword-spear combination struck. The enemy's faces were ashen. Madness alone would have disheartened no veteran—by the way they stood firm he knew these were seasoned warriors—but the combined sight of a blood-covered berserker was enough to shake even the hardiest of men. Someone muttered a prayer to Eanaigh. The Hearthwarden was the right person to talk to, but Kildanor doubted she paid attention; not even during the Demon War had the goddess intervened. He glanced back. Not one but many were praying, even the confident Úistan Cahill.

His priority was Drangar's safety; the man had feared something would happen, and he had been right. Anger lowered the defenses, allowing the Fiend to slip into his mind. What did it matter if the Chanastardhian warlord was distracted? If they were unable to free Ralgon from the demon's thrall, none of them would survive to tell that tale. Maybe he could still command the monster, but somehow, he doubted that.

Blood, spattered all over caergoult and cloak, was hissing away, dissipating into a crimson fog which briefly hung above the mercenary's head before vanishing completely. At the same pace the bloodstains burned off Ralgon, the cuts and slashes, visible through the torn leather, healed as well. No wonder the Chanastardhians were frightened. He looked first at Cahill and then at the others; some had come forward to observe the insanity, whispering frightened prayers. He shared their fear, not because the man running ineffectively against the barricade howled like a living nightmare, but because of what might happen once the creature turned on them. He had seen the light of reason vanish from Ralgon's eyes, and now the final result was visible to all.

To his surprise it was Sir Úistan who first shook off the shock of seeing this beast. Maybe it was because his mind simply ignored what was right before their eyes, or that amidst all this madness he clung to the only thing that still did make sense. Whatever the reason, the noble turned and waved to the archers still hidden atop the cliff overlooking the crossing. Addressing his cohorts, he said, "Snap out of it! This is a diversion." A very good diversion, Kildanor thought. "Ralgon keeps them busy. Camran, get a pair of bowmen into position." Cahill pointed to an intact roof. "There! Artianh, circle to the left, see if the other alleys are also blocked! Feoras, the same to the right! Braen, look for a decent position for the rest of the Bows!" He looked at Kildanor. "Anything to add, Chosen? No? Good. Proceed!"

After a moment's hesitation a look of relief spread on the retainers' faces and Artianh and Feoras took off at a sprint. He doubted the Chanastardhians would leave their flanks open to attack now that the alarm had sounded, but maybe they needed every warrior available to hold Ralgon at bay. His eyes remained on the uneven fight, though he wasn't quite sure who had the advantage. Sooner or later the Fiend would run out of foreign blood to feed its spells. When that happened, it would draw on Ralgon's life energies to keep up the healing. And when that happened the mercenary would truly have lost his struggle. Then again, his frenzy kept the Chanastardhians cowering, so that despite their apparent discipline, errors were bound to happen.

Like they did now. Quick as a hawk Ralgon's blade flashed forward, catching an enemy in the neck. Blood burst out the wound, showering the dying man's companions and, much to their disadvantage, also Drangar's face. The disturbing image was reinforced; a stubbly head caked in fresh blood. Ralgon bellowed another challenge, tried to force his way into the breach, but the Chanastardhians closed the line almost at once. It was a maneuver executed with perfection; the Chosen applauded the enemy's morale and discipline.

"Damn, they're good," Sir Úistan muttered. Then the noble said, "Chosen, what the Scales happened to Ralgon?"

He was at a loss. What could he tell the noble? Should he tell him anything at all? And what of the others? If he told Lord Cahill in front of his men, gossip would spread like wildfire, people might take matters into their hands and try to drive out the Fiend in whatever way struck their fancy. No one, not even he, knew how to handle this. He opted for an evasion. "Later I will explain what I can, milord."

Cahill opened his mouth but halted as the archers arrived. He nodded briefly. Camran saw the gesture, took it as his signal to act, held up two fingers then pointed to the roof. Morwen and another woman hurried off into the building. The others were just about to request new orders, some were gawking at the grotesque scene below, when Artianh and, a moment later, Feoras returned.

"They've blocked off the alleys on my side," Artianh wheezed, trying to catch his breath. Feoras's report was similar. For a moment the two stood there panting.

Cahill grimaced, and then said, "Dewayn, can your people create a breach for that man"—he thumbed at Ralgon— "to go through? I don't need all of the bastards down, just enough to let him finish what he's started." The sentence was underlined by another feral cry that came from below. Some of the archers and men-at-arms shuddered. Even Kildanor felt a chill running down his spine.

Dewayn hesitated, regarded the bloodcurdling situation for a few moments, and then swallowed and said, "Sure, sir."

"Make it easy and messy," Cahill replied. "I want the Chanastardhians to run in fear."

"The way he's going they'll be running away soon enough," Kildanor muttered. What was going on with the man? He couldn't have healed himself back to life; there was hardly any blood left when he had brought him to Dunthiochagh. Had the demon revived him? If so how? Too many questions were bubbling forth, and all added to the mystery that was Drangar Ralgon. The poor bastard could provide none of the answers either.

He understood why people claimed Lesganagh had blessed the man. The howling lunatic below had more things in common with the God of Sun and War than he cared to admit. For one, he was relentless, tireless, and prone to burning himself out before long. But it wasn't the god, the thing slamming itself against the wall was a demon. Yet why had it obeyed him?

"... we'll follow, understood?" Kildanor blinked. Had he just missed Úistan Cahill's entire plan? He couldn't even remember the last time he had ignored what was going on around him while awake.

"You agree with the plan?" Sir Úistan asked, this time addressing him directly.

"I'm sorry," he said, trying hard not to sound like one of those imbeciles at court.

"Get your head in the game, we're not here to ponder life itself; leave that to the scholars and priests." Shaking his head, Sir Úistan said, "Once the Bows have cleared some of the path for Ralgon, we'll let him proceed a while longer. Let him play butcher until we have the bastards fleeing, no doubt they soon will anyway." Another death wail rang up the hill. "Then, when they are running, we will follow, clearing out whatever nests remain of the bastards. And then we need to pray real hard for that lunatic down there to calm down enough so he doesn't slaughter all of them." He shook his head. "How the Scales is such a thing possible, Chosen?"

"Later, milord," he said, realizing there was very little he could say to answer the questions either of them had.

Lord Cahill nodded, closed his eyes as if to block out the horror and said, "Fire!"

Arrows whistled overhead, and true to their word each one found its target, neatly missing the berserk Ralgon. The front ranks, hidden behind their shields, were unaffected; the soldiers behind who had supported their fellows faltered and fell. Not every arrow took down its mark, but as the shield-bearers

lost their backup, the interlinked wood and metal wall faltered under the mercenary's mad battering. The enemy, suddenly aware of the threat posed by the bowmen and women,
retreated in a vain attempt to retain their coherence. Step by
vicious step Drangar pursued, lunging repeatedly for one or
another. An evading warrior lost her footing when she stepped
on an ally's prone corpse. The integrity of the entire shield wall
disintegrated.

Kildanor couldn't tell whether Ralgon was aware of the
failing defense, the lunatic was still too busy charging into the
shields held against him. Then, finally, with a gut-wrenching
roar, the mercenary was through. One of Cahill's men moved
to follow, but the Chosen held him back. "Wait," he said. "I do
not want to be caught on the wrong side of his rage." Paling, the
retainer—was it Feoras?—nodded, and stepped back.

With morbid curiosity Kildanor observed the bloody spectacle below. Screams for mercy echoed up the alley, usually they
ended with a growl and a dying human's last gasp, or whimper, or yell. At one point he thought he heard Drangar grunting "Hesmera," his dead lover's name. He saw a warrior being
picked up much the same way the mercenary had lifted Sir
Úistan off the ground, and thrown into another. If the man felt
pain, it didn't show. There was no remorse for the slaughter. He
wondered if he should have warned Lord Cahill of the danger
enraging the mercenary posed. One look at the noble showed
the man's ashen face, his mouth muttering silent prayers.

To whom should he pray, he wondered. Lesganagh probably
enjoyed the straightforward bloodshed. In a way he should have
taken comfort in the raging battle as well. Wasn't it the epitome
of everything the Lord of Sun and War stood for? Maybe it
was, but the slaughter was, in its essence, a reenactment of the
Demon War. Ralgon bashed one soldier's head against a wall,
her head rupturing like an overripe grape. The resulting shower
of blood dissipated almost immediately in a crimson mist rising around the mercenary. A man had his neck shattered by a
dismissive stomp of Ralgon's boot as he was desperately trying
to crawl away from this embodiment of war. The warrior didn't
even utter a last groan. In a matter of moments, the line had

shattered, its human remains splattered on frozen mud and ice-rimmed wood- and stonework.

But Ralgon was far from finished. He rushed after the now heedlessly fleeing Chanastardhians, uncaring about honor and battlefield courtesy. Then again, Kildanor reflected, did he fight that much differently? During Jathain's short-lived rebellion he had slaughtered as indiscriminately as the demon, and the same had happened in Harail. He had pummeled Lerainh to death with his bare hands. Was the shattering of one's skull against a wall that much different from doing the same with fists? Yes, he argued, he had been angry, but his fury had not unleashed a monster.

The skirmish had passed beyond his line of sight, and against his own advice Kildanor followed the thinning trail of corpses. The others were cautiously advancing with him. Past the wall where the woman's brains had slid to the ground, he heard the sounds of mayhem from the right. At the alley's end a house blocked the way, and the street branched. Momentary silence ensued and he wondered if he had heard correctly. No corpses could be seen in either direction. The gurgling of another dying Chanastardhian, again from the right, reassured him that his hearing had not failed.

Another scream followed. If there were enemies hidden in ambush, he doubted they remained so as a single man slaughtered their companions. Or, maybe, they cowered in shadowed corners, too afraid to show their faces. The heavy footsteps halting a few feet behind him could only belong to one man. Without turning, Kildanor said, "Think there are more, milord?" He glanced up at a pair of shuttered windows.

"If there are, they'd be bloody stupid to look out," Sir Úistan replied. The noble sounded more confident now, having fought down his fright and shock.

"I'd rather be hidden than facing this," Dewayn, who had crept up, added.

"Aye," Kildanor said, his eyes still searching the upper windows.

"What is this... man?" Dewayn asked.

"I don't truly know."

"Shall we scour the buildings, sir?" Camran asked from behind. Lord Cahill must have nodded, for the retainer snapped orders in quick succession. "Feoras, take two, search this house and its neighbor! Garlan, same for you, that side!"

Taking Ralgon along had been madness; had he told the others of his concerns, this insanity might not have come to life. It would have prevented the demon from gaining control. What if Drangar could not wrest it back from the Fiend? His musings were interrupted by a different kind of howl. He removed his helmet to hear more clearly. Twisting his head sidewise, he was able to hear the scream. Unlike the guttural yells of before, Ralgon's voice was intelligible now, reminiscent of what had happened weeks ago in the Palace's dungeon. "Let go!" the mercenary roared at the top of his lungs. Someone, a warleader most like, urged his troops to rally.

"What is it?" Cahill asked.

Donning his helmet, Kildanor didn't bother to answer and took off at a sprint. Ralgon was fighting back! How the man had regained control mattered not; the only thing that mattered was that he had.

At an intersection another mangled corpse showed the way. The others would have to follow the same signs. More bodies, all horribly mutilated, were as good as any sign for the direction of Drangar's path. Here and there he passed people who still clung to their last shreds of life. Under different circumstances he would have stopped and eased their suffering, but this was so much more important. If Ralgon was once again fighting free of the enslavement he might be able to help.

He skidded to a stop. Around the next bend a group of warriors were chanting a rallying cry. He heard the dull thud of blunt objects hitting leather, and the mercenary's pained groans amidst his angry shouts. To charge in was akin to suicide. There had to be a better way. Was he ready to enter the spiritworld here? Before he had only done so under Ealisaid's supervision. Could he do so, alone? Now? His position was as exposed as could be; the next Chanastardhian walking this way would be bound to find his limp body. It mattered little. His friend's life was at stake. Drangar was battling the demon. He had to help no matter the cost.

What was it the Wizardess had said? One could return to one's body in a matter of moments by merely thinking of it. If that was true, he might be able to help Ralgon before some foe discovered his body.

The trample of boots from behind made the decision much easier. Kildanor signaled Lord Cahill and his cohorts to stop. When they had reached him, he explained in quick words what he wanted to do, brooking no questions. He finished with, "This is important, so don't fuck it up! You will stay here, and guard my body while I help Ralgon." The inarticulate screams had resumed, mingling with the Chanastardhian chants. How anyone could take this much punishment and remain conscious was a mystery. It didn't matter. Not yet, anyway. "Guard my body," he reminded his companions once more, and then leaned against the wall, sliding into a sitting position.

The transition into spiritform was quick. So fast, in fact, that Kildanor was soaring above Ondalan even before he had fully closed his eyes. Below him were the smoky shapes of Sir Úistan and the others, as incorporeal as the houses. To the left, as expected, the thrashing, and Drangar's all too real presence. Foggy shapes surrounded his body, some holding his arms and legs, while others threw punches with wild abandon. His body flopped in synchronicity with the blows, twisting in the grip of his tormentors. He saw the shadows of the real world go through the motions of pummeling again and again. Ralgon's spiritworld counterpart was moving the same way, though there was something ghastly different about the motion. Here it looked as if more wires than there had been weeks ago were holding the man's skin and flesh. Unlike then, not just one spear protruded from the chest; there were dozens, hundreds, turning the body in a grotesque human pincushion.

Despite his all too brief experience with such a thing—there were so many more wires to tear free—he knew the slightest touch would lead to prolonged unconsciousness. Now, that he looked closer, his spiritform floating toward the screaming man, the Chosen realized there was something profoundly different about the situation.

What had looked like a bunch of elongated needles from a distance, now appeared more flexible, like fishing lines, their hooks embedded in Ralgon's body, each pull of a string coinciding with a blow in the real world. The mercenary wasn't just reacting to the physical attacks; he was fighting against a puppeteer using him like a perverse marionette! It seemed as if he wasn't even aware of the thrashing.

Then he realized another thing: in this world of shadows and silence, he could hear Drangar's scream.

# CHAPTER 5

Sir Úistan's words had angered Drangar, stoking a fury he'd thought long gone. His resolve to heed Kildanor's words and remain levelheaded evaporated in the barrage of reminders. Back in his mercenary days, he had fought knowing Lesganagh was at his side. That certainty was what had kept him standing strong. The pain of suffering the injustices at the Eye of Traksor had grown less pronounced; in a way, he realized, it was that pain that had allowed him to control the Fiend. Now he could not even steer the snarling animal within. All he could do was watch. He saw how his hand lifted the noble off the ground. He felt the Fiend's need to smash the man into the next wall. Then, to his surprise, the Chosen spoke words he could not hear, but they affected the monster. He hammered and stomped against the walls of the prison that was his own mind.

What happened then was just as shocking. He saw his charge, the attack on the building and the tearing through the opposition. Appalled, Drangar wanted to weep. All this butchery reminded him of Hesmera's death. He saw his sword flash up and down, a cruel reflection of the murder he knew he had not committed. He had never been this brutal, had he? Memories of Little Creek slammed back, half-remembered scenes viewed through the haze of inebriation. He had blamed the drink, but had it truly been the booze? What if the wine had lowered the walls holding the Fiend back? Was the monster truly a demon, as Kildanor had said? It had been a part of his life for as long as he could remember, this rage, easily controlled. Not anymore. He looked through his eyes, yes, he heard his voice, sure, but he wasn't the one seeing and snarling. Anger controlled his body.

Endless fury drove him on. How was this possible?

When the few cuts from the previous battle had vanished, Chanastardhian blood hissing away from his limbs, the question of possibility was raised to something entirely different. Why was it doing this? How was it healing him? Who had returned him from death? Was he possessed? Was it truly a demon that had taken hold of him? And if so, was it really the same as his furor? It wasn't the first time the enemies had taken a host body; that sort of thing had occurred more than once a century ago. But the demons had been driven off, beaten back to their own world! He wasn't even remotely close to the age necessary to have witnessed the Demon War! For fuck's sake, what was going on?

Through his eyes, he witnessed the slaughter, wounds he did not feel vanishing in a hiss of blood. This was his body! The silent scream reverberated inside the emptiness that surrounded him. Again and again he saw his arms rise and fall, not the polished cuts and parries he had used in the bout with Kildanor, but the reckless cleaving of a monster that cared for nothing.

His shout must have had some effect, for the malign spirit ignored still breathing, maimed people. This was his body, his mind, his muscles, and his bone. He would not allow the demon to keep him in its thrall! All too clear was the memory of what he had witnessed in the past, seeing himself kill Hesmera. This travesty was far too much of a reminder of the time when he had truly been powerless. "I am I!" he shouted, at himself, at the one controlling his body. This time the snarled declaration echoed around, gaining in strength. "No one will control my body! Not again!" Phrases mixed with words with syllables with breath until the oppressing emptiness sang with his resolve. Sound mixed with thought, and for a moment, the Fiend hesitated, allowing a Chanastardhian to retreat.

"IamInoonewillcontrolmybodynotagain!" the noise rang through his mind, the emptiness, and his body. It was maddening.

"Noonewillcontrolmybodyagain!" The creature faltered, his motions grew sluggish. Drangar felt as if someone was trying to push through the murk of sound, as if his arms and legs were being pulled one way while he willed them to stop. Now he realized he did not need his eyes to see what was going on. In a way he was looking at the outside as through a side of his skull. He glanced down, forcing his right leg to remain still, unmoving. His body faltered.

Lines held his limbs. He was no puppet! The sounds became deafening. His sword dropped to the ground, his hands reached for his head. He felt another presence here, inside of him. A throaty growl filled the air, almost drowning out the mix of syllables, phrases, words, and thoughts. Still, he howled against the guffaw. "Noonewillcontrolmybodyagain!"

"Of course I will," the other replied with a chuckle.

Now the Chanastardhians grabbed him, pinned him down. The Fiend tried to lash out but the angry echo kept up its distraction. What was this monster?

He looked up, along the gleaming lines still attached to his body. Again, he saw the feline monstrosities. One of them caught his eye. He felt the bloody stare, cowered, dreaded the thing's ire. Why was the bastard playing him like a godsdamned puppeteer? "Iwillcontrolmybodyagain!" he roared inside his mind. More of the demons were inspecting him now, some tugging at the strings; his legs shook. Drangar fought back, howling.

"Let go!"

Had he screamed these words? Or was his mind playing the final trick on him? For a moment his body ceased moving. Whipping his eyes away from the demons, he looked through his eyes again. For a moment the Chanastardhians had stopped pummeling. Then the strange tugging began anew, blows of many fists accompanied its rhythm. "Iwillcontrolmybodyagain!"

Just how strong was the demons' grip? He began to further test their domination. "Iwillcontrolmybodyagain!" A twist of fingers into a fist was interrupted by both humans and monsters, but not before his digits had fully curled. Bastards, Drangar thought grimly. The only good thing about this was that he felt none of the pain he was bound to feel once he was master once more.

"Iwill controlmy bodyagain!" He pushed, pushed, slowly

feeling the alien presence back off. Immediately the blows hit
as through a blanket. The Fiend—or Fiends?—tried to rein him
back at once. They failed. "Control mybody again!" He turned
his head, one eye already swollen shut, toward somebody on
his left.

"You will obey!" the demon's voice thundered in his head.

Drangar felt his lips twist into a grimace no one would call
a smile and said, "Fuck you!" The Chanastardhians' reply was
as swift as the demon's. Punches hammered against his head,
he felt his lip split before he was back inside the dark with the
feline puppeteers back in control. No! His body, his rules, he
thought grimly. "Iwillcontrolmybody!" Again, the tugging faltered, but the bastards still held the strings. Drangar strained
against the demonic grip.

A few futile moments later, he realized this was no physical contest. For a heartbeat he despaired. How could one puny
human make a stand against demons? Now there was nobody
shielding him, defending him. "Mybody!" the echo sounded
plaintive, not the determined holler it had been.

"Retrace your steps," the voice, Dog, had ordered. What
steps? What was he supposed to remember?

A notion tugged at the back of his mind, something he had
thought of moments before. What? What was it he had forgotten
that had helped him live? Before Hesmera's murder, before the
claws of nightmare had torn his life apart.

Was it the Scythe? He didn't want to become him again? No,
not that, he decided. Aside from her death, what had made him
Drangar? The mercenary, the bane of every shield wall, that
wasn't him, had never really been him. But...

For a moment the echoes of his voice fell silent.

But... what?

Purpose, meaning, his life had had meaning, not the bare
existence he now called living. Running away had giving him
focus, purpose. All that had returned after Little Creek, the
Fiend had remained, but never as strong. A silent presence most
of the time, until... her death. He couldn't, didn't want to go
back to being the Scythe.

And he didn't have to. In Cahill Manor his desire to rescue

the women had tamed the demon. All he needed, truly needed was… a purpose, something worth living for.

Justice. Not revenge, no death would bring Hesmera back. He would bring justice to those who preyed on the unwitting, most of all the Sons of Traksor.

"I will control!" the words reverberated through the blackness. For an instant he felt the blows smacking into his body. Pain had never felt this good.

"Bastards," he heard himself grunt.

The beating and tugging continued, but it seemed as if the latter had lost its force. His mental eyes sought his foes' faces again. When they returned his stare, it was he who snarled, baring his teeth. "I am I!" Doubts, fears, in the past he had never doubted himself, never feared much of anything. The lessons he learned at Little Creek were that alcohol was his enemy, and Lliania forgave if one was truly repentant. Cahill's words had washed away everything but the anger, and the Fiend fed on it. "I control again!" Brave words were just that, words, nothing more. He had never taken responsibility, never looked truth in the eye. Two years ago, he should have turned himself in. Justice, Lliania, knew the truth, now he did too.

"I control my body!" Drangar screamed, verbally and mentally, severing the lines fused to his body as well as breaking away from the Chanastardhians' grasp. For a brief moment he felt the howl of anger rattling through his mind. Then it was gone.

His body met the ground in an instant, the impact forcing out the remainder of his breath. With his one good eye scanning the ground for his sword, he stood, haltingly. Where was the bloody thing? A shield bashed into his back, sent him sprawling. The Chanastardhians advanced, weapons drawn, this time less intent with continuing the beating. Whereas their numbers had counted for little against the raging, blood-coated manbeast, bruised as he was, he knew he was now far easier game. His limited vision, his frantic turning of the head to keep the furious enemies in sight and, at the same time, scanning the ground for his blade, would have encouraged even the dumbest foe.

"Drangar!" the Chosen's voice hollered from behind. He dared not turn his back on the score of disciplined warriors. Racing footsteps approached, presumably Kildanor wanting to lend a hand. Creeping away from the ranks of foes eager to kill him, his hands swept the frozen ground. He understood their caution, their fear.

His left foot grazed something solid, steel scraped over earth. The enemy leader, a tallish man with the air of a true fighter, shouted, "Get him!" and Chanastardhians surged forward. When his searching hands found the hilt, for a brief moment, he felt the Fiend scream with joy. Grunting, he brought the blade up into Eagle Guard, this time he would remain in command. No bloody demons, no strings, no Fiend!

The enemy covered the last few yards the same moment Kildanor reached his side. "Don't leave this spot!" the Chosen warned as his sword rose to fend off a stab by the leading foe. The ring of steel on steel and the screech as the weapons disengaged only to meet again, brought forth another exultation of the Fiend.

"Bastards," Drangar growled, unsure whether he referred to the enemy or the demons trying to regain control. He knew he could beat the monster within, and with a snarl he countered a Chanastardhian blade on the outside, reminding the Fiend who was in command. This was his body!

Battered as he was, his parries came slowly. Again and again, Kildanor jumped in to deflect a blow he had not seen. Limited vision, dizziness, a multitude of bruises, he tried to shut the pain away but it remained. He was master of a failing body. Stumbling, only the Chosen's helpful hand and a lull in the fighting prevented him from hitting the ground.

Drangar needed to think, quickly, for the enemy was advancing once more in closed ranks. Cahill Manor, a goal, confidence, the words rattled through his numbing mind. If he made sense of them, the plan to lure Mireynh's attention away would work.

Had he healed himself in the turret room, or had that been the demon? Was it wise to even consider allowing the Fiend back in? Barely remembered sentences, the evaporating of blood, wounds closing, flesh charring and growing back;

magic, all of it. Forcing fact onto an uncertain world was what Ealisaid had said. Was that what his father had been afraid of? That he, by accident, would learn the same type of magic the demons employed? Could he force the fact of healed flesh onto his bruised body?

Gritting his teeth, Drangar decided to try. If he failed it barely made a difference. He imagined his face, hale, unhurt. Blackness…

"Get to your senses, man!" someone shouted, shaking him.

His head throbbed, the pain almost unbearable. A purring laugh resounded through his mind. Opening his eyes, he squinted as far too bright light pounded into him. Shapes peeled out of the luminance, shields, helmets, and spears.

"To arms!" the voice roared.

Kildanor!

Ondalan, it all came back in a flash. Forcing his body to health, creating fact from possibility. The enemy was nearly upon them. Drangar blinked tears from his eyes. Both eyes! It had worked, but the agony and fiendish laughter within his skull almost made him throw up.

Then there was no more time, for the Chanastardhians had reached them. Instinct took over.

"Stay put!" Kildanor reminded him.

Now, in full command of his body and senses, Drangar still felt detached, as if this was less real. He stabbed at the helmets poking above the tower shields.

For an instant it seemed as if the dark shadow would step in again, just as the warriors retreated to prevent being impaled by his sword. A mental snarl kept the shadow in check. Again, he stabbed. Kildanor was employing the same tactic. The Chosen's plan revealed itself a moment later.

Arrows quivered in a pair of heads before him, and another two to his right. The falling warriors created a breach. Not waiting for his companion to urge him on, Drangar darted into the opening. Surprised shouts and the ring of steel told him the Chosen was right beside him. Again, he felt the Fiend tug. "I am in control!" he roared, bashing aside two slashing blades. He used the momentum to pivot, stomping his right boot into the side of one opponent's knee. The monster rejoiced, cheered the subsequent crunch and the man's pained scream. His snarl silenced the demon.

Dodging a pair of thrusting spearheads, he slashed his blade in an arc, decapitating the second swordsman. With grim determination he now fought on two fronts, one within, the other without. As blood splashed into his face, Drangar drove his blade into a woman who was trying to stab him from the side. At the same time, the Fiend roared once more, stronger than before. In the moment it took to reinforce his defenses, the spearmen drove their weapons at him in unison. At the last instant, with steel points almost scratching his armor, he managed a desperate parry. The two soldiers, their faces blurred from blood running down his face, had overeagerly advanced well into his reach. A horizontal slash penetrated their chainmail. He saw the look on their ashen faces as their guts spilled on the ground.

"Retreat!" the warleader shouted. Glancing about, Drangar saw there were few enough Chanastardhians to obey the order.

Arrows, he now realized, had cut down most resistance while leaving himself and Kildanor virtually untouched. Dewayn certainly was true to his word. All he had to do now was lure Mireynh into sending more troops here, preferably the rebel noble Kildanor had mentioned.

Two more Chanastardhians hit the ground, missiles in their backs. He had to act fast! Presumably the archers knew to leave at least one survivor, but one could never predict such things in midst a battle. Drangar followed the handful warriors fleeing Ondalan, waving his sword in a way he hoped would tell the bowmen to stop shooting. Another Chanastardhian went down. Then the whistle of arrows stopped.

His legs and feet ached; even breathing felt impossibly hard. New bruises had replaced old ones. It was as if the Fiend was now trying a new tactic to usurp command. It promised healing, fast and quick relief from the aches. Remembering the instant of unconsciousness, he snarled his refusal. Instead, he sped up, sprinting after the enemy. Again, the shadow leapt forward, trying to dominate.

Growling, snarling, Drangar caught up with the rearmost soldier. He didn't bother to aim his blow, bringing his blade down in a quick slash; cutting off the woman's left leg at the knee. He was past before her body connected with the ground. Only three were left, including the leader.

Another one, a chubby bastard, faltered, stopped, gasping for air. As he passed the man, he brought up his sword, the blade flashing briefly across the exposed side of the neck. Then he was upon the remaining pair.

Both had freed their horses, the leader already in his charger's saddle. The other one—Drangar noticed he was also garbed in better armor—had a foot in the stirrup and was glancing his way, eyes wide with terror.

Holding his sword like a lance, he covered the remaining distance in a single lunge. The nobleman's chain surrendered to the weapon's point just as easily as any other armor would have, the hammered steel sliding effortlessly into the man's abdomen. For a moment, the Fiend's cheer mixed with the Chanastardhian's dying groan. Drangar tried to ignore both. His scowl had the added effect of drawing the other nobleman's eyes his way. "Tell Mireynh, Drangar Ralgon is here, and demands the promised reward!" he said, his last victim still impaled on his blade. Despite protesting muscles and the need to vomit and weep at the same time, he held man and sword aloft, so the Chanastardhian slid down the entire length of steel until he came to rest against the already bloodstained guard. "Tell him he owes me!"

The horror in the man's eyes was even more pronounced now, and Drangar tried to retain his uncaring, unstrained face as he held the sword in a two-handed low guard. "I am Drangar Ralgon, and I demand the reward Mireynh promised. It's long overdue." The effort almost made him drop the blade, but determination prevailed. "Now, get to your pathetic High General and tell him, understood?" His stare still held the Chanastardhian's, and finally the man nodded, his entire body reflecting his dread. Turning his horse, the warrior galloped off.

As the noble disappeared behind a hill, Drangar finally let go of his sword and the mask of the hardened killer. He fell to his knees and retched. When his stomach was empty, he wiped bloodstained tears from his face and looked back at the trail of bodies left in his wake. Were his killings so different from those of the Fiend?

Not much later, after Lord Cahill's men had brought horses and wagons into the village and had relieved mortally wounded foes of their prolonged suffering, the others inspected the ruins. Sick of death, Drangar watched from a distance. What had Kildanor said earlier? Or was it Cahill? He didn't remember. The people of Ondalan had fled their homes before the Chanastardhians had arrived. Only those few skilled in archery had stayed behind. Yet why would a conqueror of an abandoned, burnt out village demolish the place even further? Had the enemy done more than simply hold the place against a handful of defenders? Did it even matter?

Before, be it in Little Creek or Dunthiochagh, he'd not seen what the Fiend was capable of. Even the glimpse into the past had not revealed the sheer disregard for life the demon had shown today. The bloodstains on his armor glaringly reflected the deadly work. But some of the slowly blackening crimson was not the work of the other possessing his body. There were a good half-dozen that had fallen by his hand. He recalled the battles he had fought, more clearly now than during the past few years, but never before had the killings etched themselves so strongly into his memory. Slaying a man from behind, there was no honor in that. All the Chanastardhians had done was to follow their lord's command. If only he could find some justification, anything that would make the slaughter easier to comprehend. He did not want to be the man the others fearfully regarded from a distance. If only he felt as true in his actions as he had in Eanaigh's temple.

If only…

He ran an ungloved hand along the cold stone of a wall. Not only had fire devoured the roof of the house, but mortar had been scraped out and rocks removed so that its top looked as uneven as a mountain ridge. All evidence spoke of only recent abandonment, and the scratch marks on plaster and stone were fresh, underlining that fact. Drangar circled the ruin, found the entrance, and stepped into the enclosed space that had once been the common room. The remains of wooden furniture were yet another reminder of what had taken down this house. In the crisp air of the foothills, the tang of burnt wood stood out, and though some of it carried the scent of singed shingles, there was an even fresher note underneath the layers of smell.

Guided by his nose, he looked around. Near the fireplace, its brickwork chimney still standing, he saw a few rags that had miraculously survived the flames. While everything else had gone up in smoke, why had these strips of cloth survived? He knelt and inspected the fabric. The flames hadn't even come near this stuff! Instead he discovered teeth marks and dried blood stitching the cloth.

For a moment he halted, closed his eyes, and snarled back the shadowy creature that rejoiced at further evidence of violence. The Fiend scoffed as if his determination merely amused it, and then, finally, it retreated. Was he mad? Was it merely a figment of an insane mind, this monster? Even without Kildanor's claim, he would have dismissed such a thought. He had met mad people before, lunatics who thought themselves Danachamain or elves of old, knew these maniacs truly believed in their delusions. None of them fought back like he did. On top of it, he hadn't even heard this fiendish shadow pronounce it was somebody or other. No, there was a presence in his head, one of those feline bastards who pulled the strings. Given that the Chosen had described the same creatures and identified them as demons, he knew he was not mad. "Not that this makes it better," he muttered glumly.

Unearthing the mystery of the missing rocks and now the bloodstained rags kept him busy. He did not want to think of this. Besides, he feared the Fiend knew exactly when he considered its presence and used that thought to reassert dominance.

"I control myself!" he growled, and then picked up a poker to prod the fireplace's ashes. Oddly enough they looked fresher, more recent than the fire that had taken out the roof and interior. He halted his thrust; a terrible thought entered his mind. Had the bastards branded and tortured survivors? He sniffed at the rod's tip. Burnt flesh. Looking closely, he even saw traces of blood. His gaze wandered back up to the disfigured walls. Up there, in all likelihood, builders had put thinner stones to close the gap between wall and roof. What would they need slabs of stone for? The answer came in an instant. "Cairns," he muttered. Cremation was unheard of in Chanastardh, villeins got a hole in the ground, freeborn a box if they could afford it, again lowered into the ground, and the rich got cairns. "If the ground is too resilient even freeborn and villeins get cairns," he concluded his thought aloud.

He stood and went back to the alley, inspecting the remains of other nearby houses. Many of them lacked the slabs that made up the upper part of the walls. A cursory inspection of these other fireplaces unearthed a few similar strips of cloth and the occasional bloodied poker.

"What the Scales are you doing?" Kildanor's voice sounded from behind him as he knelt at yet another chimney.

"Trying to make sense of the things I can make sense of," he replied. He stood and passed the Chosen. "At least some of this fucking world still does." When the warrior fell into step beside him, and he saw no way of getting rid of him—killing him would solve many of his... this was the Fiend whispering, it was trying to tempt him, instead of roaring for control—he continued, "Found bloody cloth in some of the ruins, and ashes too fresh to be from the fires. I want to find out if the bastards tortured some of those who stayed behind."

"You could ask the survivors," said the Chosen.

Drangar hoped his scoff sounded genuine. "They'd lie most like, and I will not resort to violence again."

# CHAPTER 6

At first the ladders were few and they were short of things to do. So far General Kerral's warriors manned most of the wall east of South Gate and had things well under control. Rhea and Briog stood on the side, watching the few ladders that were put up topple back down. Several fighters had learned the lethal way that the Chanastardhians were prepared; they dropped dead with arrows imbedded in skulls and throats. Danastaerian Bow-Captains had already ordered archers to nearby rooftops. The higher vantage points allowed for a greater field of fire. Besides, Rhea noted when the first missiles took out a bunch of determined enemy soldiers attacking a little spot of battlement, the archers were of far more use against unshielded foes; they would have wasted their ammunition on the well-protected warriors below.

The battle went in their favor; fallen enemies were tossed onto the Chanastardhians climbing the ladders, and their own dead were allowed to fall into the city proper where carters waited to take the corpses from under the boots of the living. So far Rhea had seen few corpses dropping into New Wall Street. But she knew the enemy had vast reserves and once the sling-thrower crews got the angle right, the boulders that were now still crashing into buildings would strike the battlement. So far this had not happened, and at this range it might never happen at all, but she had learned very early in life that never was as finite as always.

Her silent prediction came true in the early afternoon. The two Chanastardhian slingthrowers had their aim improved, or worsened, she thought wryly. It all depended on where the observer stood. For Dunthiochagh's defenders it had certainly worsened. The boulders had not reached the battlement yet, but they were getting closer. The rate at which the engines were firing was abysmally slow; she had given up counting between each salvo. At this extreme range the bastards were firing blindly, and quite effectively so. Already the abandoned building behind them sported a pair of massive holes; its inhabitants had fled across the river the moment half-frozen, half-rotted strips of human flesh had rained down onto the earth. Rhea didn't blame them. To her surprise a good number of chubby merchants, tradesmen, and tradeswomen remained, armed and armored in well-tarnished but serviceable gear.

Now the enemy slingthrowers again gave muted twang. They had missed the wall so often that only the Bows atop the roofs paid attention to where the missiles struck. This time, however, the Chanastardhian engineers got lucky.

To her left both stones touched the battlement, skipped into the assembled defenders and off into the roofs beyond. It all happened so blindingly fast that as soon as the sound of the 'throwers reached her ears, two blood-smeared breaches split their lines, and a pair of roofs crashed down with two-score archers standing on them. Into this moment of shock, Rhea was as stunned as the others, when none of the defenders lifted a finger or moved a foot to fill the gaps, a wave of enemy fighters mounted the battlement.

They were already pulling up ropes that held stacks of tower shields. So well-trained was this warband that in mere moments, they had complete control of the crimson strip of wall. Joining those already on the battlement were half a dozen lightly armored Bows, weapons ready in an instant. They began to pick their targets in a routine manner that Rhea had only seen in seasoned hunters. When those already on the wall were joined by a yet another group, this one led by a giant in plate armor wielding a greatsword, and none of the Captains or Wardens reacted to the threat, Rhea shouted "To arms!" to the Riders waiting below.

Now, as they gathered on the battlement, swords and shields

in hand, a warleader, further east of the breach, finally reacted to the intruders. Unfortunately, the enemy was ready for them. In quick succession, before the Riders had advanced more than a few yards, soldiers blocked their paths with a wall of interlocked shields.

"Bastards," muttered Briog, voicing her thought. Whoever was in charge of the beachhead knew what they were doing. She had an idea.

"Fetch the horses," Rhea ordered, getting some incredulous stares from her companions. Then the others realized what she had in mind.

Gail Caslin snorted, saying, "Woman, you're crazy! But it can work." The Caretaker hurried after the others.

"Fetch Talaen, will you?" she called after Gail, and received a nodded affirmative. Then she turned to the nearest Sword-Warden who, finally, tried to organize an assault from this side of the breach. "Warden!" Rhea shouted.

The woman turned a one-eyed glare at her. "Can't you see I'm busy?" she snarled, and returned to hollering orders at a score of warriors that headed for the enemy. "Get them off my wall! Shield on shield and spears atop, aim for the fucking heads!" Rhea searched for her companions, and found them leading the chargers up the nearest ramp. Unfortunately, the bloody thing was some fifty yards west.

"Gods," she whispered, "hurry up!"

By now the Chanastardhians' beachhead had swelled outward. As one they pushed the defenders back with their wall of shields, spears and lances flashing out, much like the Warden had ordered. A cautious glance to the ground on the other side of the rampart showed more enemies climbing the ladders.

"Make way!" Fynbar shouted from behind. His order was answered by exasperated insults, as the defenders stood aside, either closer to the merlons or off to the rear. By now they all kept their heads down, the slow learners had died quickly enough.

"What the fuck are you doing?" the warden, accompanied by a warleader, snarled.

Rhea turned from the approaching line of horses to the warriors, a grim smile on her lips. "We intend to breach the breach.

If you send infantry in there,"—she pointed at the troops pushing against the enemy wall, half of them already dead—"you won't ever reclaim that wall and the number of foes will grow with each breath! Horses will do the trick!"

"You're crazy!" the woman retorted.

"We'll get the job done," Rhea said confidently. To the warleader, she added, "We can break through the wall, but only if you clear enough room for us to charge." A quick estimate told her the enemy was some hundred yards away. "It'll be tight, sir, clear us the way if you please." The Sword-Captain nodded, frowning, as he inspected the breadth of the battlement.

"Three horses abreast, if you're lucky," he said, "if we clear the entire length of it. But..."

"No," interrupted Rhea, taking Talaen's reins from Gail, "if you withdraw, they will follow all the more quickly."

The noble seemed to have an idea of his own. A grim smile formed on his lips. To the warden, he said, "Lynne, get your five best, take them against the enemy." The subordinate frowned. Beside them the groan of wood and the wails of falling soldiers indicated a ladder had just been toppled into the milling army below. "I assume you have a horn or some other sort of signal?" he asked, looking at the double row of riders.

The horses, although used to combat, were skittish. Rhea couldn't blame them. What living being in their right mind would want to stand in midst of any sort of battle? "Aye," she answered, scratching Talaen's muzzle. That always calmed the mare. Then she understood what the captain had in mind, and saw Sword-Warden Lynne did as well. "That's still a drop of a couple of yards," she told the woman.

Lynne grimaced. "Aye, but ain't it better to die whilst trying to get those bastards out of the city than to wait on death?" she replied. "Maybe yonder Caretakers can take care of our broken bones once we touch ground?"

Gail, Briog and Fynbar, the only ones close enough to hear, answered at once. "Sure."

Turning to her commander, Lynne said, "It can be done, sir." To the Riders she added, "Just make sure we have time to make the dive, will you?"

"Count on it," Fynbar answered.

In a matter of moments, Lynne had assembled her warriors. Burly men, all encased in splint armor and well taller than the average man, they each had a sword in one hand and a solid-looking shield in the other. The Warden took the shield from her back, strapped it to her forearm and drew her own blade. "We'll tell those we pass to back off."

The Riders were equally prepared, and as the half-dozen fighters trotted toward the enemy shield wall—how far had they come, Rhea wondered. Five yards? Ten?—they mounted their chargers, strapped tear-shaped shields to arms, and drew their lances from the hoops of their saddles. "Keep your heads low," Briog reminded. Rhea and the others smirked. It was not the first time they charged into an enemy under fire.

From the east, Chanastardhian arrows kept their own Bows at bay, but as the occupied area grew in width, so grew the distance between the shields protecting them. The archers of Dunthiochagh inflicted more and more damage. And still the enemy swarmed onto the wall.

By now Warden Lynne and her veterans were almost upon the enemy. "Let's go," Rhea said, nudging Talaen into a canter. Horseshoes clattered on stone; the others were with her. Warriors parted in front of them, to the left and right they went, pushing off those enemies who had just found footing on the battlement, or cheering the riders on.

The half-dozen hammered into the enemy shields. For a moment it seemed as if the defense would break altogether. Then the Chanastardhian line straightened. Sixty yards. Was it possible that Lynne was actually clearing space for them? Forty yards, she thought. "Fynbar, horn!" she called.

As the single note rose, she spurred Talaen into gallop, just as the six, no, five warriors jumped clear of the enemy's shields and dove off the wall. She heard Gail whisper the same prayer to Eanaigh that was in her mind. "Goddess, protect these brave souls."

The sudden absence of pressure made the enemy lose their coherence as they stumbled forward. Rhea and Gail were the first in the line at ten yards away. Horseshoes showered the stone with sparks, and they lowered their lances, the gleaming points aiming straight at the faltering Chanastardhians. A pair of shield-bearers had the presence of mind to dive out of their way, further reducing the effectiveness of the wall. Rhea didn't see where they went down. Talaen crashed into the enemy a moment after her lance had impaled two soldiers. Against infantry the method of one rank steadying the next was good enough, provided the line was even. When already in tatters, those who remained in formation were easy killing for cavalry.

She let go of her lance. It, and the pair twitching on the shaft, went down. For one frightening moment, it felt as if Talaen had lost her footing amidst the enemy bodies, but then the mare surged on, into the next cluster of foes. Amidst the near stumble, Rhea had trouble drawing her sword. Finally, she slashed down to her right, noticing that Gail was no longer beside her. The steady beat of hooves reassured her that the charge was continuing. There was no time to look for her friend; danger lay in front, what lay behind was up to her comrades to deal with.

Close to the inner ledge stood the archers, in front of them the soldiers wielding the shields. Had it been possible to give Talaen a reassuring pat, she would have done so. The mare trusted her guidance, but sure could have used some encouragement, some show of support, considering what she intended to do now. Rhea fended off a halfheartedly aimed sword—the enemy still confused—then spurred Talaen into a fresh burst of speed, reining the charger as close to the ledge as possible.

Talaen's tremble was a sure sign of how frightened the mare was, and still Rhea sped on, driving Bows and Swords off the wall to the wild cheer of the Danastaerian archers atop the roofs. Before her, the distance shrinking by the heartbeat, the Chanastardhians had finally managed to come to their senses. A wall of lances formed, spears, polearms, a hedgehog of weapons. Already it was too late to turn. Talaen, sensing her tension and frightened by the massive obstacle, veered off. In her panic the charger went left, there at least she could see the ground, even if it was far too much of a leap. For a moment Rhea thought they both might actually make it. Then the mare's front hooves impacted on the cobblestone, slipped. Rhea tried to jump clear as Talaen's legs snapped and the horse wailed in pain. She struck cobblestone hard, slid into a nearby wall, banged her head. Talaen, her thoughts were a jumble, but she knew her duty to the loyal trusting mare. With the world whirling around her, Rheanna stood, stumbled, went to her knees, and then tried to stand again. Finally, her legs steadied. Dizziness rushed her like a wave, and despite the splitting headache and a shoulder that felt half-torn out, she made her way to the pitifully whining mare.

Talaen, despite the obvious pain, tried to stand. The splintered bones of her front legs scratched ineffectually across the stones. Rhea wept, failing miserably at soothing the animal as she cut her mare's throat. "May your life be a better one in the next world," she said, grief gripping her heart. "May Rauggeeth know your quality, my dear friend," she whispered. For a moment, it was as if the world around her had stopped, but then the clash of arms and the screams of the dying engulfed her once more.

On top of the wall she saw fewer than half of the Riders were still in the saddle, reeling back from the bristling Chanastardhian spears. Surging around her friends came foot soldiers, shields raised, intent on driving the foe back even farther. Gavyn and Briog, swords in hand, stood amidst the dead and dying, fending off enemy steel in a wild dance of blades. If Gail, Fynbar, and the others still lived, she could not see. One last look at Talaen then Rhea trotted for the nearest staircase to join the battle once more.

Numb, her shoulder aching, she was barely able to move the shield; yet still she was determined to keep on going. Her friends were up there.

When she reached the battlement, infantry had reclaimed the ground lost to the chance breach caused by enemy 'throwers. Amid the roiling soldiers and horse, the Riders tried to get off the wall once more, she spotted Briog and Gavyn dragging Fynbar away from the melee. Their faces were drawn, that much she could tell even from the distance, and as they drew closer, she saw that Fynbar was barely clinging onto life. His armor was pierced in at least three places, his right arm hung in tatters, and copious amounts of blood covered his face. She hurried to his side.

"The rest?" Even to her ears the question sounded hollow, and the silence of her comrades returned a grim answer.

Briog grunted. Then, to the warriors crowding behind her, he shouted, "Clear the godsdamned way!"

"Can he...?" she fell silent.

As Gavyn threw her a warning glare, she followed them down the same stairs she had ascended only moments before. At its foot the two men put Fynbar down. "Eanaigh," Briog said, his voice reflecting the pain she felt, "we all are mortal. We live, we die. I ask you for the strength to heal this servant of yours. Always has he worked to remind people to live and let live, only has he ended life when necessary. Please, Goddess, grant me the might to cure him." Gavyn, kneeling down beside Briog, added his whispered prayer, and continued chanting while the older Rider closed his eyes and waited.

Then the air around them began to sing. The stench of blood and sweat and feces was drowned out, overshadowed by the scent of freshly tilled earth, roses, even of sex. From experience and long talks with the various Caretakers among the Riders, she knew the aroma was different for everyone; those near the ritual smelled that which reminded them of life. It was a rare moment, for although the gods were ever watchful, Eanaigh rarely intervened in fatal cases. Nature was struggle, and the Lord of Growth and Struggle, Lesganagh, was its ultimate judge. A sickness might be cured, yes, though whereas Lesganagh allowed things to unfold as they did, his daughter and wife, the Lady of Health and Fertility, took a more active stance, every once in a while.

"Thank you, Lady," Briog muttered, awed.

Fynbar's wounds stopped bleeding, his breathing became steadier, yet the gashes and holes remained. Eanaigh gave her priest a chance for life, the healing he had to do by himself. "Stretcher!" Gavyn shouted, and a moment later four fighters trotted their way, between them the couch. Rhea thought they looked familiar, but it was Briog who recognized them.

"Take good care of him, brethren," he said. "The Lady

stopped the bleeding. This is the time you can prove you are truly repentant." Now she remembered. These armored people belonged to Morgan Danaissan's ilk, they were those who had accepted duty on the wall instead of the judgment Cat's son had given the former High Priest.

Gently, the Caretakers put Fynbar on the stretcher and carried him off. "I saw what happened to Talaen," Gavyn remarked. She would have been surprised, had he said more. They were lucky to be talking at all.

"We have to get fresh horses," Briog said, looking past Rhea. The clatter of horseshoes told her that the other surviving Riders had finally descended from the wall.

"All life fades," Gavyn added. The proverb was old, no one knew from which faith it originated, and everyone claimed their church had first come up with it. In the end it didn't matter, what was important was the sentiment.

"Aye," she muttered.

On their way to the stables, losses were tallied. Edmonh, Gail, Diorbail, Kieran, Aehill, and five others had not survived the charge. Their only comfort was that they had managed to weaken the Chanastardhian foothold. Upon arrival, word reached them that a heavy company of Horses had used a similar tactic against the western flank of the enemy. The warriors hadn't been as successful, the only good thing that had come of this second assault was that the enemy Bows had been slaughtered, both by lance and arrow. Now they were trapped on a stretch of battlement four yards wide and fifty long. More were said to be pouring up the ladders, but with Pikes below on New Wall Street and Bows atop nearby buildings, this inflow was slowly spilling bloodily over the edges.

"With so many of them on that strip of stone," Briog concluded after the Horse-Captain had related the news, "the 'throwers will ignore that part of the ramparts."

"There are more than enough other places they can fire on," Rhea said, voicing her doubt.

From the wall thundered a victorious cheer.

"What's that?" Kyleigh asked.

"Let's find out," Gavyn said, and mounted his new horse.

They saddled up, and on their way back down Trade Road, Rhea tried to get used to her new charger's height and temperament. Talaen had been smaller, sleeker. This horse's powerful muscles propelled them forward with an easy grace, and despite his great size, he was younger, well trained certainly, if the Stablemaster could be relied upon. But the stallion seemed much wilder than the mare. This steed couldn't be called skittish, though his temperament might make him shy in the middle of a fight. She hoped she was wrong.

Nerran caught up with them when they arrived at South Gate. The Paladin accepted their losses with some colorful curses, and then broke the news to them, "We only have to worry about one of their 'throwers now." From the looks on their faces, Rhea knew her friends were as reluctant to cheer for this minor victory as she was. "Princess," Nerran said, addressing her in a tone that vaguely echoed his usual light-heartedness. "Good plan, charging down the wall."

Considering their losses, Rhea didn't feel ecstatic about the praise. She silently bobbed her head in acknowledgment.

"Where to, chief?" Briog asked. The Paladin's scrutiny turned from her and onto the Caretaker.

"The breach," Nerran replied. "No bloody idea what we can accomplish, but Princess Rhea's presence might bolster morale." She opened her mouth to voice her dismay. Nerran must have anticipated her reaction, for he said, "Lass, I know you do not like to be put on a fucking pedestal. Trust me, neither I nor any of the others here will do or allow such to be done. Once this is over, provided we live through it, you'll be our little Princess again, understood?" The chuckles around her were weak, subdued.

She nodded. "Very well, chief; let's play through this mummery then."

"It ain't no mummery, lass, but war," Nerran growled, reining his horse. "Never forget that."

By now the sun had almost set, stars were appearing in the black-tinted eastern sky, and the mist billowing out from man and beast grew in density. "Fucking cold," Gavyn muttered. None of them answered.

Atop the wall the defense was still going strong. Arrows, shot from the houses to their left, whistled through the air. The Bows shot sparingly. Full volleys into the enemy below were pointless; the only targets worth shooting were those fighters that reached the tops of the ladders. Here and there forced shouts of victory briefly silenced the groans of the dying, only to be replaced once more by the clash of steel and the screams of the newly wounded. War, Rhea determined not for the first time, was a stupid, senseless act.

The Chanastardhians, she saw when the enemy bastion on the wall came into sight, had fortified their position.

"Just like before," Gavyn grumbled.

"Only difference is that they don't advance," Kyleigh said, frowning. "They're waiting for another lucky shot?"

Rhea shrugged, but Nerran spoke before she could voice her opinion. "Buggers are trying to decide what to do. This is the only place they could really force entry, so far."

"Maybe they just gather their strength," Kyleigh suggested. "One forced assault to either side and they could wipe the ground with our Swords up there."

"So why aren't their crossbowmen shooting?" Briog asked, pointing at the soldiers brandishing the weapons. "Our Bows are visible enough."

"Shit!" Rhea swore as she saw the ripple go through the Chanastardhian lines. Then, scant a heartbeat later, the western enemy flank lashed out pushing their shields against the defenders. With each shield-bearing soldier supported by at least two others the thrust was impossible to counter; still, some of their soldiers tried to stem the tide.

In a matter of moments, arrows shot from roof-bound archers whistled into the milling mass of fighters, felling some. Most shots, however, glanced off armor or struck the steel-reinforced shields. She could only guess how fast the enemy was going, five feet, five yards, ten yards. An unstoppable wave crashed against faltering Danastaerian defenses. The crossbows remained silent.

"What the Scales?" Nerran swore, eyes pinched against the last glares of the sun. Then he let out a gust of air. "Thank the gods! Thought the woman would never come back!" he exclaimed, pointing.

Rhea followed the direction of his finger. Above the houses— flying!—was a woman. The Paladin wasn't the only one who had noticed the newcomer. From the Chanastardhian troops a concerted shout erupted, "Wizard!" An instant later crossbow strings sang. She couldn't see whether the Wizardess, Nerran hadn't mentioned her name, had been struck. The thing she did see was the sorceress performing some sort of ritual, and in the blink of an eye the entire stretch of wall was empty.

# CHAPTER 7

"So," Paddy asked her when they had put enough distance between themselves and the camp, "what shall we do until nightfall?"

Anne smiled happily at her cousin. "Haven't had venison in a while. Porridge gets tedious." The others groaned in agreement and soon the two best archers hurried off into the woods south of them.

"Shame really, to cut down all those trees," Dubhan muttered. In the Chanastardhian highlands the pines and occasional oak were treasured for their ability to keep the soil in place; she silently agreed with her old weapons-master. "Ever seen what the buggers did in the coastal areas?" the old warrior asked.

By now she had learned that her squire was fiercely proud of her heritage, and knew Gwen would be goaded by such a remark. The lass didn't disappoint. "Without ships, getting goods from one place to the other would be tedious! And besides," the seafaring young woman added, "who needs mountains anyway? If you lived in the plains, all that timber wouldn't matter to you anyway, because the soil stays put."

"Speaking of timber," Alayn interjected, "I'm gonna find us some fuel to burn. Who's with me?" Ardeen and Natheira joined him, and the threesome headed for the wasteland of tree-stumps and cut off branches that surrounded them.

They returned quickly, arms loaded with twigs and branches to feed a decent-sized fire. In the hollow, behind one of the taller hills, flames would go undetected. Smoke was a different matter.

Despite having had little rain in the past few days, the frost had sealed the inherent moisture within the wood. Had they not all been, with the exception of Gwen, of House Cirrain—trained at survival from a very young age—this would have presented a problem. Soon nearly smokeless flames danced atop the gathered wood. Paddy produced a skin of wine from one of his saddlebags and passed it around.

Anne always wondered how her cousin managed to smuggle in any amount of comfort. She decided she didn't want to know. When the skin reached her, she declined, stood, and walked from the fire.

She didn't go far, only a good score of yards were between her and the others, their muted voices still distinct in the crisp air. All of them, she knew, had already made a decision, and still the path before her made her skin crawl. Why had her father broken with Herascor? Duty or honor, the words echoed in her mind. The reason that House Cirrain had risen against King Drammoch lay in these two terms. Mireynh had interpreted the royal orders regarding her person, she was sure of it. Treason wasn't tolerated back home, and still her father had committed it, and had pulled her down with him. Not that she wouldn't have followed him. And if this oath breaking had reached Herascor weeks after the actual act, given the distance and lack of general communication, it was clear that Wadram Cirrain had taken matters into his own hands even before she and the others had joined Mireynh's army. Why hadn't her father sent word? They would have never crossed the border. They would have stopped on the spot and returned home.

The choice was made; she would desert. Still, her heart felt little comfort in the fact that she was doing the right thing. Had news of her father reached her before the slaughter of the Danastaerian turncoats she might have reacted differently, at least until the arrows struck down the retreating allies. In a way Mireynh had decided for her which path she should take. Little comfort though this was. Before them was the long journey north, through hostile territory. If someone recognized them, they were done for. Duty and honor laid before her a straight and narrow line of what to do. "Sit out the winter and then get our asses back home," Anne muttered. "The passes are probably shut with snow now anyway, pointless to leave immediately."

But if Dunthiochagh fell... the thought trailed off. Ifs and whens were the herald of hesitation, and she refused to go down that road. The city had never been taken, and even though her countrymen—it was natural to call them thus—counted more than the citizens of the town on the Dunth, Baron Duasonh had a weapon of unequaled strength at his side. With a wizard's aid, all of Mireynh's soldiers would not be enough.

What about Gwen? Wistfully she looked back at her squire, lounging with the others around the fire. The lass wanted to accompany them. Neither Anne nor the daughter of Illar Keelan had a great love for the bickering, backstabbing bastards that were the crop of Chanastardhian aristocracy, but House Keelan would be marked traitor to the crown, as was House Cirrain, if the eldest daughter fled with them.

Footsteps crunched through the hoary grass. Anne turned and saw Paddy approaching, wineskin in one hand, the other easily resting on the pommel of his sword. "You always frown when you're deep in thought, cousin," he remarked when he came to a stop beside her. Her sigh prompted him to add, "Very deep thoughts indeed."

"It's Gwen," she finally said.

"Easy for us to desert, we already are marked traitors," Paddy agreed. "You can't change her mind?"

She looked past him, at the somber yet somehow spirited crowd around the fire. "She's stubborn."

"Aye, that she is."

"I don't know what to do. If she comes with us, she condemns her family."

"She won't turn on us if we leave her behind?"

Anne snorted. "You want to hogtie her?" She regarded her cousin. "She despises our fellow noblefolk as much as we do. The bastard Farlin tried to rape her; the gods only know what someone like Duncan Argram would do."

Paddy remained silent for a while, and then said, "Hostage."

Immediately she caught on to the idea, berating herself for not thinking of this obvious ploy herself. "Mireynh's bound to send others with us, someone will see us deserting, switching sides, taking Gwen with us for ransom."

"Even if the lass's family has no money to buy her freedom, aye," her cousin said, grinning at her. "Your thoughts are always far too complicated, knucklehead."

Playfully she punched him in the arm. "Imbecile."

He shrugged, saying, "Occasionally." Then, "So, we'll do what few of our House have done before?"

"You mean aside from my father and the others?"

"Aye, well, all right, not so few."

"Defection, treason, call it what you will, removing ourselves from the army is the only way to prevent the king from either ordering our executions or using us as levers to make father compliant."

"I wonder why he did it," said Paddy.

She shrugged and turned to head back to the fire. "Must have had his reasons. Let's rejoin the others."

The hunters, Genice and Connar, returned some time later. Having been wedded for almost six years, most of which they had spent tracking and hunting wild goats and wolves, Anne had expected them back soon after the wood-gatherers. Paddy's wineskin was long empty; the skin of spirits supplied by Dubhan, was also nearing its end.

Genice and Connar were not alone. The man accompanying them must have evaded the lookout and rejoined the couple a short way before they made their way into the hollow. At once they jumped to their feet, weapons ready, Anne first among those standing. The couple was still armed; a buck was slung over Connar's shoulder. On the surface nothing seemed amiss, but the newcomer was proof that this was not so.

Then she spotted the single ear of wheat pinned to the stranger's cloak. "Halt!" she snapped. "He means no harm." By now others had detected Eanaigh's symbol, the commonly accepted sign for peace.

Genice looked around, shaking her head. "Really, do you think my husband and I incapable of dealing with one person trying to follow us?" The stranger and Connar snorted, sharing a glance between each other. "He followed us while we tracked the buck. Caught him first, and then the meat."

"I'm Rhygall of House Grendargh," the stranger introduced himself.

"And what do you want from us, Rhygall of House Grendargh?" Paddy asked, voice more tense than Anne had heard in years.

"Funny, I wanted to ask you lot the same," the man said. "Mainly I wanted to know if Genice and Connar here were speaking the truth." His words were underlined by a multitude of creaks as bowstrings were pulled back.

Her people were good, even in this seeming complacency they had not lost their wits or senses. Almost as one—Gwen was a tad slower—they whirled and faced the arrowheads glinting in the setting sun. "What do you want?" Anne snarled.

"Questions answered before my people riddle you with holes," the Danastaerian replied in a frighteningly calm voice. "I ask, you answer, understood?"

Dubhan was the first to throw down his sword. "Bloody pointless this. They have us surrounded."

"Our lookout?" demanded Anne, furious at the ease with which they had surprised them.

"Eating roasted chicken," Rhygall Grendargh said, "for now at least."

She tossed down her weapon. "Ask then."

"Are you truly not after us?"

Genice and Connar must have already answered that question, Anne realized. Rhygall only repeated it to confirm what he already knew. She poked a thumb back at the fire. "Does this look like we are hunting anyone?"

"Except for the buck, of course," added Paddy who had begun skinning the animal.

The ensuing levity leapt from one House's warband to the other, and when she was certain the hidden archers had eased their bowstrings, she said, "Aye, we were hungry."

Rhygall of House Grendargh halted his chuckling and nodded, whether it was at her or at his hidden Bows, Anne couldn't tell. "What brings you here?" Again, she suspected the query was to confirm what he already knew.

Anne looked at the two hunters. Connar shrugged. "You really think it took us that long to shoot one lousy buck?"

"Is it true that you intend to desert your army and join with Duasonh's forces?" Rhygall rephrased his question.

"Aye," she replied. "And assuming these two haven't told you I am to wed some mongrel mountain dweller or another absurdity, you can consider all they said as confirmed." She looked at the hunters, nodded briefly. "Good job."

"Well," Rhygall said, "We're out to shoot us some raping Chanastardhians to put up on the mantelpiece." One look in the man's eyes and Anne knew the statement for what it was: cold-blooded vengeance sworn. Not that she couldn't sympathize with them.

"House Argram did the foraging."

Another of the bowmen spat. "Those sons of whores did more than just take our food."

"We're all aware of that, Duncan Argram has received twice the punishment his troops got. Forty lashes." The number drew a gasp from the Danastaerians. "If you want to hunt an enemy, circle 'round and harry the eastern flank," she continued. "If the gods are with us, we will be eastbound sometime soon."

"Plus," Paddy added, still busy with the buck, "House Farlin's troops are there, and the stupid fucks are too inept to mount any sort of pursuit. Try your luck there."

The Danastaerian noble nodded his thanks. Then, for the first time, she spotted the hidden archers, clad in earthen colors, sprinkled with the occasional green, they were hard to discern even in the open. The group counted some two score, those visible to her at least, though she couldn't be certain there weren't more. All of them carried a flimsy looking staff, far too slender to be either an unstrung bow or any sort of spear. One of the mottled warband tossed Rhygall the second branch she was carrying, and now that it was up close, Anne had the chance to inspect the thing. The noble gave strange hand signs, accompanied by a series of whistles, ignoring her scrutiny.

At first glance the staff looked like a strangely ornamented fishing rod. Only after a few moments did she notice how bloodcurdling the scrollwork imbedded in the wood really was. Amidst knots that looked more and more like entrails were scenes of grisly torture, intermixed with pictures of beings reclining on couches, obviously observing the suffering around them. All of those beings were not human, their features too elegant and cruel at the same time. Even in the victims' faces the hint of cruelty was still present. Then she saw the cord wound around the staff.

Rhygall must have noticed her disgusted curiosity. "Elven warbow," he said. "They look almost as unpleasant as humans when dealing with an enemy."

"It's so slender," she replied, unwilling to meet the Danastaerian's eyes. The almost reverent care with which he handled the grotesque instrument of death sent a shiver of dread down her spine.

"Steeloak," he said as if that explained everything.

"How did you…?"

"We've traded with Gathran since settling here."

Now she looked into his face. "You know elves?"

At that Rhygall laughed. "Milady, there haven't been elves in these parts for nigh on a hundred years. The bows have been in our possession since long before the Heir War, heirlooms if you will." By now the brown-green mottled archers were gone, only their leader remained. A succession of whistles sounded from the distance. "Enjoy your meal," the Danastaerian said; then he hurried after the others.

Even with the city a few miles away they heard the thrum of slingthrowers and the crash of boulders. Anne anxiously paced the perimeter, waiting for a sign to return. How long had the other patrols spent away from the camp? Already her friends were annoyed by this one question none of them could answer. What happened if Mireynh decided not to send House Cirrain? They would have to strike out on their own. Scales, she didn't even know what they were to do when they were with Duasonh's forces. From what she had heard the Baron was a decent man. He had promised her support, but how and when was a different issue. First the siege had to be lifted. And then?

Most likely Duasonh hadn't thought that far ahead, because even if he managed to drive Mireynh off for the winter, what happened next year? She doubted the High General would return to Herascor without having conquered all of Danastaer.

The sun was inching down, soon night would fall. Returning in the dark was akin to suicide, far too many ruts and holes dotted the landscape, not to mention the stumps left behind by the lumber parties. Best to return now. By the sounds of the 'throwers the battle was still going strong. Dunthiochagh was holding. And why shouldn't it? Mireynh had been unprepared for either siege or escalade, too comfortable in the thought that some traitor would open the gate. She shook her head clear and stepped into the makeshift camp. "Let's be gone," she said.

The camp looked different. By chance a few boulders had skipped and bounded through the tents, plowing down horses and warriors alike. Their host was huge, and the losses from the slingthrowers were minor, or so a Sword-Warden informed her, playacting the concerned warleader. She sent Gwen with a group of four to retrieve her tent, determined to sleep in the company of her band in case the hoped-for order come in the morning. Then, escorted by Paddy and Dubhan, she rode to Mireynh's position.

The closer they got to the city, the clearer recent events became. Long rows of wooden roofs seemed to home in on the city, providing shelter from enemy arrows. Some of those contraptions had already been reduced to blood-soaked kindling, but the majority remained standing. Beside her, Dubhan snorted.

She threw him a questioning glance. "Hmm?"

"Foolish, if you ask me," he grunted. "We have only one 'thrower remaining." He pointed in the direction of the two holes dug for the siege-engines. The farther one was just now lobbing another rock at Dunthiochagh, while the other was surrounded by a host of warriors who, in the flickering torchlight, were busy with repairs. "It'll be a bitch without proper artillery support."

Most of the soldiers they passed were bruised, some with

broken bones perhaps, but most showed only signs of exhaustion and frustration. "There's still the reserves," Paddy pointed
out.

"Aye, still won't do much good unless they manage to dis-
lodge a part of the defenders and gain a foothold on the wall."
The old warrior spat on the ground. "Look at them corpses."
He motioned to a score of men and women carrying off their
slain comrades. "Most of them have been stabbed in the back,
not by anyone's intention, mind. They just fell in a bad spot,
mate."

Anne looked north, at the wall lined by ladders with milling, eager soldiers at their feet. Farther to the east, she saw, a
whole stretch of wall that actually was held by—what should
she call it anyway? Chanastardhians, Enemy—the attacker,
House Argram's banner visible even from this distance. "What
about that?" she asked, indicating the spot. In the gloom of twilight, the only good light source were the flames of some of the
wheeled roofs. "They... we're already occupying a piece of the
wall."

Dubhan spat again. "So? Do you see a steady stream of people rushing up the ladders? They are on the wall, sure, but the
buggers can't move on."

"Think they..." she fell silent. Now House Argram was
on the move once more, pushing back against the defenders.
For several long heartbeats it seemed as if they would actually
manage to take a long swath of battlement, and then—she had
to rub her eyes to make sure she was not seeing things—the
entire contested length of the wall was wiped clean. "Gods!"
she hissed.

In a wide arc bodies tumbled through the air, crashed
down onto frozen ground, onto wooden roofs, barreled into
unprotected archers. Then, from the hill to their left, she heard
Mireynh's unmistakable roar of anger.

Tugging her horse's reins, she wheeled the mare around,
and applied pressure with her thighs. "Come on, let's see how
the High General's faring," she said, as the charger took off at
a light canter. Paddy and Dubhan followed. Again, their path
took them through clusters of wounded and beaten soldiers.

Others, looking eager and fresh, went the other way, straight for the mobile roofs.

When they reached the command hill, Anne's attention was immediately drawn to the man on a visibly exhausted stallion. Upon closer inspection the rider looked even worse. Not a spot on his surcoat and armor was free of caked blood, though none of it seemed to be his own. A gory patina that accentuated his jutting cheekbones marred the man's face. It seemed as if he had wallowed around in a butcher shop's muck. Dubhan and her cousin must have thought the same, for both men swore under their breaths.

Then the blood-caked face turned her way, and she was finally able to identify the rider. "Braddan," Anne whispered. Of all the nobles, she despised the scion of House Kirrich the least, Gwen was the only true exception but still, to see him like this stunned her.

"Trileigh!" Mireynh snarled. His eyes were focused on the empty spot of wall that was filling with Danastaerians. "Before anyone goes up there again, make sure they got the Wizard! And get a count of dead and wounded; that was House Argram up there; get a healer to Sir Duncan right away."

"Sir!" the nobleman confirmed, turned, and called for a runner. "Fetch some healers and someone from House Argram, tell them to do what's possible and count the dead!" he briefly summed up the order, and then added, "Make haste, damn you!" The runner rushed off.

"Damn those wizards!" Mireynh shouted. He turned to Braddan, his face betraying conflicting urges. Anne could only imagine how the High General felt, not having known the man for that long, though the anger and shock at the devastation atop Dunthiochagh's wall was slowly being replaced by a worried scowl.

"Gods, Kirrich," Noel Trileigh said. "What the Scales happened?" That Mireynh remained silent and did not lash out at the Lord Commander suggested something serious had passed between the two.

"My... my lords," Braddan stuttered. He looked weary, and up close it was not only from the patina of blood. The haunted, wandering stare, eyes that rarely remained steady for more than a few heartbeats, darting, furtive glances as if Jainagath himself was trailing the noble.

"Gods, man," Mireynh grumbled. "Pull yourself together."

"Maybe he needs a drink," Paddy suggested. As always, her cousin had no respect for any sort of etiquette, speaking even when his opinion was not wanted. That the High General merely waved for a page to bring a tray of bottles, however, was enough evidence that Mireynh had other things to worry about. Her reproachful glance was answered with a mocking wink.

Anne waited, along with the others who alternated their attention between the exhausted nobleman and the once more well defended wall. Finally, after several long pulls from a bottle of wine, Braddan had dismissed the goblet with a fierce shake of the head, and an equally long time with a jug of spirits, he spoke. "Horror, slaughter, Ondalan's in his hands now," he muttered, words spilling franticly from his lips.

"Godsdamnit, man," Mireynh snapped. "Has the booze gone to your head already? Speak sense!"

"He said he wants his reward!"

"Calmly, Sir Braddan," Noel Trileigh intervened, casting a reproachful glance at his superior. Something had definitely changed. "Tell us what happened at Ondalan, there is no need for panic, you are here among... friends." A quick look about told her she was not the only one to have noticed the slight hesitation in the Lord Commander's voice, although Mireynh was too busy shifting his attention from the faltering escalade to the wounded and back to Braddan Kirrich. Dubhan moved not a muscle, but his lip twitched in a slight sneer; Paddy's right eyebrow was gently arched. "Tell us what happened, calmly," Trileigh repeated.

"At noon he came, with a score of others. The perimeter must've been taken completely by surprise, for only after a blast from the horn signaling immediate danger were we alerted. I rallied my men, trained veterans mind,"—Anne knew House Kirrich's well-disciplined infantry—"and as a wall we advanced, blocking the path." Braddan groaned, requested the spirits with a wave of his hand, and took another long pull from the bottle, the liquid spilling down his blood-caked chin.

"One man had taken the sentinels posted in the village stronghouse. He stormed at the wall, again and again, like one possessed. I gathered the others to bolster our defense. And the madman just kept running and running against the shields." A shudder ran through Braddan. "They pierced him, stabbed him, but his wounds closed. And then the wall faltered." He let out a dismayed wail. "Arrows from his allies opened a gap and he was amongst them. Those who didn't flee were butchered on the spot."

Anne looked over to Mireynh whose gaze had stopped roaming, eyes intent on the raving warleader. Was that a glint of recognition in his eyes?

"We retreated around a bend, and waited with a new wall in place." Braddan took another long pull from the bottle, the booze cleaning his chin, bloody droplets splattering on his surcoat, mixing with the gore there. "He followed. Then, as he stood before us, he faltered, stopped. When he remained unmoving, I ordered my troops to take him down most painfully." A shuddering breath and hacking cough later, he continued.

"I was with them. We charged, beat him down, kicked, scratched, pounded, and he just hung there, took the blows as if they concerned him not! Then he looked at us, cursed us, and took us apart with his bare hands at first, and then with his sword. He was mad with rage, but he did not heal anymore. My cousin and I fled. He followed, ran my cousin through, and with his still twitching body impaled on his blade, the sword keeping poor Ailan's legs a foot above the ground, he demanded that I relay a message." Quivering, wavering eyes met Mireynh's as he waited for the High General to respond.

Mireynh was ashen, even with the walking dead and the shattered lumber he had kept his emotions hidden. Now they were plain on his face. "Speak!" he whispered, his hushed voice still carried to her ear, and Anne heard the rage and grief within.

"He said to tell you, Drangar Ralgon is there, and he still wants the promised reward. That you still owe him," Kirrich stammered, his haunted look intensifying.

The High General's reaction was different, but just as

shocking. "Damn you, Ralgon, you whoreson! Fucking bastard! Should have put his accursed head on a pike when I had the chance!" He turned to a drummer. "Sound the retreat, son, we have other things to do." Anne felt her eyes grow wide.

"Sir!" Trileigh intervened.

"What?" Mireynh glared at the Lord Commander. As she stared on, incredulous, she noticed for the first time that the High General's bodyguard had inched closer to their charge, hands on their weapons. It did not look like they were trying to protect him.

"We have a city to worry about, an escalade! You cannot commit the entire army to the capture of one man! That is madness, sir!"

"Bastard Ralgon won't get away this time!"

"The army will not hunt down this friend of yours, Mireynh." She wasn't sure the words had actually been spoken, so hushed had they been. One look at the High General and the Black Guard at his side, with Mireynh's face plunging from furious red to a deathly pallor in a heartbeat, told her she had not imagined it.

"Damn this fucking...! Runner!" he roared, and as a young woman rushed to his side, he continued his verbal abuse.

To the girl he said, "Get Lord Argram here!" Anne felt her heart sink; that he would send the butchers of House Argram there she had not anticipated.

The runner was about to hurry off when another returned, leading a horse. On a stretcher, attached to the saddle lay Sir Duncan. Her spirits rose as she saw how beat up the nobleman was. The right leg was splinted, covered in bandages. His left arm hung limp in a sling, also splinted and bandaged. "Belay that!" Mireynh snapped.

"Fucking wizard," Argram muttered drowsily.

"The healers gave him ophain to keep him calm," the runner explained.

"Damn those wizards!" Mireynh snarled. Then his sight fell on her and his face lit up. "Cirrain!"

"Sir?" she replied.

"Rouse your warband."

Playacting had never been her strong suit; the recent days deceiving everyone around her, however, had improved her skill. "Sir?" she asked, trying to sound confused. "We've been out hunting Danastaerians all day."

"Damn you, woman, I thought your kind was highland-folk, trained to fight wherever and whenever."

Paddy, by far the better liar, snapped, "House Cirrain is always ready, milord!"

"Good!"

"Your orders, High General?" she asked, throwing a glance at the Black Guards who had now returned to their customary positions, their faces betraying no emotion.

"Take two score of House Kirrich's warriors with you and head to Ondalan! Bring me Drangar Ralgon's head on a pike!"

"Yes, sir!" To her companions she said, "Let's get going, we have a long way ahead of us."

"And Cirrain."

"Sir?"

"Be careful, the bastard is very dangerous."

"We can handle it, milord," she said confidently. They took off, heading first to their tents, and then to freedom, rebellion, and war with their own country.

# CHAPTER 8

Ysold's voice was still pounding in her head as Ealisaid swooped over the Dunth toward the wall that encircled the southern portion of the city. In the final moments of sunlight, she saw pockets of fighting everywhere. From this high up it was hard not to. For a moment the myriad flickering flames, the screech of steel on steel, the shouts of the dying, and the curses of the living painted a tapestry of destruction. Then, with a clarity that had previously eluded her, she discerned more detail. Most melees were in control, and the Danastaerian forces dealt with the enemy swiftly. The area west of South Gate was contested, yes, but not so fiercely fought over as the east.

The enemy's roofs, corridors through which the attackers could advance unhindered, spread from the wall like the spokes of a wheel. Jutting out like fingers from the ends adjacent to the wall she saw ladders, three or four to each corridor, and up those the Chanastardhians came. Most were sent sprawling the instant they reached the battlements, but in the east the enemy had gained a foothold.

Now they were battering back the defenders, gaining even more ground. Here the enemy had put up a good dozen ladders, and up the ladders came scores of warriors, bolstering the twin assault.

Her magic was needed here! She wished she had more time to perfect the battlespells, but given the situation, this was impossible. Gritting her teeth—the wind was as icy as it had been in the Shadowpeaks—with tears streaming down her cheeks freezing to nothingness the same instant, Ealisaid swooped for the embattled wall. The chill air caressed her body through the seams of her dress; she shivered, ground her teeth, and sped on.

The closer she got the more distinct the sight became. With the sun now beyond the western hills, torches and burning roofs were the only illumination left. The breach was worse than she had initially thought. If the Chanastardhians kept pushing like this, and more people scaled the wall with every heartbeat, the wall would not last much longer. A valiant group of infantry-men tried to stem the tide of steel flowing toward them, but the enemy crashed into and over them. She saw reserves rushing for the wall, too late.

"Wind," she muttered, "remember your strength. Remember how it felt, crashing through the mountains, across the sea, rip-ping with you everything in sight." The cold around her inten-sified then eddied away; the air remembered.

Now that she knew what to do, directing the magic was easy. But she had to get closer to ensure that she cleared the entire wall. Through the stiff gale, her dress and hair whipping about her, stinging her face and legs, she dove for the ground and swung into position a few yards above the nearest roof.

The wind followed, went lower.

When the blast closed in on the enemy, just before the wall was to be swept clear, somebody amidst the foe shouted "Wizard" and before Ealisaid even realized what was going on, three score crossbowmen took aim and fired at her.

The gale struck from behind and below, but the bolts flew unhindered, and though she tried to dodge and weave, the strain of the past days made her slow. As the combatants atop the bat-tlement were blown clear off the wall into the forces beyond, the first missile pierced her thigh. Ealisaid let out a scream, which was redoubled when a second and third bolt struck home. The bowmen had spread their volley, many shots missed, striking chimneys, and shingles. A fourth and fifth punctured her; she plummeted down, coughing blood and screaming in agony. The last thing she saw was a band of Swords retaking the cleared wall. Then she hit the roof.

"Someone sure looks over her," a man close to her said.

"Will she live?" another asked.

"Hard to say, Cumaill."

The Baron was here? Ealisaid strained to open her eyes. A sliver of light flashed into her, sliced into her mind.

"She's coming to." Now she knew it was the Baron; his voice was one of a kind.

"Would've been better if the lass had just died like most of the poor sods she dumped on the other side," a third voice grumbled. "That hothead Kerral is furious, can't blame him." Was that the Paladin? Nerran? "Why didn't she check with us first?"

"Same reason your princess got half your Riders killed, she thought there was no time," the first man retorted, and then said, "Can you hear me, Lady Wizard?"

She wanted to nod, instead hot pain coursed through her neck. A whimper escaped her lips.

"Will she live?" the Baron asked again.

"No idea, the bolts alone were enough, lung pierced, some tendons ripped. The fall did the rest."

"Can't you pray for her health?" Duasonh said.

"Prayers help the spirit, rarely the body," the Paladin said with a derisive snort. "A Caretaker's blessing is that he can treat a wound without risking infection."

"But I heard what happened to Fynbar," the Baron interjected. "He was healed."

"Rumors spread like wildfire; he was brought from the brink of death, but he still has to heal," Nerran grunted.

"Aye," the third man agreed. "If you want me to, I can cut her and try to mend whatever wounds there are. It's dangerous; the blood loss might kill her just as well."

"As if the bolts and her fall aren't doing that already," Duasonh muttered. "What's the Lady of Health and Fertility's job if not to heal the ill and injured?"

"The Lady rarely heals those who are dying; otherwise we'd have no death…"

"So, she is dying!" Duasonh said. "That won't do. She can help end this nonsense."

"One mage cannot defeat an army," Nerran said. "Besides,

the way she is going she will likely kill as many of ours as of theirs. The lassie isn't fit to do battle even if she were healthy."

"So what, pray tell, do you Caretakers do? Just take care of people, tell 'em all will be well and not lift a finger?"

"Bullshit! We mend wounds, we make sure crops thrive, but bringing back one who is already toeing the Bailey Majestic is... well... a miracle. Eanaigh guides my hand during surgery, whether the one cut open survives is up to themselves."

"Then sharpen your knife, you're going in."

She wanted to scream, tell them she could hear them and that they were discussing cutting open her body while she was wide awake. Why was she unable to enter the spiritworld? And where was Ysold to talk some sense into this trio of jesters? Another thought struck her. What if the Eanaighist wanted to cut her open while she was awake? Her entire body ached as it was, and though she couldn't speak, she could listen, perhaps even scream.

A door opened. "My lords?" a woman said.

"Fetch Winna from the Lady's Temple," the Caretaker said. "Tell her she is needed here, and ask her to bring the ophain; we need to send someone to sleep."

"Certainly, High Priest," the servant replied and the door shut again.

"Ophain?" Nerran said. "Strong stuff."

"Aye," the Baron agreed. "Didn't know you had drugs like that at the place."

"It'll slow the heartbeat and make her as oblivious to pain as possible. And yes, we have things like that at the temple; after all, even though my predecessor made people pay for what should be given freely, our duty is to tend to the ill and injured."

Consciousness came and went. The voices faded in and out. One moment Paladin Nerran was there, the next he was gone. Then he returned, only to fetch the Baron. Someone else came, Winna most like. The two Caretakers conversed in hushed tones. Only fragments reached her ear, even less penetrated her mind.

"... so many wounded..."

"... the Baron..."

"... at her... dead for... the fact..."

"… save her…"

"… kill her…"

"… all we can…"

Her head was lifted carefully and tilted back. For an instant her eyes fluttered open. She saw an older woman, looking at her through weary eyes. "Drink," the Caretaker ordered. Ealisaid wanted to laugh. How should she drink this when even breathing was painful? It was dark once more.

"No, we need to get it into her blood."

"What do you suggest? We pour it onto her wounds?"

"Close."

Though her body was numb, she felt the blade cut into her arm, but not because of sharp pain. The steel was cold. "Keep her down!" She wanted to roll away, prevent more harm coming to her body.

"You're crazy, High Priest!"

"Cumaill wants her safe, so I do my godsdamned best to save her. Hand me that tube."

"That thing is bigger than the entire vein!"

"You have a better idea, something that we can use now? No? I didn't think so."

"You need to stop the blood flow!"

"Tie her arm."

By now she was almost beyond caring. Through a haze she heard voices, the argument. The excruciating pain that stabbed into her vein was like the bolts that had pierced her. Suddenly, it felt as if she was floating. Then…

She came to again. Her head felt worse than before.

"The goddess was with us." The voice sounded like the High Priest's. "Did you feel her?"

An uncertain laugh. "I'm not sure what I felt."

A door opened, and heavy feet stomped in. "Gods, what a bloodbath!" Was that the Baron?

"Not worse than the battlements, really," a fourth voice—the Paladin's?—said.

"You didn't kill her?"

"If she lives through the night, she might make it, if not, I'm sure Jainagath won't mind yet another soul to take to the Scales."

"How many of ours died during this madness?" Duasonh asked. "Not the entire assault, mate, I mean how many did she kill?" The question should be how many still lived because of her action. She wanted to scream, protest, but the pain in her head redoubled. Though she found it easier to breathe, she remained as she was.

"Had she not done it we would've lost one-half of the city, lad," the Paladin said grimly.

"So that makes it right?" the High Priest asked. If she could only open her eyes! She wanted to defend her actions. Was the spiritworld a possibility? Maybe. She had to try. The first calm breath she tried to draw sent blazing pain through her body. Scales! Talking to Ysold in spiritform was out of the question as well.

"Lad, you've never seen or been in a real battle; the skirmish here in the Palace doesn't count. If you win, your actions were right, if you lose, well, then it won't matter fuck all if what you did was right or wrong. What the Scales is she doing?"

"Give her something to make her rest; having her conscious won't help," Duasonh ordered. "You can send her to sleep?"

"Of course I can."

"More ophain? Is that wise? She's just been cut open and sewn shut," Winna said.

"It's out of our hands now anyway."

"No more pouring it through the vein!"

"What the Scales do you mean?" Nerran grumbled. After a short pause he asked, incredulous, "You put that into a vein? Braigh, you are crazy."

"I knew it would work."

"True, you couldn't have made it much worse."

"This time she'll drink the ophain."

"Then don't just stand there, if she lives there might be some who'll bitch about her actions, but in my book she did good. The lass has spirit. Too bad she doesn't know spit about defending herself."

Something dribbled down her throat and she swallowed. The voices faded away.

# CHAPTER 9

## First of Cold, 1475 K.C.

"You truly intend to abandon the city?" Fiacuil asked, the look on his face showing that he battled with concern and comprehension. The Black Guard still served his master, Mireynh had seen no indication otherwise, but still he felt a sort of kinship had grown between them.

"Abandon it?" the High General said. "Hardly, my friend." He thought a glimmer of pride briefly illuminated the younger man's face. Maybe he was probing the waters; maybe having Fiacuil as an ally would ease the High Advisor's inevitable blow. Right now, it hardly mattered. His family was less important. The tactical situation here by the Dunth mattered not. Last time, he would have had a mutiny on his hands had he hammered the bastard Ralgon to the next wall. This time, none of his soldiers cared. "I've halted the escalade, not given up on conquering the bloody town. The King's spies have failed us, and I've done everything in my power, in our power, to take the city. Now we'll sit back and consider our options."

"My lord, the High Advisor will not look kindly on any delay," the Black Guard replied.

"I did the best I could do given the fucked-up situation we faced," he snapped, regretting the outburst almost immediately. "Forgive me, my friend, matters have been tense."

"Think nothing of it, milord."

"You probably know better than I what is at stake here," Mireynh said in a calmer tone. "Scales, who knows, maybe you are under as much compulsion as I am." As the words left his mouth, he wondered if this had been too much.

For a moment Fiacuil remained silent, and then said, "We all do our duty to the best of our abilities." It was neither the confirmation Mireynh had hoped for, nor the firm denial he had expected. The guardsman's statement could be seen from both positions and still make sense. For now, it had to suffice.

"Assure the High Advisor I will stay the course, even if we have to wait until next year." Mentioning only the title, not the name, was intentional, a test to gauge the Black Guard's reaction. Fiacuil remained silent. "Winter's almost upon us, and even though I have no doubt that our warriors are hardy folk, the snow works to Duasonh's advantage. With one slingthrower gone, taking any part of the wall is dependent on luck, and I am tired on relying on chance to get things done." Now he had to wait, the bait was laid out and all the Black Guards had to do was follow the line to its logical conclusion. No, it wasn't his fault the bloody city still was in Danastaerian hands, had he had his way the army would have taken 'throwers and other heavy equipment with them. He saw understanding dawning behind Fiacuil's eyes. "Now, if you excuse me," he added, giving his voice an extra note of having other matters on his mind, "there are things I need to see to. An army unfortunately does not run itself. There are lists of dead and wounded, and I need to assess the situation completely."

"Certainly, milord, I understand." The warrior saluted—a first, Mireynh remarked silently—then left the tent.

To Fiacuil he had spoken more confidently than he truly felt. It seemed moot to discuss whether it was wiser to waste the army on wall and plain, maintaining the siege and assaulting the city on a daily basis, or retreating to Harail to regroup. In the end, the result was the same: the High Advisor had to wait. Not that he knew what the bastard had in mind. When he had been told the invasion was to happen in late autumn, he had first decided the King was mad. Then, with the revelation of the mind behind this plan, he had attributed the High Advisor with the same disease of the mind.

But the bastard had prepared for Danastaer, and as leader of Chanastardh's army he had been forced to obey. Actually, he had made the best of the situation. If only the spy within Dunthiochagh had been more reliable.

Now he was trapped. The future looked gloomier by the heartbeat. No doubt the High Advisor would vent his displeasure on Mireynh's family. Why had he agreed to become leader of a regular army in the first place? As mercenary general he had been content. Until... "Ralgon!" the name hissed from Mireynh's lips. "Damn you!" His life had changed the day that whoreson had tossed his boy's head at his feet.

All this was Ralgon's fault. Had the bastard not killed Kirran, Mireynh might have never opted for this life of servitude. He hardly dared to hope Anne Cirrain would capture the cutthroat, would have preferred Duncan Argram hunt him down. If it hadn't been for the Baron's pet wizard, the hulking nobleman would be halfway to Ondalan now. Argram was ruthless enough to carry out any mission, no matter the cost. Scales, even with his arm and legs braced Argram was a far more efficient leader than Trileigh, even though that man had his uses.

"Sir?" someone asked. Mireynh turned and saw a young man poking his head into the tent. His complexion and features were similar to that of Sir Duncan. "Murray Argram, milord General, here as requested."

"I asked for a report, not a visitor."

"I have the information," replied young Argram proudly.

"Well then," he said with a sigh, hoping that at least one part of the planning had gone as intended. "Come in."

Murray Argram was almost as tall as the Argram heir, though he lacked the elder's muscled physique. Still, his salute was crisp and he wore the scabbarded sword with the ease of an experienced campaigner. "Sir," the lad said, standing at attention.

"Well?" Mireynh asked impatiently.

"The Lord Commander's tactic proved successful, sir."

"Did it now?" he asked. Maybe Trileigh was no fighter, but as a tactician he might be useful come spring.

"Aye, sir." Young Argram fingered in his pouch and pulled out a folded paper. Opening it, he began to recite, "Of the hundred atop the wall forty-one were killed, the rest, like my cousin, were injured, some suffered only a dislodged shoulder or a few broken fingers, more had serious breaks, and a few had to undergo cutting." A moment later, he added, "Sir!"

"The numbers are of minor interest," Mireynh spat back, annoyed. Too many good people had been injured or killed. "What I want to know is if the wizard is dead!"

"She flew into the cluster of bolts, just as predicted."

"And?" he prompted. Even if they retreated to Harail to sit out the winter, with the wizard gone Duasonh would only be able to muster natural defenders. Natural he could deal with; the supernatural would make the next siege unpredictable. Who knew what sort of destruction the sorceress could unleash with a few months' respite?

"At least a score of Crossbows saw her hit and crash into a building, sir. None could confirm a kill since they were all pushed off the wall, sir."

"Chance a guess," he said. "Could anyone survive such a crash?" He had seen people live through a lot of punishment. The human body was quite resilient, and since he had no idea how many missiles had struck the wizard, and more importantly, where they had hit, eyewitness reports might prove more conclusive.

"One claims her chest was punctured; nobody could confirm it, though. Unfortunately. They all say she was flopping about the air pretty wildly before crashing. If I were to guess, I'd say she's dead, but as my da always says, anything's possible, sir." His face must have darkened for young Argram uncomfortably shifted his weight from one foot to the other.

"Thank you," Mireynh said with a nod that he hoped looked less angry than he felt. "Send in my aide, and tell your cousin I demand his attendance at once. Dismissed!"

The young nobleman gave a shaky salute, turned about smartly, and strode out. When the flap had shut behind the youth, the High General went to his chair near the small iron oven, and sank down into the furs. "Fucking wizardry!" he swore, clenching his hands.

Mireynh was just about to slam both fists onto the tabletop

when his aide entered. "Milord General, I would advise against that. The Caretakers said any strain to your body would put more pressure on your back."

He cast a scathing look at the young man. Sycophantic as Nairn was, he was still efficient in looking after his needs, even if his overeager nature annoyed Mireynh on a daily basis. "Nairn, thank you for your consideration," he said, not trying to hide the sarcasm tinting his voice. Nairn merely nodded in his typical way. Whether the man was mocking him or being serious was impossible to tell.

"Your wellbeing is my chief concern, milord." Was there a trace of irony in his voice? He couldn't tell. With the Black Bastards and Bitches it was easy. They never hid their intentions. Nairn, however, was a trained courtier; at least he behaved like one. Or maybe he was just getting paranoid.

"Send runners to the warleaders, ask them here at once," Mireynh said, and then added, "When that's done, start packing my things, and yours as well."

"We're leaving?" Again, no hint of emotion marred the aide's face.

"Aye, in a week or so we should be back in Harail."

"Let's hope the snow waits until then, aside from the Elven Roads these trails here barely deserve to be called trails."

"True enough. Now get to it."

Nairn bowed, saying, "At once, milord." Then he hurried out, adopting a casual, yet purposeful stroll. Mireynh had seen these antics so many times he didn't notice.

A feeling of dismay rose as he glanced at the tattered reports stacked on his table. In all likelihood most were merely wounded, like House Argram's warriors, but the death toll would be high. Maybe one or two hundred, at least he hoped it were that few. The corridors had prevented the enemy archers from shooting feathered death into the infantry, but the sling-thrower rocks had drilled through some of the roofs. "Perhaps there're more," he muttered.

He had just taken the first report—he didn't mind the state the papers were in; given last night's fighting the Wardens and warleaders had better things to do than to find a suitable spot

to write—when a voice outside shouted, "Message for the High
General! Let me pass!"

It had to be urgent. Usually the couriers were a quiet lot,
passing through camp like any other rider. That this one
announced his presence so loudly underlined his importance.

With a grunt he rose. His back ached, courtesy of being in
the saddle longer than he had in ages. Nairn would have sent
for a healer. He grimaced. The Caretakers had better things to
do than worry about one old man's back. There were too many
wounded, and he refused to draw any Eanaighist away from
where he was needed. Gritting his teeth, he went for the flap.

Before he was halfway there, the fabric was pushed aside
and a haggard looking man came in. The messenger gave a
weak salute. Judging from the state of his clothes, the chap had
not slept for days.

"Milord General, urgent missive from Herascor."

Wearily he returned the salute and took the proffered scroll-
tube. Both King Drammoch and the High Advisor had sealed
it. He was far too tired to hide his surprise. This, indeed, was
urgent. "Thanks," he muttered absentmindedly. "Take one"—
he pointed at the tray laden with bottles—"and tell my cook to
fix you something. Dismissed." What kind of booze the courier
made off with didn't concern him, the man's presence forgotten
by the time he broke the seals and sank back onto his chair. Two
seals, no other message had been secured this way, it had to
be very important. He reached inside, withdrew the rolled-up
parchment and read.

When he was done a second time, the first of his warleaders
stood before him. "Fucking Scales," he muttered, and took in
the full of the writing once more.

"Make a hole," someone in front of the tent said. Irritated,
he looked up and saw four men in Argram livery carry inside
a litter bearing their lord. Weary though all of them looked, the
warriors managed to clear the path before an accident could
occur. He barely noticed.

"Milord?" Noel Trileigh sounded as tired as he felt. He
looked at the Lord Commander; the noble not only sounded as
he felt but looked the part as well. Wordlessly he held out the

message, if he couldn't share this information with Drammoch's cousin with whom else then.

"Read, tell me what you think," he grumbled.

Nairn passed out mugs filled with steaming tea. His, as always, was spiced with a bit of mead. Dully he nodded his thanks. How the Scales was this possible? He burned his lips on the liquid, but hardly felt the pain; the dull ache in his stomach overshadowed such paltry things as scalding tea.

He felt betrayed, angry, and empty. Ralgon would escape once more. He had no doubt that the bastard was at Ondalan; Lord Kirrich's description too precise to be an empty tale. If only he had been able to get his hands around the Scythe's throat. The enthused determination he had felt only moments ago was gone. Did this war really matter? Did his family matter? Kirran was dead, and his killer had eluded him again. No, he decided. Not if he could get to Ondalan within the day! "Nairn, get my horse ready! Killoy, have your Horse saddle up!"

"Sir?" Killoy asked, looking at him as if he were mad.

"You heard me! We need to get to Ondalan!" he roared. "We need to catch him!"

"Catch who, milord?" the cavalry leader said.

"The bastard who's taken the place!" he shot back. Noel Trileigh cleared his throat. He glared at the noble, "What?"

"Cirrain has most certainly fled, General, what needs to concern us now is how to keep more mischief from happening."

"Ralgon is getting away!"

"Who?" Sir Duncan asked.

"We can still catch the bastard!" Didn't they understand?

"Sir, whoever this Ralgon is," Trileigh put in, "we have to think of the invasion, and the code, and the spy in our midst, not some personal vendetta. House Cirrain hasn't been cleared of treason; the message that said so was a forgery." When had this fop become so levelheaded, he wondered. Then he realized just how the hope of capturing Ralgon distracted him. Gods, he had matters of more importance to attend to.

He looked at Nairn who had remained inside, staring at him like he was some kind of ghost. "Forget what I said," he muttered, embarrassed that one such as Trileigh had reminded him of what was important. "Killoy, don't gather the Horse."

"What does the message say?" demanded Sir Braddan.

"It is written in the clear, no code, signed by the King and the High Advisor," Trileigh answered, his frown shifting from the parchment to Mireynh and back to the missive. "House Cirrain is still in open rebellion, and we are to put Anneijhan of House Cirrain and her troops in chains and send them to Herascor." His look returned to Mireynh. "The message saying House Cirrain had returned to its senses was written in code, this one is not. Yet I know my cousin's hand, no scribe wrote this. I suspect there was no time to encode it, things with House Cirrain and the northmen seem urgent."

"Are you saying Duasonh got a spy into our camp who cracked the code and managed to sneak in a forged message indistinguishable from the official one?" Duncan Argram said from his litter.

"Aye," Trileigh replied. Why hadn't he seen the obvious connection? Had his hate for Ralgon blinded him so much that he couldn't see the obvious? Mireynh was angry with himself for being blinded by his reawakened thirst for revenge.

He scoffed. All heads turned to regard him, and, trying to keep the anger from seeping into his voice, he said, "That makes things easier. We all can agree that even though we have superior numbers, Dunthiochagh's defenses are holding and we will waste resources trying to get inside without the support of more artillery."

"Bloody wizard bitch," Argram spat, others muttered in agreement.

"We can't confirm whether Duasonh's wizard is dead or not, but we have to assume the worst." He halted, seeing the head of a Black Bitch poking inside, listening. She was not staring daggers at him, and he dared to hope Fiacuil had been able to sway their opinions. If not, it was still best to proceed.

"Without proper equipment we'll never be able to take the entire city. It's getting colder, and the clouds gathering around us are heavy with snow," he continued. "We'll retreat to Harail, wait out the winter, building new artillery, and licking our wounds. Duasonh will no doubt do the same, but even if there is no siege, with all the food we have foraged, people within Dunthiochagh will starve before Seed. Next year we will succeed."

Silence followed; he watched them ponder his decision. Some certainly would voice the issue of freeborn and villeins having to return to their fields before Seed, but he had a reply ready for them.

It was Lord Kirrich who spoke first. "Sir, with the beginning of next year we need to be home, on the fields. Planting takes priority, otherwise we all will starve."

"The High Advisor has assured me that all will be taken care of."

"How?" the noble wanted to know. That anyone would question the High Advisor's word was one thing, he could live with that. But one of his warleaders putting his word to the test was quite another.

"All will be settled," he answered coldly. "Dismissed! We're heading back to Harail."

As he watched the noblemen and noblewomen file out, he saw meaningful glances exchanged by Kirrich and Killoy. He understood their unease, both Houses were largely dependent on agriculture, and the vague promise he had given them—if he were honest with himself—did not sound truly convincing. On the other hand, by now he hoped the nobles trusted his judgment. The moment his word was questioned would open a new rift of distrust.

When Sir Duncan's litter had been carried out, the only people left were Nairn and Lord Trileigh. "Leave us," he told the servant, and when the sycophant was gone, he turned to the Lord Commander who calmly regarded him.

"You are a learned man, Trileigh." The other acknowledged the compliment with a nod. "When I was told of the planned invasion, I was skeptical, to say the least. You know I'm not fond of traitors, there's a reason for that."

"I assume it is this Ralgon," the Lord Commander said. Then he hesitated, frowning. "Is that Drangar Ralgon?"

It was his turn to be surprised. How would one such as Trileigh know of the bastard? "You heard of him?" Mireynh asked, his voice betraying nothing of the resigned anger he still felt at having his son's killer elude him once more.

It took Trileigh a moment to reply. Then he said, "Aye, he butchered his way through a lord's castle to free a nobleman's daughter." Chuckling, he added, "The reward promised for the girl's return was a distraction for the father's villeins and relatives, the fool had bartered the girl away, receiving a hefty dowry to pay off his debts."

"I take it the rescue wasn't well received," Mireynh asked.

"Not from the father, no, but to his family and villeins Ralgon was heralded a hero, so he had no choice but to reward him. Next thing that happened was the groom putting out his own reward for Ralgon's head; ever since he hasn't set foot on Chanastardhian soil." There was a brief pause, Trileigh studied him, and he wondered what was going on in the noble's mind. "Ralgon has a knack for stirring up trouble, hasn't he?"

"Aye," Mireynh replied, and before he could say more his second in command continued.

"Sir, vendettas will not help the war effort. In all likelihood Lord Kirrich was allowed to flee so you knew he was there and to distract you." He paused a moment, then said, "We should have abandoned this venture right after we found out that the gates are closed. Now the best we can do is leave and wait. Your choice is the correct one, and I will say as much in my report to my cousin."

Mireynh stared, unsure how to react to the revelation that Noel Trileigh was personally reporting to the King.

His ire must have shown on his face, for the King's cousin said, "Not to worry, sir. I did not spy on you nor work against you." There surely was more to the man than he had thought. To a degree he was still the fop who had demanded that his tent be fortified with a flimsy palisade; his tent here was surrounded by a moat that wouldn't stop a squirrel, for gods' sakes. But now, for the first time, he saw the royal cousin as valuable ally. Maybe not all was lost. "I will make sure this retreat will not be seen as failure," Trileigh finished. Then a frown creased his forehead, "Why, pray tell, do you want Ralgon so badly? He's just a rogue."

Just a rogue, he thought, struggling to keep from snarling at the man. "He killed my son." Let the noble keep guessing. Even though he began to like the man, he was not ready to relive the entire story by relating it to anyone.

Trileigh must have guessed there was more to it, but thankfully kept silent. He nodded, saying, "I'll see that we are on our way by noon."

Before the noble had reached the flap, Mireynh said, "Make the patrol big. Last night's interference by those damned archers on the eastern side might just invite those bastards to harry us further when we retreat."

"Certainly, sir," said Trileigh then left.

A few moments later, he had just begun to fold the assorted papers into a bag, Fiacuil poked his head in. "A word?" the Black Guard asked.

"Sure, come in." Had he already succeeded in convincing his fellows? Mireynh was eager to find out, but knew he couldn't do so overtly. Tying the bag shut, he said, "So, what can I do for you?" If the Black Guard suspected manipulation, he didn't show it. He began to roll up the maps, looking up at Fiacuil. "Come on, we haven't got all day."

Finally, the guardsman said, "What about the dead? Shall we just leave them here?"

He paused, the rolled-up maps halfway in the scroll case. The dead, he had almost forgotten about the corpses littering Dunthiochagh's wall. For a moment he pondered what to do. In Chanastardh people were buried in cairns, and though they had some stones, courtesy of Danastaerian slingthrowers, it would take days to bury them properly. Besides, Duasonh had already sent walking dead to harry them before. Who was to say the Baron wouldn't try the same trick a second time? He called for Nairn. His aide entered a few moments later.

"Send a messenger to Dunthiochagh, under colors of truce. Inform them we wish to retrieve our dead and grant our gracious enemies the same, understood?" Nairn bobbed his head and left. To Fiacuil he said, "We'll burn them."

"Very good, milord."

When the flap blocked out daylight once more, and he was

alone, Urgraith Mireynh looked at the old suit of armor hang-ing from its rack. He hadn't truly been aware of how much he'd wanted to be part of the escalade, to once more feel blows glance off the steel, to once more enjoy the sound a sword made when it slid into an enemy's entrails. Dunthiochagh was that enemy now, the army his sword and armor, and though he wanted to drive this sword into the enemy's guts, his thoughts and desires were once more directed at getting out from under the High Advisor's clutches. Noel Trileigh had set his head straight. Ralgon was just a rogue; there were thousands in the world, and maybe, just maybe, he was in part to blame for Kirran's death. That realization lifted a great weight off his shoulders, and for a moment he felt like a young man again.

For the first time in years, his back no longer ached. Wistfully he smiled and stroked the steely rivulets engraved on the breastplate. The weight was gone, and with it the pains in his back. Perhaps he would be able to stand atop the bloody walls of Dunthiochagh in his armor, sword in hand.

But first, there was the trek back to Harail and the com-forts of the Royal Palace. In three months, he'd show Cumaill Duasonh just what war truly meant.

# CHAPTER 10

It was amazing how the sound of the whetstone running down the blade calmed Drangar. Despite the chill that had increased tenfold since sundown, he didn't join the camp Sir Úistan and his men had erected in a sheltered depression near the river. Their looks convinced him he was not wanted there. Not that he blamed them. Instead, he had remained here, on the eastern outskirts of Ondalan, alone. Too many things were going on in his mind, and he still tried to make sense of them.

To his right, a small fire struggled to give him warmth, impossible really in this last night of fall. It still provided needed illumination. To his left lay a discarded cloth, smeared with blood and oil. How easy it was to clean the blade; his hands, face and armor had fared worse. All in all, the blood had penetrated the layers of cloth and leather, crept into the fabric, and remained there, in an almost frozen state. The only thing that did not have the metallic smell was the cloak he had discarded before the madness had begun.

Up and down the whetstone went, as he relaxed. Shortly before dawn the fire went out, and he sat there, still. The outer darkness felt almost familiar by now. Unlike the Fiend that lurked within, it was comforting to know that now only the chill affected his body.

Drangar watched the sun creep across the eastern horizon, still pondering who and why he was. Yesterday's slaughter was unlike anything he had ever consciously experienced. Sure, there was the fury at Little Creek, but even then, his inebriated self had retained some measure of control. At least that was what he had told himself time and again. Had he been unaware of the Fiend back then? He knew he had never felt this dark presence the way he did now, and he certainly was no miracle in the sense that some god or other had returned him to the world to fulfill some divine mission. The gods could be cruel, but even Lesganagh never condoned meaningless slaughter. Slaughter, yes. Judging from what he had read in his youth, the Lord of Sun and War was pretty straightforward when it came to destruction; though like everything else there always was a reason, an explanation behind it. He had seen some of his victims, and if there was a reason behind the evisceration of one and the tearing-in-half of another, with bare hands, he could not see it.

"No wonder the others shun me," he muttered. But even had they wanted him there, he would have chosen solitude. He remembered watching the assault on that first house, recalled his anger at himself as Sir Úistan had listed all his faults. It began to blur, fragments of bloodstained visions; his sword stuck in a Chanastardhian's skull; racing up the stairs; his hands in a woman's belly. Gods, what kind of creatures did such things?

Even though he had seen himself cutting Hesmera to pieces, he remembered none of it. Had the puppeteers taken control then? If that was true, could the Sons be in league... No! He shook his head, dismissing the notion. Something else was going on here.

Approaching footsteps halted his musings. Drangar turned and saw Kildanor. The Chosen's face was drawn.

"Been out here all night?" the warrior asked, leaning against the wall he had put his sword up against.

Drangar regarded the man, wondered if the distrust present in Lord Cahill and his men was present there as well. "Aye. Had a lot of thinking to do."

"About the cairns?"

He shook his head. "No, they had to bury some dead, hidden archers in the east." Absently, he picked his nose, scratching the inside with his thumb. Then he turned and faced Kildanor. "I saw the slaughter, mine and the Fiend's. How do I know it isn't me killing all the time? There isn't that much difference after all." Finally, he had put into words what had been bothering him through the night.

Kildanor heaved a sigh and sat down beside him, facing him squarely. "You think the demons guide your hand even when you are in control?" The Chosen scoffed, and held up a hand before Drangar could snap a reply. "That trail of bodies, of parts scattered in your wake, first time you've seen those?"

Irritated, he shook his head. "Of course not."

"Then why ask such a stupid question? Old reflexes came to the fore, like our last bout at the manor, remember?"

He did, barely, flashes of steel, dodging, parrying, losing track of time. Despite this, he nodded his head. "Aye."

"As a mercenary, did you not kill enemies?"

"I never looked back. Only see their faces."

"At night, in dreams? Same happens to me, only I have a few more decades of killing and bloodshed on me."

"I was searching for a wrong these bastards had done, hoping that would explain the violence. You know, sword of Justice and all. They didn't murder, torture, betray, or cheat. They just did their jobs."

He took a deep breath then continued. "I was afraid. Before Sir Úistan made me angry, I mean. Yes, I thought I could remain in charge. At the manor it worked; I was able to control whatever is inside of me." He saw the Chosen frown. "Yes, there is something else inside of me; I can feel it even now. It is angry and wants out, and I think that whenever I lose control it gains more ground." He chuckled.

"I realize how insane this sounds." He paused, scratching his chin. "You saw me, what I did. Or rather what my body did. Do you really think me capable of tearing a person in half?" The Chosen's expression didn't change. "Bleeding Scales, come on, man! You damn well know that tales get embellished, and if I had killed as many enemies as the stories say I did, don't you think we'd have very few standing armies left?"

"I saw the demons," Kildanor reminded him icily.

"And I freed myself." He spat, looked to the sun that was now fully visible. "Do you think I enjoy the bloodshed?" The Chosen remained silent, regarding him. "Do you think I like dreaming of Hesmera's pieces scattered all across the floor?" He poked his finger at Ondalan. "Do you think that knowing I tore that woman's spine gives me warm and fuzzy feelings?"

"Then why did you follow my order?" Kildanor retorted.

He opened his mouth, but the reply did not come. He wanted to know that answer as much as the Chosen did. It was like what he encountered whenever he tried to remember willing his sword into his hand. Finally, he said, "I don't know." The Chosen regarded him evenly. "Fetch a Lawspeaker, if you want to, but I am not lying to you."

"Is it constant?" Kildanor asked a moment later.

"Is what constant? The struggle?" Drangar said.

"Aye."

The answer came easily enough; after all, he had been pondering the issue the entire night. "Until recently I wasn't even aware there was a struggle going on. After Little Creek I thought I had just gone mad with the injustice and all. I could feel the furor, sure, but always thought that was just me being angry at shit, and believe me there is enough shit to fill a bunch of lifetimes. I gave it a name, Fiend, after Little Creek, not that I was aware of it as an entity."

"You channeled it before?" the Chosen wanted to know.

Drangar considered, then shrugged. "Consciously? At the manor, yes, I did; no idea how. Maybe I had some leverage because I was angry at something other than myself and wanted to save the Ladies. Cahill just made me furious."

"And on the battlefield?"

"That's easy, I was mad at my father most of the time..." he fell silent, regarding the Chosen. "Say, if the bastards who attacked me in the Shadowpeaks were Sons of Traksor, they must have a reason for wanting to see me dead. Other than sheer maliciousness, I mean." He chuckled. "If I was in some way connected to those demons, wouldn't they know? And if so, why the Scales did they let me live in the first place?"

"In their place, would you have killed yourself?"

"Scales, yeah!" he replied in a heartbeat. "We were trained to fight the demons any way possible."

"But you are no demon," Kildanor said. "So, what are you?"

Drangar closed his eyes, suddenly weary. "That is something only the Priest High of the Sons of Traksor can tell me."

He rubbed his face, yawning. "Guess the conversation with daddy dearest will take a completely different turn."

"Why was it different?" the Chosen asked. "Why could you control yourself before? It can't just have been your focus."

He blinked, looked at the warrior and said, "I still had something to live for, I guess." Speaking out what had been bubbling up inside of him was hard. Not even with Hesmera had he shared all of his feelings. "When around her, the shadow withered." He paused, thinking. "It never completely went away, but I found a measure of peace."

Kildanor squinted, scratched his temple. "You said those who had wanted you defenseless did it because they wanted to kill you, right?" He nodded, frowning. What was the Chosen getting at? "What if that potion had an effect on you that was unforeseen? Maybe only part of their illusion worked, and this demon of yours did the rest?"

Could that be possible? It didn't matter, and he said so.

"Nothing of this matters now, only that this Fiend, or fiends, or demons, are now able to slip past your defenses even when you are not in any way poisoned," Kildanor countered then fell silent, looking thoughtful. Drangar didn't know what to say; so little made sense as it was. He tried to recall other instances where he had lost it the way he had yesterday.

Into his musings, Kildanor said, "Ever been to an old ruin? Something really old?"

He frowned at the Chosen. "Most of the shit built before last year is considered really old by some idiots."

"No, I meant have you ever been to a place..."

His derisive snort silenced the warrior. "I know what you meant. No, I have never been the type to go plundering tombs. Doesn't sit well with most folk, grave robbing. So, unless something mundane has been possessed by an evil spirit, I am haunt-free."

"Except that you aren't," remarked Kildanor.

"But why?" He was tired of the endless debate, internal or external. "Until I reach the Eye, there won't be any answers," he grumbled. "And this talk isn't helping any, won't change a bloody thing. Why do you help me?"

"I have my reasons."

"So, you'll be what? A wet-nurse?" he muttered.

"You can't be that moody a bastard, can you?"

"No, I like to go to the opera before I eviscerate people," Drangar snapped. Then, more calmly, "Sorry, just too much shit on my mind that doesn't make any sense. Of course, I appreciate your offer. If all else fails you can stand next to me and kill me for the next few centuries."

Kildanor snorted, and he joined the laughter. It felt good to laugh again, even if the matter was not truly humorous. The moment of mirth lasted only a few heartbeats, and, almost reflexively, Drangar felt his face revert to the cold mask he had worn for more than two years. Looking at the Chosen, he said, "Just when I hoped the entire affair over, the shit gets flung right back into my face."

"Maybe it isn't that bad," the other replied jovially, but his tone changed in the end.

"Bloody difficult to maintain a charade when the world is this fucked up, eh?" Drangar remarked.

This time there was no hint of humor in Kildanor's eyes. "Too true, my friend." He was about to say more when another set of footsteps approached. Both turned and saw a grim-faced Úistan Cahill approaching.

Lord Cahill avoided eye contact with him and said, "The men would like to have breakfast with you." That Drangar doubted very much, mainly because he would certainly not like to share breakfast with himself. He looked at Kildanor who responded with a brief nod.

"Very well," he said with a reluctant sigh. "Though, truth to tell, I am not hungry." It was the truth; he hadn't eaten since before the attack yesterday, and with the images of his hands tearing two fellow humans apart still in his head, he doubted he would feel anything remotely resembling hunger again.

"You need to eat," Sir Úistan said, finally looking at him. It was as if Lord Cahill tried to summon up the same friendliness he had shown before, the same patronizing way he addressed his servants. He tried and failed. Drangar didn't blame him, had there been a mirror, he would have smashed his image to pieces. Did Sir Úistan think himself responsible for the carnage? Maybe it was good to be around the others. A last swipe of the stone, thumb touching blade and point, mainly out of habit and not to truly feel if the edge was honed—a night's work of sharpening would have brought an edge to a maul—and he stood.

To Drangar's surprise the mood around the fire was less subdued than expected. Who knew what kind of self-preserving rationale the men and women had come up with? Feoras's warm greeting was only a charade; the horror still lurked in the servant's eyes. But he had not the heart to respond to the well-meant banter that haltingly restarted when he sat.

Someone handed him a mug, and, after making sure it contained no alcohol but tea, he drank. Bread was passed his way. Absentmindedly he tore off a piece and ate, chewing listlessly. What the Scales was going on with him? The thought was always there, not even the forced cheerful noise around could drown it out. He went through the motions, bite and chew, drink, and swallow, but what should have been refreshing tasted like ashes. He knew far too little to make sense of this tapestry of madness; too little about the Sons, too little about the demons, and ironically enough, it seemed, too little about himself. In a way the slaughter of those Chanastardhians had wounded him almost as much as Hesmera's death.

With a start he sat up. Hesmera, his anger at Darlontor, even Little Creek had one thing in common: it was personal; it affected him personally. Not her killing, but fighting for her, fighting to impress her. It really had been a personal matter. He remembered the faces of those he had killed, even the villagers. Always he'd had a private reason to be angry, determined. The only killing he hadn't been able to recall was Hesmera's. Maybe the nightmares were akin to the flashes he had when thinking about his one-man assault on the Chanastardhians. Kildanor was right! The potion the bastards had sold Hesmera had done so much more than just make him see weird things! It had eased the bonds of the Fiend.

"That doesn't explain it being there, though," he mumbled through the saliva-soaked shred of bread in his mouth. He swallowed, acutely aware that the banter was gone.

"What being where?" Camran asked.

He ignored the servant and caught Kildanor's gaze. "We need to talk," Drangar said, standing, and walked into the open before the Chosen could react.

The crunch of a single pair of feet and the jingle of chainmail followed him. A slight glance back showed it was Lesganagh's warrior. He breathed a silent thank you, and didn't stop until the house inside which he had brutally killed the Chanastardhians loomed before them.

A moment of hesitation, and then he entered.

Inside, he turned to face the Chosen who was right behind him. "I think you are right," he began.

"About what?"

"That the potion I drank two years ago loosened something inside of me." Drangar paused, considering how to continue without appearing completely mad. "When I was angry, I always was more powerful, stronger. I've never forgotten a face of anyone who died by my hand. Except..." He couldn't believe how difficult it still was to speak openly of...

"Hesmera," Kildanor supplied.

"Aye," he said, acknowledging the help with a brief nod. He searched for the right words. They came haltingly. "Whatever this Fiend, or fiends, is, it never truly manifested itself before... her death. I have nightmares about my killing... her, but until I was shown the past, I never knew what really happened. Yesterday I saw, as if my eyes were windows through which I looked, because I was fighting back. I was aware of the monster taking over."

"So infuriating you set that thing loose?" He nodded. "But why then did you obey me?" the Chosen wondered aloud.

"Bloody good question," he said. "I can't recall ever obeying anyone, not really."

Kildanor laughed softly. "Now that I can imagine. Still..."

"Aye, still a damn strange thing, and nothing that we can solve here and now, it just might be a good idea to remain calm." Drangar held up a placating hand. "I literally tore through a bunch of people. I certainly don't want to see that happen again."

"Agreed."

To Drangar it looked as if the Chosen was about to say more, but hesitated. "Speak your mind," he prompted.

"So," Kildanor began, sounding as if he was truly thinking out loud. "How can we make certain the demon will remain trapped when we engage some foe? I mean, is there a way for you to fight and still remain yourself?"

He had already wondered about the same thing; after all, they were at war. "I need something worth fighting for," Drangar finally said, realizing that such a thing, or person, was very difficult for him to find. A sad chuckle escaped his lips. "Bright thought that, isn't it?" The reply he got was a shrug. Revenge wasn't a good enough reason, anger even less so; what might have worked in the past had been obliterated by the Sons of Traksor's marvelously insane and insidious plot. Love, he thought, might be an answer, and the double failure of the Sons became even more obvious. By using him to kill Hesmera they had not only loosened whatever restraints had been in place against the Fiend, they had also obliterated yet another anchor for him to hang on to. "Fucking idiots," he grunted.

The Chosen nodded. "They shouldn't have done that."

He gave Kildanor a sardonic look. "Really now?" He knew that the warrior hadn't meant it the way it came out, but the misplaced levity broke the ice. "You know, oh Chosen of Lesganagh, you are a right bastard."

A moment passed, and then Kildanor said, "Takes one to recognize one, eh?" They laughed, briefly. "We'll figure out a way, and then we'll get to the bottom of this."

"I hope it is a bottom I like," he replied, feeling better. "Come on, they can't be done emptying out those storehouses, can they?"

They headed out together, and for a moment Drangar really felt at ease. But the gloomy thoughts returned during the monotonous haul of sacks and barrels filled with raw iron.

By late noon it began to snow. The wagons were loaded and on their way back to Dunthiochagh, accompanied by half the retainers. Lord Cahill had been loath to leave a single one behind to welcome the Chanastardhian deserters, but a firm reminder from Kildanor changed the noble's mind instantly.

Snow on the first day of Cold was a rarity. Winter usually took its time to cover the world in white. This year, for a change, the calendar was true to its word. With the coming of snow Drangar's chance to leave for Kalduuhn before the beginning of next year was as thin as the sheet of ice he watched forming in a puddle. Dismayed, he flicked a pebble onto the ice, shattering it. It was getting colder still. He pulled the cloak taut about his shoulders and watched the fog of his breath mingle with the falling snow.

"Riders!" Feoras called out. The man was on lookout near the southwestern road, and he was glad that it wasn't Camran who had stayed behind.

"Banner?" Lord Cahill asked.

"Some mountain, tied to its lance is a blue ribbon," was the answer.

Kildanor who had been huddling near a low fire, stood, crossed over to Drangar, clapped his shoulder, and said, "C'mon, let's greet our guests."

"What if it is a trap?" he asked.

"Would you feel more comfortable if I put you on a leash and made you real angry?" the Chosen asked.

Drangar shook his head. "Fuck you!" he retorted. He knew Kildanor had spoken in jest; still, he wondered how he would ever find anything or anyone worth fighting and, more importantly, living for.

When the Chanastardhian warband rode into Ondalan, the woman he saw made him wonder how he could have ever worried about that at all. He stared, and didn't care anyone nearby could see him ogling the breathtakingly beautiful woman. Sure, she was no Hesmera, but for the first time his thoughts about her did not hurt as much as they usually did. Before him on a horse sat perfection, and suddenly he knew there indeed were things worth living for.

In a rare moment of self-consciousness regarding his appearance, Drangar pulled up the hood of his cloak to hide the clusters of stubbly hair that were slowly returning. He had enough possession of his senses not to check his breath or see if his hands were clean. If any woman worried about things like that out here in a warzone, he was certain it would not be her.

# CHAPTER 11

"Princess!" a snapped command woke her. Lightbringer's eyes fluttered open, and immediately she squinted against the luminescence bathing her cave.

At first, she was unsure of where the light was coming from; it was everywhere. Then, as her sight adjusted, she saw them. Trying to retain some grace, she stumbled to her feet. Millennia of etiquette had never been wholly erased, and, although the motions came haltingly, she went through the proper ceremony of greeting Those Who Came Before. Clawed hands went crosswise to her shoulders, chest, thighs, and finally, as she kneeled, to the ground. "Ancestors, I hail you," she repeated words unspoken for eons. They felt wrong. Hadn't she earned the right to be treated as equal?

"Equal?" one of them echoed her thoughts. She couldn't tell who had spoken; the illumination was too bright to differentiate between the twenty-four first ones.

"You are not," another said. Male and female voices of her race had always been hard to distinguish, and it had been millennia since she had last heard any of them speak.

Of course, she was equal! She had done more, accomplished more than any single one of them. She had freed the elves from slavery, had taught them a safer way to use magic, she had even reminded them to release humans before there would be another Great War. How could she not be equal to them?

"Don't be petulant, girl."

"But I've done so much!" she complained aloud.

"You never abandoned your ways, always sacrificing those you claim to protect!"

"I can't!" she retorted, realizing that she sounded like the Royal Princess of Hrecknast, spoiled beyond belief.

"You have never even tried!"

"You never led by example!"

"You told the elves it was wrong to use life to force magic, but did so yourself!"

"These ashes, this place, witnesses to your failure!"

"Hypocrite, teaching one thing and doing the other!"

"Know that even if you were to defeat your brother, as long as you do not abandon your unacceptable ways, the war will never truly be over, not as long as you do not change!"

"But I set things in motion." Even to her ears the words sounded weak.

"We turned our back on our children's children because of what you all did, what you still do."

"Even now he plans their return. His followers have wrought horrors and perversions upon the world that prevent even the gods from seeing what they are doing. The Kumeen Mountains are dark; Naghturuu'klanagh's magic saw to that."

"Can't you pierce it?" she wondered aloud.

"We are servants to the gods; you decided to guide events."

"You took it upon yourself to change the world."

"To truly change the world, you have to change as well."

The brightness didn't waver, and still the only thing Lightbringer saw were silhouettes painted onto a gleaming canvas. These were her ancestors, the first ones, and they had forsaken the world before she had been born. "Teach me!" she pleaded. "I want to learn!"

"You taught the elves, teach yourself!"

"Let your past go, child."

"Your machinations have born many fruits, but you have never eaten one of them."

"If you are unable to heed your own teachings you will never bring the desired change."

"You have the discipline, the focus; you would not be here pulling strings otherwise."

"You helped the human prince, Tral."

"Him you taught an amalgam."

"And you claimed it came from Lesganagh!"

"You do not serve Him, or any other god."

"He let it pass, for even we fought your brother's hordes on behest of His clergy."

"If you want to change the world, change yourself!"

With that final advice, she was alone once more, the ancestors gone. Her knees ached from remaining prostrate on the ground. She stood uncertainly, fists clenching. Had she really thought herself equal to them? If she was completely honest with herself, she was forced to admit they were right. Humility was lacking just as much in her vocabulary as it did in Naghturuu'klanagh's. Now, even though she had lived with his name all her life, the shortened version the humans used, Turuuk, felt much more familiar.

Unlearn everything she had ever learned? The mere thought was daunting, frightening. She had never truly considered it. Part of her recoiled at the idea; the habits of millennia had become so ingrained that even thousands of years after her kind's defeat, using the blood of others came as natural to her as breathing.

She had tried to explain it to Cat, but now realized her fear was talking. Could an old dog still learn new tricks? This question she had never truly considered. Teaching young pups was easy, the elves had learned quickly enough, as had Prince Tral, and in turn, his followers. Even the human wizards had excelled at it. But none of them had been truly weighed down by a lifetime that had outlived the ages.

And who could teach her? More importantly, who would teach her? Elves? Certainly not. If the Elf Lloreanthoran were any indication, they would sooner wet themselves. Humans? There was no one... She hesitated. That there were no humans capable of teaching was wrong. The Phoenix Wizards were gone, and that whelp of a sorceress would not really suffice as a teacher. But there were others, the followers of Tral Kassor first and foremost. And their location was very suitable for launching an attack at her brother's stronghold, when the time was right.

The students would become the teachers, and the teacher

the student. And maybe she would be able to find out what had really happened to Cat.

With practiced ease she began casting a teleportation spell, and then suddenly, she halted. If she were to unlearn and learn anew, she had to start now, not when she reached the Eye of Traksor. Never in her entire life had she walked that far. The eastern part of Gathran was considerably wilder than the west, and the Elven Road had fallen into disrepair in the last century.

A hike through the forest it was, then. She would have to hunt for food, yet another thing she had never done before. Back in Hrecknast it had never been necessary, and after the Great War when the servants were gone, and the whole of the sunargh people had been wiped off the face of the world, magic had provided her sustenance. Magic and blood had made her as lazy as the elves of Gathran. Fear almost made her abandon the journey before it had begun, but the appearance of the twenty-four ancestors was a sign she dared not ignore.

The moment she stepped out of her cave and into the tangle of trees that was eastern Gathran, the chill of winter rushed in on her. With a groan she realized there was much more to traveling than just hunting and walking and fire making. She needed the right clothing as well.

And with what should she hunt? Swallowing her rising despair, she began to walk. If she were to relearn magic, it was best to relearn life as well. She would live stark, primitive, as if she were the first being to walk the world. Like one of the for-bears, her ancestors who were first given the light of reason by Lesganagh, first of the gods, she would make her way, unhampered by trappings she had lived with for thousands of years before she had helped the elves rebel. With that in mind, the cold seemed to barely reach her feet.

# CHAPTER 12

A t the break of dawn, the assault had lost none of its ferocity. Again and again the Chanastardhians charged the wall,
but the defenders prevailed. Only a few were dead, on each side.
Cuts and bruises were prevalent, and those who had died had
been kicked off the battlement. The healers and pallbearers had
their hands full with the wounded; the dead were of little concern to either side.

Strangely enough, even with Gail and several others missing, Rhea felt the same. She was far too weary to bother with any
thought not dedicated to saving her hide and keeping the enemy
off the wall. At midnight some fresh troops had been brought
in, but seeing that her fellow Riders remained, even Nerran who
looked beyond tired, she refused to be relieved of her duty. The
wizard-wrought clearing had allowed them to retake that section, and it had remained in Danastaerian hands ever since.

The grind of slash and stab and kick was now a reflex;
Rhea felt like a sleepwalker, going through the motions burned
into her body, almost like riding. Had anyone ever told her she
could fight while asleep, she would have scoffed at the notion,
now even this thought slipped from her mind, as she cut at a
Chanastardhian's head. With a shout the enemy woman flung
herself backward, off the ladder and into the milling mass of
soldiers below. A moment later the next in line poked his helmet
above the merlon. Before her weapon was ready to strike, someone beside her lodged a halberd into the ladder's wood and sent
the entire thing rocking back. In a flash of clarity, Rhea let go of
the sword and helped the man finish the job. The ladder went
down.

She had barely retrieved her blade when, a few yards to the right, a concerted assault began. The battle cry and subsequent clash of arms drew her attention, and she saw a trio of well-armored enemies mount the wall at the same time. The soldiers launched themselves at defenders who looked as weary as she felt. It wouldn't take them long to widen the gap to a degree where those who were just now pouring across the battlement would be able to fight as well. A glance at the Pike whom she had helped only moments ago, and then she charged off. The soldier, his halberd leading, was right beside her.

In silence they covered the distance, crashed into the flank of warriors still trying to get their bearings. They cast them off the wall. Their ladders followed a heartbeat later. By now the three enemy warriors were batting off swords and maces and axes beating at them from all directions. They were back to back, and although they fought well, a sudden arrow into a helmet's face-plate ripped the defense asunder. A moment of violence later, three corpses, weighed down by heavy armor, were thrown into the attackers.

Rhea returned to the section of wall that was her killing field. The Pike, she didn't bother to mark his features, was at her side. By now the ladders had been righted and the dance began anew.

None of them truly noticed the moment when, at noon or so, the assault stopped. It looked as if everything had just been covered in a translucent veil; then the lack of arms clashing and absence of grunts and cries and howls registered in her mind. Blinking dazedly, Rhea looked around and saw the other defenders were just as surprised as she was. If this was victory, she didn't feel it. The Pike, her unlikely brother-in-arms, gave an uncomprehending laugh, others near her gasped, their mouths and faces distorted in base relief. For the first time, at least it felt like the first time, she noticed the cuts and bruises she had suffered.

Until now, with the constant fighting, she had barely felt the frosty air. Now, as the tension of combat fled her body, the chill of winter rushed in without mercy. Her teeth chattered, and her lips trembled. It felt like she had been tossed in ice water; she felt just as helpless.

The Pike hung on to his weapon for a moment longer, and then joined her on the cold stone. Rhea hadn't even noticed her knees buckling. Near her, embedded into the heavy granite foundation, stood one of the massive ovens guards usually gathered around on their tours of the wall. With fingers that were as numb as the rest of her body, she clawed her way to the iron monster, only to realize upon arrival that the fire had gone out during the night. Amidst all the fighting, who would have found the time to feed wood to the flame? With the cold driving out the last shreds of heat left in her, freezing sweat soaked her undergarments, and she had no strength left to crawl any further.

Then she felt someone pull her up and wrap her in something heavy. She opened her eyes and saw an old woman, a merchant's wife judging by her clothes, wrapping her in a blanket. The woman looked weary and afraid, and deep gratitude overshadowed her exhaustion.

"Have some soup," her savior said, and a moment later she felt the hot rim of some bottle scorching her split lips. Rhea didn't care how much it hurt; she drank greedily. "Not too much, dear, there are others who need it, too." The blessed warmth, she couldn't even tell what kind of soup it was, left her lips and the woman walked to the next warrior who was already wrapped in a blanket.

As some life returned to her tired limbs, she struggled to her feet and looked around. All around her she saw the same thing: townsfolk, mostly wives, but also children and elderly folk, were walking among their defenders, bringing blankets and hot drink. How many there were she couldn't tell, not that it mattered. Those same citizens had, only a week ago, complained about the presence of so many warriors inside Dunthiochagh. Now that animosity was gone, replaced by a caring gratitude only found in people who had just realized how much they relied on those they had scorned. Better late than never, she thought.

A girl, she couldn't have been more than six or seven summers old, walked up to her, eyes wide with fright and bewilderment. In her small hands she carried a bottle, saying, "Ma says you have ta drink, brings back them spirits. Just one sip, more wanna drink, ma'am."

Rhea took the container and made sure to fill her mouth with just a little of its contents. She was glad not to have poured in more, the stuff, whatever it was, burned her mouth, lips, and chin. Scales, even her throat hurt as the liquor ran through it. Only years of drinking booze with her friends stopped her from coughing. She returned the bottle, not trusting her voice to thank the girl.

The lass beamed at her, waved goodbye, and skipped to the next warrior, addressing him with the same words: "Ma says you have ta drink, brings back them spirits. Just one sip, more wanna drink, sir." The man-at-arms, so tattered was his surcoat Rhea couldn't even tell whether it was a Sword, Pike, or Lance, drank. His eyes bulged, color crept back onto his pale face, and the girl was off again, smiling broadly. Whatever was in this bottle, its contents were potent.

More children came. Some looked frightened enough to cower from the blood spattered on the stones, but others, obviously used to at least some sort of bloodshed, carried armfuls of firewood, and set about rekindling the ovens. There even seemed to be some reserves coming up the stairs.

One of them, she recognized a moment before he stood in front of her, was Nerran. The Paladin looked weary as he inspected the situation. The Baron joined him. Duasonh looked just as tired, his shredded surcoat and haphazardly bandaged wounds were ample proof that Dunthiochagh's ruler had not sat idly by and let others do the fighting. Nerran, despite his exhaustion, seemed in better shape, she noted wryly. She had seen neither of them during most of the night, but judging from their appearance they had been in the thick of it as well.

Duasonh offered her a weak smile and a nod. She owed him no allegiance, and he knew it. It was Nerran who spoke. "Think they are regrouping, Princess?"

Gods how she hated that title! Suppressing her ire, Rhea said, "No idea, chief, we gave 'em a good deal of bloodied noses, but if it hadn't been for that Wizardess we might have lost half the city." She tried but couldn't keep the scorn from her voice. Gail and the others had been in that captured stretch of wall, and that bit of sorcery had literally wiped out the chance to find them.

Losing anyone was hard, had always been hard on her. Far too many bad memories of living while the ones closest to her had been left behind—left for dead. If the others had been alive when the Wizardess had worked her spell, they had surely died when the magic had hit the wall.

The Baron, probably sensing her resentment, cleared his throat and then spoke. "The Lady Ealisaid did what had to be done; there is no point in arguing that." He sounded tired.

"Tell that to those who lost someone in that assault," she replied bitterly, though a small part of her kept arguing that the sorceress's intervention had probably saved more lives than it had taken. Maybe—she had never truly thought about it—the end did justify the means. Maintaining the law was one thing, but was it the law of man or the law of gods she was supposed maintain? The laws of man elegantly stepped around certain entities, first and foremost among them the very nobility she had belonged to. There was freeborn and villein right, and noble right; those Lawspeakers who disagreed with what a lord did never raised their voices again.

"They would've lost more than just their sons and daughters, Rhea," Nerran said, putting a hand on her shoulder. He rarely used her name; he mostly used the hated title. Surprised, she looked up and saw the grief she felt reflected in his eyes. "Just remember that they went into battle knowing the risks."

She wanted to argue, deny that fact, but she could not. Instead, she nodded her head in silent agreement. The pain of loss was strong; she felt very much reminded of the life she had left behind all those years ago.

"Good girl," the Paladin said, squeezing her aching shoulder. "Even the Wizardess did her job."

"Not as expected but it worked," Duasonh added, and then turned to walk among his warriors.

"There's gonna be some people demanding payment for what the Wizardess did," she muttered.

"That's been going on since she blew those houses to rubble," the Paladin said. "Don't worry, lass, the Baron will put her to trial once all this is over."

She had heard some of the rumors. Still, now that she

thought about it, maybe in this instance her deeds in defense of the city should be weighed against the destruction and death she had caused. She remained silent.

"Got some inspecting to do, lass," said Nerran, giving her shoulder a final squeeze, then turned to follow Baron Duasonh. "Get your wounds looked after" were his parting words. She watched until he was lost amid the milling of warriors, healers, women, and children of the city.

"Some soup, m'lady?" piped a voice beside her. A boy and a girl, brother and sister by the look of them, stood there, holding a cooking pot by its cloth sheathed handle. The girl held out a ladle, which she gratefully took. Her brother looked about, unease and fear plain on his face.

"Ma said we'd find da here," he finally said.

Rhea sampled the broth. Invigorating as it was, the worry about what she should tell the child who seemed younger than his sister soured the taste. The girl kept her resolve, and only for a moment did she show her own dread. "Where's your ma?" Rhea finally asked.

"Tending the wounded near our house," the lass replied. She reckoned that the clothes the children wore did not suggest they came from the Westgate slums. They were dressed in robust yet elegant cloth, meant to be both practical and warming. She wondered if they were a carpenter's children. Not that it mattered.

"Why did she send you two here?"

"We wanted to help, and Aydan"—the girl nodded at her brother—"wants to become a warrior when he grows up, like da had been before we were born." Rhea could guess the rest. The mother probably wanted to discourage her son from becoming infatuated with war. Judging by the look on little Aydan's face, she had succeeded.

She took another mouthful of soup, and then dismissed the siblings who promptly went to the next one along the wall. Rhea continued to watch, wondering what the world was coming to. Before the two passed out of sight, their soup being drunk again and again, she saw the boy's eyes acquire the same expression as his sister's.

Fynbar lived; at least the Caretakers assured her he would not die. Of those who had led the insane charge with her, Gail, Edmonh, Kieran, and Kyleigh were still missing, most likely dead. They were trying to find all of their comrades, and Rhea wondered if there was even a point in reforming the Riders once this was done. Gail, Kyleigh, most of those who were casualties she had known for years, and there was nothing casual about the losses. Nothing at all.

The cot Fynbar was resting on was one of many, all located in a warehouse that had seen better days. Then again, most buildings near Westgate had seen better days. The place stank of tanning, but the stench suppressed the fresh stench—feces and urine and blood of the wounded and dying. Maybe that was why the healers had chosen this building. Courtesy of Eanaigh a patient did not have to be kept in a clean environment, the knives and saws and strings blessed by Caretakers sufficed to keep infection at bay. Those who lay here were the hopefuls, those who might live through the night. With so many Caretakers among the Riders it was hard not to pick up a thing or ten of Eanaigh's philosophy. The Caretakers usually killed those too severely wounded on the spot: on the wall, the street, or wherever they had fallen. A merciful death, one strangely enough in tune with Lesganagh's tenets, especially if one considered that the Lord of Sun and War's faith had been banned for so long. Some things just carried on, no matter the dominant philosophy. The gong was struck thrice a day, and those unlikely to survive were released into Jainagath's care.

Lliania sure had her hands full today, she thought with a sad smile, not only with the dead from this battle, but with the thousands of others all over the world. Lady Justice's work was never truly done. Then again, neither was Jainagath's. Even now the Deathmasks were preparing the funeral pyres.

More wounded were brought in, while the dead were carried out to make room for those who might make it. Caretakers performed surgery; arms and legs littered the floor, gathered on wheelbarrows to be brought out and burned along with the corpses. Worried mutterings arose when an apothecary

apprentice loudly proclaimed there was no ophain left anywhere within the city. And sure enough, before the sun had
touched the horizon the groans and shrieks rose in volume.
Healers had to saw off maimed limbs without sedation.

Then, despite the tapestry painted by wails and blood and
casually dropped old bandages, an excited mutter went through
the warehouse. "They're retreating," someone exclaimed.
"Buggers are running!" another added. Then the individual
shouts bled into one another, and elation mixed with agony and
weariness. She had taken her last look outside with the guarded
knowledge that soon the fighting would begin anew, and
although tired she knew sleep would elude her. Now, despite
grogginess, she made her way past patched up men and women
who had, luckily, escaped the Caretakers' knives and saws.
Some of those warriors looked worse than others, while a few
had begun a grim game of knucklebones. Judging by the shape
of their hands, and the pristine yet somewhat bloodied condition of the bones, Rhea choked down the bile when she realized
this particular game was actually played with their own lost
digits. She hurried on and soon stood outside, sucking in the
fresh, crisp air. Only now did she realize how bad the air inside
truly was. Thankfully the wind came from the east, and the
pyres, which were already burning, were further to the west.

Had the Chanastardhians really given up? For weeks the
enemy had been quite persistent, had almost taken the wall.
Could it really be true? A snowflake spiraled down, landed on
her cheek, and melted. Another followed. Then the sky seemed
full of them. Winter had come at last. Was this the reason for the
retreat? Already they had spent most of their time in the cold.
Maybe.

Another stretcher was brought in, its occupant barely alive.
Rhea glanced at the wounded warrior's face. It was terribly cut
and bruised, and in the last moment, as she was turning away,
she saw the bracelet. "Gail!" she exclaimed and went to the
Caretaker's side. Gail looked horrible. Rhea wasn't even sure
she noticed her.

"You know her," one of the bearers observed. The man had
neither the trappings of a Caretaker nor those of a warrior. A lay

follower, she suspected. "Good," he continued. "Talk to her. No, don't take her hand or anything, pretty banged up; if she's to live, any unnecessary movement will do even more harm. She's hanging in there, tough little lady."

Rhea barely remembered her grandma's passing, knew not how to act, what to say, so she just began talking. Nonsense, issues of horsemanship, that winter that had arrived on time, she reckoned it might just be enough that Gail heard her voice. She followed the bearers to an empty table, another laywoman wiped the worst of the blood off the soiled surface, and then Gail was laid upon it. A Caretaker, a woman she thought she recognized, stepped up and inspected Gail with weary eyes.

"She's one of yours," she said, whether it was to her friend or the healer she didn't even know.

"Gail Caslin," the woman muttered. "Bloody light's fading," she cursed. "Lamp!" A lantern was brought and now, with twilight dispersed, Rhea saw the extent of her friend's injuries. Gail was torn to shreds, not a patch of skin had escaped intact.

"Can you do anything?"

The Caretaker wiped her brow with a bloody hand. "No idea. Looks pretty bad." How the words pretty and bad went into the same statement was something Rhea would never understand. A shuddering breath went through Gail. Her body shook, violently. The female Caretaker put both her hands on her chest and prayed quietly, asking Eanaigh for guidance. Then, with a resigned nod of her head, she took a bloodied poker, saying, "I see you on the other side, Gail Caslin, may the Scales of Lliania judge you by who you are and what you did. I see you on the other side, sister." Before Rhea realized what was happening, she plunged the poker into Gail's heart. She let out a horrified scream of denial as Gail shuddered one final time and then lay still.

Seemingly uncaring, the healer addressed the bearers. "Take her outside, priestly burning for her, remind the Deathmasks." As the two men unceremoniously returned Gail's corpse to the stretcher, the Caretaker waved the next pair of laymen forward. "Put him here, maybe he has more luck." She gave a sigh, and despite her renewed grief Rhea saw none of the deaths truly went by this healer unnoticed. There were just so many wounded and dying and so few healers. It was an impossible battle, and the Caretakers fought it anyway.

Gail had returned into her life from the dead, if only for a moment. Now the pain of knowing she was gone felt all the more acute. Dumbly, not noticing what went on around her, she stumbled outside and let the snowflakes wash away her tears. This loss felt far more intimate than the knowledge of her parents' death.

# CHAPTER 13

For most of the way Anne had tried to figure out how to get rid of House Kirrich's warband. Forty heavy Horse was a force to reckon with; she and hers knew mountain combat, not mounted combat. If these warriors somehow got wind of what was truly going on and had time to prepare, they would plow right through her warriors.

By the time Ondalan came into view, she had decided. "Captain," she called to the Kirrich leader. With practiced ease the man nudged his mount to her side.

"Ma'am?"

"I want you to circle the village, get them from the east. Those Danastaerians will be caught between hammer and anvil," she said. "Wait, and upon my signal, a single trumpet blast, you will charge. Do not attack until that note, understood?"

The look the warrior gave her spoke volumes, all of them filled with meaningless drivel of highland ignorance and lowland superiority. "Yes, ma'am!" the captain replied and prodded his horse into a canter.

A few breaths and barked commands later, and the two score of heavy cavalrymen detached from the numerically inferior House Cirrain force, heading southeast to circle around Ondalan. Seeing them leave, Anne let go a long breath of relief. Being able to meet the Danastaerians without initial interference of that stiff-necked, arrogant lowlander was nearly as important as getting away from Mireynh in the first place.

"That went smoothly," Paddy said as his horse fell into pace with hers and Gwen's. "What's to be done about them?"

She hadn't thought this far ahead. The Horse were supposed

to assist them in capturing this Ralgon character; once they realized Ondalan was their staging ground for desertion they were bound to either interfere or report back, most likely both.

"Simple enough," Gwennaith Keelan said. Obviously, the squire had given this far more consideration, which, given her experience with sailors and pirates, was very much in her nature. "We kill them."

A quick glance at her cousin told Anne he had considered this option as well. In a way she balked at the prospect of fighting her countrymen then remembered there was no other option. House Cirrain was in open rebellion against the King; her father already was ordering fellow Chanastardhians to be killed. Had she truly believed their escape could have been accomplished without bloodshed? "Aye," she said grimly, "kill them."

They crossed the last hillock, and before them spread the ruined mining village. Somewhere, off to the eastern edge of the settlement a smoking fire burned. Given the climate and general state of matters here, it was a wonder anything flammable was left at all. From the look of it the Danastaerians cared little about subtlety. On a nearby wall sat a lookout, feet dangling lazily, the longbow unstrung on his thighs.

She searched the periphery and saw things were not as casual as they seemed. In the shadows of at least two doorways stood archers, arrows and bows ready. "Ribbons," she ordered, dropped her left hand into the folds of her cloak and retrieved the same blue scrap of cloth she had used the night the walking dead had attacked. She let go of the reins entirely, and tied the rag to her arm. A sweeping glance confirmed the others were doing the same.

The ribbons had been a last moment addition to the plan, delivered by the bodiless voice of a young girl. It made sense, really, when one considered that anyone could carry House Cirrain's banner, Anne was the last to dismiss the suspicion that might still linger in Mireynh's mind. The High General could have ordered the Kirrich to keep a close eye on her. That the heavy Horse had followed her order at once told her this was not the case, but the cloth was an added, and welcome, precaution.

In the shadows, the archers relaxed visibly, yet they

remained as they were, hidden, ready to attack should things turn sour. She didn't mind. In fact, it told her something about the discipline of these Danastaerians, and the foresight of their leader.

As they rode closer, the man atop the wall leapt to the ground and vanished into the ruins, most likely to inform his master. She heard Dubhan clear his throat, muttering some curse under his breath. The aging warrior had voiced his concerns about entering Ondalan openly, thinking the entire thing a setup, a trap. She had dismissed the notion, but now, as the ruins loomed to their left and right like broken teeth, a hint of worry crept into her mind, and she shifted nervously in her saddle.

Nothing.

The thirty-two riders entered the village square, and for the first time since passing into Ondalan she had the chance to scrutinize their surroundings. Blood, maybe a day old, was splattered about the place, though no bodies could be seen. Somebody must have fought a vicious battle. One wall sported the gore-smeared silhouette of a person that had apparently been thrown against the brick and wood construction and left this image. Anne understood why Dubhan had expressed his discomfort in his own special way. Whoever had done this had left a frightening reminder of barely remembered tellings of the Demon War. She swallowed, half expecting a shadowy, feline monstrosity to jump them at any moment. Behind and beside her, the others must have come to the same conclusion. Leather and chain creaked as her comrades shifted uneasily in their saddles. A few whispered prayers to Eanaigh and Lesganagh reached her ears. She couldn't blame them; the sight was eerie. Dubhan cleared his throat once again. Swords were loosened in their sheaths, the sound of steel detaching from leather unmistakable.

Anne checked her own right hand and found it clasping the hilt of her weapon. Another leader, she thought with scorn, might have attempted to hide her discomfort. Here among friends, however, the show of concern was viewed as prudence.

Then, from two different directions, three men entered the

square. One of them, older, built like a true fighter and sporting the armor and pristine surcoat to prove it, scowled, not at her, but at the pair who joined him from the east. This knight surely had to be the Danastaerian's leader. The other two stopped next to him, the lean one was almost bald. He scanned her band, his eyes opening in an expression that might have been surprise as well as worry and pulled up a hood to hide his features, while the other seemed to take a casual interest in them.

Beside her, Paddy whistled through his teeth. She was about to inquire what was on his mind, when she saw that the hooded man's caergoult armor was almost in its entirety of a red-brown coloring that could stem from only one source. That his breeches were of the same dye only elevated the suspicion. "Damnation," she whispered. If there had been a bloodbath in Ondalan, it had been this man doing the bathing.

"Guess Lord Kirrich wasn't exaggerating," Dubhan growled. "Bastard looks like he wallowed in it, too."

"Ralgon?" Connar suggested. She heard the lump in his throat forming.

"From what Kirrich told Mireynh, I'd say so, aye," she replied, still eyeing the unlikely trio. If this one man had truly caused such havoc alone, it was no wonder the nobleman had been a wreck. It also explained the scowl the older man had cast the blood-dyed warrior. Ralgon, if it was he, was certainly someone to worry about.

"Let's go," she said, letting her horse canter up to the three-some. From under his hood the man that she suspected was Drangar Ralgon seemed to be looking at nothing, not that she could truly tell, the cloth hid his eyes.

To her surprise it wasn't the nobleman who greeted them, but the younger man beside him. He stepped forward, bobbing his head in a quick nod. "Anneijhan of House Cirrain?" he asked in a voice that promised quick death.

"Aye, I am she," she replied. "And you are?"

"Kildanor, Chosen of Lesganagh and Advisor to the Baron Duasonh. This is Lord Úistan..." She barely heard the rest of the introductions. A Chosen! Here? She had trouble containing her excitement. The warriors of Lesganagh were considered a myth, even though Mireynh proclaimed they died just as easily as any man. Then she remembered the brief engagement in Harail, and the face of the whirr of a swordsman who had hewn his way through the Chanastardhian lines to reach his brethren. That same man was now standing before her.

"An honor," she said.

She wanted to ask him about his duties, but Paddy interfered before she could begin. "My lords," he said, "Padraigh of House Cirrain." He received acknowledging nods, and then continued, "We have time to speak later on; there is a force of forty heavy Horse coming this way from the east. Best prepare for their arrival."

"Not yours?" the older man asked.

"Nay, milord," Paddy answered. "They were forced on us by the High General. He thought it wise to send more than just us thirty to capture one Drangar Ralgon."

The hooded man scoffed, confirming her suspicion that this was indeed the one person with whom Urgraith Mireynh had lost his temper.

"Very well then," the noble said. Others must have observed the exchange, for he merely looked to a nearby ruin, nodded briefly, and a score or so people scuttled across the yard, heading eastward.

Then, turning to the other two, he said, "I think we're able to handle them on our own." To her he added, "But would you care to join us? After all, this is also in your best interest."

Anne looked her companions in the eye, ignoring Gwen for the moment. Paddy and Dubhan shrugged their shoulders in a dismissive gesture, and the others seemed equally uncaring. "Sure, milord, we'll fight."

"After all," Ralgon grumbled, "that's what rebellion and desertion is all about, eh? Fighting."

For a moment she was tempted to reply, and then thought better of it. The stranger's mood seemed somber at best, and she wondered why anyone would keep company with him. "Let's go, folks," she told her troops, dismounted, and retrieved the short lance tied to her saddle. The others followed her example. Grunts of displeasure mingled on the square as they stretched the knots and kinks of the long ride out of their muscles. Gwen, she saw, had remained on her mare, glaring at her. The question whether she was to come along as false captive had never been truly answered, but with the intent of killing the Kirrich soldiers it became a moot point.

"Keelan, this'll be your first real battle, stay alive," she snapped at the young woman who brightened instantly, and was on the ground, spear and shield in hand in an instant.

"Yes, ma'am!" Gwen said, and Anne could see how the squire struggled to restrain her excitement.

Lord Cahill asked, "Ready?" Then, after receiving her affirmative nod, said "Good, let's go."

They took off through the ruins, following the general direction the score of warriors had taken a little while before. On the way Anne saw more evidence of Ralgon's path of destruction, though, thankfully, there were no corpses littering the street. Briefly she wondered what had happened to those Kirrich warriors unfortunate enough to be slaughtered by this animal, and couldn't find an answer. Lord Cahill was preoccupied, and the others, having arrived with her, were no help either. From the look of him, she considered Ralgon perfectly capable of hacking his enemy's remains to pieces.

When they passed the last building, before she even saw the warriors hidden among the craggy rocks, Anne realized she had erred at least in this issue. Whoever had built these cairns had firsthand knowledge of Chanastardhian burial rites. Sure, they looked crude, probably housing more than one body apiece, but they felt... right, fitting. Who had built them? It mattered little, though she was relieved to know that this hooded stranger had not just cut the dead to ribbons and discarded the remains. Then again, maybe the victims had merely died and been buried, who knew? Some cairns were smaller, built for individuals instead of mass graves; in wake of the stray attacks that had been reported, Braddan Kirrich and his troops had in all likelihood erected these.

Then, with a surprising suddenness she was pulled off to the side, into a crevice. Silently cursing her own lack of focus, but retaining her silence, she regarded the Danastaerian noble who had tugged her out of view.

"What's the sign?" Lord Cahill asked.

"Single trumpet blow." Her reply came just as hushed.

"Well then," the noble whispered. "Grab a few of your warriors and make a lot of noise, and then sound the signal."

She gave a brief nod in reply and hurried off, hunching until she reached Dubhan, Connar, and Natheira. In quick words she explained what was expected of them, scowled at Dubhan's disappointed expression, and then moved on back to the ruins with the three warriors behind her. That she had to be the one to play bait had never occurred to her, it wasn't truly honorable. But, she reminded herself sternly for hopefully the last time, neither was desertion.

One set of footsteps behind her halted every few yards. She turned and saw Connar had fallen behind. Right now, he was scanning the horizon, most likely for any signs of the heavy Horse. As a hunter, his eyesight was keen, and his experience at tracking gave him an extra advantage in most situations. The others halted beside her, hunched down behind the remains of a cart. Connar took his time. She didn't see his face but knew the expression he made whenever he scrutinized an area, the intense concentration, the lids closed to razor-fine slits, his lips pursed.

Finally, the hunter turned and caught up. "Kirrich keeps out of sight," he reported, voice even.

Behind her, she heard Dubhan's distinctive snort. "Look at that," the old warrior muttered, delighted.

"What?" she hissed, glancing back at him.

He had crept a little further, and now was peering into the nearby ruin. "Enough stuff here to make a lot of noise," he replied in a whisper.

They hurriedly joined him, and she inspected the building the same way Dubhan had done by peering through a torn part of the wall. Inside, piled against a wall were the wooden tower shields Kirrich infantry preferred. There was no sign of the weaponry and armor. Most likely the Danastaerians had scavenged everything metallic and left the shields behind, seeing no real use for them. For their distraction these would certainly work.

With a grim smile she approved, and moments later they each had a shield in hand and headed for the square.

Even at a distance the sounds of battle seemed intense. At first there had only been the thunder of hooves pounding the frozen ground, the shrill cries of horses and riders, and the clash of arms. Dubhan returned the horn to his pack and looked at her. Anne knew how he felt, all of them were people of action and this passivity went against every instinct. She also knew that even if they managed to rush back to the ambush, the battle would likely be over by then. A shake of the head earned first a scowl, and then a resigned sigh.

The Chosen and Ralgon had trundled over, and while Kildanor looked tired, the other's features were still hidden beneath his hood. Ralgon slumped on the central well's wall and pulled back the cloth covering his head, revealing his bald, somewhat gaunt cranium upon which hair was patchily growing. He scratched his scalp and regarded her. A wry, sad smile formed on his lips, never reaching his eyes.

"Shun me," he said, "it's what I'd do."

The Chosen wiped a hand over his face. "Don't listen to him, he's just..." he faltered.

"What? What am I?" Ralgon retorted. "I saw the corpses. Scales, I buried the poor bastards."

"We still have no idea what is going on!"

"What is going on?" Ralgon's voice was a mix of hysteria and fear. "I tell you what is going on!"

"Not here," interrupted the Chosen.

It was then, when the bald man snarled at Kildanor, that she saw the deep hurt and worry in his eyes. Ralgon looked about, as if searching for something. "I shouldn't have come." He was oblivious to their presence. Even the noise of battle perturbed him little. "Cahill shouldn't have had me come!"

"We needed Mireynh to know you are here!"

"Well, it worked; only thing that is wrong with all of this is that I feel worse than I did when I saw Hesmera." He looked east. "Sir Úistan and his men shun me, and rightfully so." He took a deep breath. "I thought I was ready, but how can I be ready when I'm in control only half the time?"

What the Scales were they talking about? It sounded as if this man had done murder without being in command of his senses. Anne had seen berserkers—they all had. Highlanders who first drank themselves into a furor, and then rampaged through enemy lines, not much control there, she knew. Was this what they were talking about? She doubted Ralgon was aware of or cared about their presence. It seemed as if he was talking to himself, with the Chosen providing apparently much needed reason.

Beside her, Dubhan shuffled his feet. She looked at the old warrior; he returned her stare. It spoke of the discomfort she also felt. They were privy to a conversation that should have been private. To the east the ring of steel on steel and the cries of wounded and dying slowly ebbed away. Though curious at how the talk would proceed, Anne heeded her gut. It was wrong to spy on this, even unintentionally. If Ralgon had been in full control of his mind, he would have been aware of his surroundings and the audience. He was not, and although he showed no true interest, the Chosen was, and tried to compensate for his companion's lack of well-being. Again, Kildanor glanced their way, his eyes speaking where his mouth could not.

Anne nodded her understanding, and said, "Come on, let's see what's happening."

# CHAPTER 14

Drangar Ralgon was a mystery, had been a mystery since Kildanor had first laid eyes on the closing wounds. Injuries that had killed the man, and yet he was alive, sitting here on this walled-in well. The Chosen knew what he had seen, not just the torn apart bodies, but also the almost senseless assault on a splendidly maintained shield wall. He had seen Ralgon coated in blood that had evaporated, closing his wounds in its wake. Things he had witnessed only once before.

During the Demon War.

By now he was convinced that a connection existed between the Fiend and the demons he had seen. Ealisaid had explained things, the forcing of potential into fact. For a moment, when Drangar had freed himself from the demonic yoke, the surge of bloodmagic had returned, and the mercenary's wounds had closed. Had he not seen Drangar swoon, he might have said the man was perfectly capable of harnessing his life force into magic. The visible cuts and bruises, however, told him otherwise.

Ralgon was no demon. That much he was sure of. Exactly that much. How the feline creatures had gained a foothold in the mercenary's mind was a good question. An even better question was why. The connection between demons and man hadn't truly been severed when he and Caretaker Gail had entered the spiritworld, and he was certain that one minuscule thread still remained. Unnoticed by the Chosen or Drangar, the Fiend bided its time, waited for the right moment to seize control once more. Gone were the naïve attempts to explain facts as miracles. Maybe Drangar was blessed by a deity, Lliania most like, but it mattered little for none of the gods did much to help the poor sod.

Even the theory about Drangar possessing the knowledge and the skill to perform bloodmagic was ludicrous in light of him fainting whilst healing himself.

He did not regret his decision to help the man solely out of friendship, but now he didn't just want to see him safely to the Eye of Traksor. Kildanor needed to find, and fight, the source of this threat.

The four Chanastardhians across the street, the well and truly battered shields cast aside, looked as if they were trying to not pay attention. He couldn't blame them, would have stared as well had he been in their place. In terms of etiquette Ralgon cared little about who was privy to his thoughts. It most likely had to do with his two years of isolation. Talking to animals only blunted one to the proper time and place for speaking one's mind.

"I think in a way Lord Cahill understands," he finally suggested.

As expected, Ralgon's head snapped up. "You're joking, right?" The twisted grimace of his face resembled a mismatched figure: half snarl, half resignation. "How the Scales can he understand when I can't? And don't tell me you can also." A sigh, and then his face relaxed. "I tried to make sense of it last night, I mean after I found the teeth marks on these scraps of cloth. I thought maybe, just maybe, I had done something fair, in the end.

"That maybe those poor bastards had tortured some hapless soul." Silence followed. The struggle inside was evident on Ralgon's face. He made a motion to rake through nonexistent hair and hesitated, probably remembering he had none. "I wanted to find a reason for what I did." His voice sounded pleading. "Maybe, had they tortured anyone, what they received would have been justified. Even in the village my fury had reason. Lliania shat on me; I judged a High Priest with no interference of Coimharrin's. I hoped what I had done here was something like that, divine will or whatever you wanna call it. Nothing! Senseless!"

This at least explained the almost frantic search for clues regarding torture. Ralgon had wanted to purge the guilt, and

Kildanor wondered what he would have done had their roles been reversed. He was at a loss; there were no comforting words, no pat on the back to make things easier for this shell of a man. Another glance at the Chanastardhians showed they had drifted off toward the din of battle. Turning back to Ralgon hammered in the realization that a Chosen of Lesganagh, a warrior, a defender, and a killer, was not the right person to give advice about matters of the soul. Had he been asked to reveal tactics, or even provide protection, the answers would have come easily, but here there was nothing he could do.

The group of more or less allied forces left Ondalan shortly after noon. Thanks to the ambush and the archery skills of Lord Cahill's retainers, they had suffered few casualties. With firewood a rare commodity in the treeless foothills, the Danastaerian dead had been interred alongside the enemy warriors in the cairns their countrymen had erected. Now they made their way through the swamp.

It seemed as if winter had waited until this very moment to lash out; snowflakes were everywhere, limiting their vision to a few yards. Thankfully they had crossed the Dunth at the onset, a little later, and to traverse the ledge would have been to slide into the cold waters of the tributary.

The white stuff only melted in the higher reaches of the Shadowpeaks, feeding streams that usually only trickled down the cliffside. When they hit colder areas some of these froze, while others continued on. Before long, Kildanor knew, the face of the mountains would look like a single wall of ice. Down here the snow blanketed the already frozen marshland, hiding all sorts of nasty surprises, and still they had agreed that by traveling close to the crags they would be protected from the snow on at least one side. Closer to the river visibility would diminish to the point where any step might lead to broken legs or drowning. Here, underneath the slowly freezing cliffs, it was only broken legs, and even these could be avoided if one stuck to the path of planks that crisscrossed the marchland. Fortunately, Sir Úistan's archers knew their way around this place, even with visibility as bad as it was.

Most of the time they rode or walked in single file, which kept conversation to a minimum, and soon, after crossing the first of the two tributaries on their way, even those hushed conversations died under the permanent onslaught of wind and snow. The going was slow, even on the wider strips of firm soil. As predicted, Ralgon was shunned, but the man also isolated himself from the others.

Kildanor didn't know if leaving the mercenary to form the rearguard was a good thing. Left to brood, who knew what kind of mad ideas he'd have next. Still, even his tentative attempts to start a conversation were rejected. After a while he merely turned to see if Ralgon was still with them.

A cloaked and hooded figure leading a horse slowed its pace until it was beside him. Only when the figure spoke did he recognize Úistan Cahill. "What the Scales is going on with him, Chosen?" the nobleman asked without preamble. Of course, he was talking about Drangar. "No, let me rephrase that. What the bloody Scales happened to him in the village?"

He couldn't tell if Cahill noticed his shrug. Revealing the truth might upset the band to the point where Drangar would be cast out, so he lied, "No idea, milord."

"Come on, man, he ripped a woman in two and tore open the chest of another," Cahill grunted. "What he did is not human."

"Not the first impossible thing he's done," Kildanor said.

"Explain."

The Chosen didn't like being ordered around by anyone who was not the First or Cumaill Duasonh. Cahill was the leader of this expedition, certainly, but he treated Kildanor as if he was one of his retainers. Shunting his ire aside, Kildanor said, "He died and came back, for starters." This time he intentionally omitted the honorific, if Cahill noticed at all, he couldn't tell. "Then the entire affair of him breaking through magical bonds by sheer force of will."

"So..."

He denied Cahill the chance to continue, thinking it best to speak about the conclusions he had already dismissed. At least they made sense. "He used magic to escape that cage, channeled his own life force into tearing through that cage. He says he can't remember using magic, and I believe him, but some part of him can, and does call on it quite well. It was that primal part of him that butchered the Chanastardhians." He paused, glanced back at the snow-shrouded figure stomping determinedly through the ever-higher piling snow. "He is struggling to understand, same as you are." In this wind it was impossible to tell sounds apart, so the conversation was probably safe, although he doubted Ralgon would care had he heard them.

Cahill made a sound that could have been a snort, he wasn't sure. "So, what are you telling me? Should I worry? Is it safe to keep him in my house? Provided we make it home, that is." Was Sir Úistan really asking him for advice? "Please, I don't want a potential monster in my home."

"Everyone can be a monster," he stated. "Under the wrong circumstances." The memory of his brothers' betrayal was there, still, but the pain was missing.

"Well?" Sir Úistan asked as if he hadn't heard his words.

"You must have heard of the Scythe before he came to stay as a guest," he said.

"Aye."

"So, you already knew what Drangar Ralgon was capable of, not only considering the tales of his battle prowess. After all he killed a woman who was friend to both your wife and your daughter, and you probably know that there wasn't much left of the person Hesmera."

"Aye."

"So why do you worry now?"

"Because he convinced my women he did not do it, claiming something had controlled his body," Lord Cahill replied, a note of doubt creeping into his voice.

"Well, he claims the same thing now. As long as he isn't angered it's safe." Safer at least, he added silently.

"You think he just needs friends to talk to?"

"Maybe."

Before nightfall Dewayn and Morwen guided them to a cave. At first the Chosen had frowned at the hole in the rock. Then, as horse after horse was led inside with no apparent end in sight, he understood that the cavern behind was in no way represented by its entrance.

He entered last, following the brooding Ralgon. Inside the snow had only penetrated the first few feet, forming a by now well-trod ramp leading down into the calm interior. To Kildanor's surprise it was stocked with enough firewood to heat an entire village all winter, and soon all of them were huddling near the flames, trying to warm and dry their bodies. Steam rose from moist clothes, both worn and laid out in front of the fire. Wind-driven snow had penetrated everything.

Even the horses huddled close. Rubbed dry, they were slightly more resilient than their riders, who were glad to have a little extra heat in their backs. As the fire grew in size, it didn't take long for this part of the cave to become almost too hot for comfort, and after the last shadows had given way to night Kildanor regretted the lack of a window.

Ralgon stared into the flames, a hand absently scratching his charger's muzzle. Occasionally the mercenary stole a look about, eyes searching the faces of those in his field of vision. Always they lingered on somebody, and Kildanor had to turn and try to imagine the line Drangar's eyes were drawing to find who he was looking at. Of course, he had noticed the sudden hiding of the face, the drawn-up hood, but never in his life would he have thought it had been because of the girl.

Drangar's brooding mood made him doubt the man would even consider a woman, especially after he had torn apart the Chanastardhians. The acts of violence reminded him of the Cherkont Street murder, but not in the way they were executed; Hesmera had been cut to pieces. No, it was the sheer abandon of the act. Had Ralgon not managed to wrest control from the demon, not a single enemy would have left Ondalan. But if this sort of ferocity was something that had not happened before the murder, why had it occurred in Cherkont Street in the first place? Little Creek, Ralgon had mentioned the village, of how he had killed the people there. He had in no way indicated that the level of violence had been anything more than the slaying of villagers.

He watched the mercenary, tried to figure out what was

going on. There was a connection to the demons; of that there was no doubt. The important questions were "Why" and "How." His promise weighed more heavily now, but he was determined to see it through. Maybe this was because it gave him a chance to face Ethain and Ganaedor; perhaps it was merely the desire to do something that had nothing to do with great armies moving. He didn't know, and if he was honest with himself, it mattered little. Not that he could relate with Ralgon, he doubted many could. It just felt right to help the man. He only hoped that the solution to this problem was within easy reach.

Supper was an easy affair, porridge, which the thirty or so Chanastardhians ate with much grumbling. Until now, no one had spoken more than a few words at a time. All this changed when Camran began to ladle out the gruel. Apparently, their new allies had seen more than their fill of the stuff. Even Lord Cahill grimaced. As Kildanor had expected, the only one to eat without any complaint or show of distaste was Drangar. The Chanastardhian to his right slumped down with a relieved sigh then elbowed him.

"Say, mate," the man mumbled with full mouth, "what's the deal with the chap?" He nodded toward the blankly staring mercenary.

He regarded the warrior and recalled him to be one of the four who had called the cavalry into an ambush. "What?" he asked, after swallowing a spoonful of porridge. The last thing he wanted was to make Drangar into a hero. Seeing the man's curiosity, he wondered if it truly was only that or a part of some silly bet.

"What's his troubles?" the older warrior pointed his spoon at Ralgon. "All that gloom and doom. And was that really blood all over his armor?"

The nearby conversations quieted down. Kildanor glanced about and saw that those Chanastardhians sitting close were watching and listening intently. He was about to answer, when Úistan Cahill spoke.

"Nothing like a good bloodbath in the morning, eh?" the nobleman said, his voice a perfect imitation of hardened veteran.

A look at Sir Úistan was rewarded with a brief nod, and when his eyes wandered over to Ralgon he saw a slight, grateful smile play about the mercenary's lips.

The Chanastardhians roared with laughter, while House Cahill's retainers remained silent, their guarded looks going everywhere but at the mercenary. Even Sir Úistan, despite his apparent good humor, seemed more relieved than at ease. He didn't blame the nobleman; the sights of the rampage had brought forth a loathing and terror he hadn't felt in decades. There was something deeply disturbing about all this.

Soon the warmth spread farther from the fire, and Kildanor walked off to find a place to sleep. His boots and socks were thankfully dry once again, and even his gear, most importantly his bedroll, had lost most of the moisture. He was surprised when the footsteps that had followed him turned out to belong to the redheaded girl who had stayed close to the Cirrain woman most of the day. Whether she looked curious or annoyed was hard to tell this far from the fire. Shadows flickered off the walls, and with the flames in her back, he barely made out her face. For a long moment it seemed as if she would merely stand there and look at him, and then, finally, she broke the silence.

"What happened to his hair?"

He instantly knew whom she meant, and was surprised by the lack of disgust in her voice. All he could detect in those few words was interest. Apparently Drangar's covert looks had not gone unnoticed. Opting for a variation of the truth, he said, "Went through flames to rescue the Lord Cahill's wife and daughter." It was quite close to what had really happened.

She must have sensed that there was more to it, which, given the others' obvious discomfort, was quite easy to deduce. Her eyes narrowed, that much he saw in the shadows. "So why does everyone act like he's a leper?"

He wished for better light, if only to gauge her intent. Surely rumors of what had passed between him and Ralgon had made their rounds, but the way she asked did in no way feel like the probing of a gossipmonger. Still, it was not for him to tell of things the mercenary kept to himself. "I can't speak for him, young lady; ask him yourself if you must."

"I tried, to strike up a conversation, that is. He barely replied. Said something along the lines of not wanting to involve any more people. Not in so many words, of course."

The statement piqued his interest. Kildanor regarded the woman in earnest for the first time. She had long, curly red hair; her age was more difficult to guess. He had started to ignore signs of attractiveness over the years. There was no point in falling in love when the person of one's desires and affections would grow old while he stayed young. She was pretty—Ralgon obviously had an eye for beauty—and there was somberness in her eyes he rarely saw in any but the most hardened of veterans.

"Well?" she asked.

For being so talkative in front of an audience this morning, Ralgon now wore his moodiness like a cloak. He smiled sadly, shook his head, and replied, "Have you seen the cairns? The ones outside of Ondalan?" Her head bobbed up and down. "He buried your countrymen there."

"But that's a decent thing to do," she said perplexed.

"Well..." He paused. "What's your name?" In all this he had forgotten what little remained of his etiquette. The few women he socialized with in the Palace had all known him for ages, Scales, many of them were guardsmen's children that he had known him since they were little. "I'm..."

"Lord Kildanor, Chosen of Lesganagh," she finished for him. "Gwennaith of House Keelan."

"Never was a lord," he said. "Kildanor will suffice."

She nodded. "Everyone calls me Gwen."

"Well, then, Gwen. It was decent of him, but I doubt he did it because it's your tradition." He paused, looked over to the fire. Drangar still stared into the flames. "He wanted to bury memories, I think." Not that the gesture helped much, but speaking silently, he added, "He killed most of them."

He could almost see her eyes grow wide, disbelief evident in her voice. "You're joking."

"No, and the way he killed was..." he searched for the right word "... frightening."

"That's why he's alone then?" A trace of concern seeped into her voice, and he was unsure whether it was for the man or the situation. He remained silent, spreading his bedroll. "Thank you," she finally said and left.

He watched her as she went to the Cirrain woman's side and talked. Ralgon seemed to take no notice, staring into the flames. Kildanor knew what it was like to feel alone in a crowd, the only place he did feel understood was with his friends, and the other Chosen. If the mercenary's two-year-long isolation had not robbed him of his social skills already, this confinement within the group he had killed for surely did the job.

He slipped out of boots, into the blankets, and waited for sleep. If they were lucky, they would reach Dunthiochagh tomorrow. But somehow, he doubted luck was on their side.

# CHAPTER 15

They had retrieved Ben's remains shortly after the strike of the noon-gong. Living in the path of the enemy's slingthrowers under the nightlong bombardment, they had noticed the sudden silence long before the news of the Chanastardhian retreat reached them. It felt unreal. Ben was dead.

Jesgar sat in front of the hearth. His mug of hot wine had gone cold long before, and he stared into the sliver of flame still burning inside. Outside, like so many other dead, his brother's corpse lay, snowflakes already piling high upon it. Someone was busy about the house. His mind blank, a bruise of pain, emptiness filling his heart, he barely recognized the sounds. The voice that spoke to him now sounded distant. Who was here with him? He didn't know. All he saw was stupid, arrogant, know-it-all Ben taking the torch and stepping to the battlement, ignoring everyone's protests and warnings. Then Ben thudding onto the stonework, two arrows lodged in his head. The shafts had broken, now it looked as if two snowy nails were stuck in his face.

Ben was dead, and he was left with... what? The smithy? Ben was dead, because of his damned pride. His brother had always seemed immortal, a towering mountain, immovable, rigid. Now he was merely rigid, not towering above anyone. He was out there, in the yard, two arrows lodged in his head. Was he cold? Maybe. He was out there in the snow, freezing. "Little brother," he had always said, "when you go outside in the winter, always make sure you have your cloak with you."

Jesgar stood, walked to the pegs in the wall, the ones for the coats. Gentle but firm hands gripped his shoulders, steered

him back to his seat. Someone spoke; the voice sounded soothing. He didn't hear what it said. The mug thrust into his hands
was hot. More wine. Another log landed in the fire. Sparks flew,
wood crackled, flames licked. It all seemed so pointless.

He tried to lift the hot beverage to his lips. His hands shook,
and liquid spilled over, like it had before. That much he could
remember. He'd had hot wine over his hands all day, ever since
he had returned home. Home, the home where he had lived
with his brother and—the name returned haltingly—Maire. A
cloth came into view, wiped his hands clean. He should have
felt the burn, but didn't. He was hollow, his body, his mind, his
heart. Ben was dead.

And he had never had the time to really tell him how much
he loved him. Now he was outside, lying in the snow, two arrow
shafts sticking out of his snowed-over forehead. Now it was too
late to tell him anything.

Someone—Maire, he forcefully reminded himself—held the
mug to his lips. He drank. For the first time the liquid that penetrated his mouth did not taste like ashes. His eyes left the flickering flames, found her face. She looked weary, as if she had
cried a lot. She had lost her husband, he realized. She was the
only family he had left, and the thought made him understand
why she seemed so exhausted.

Maire hadn't slept either; she had stayed with him, taken
care of him while suppressing her pain. Now, mingling with
the misery he already felt was guilt at having been the one to be
cared for. He was an adult, a man, he reminded himself. It was
his duty to give comfort to his sister-in-law, not the other way
around.

She was still holding the mug to his lips, as if he were a
child. Catching her eyes with his, he lifted his hands to hers
and took the drink away. At that moment it seemed as if life
not only returned to him, but to her as well. "My fingers are
raw," she mumbled, showing him her right hand. "Too many
arrows," she explained.

His confusion must have shown, for Maire frowned then
slapped him across the back of his head. "Get up and make
yourself useful," she grumbled. "I've spent too much time

mothering you." A coat was thrust into his hands, and a bag of coins. "Your brother and I didn't plan it this way. We should've been old and wrinkly. We put the money aside, for the funeral." He gasped, but she spoke on, "Go to the cemetery in the noble district, the Deathmask knows what to do."

"You planned all this?" Jesgar finally managed to stammer, still holding cloak and purse, not moving an inch.

"Of course we did," Maire replied. "Your brother may have been a thickheaded oaf on numerous occasions, but he was no fool." Now he saw that underneath all her furious actions, grief lurked and stabbed at her. "Listen," she continued, drawing a deep breath. "We all die, Ben knew that as well as I do, and you should. We prepared for it, started preparing for it when your da died." She took the cloak from his hands and fastened it around his neck. Next, she pulled the hood up. "It's snowing like the heavens got nothing better to do, so you get there now before we are all snowed in. Take the corpse with you, on a wheelbarrow. Tell the Deathmask not to wait; we don't want much fuss be made about it." Beneath all this determination he heard her misery. "All's been arranged."

Instead of obeying his instincts, which told him to embrace Maire, Jesgar nodded and headed out. By now Bennath lay underneath a mound of white. As he closed the door, he thought he heard Maire sob.

Despite the ever-present snow piling high in the streets, hundreds of people hidden in layers of cloth were about. It seemed as if most of the wounded had already been cared for, because the only warriors he did see were ones who carried fallen comrades. Some had commandeered a wagon, with the dead piled high on top of it. But most were townsfolk. Women and children wandered the streets, searching for husband or father, their shouts muffled by the snow. If he saw familiar faces, he wasn't aware of them. The load of his cart wasn't heavy, not as heavy as he had always imagined Ben would be. Navigating the ruts and piles of snow was far more difficult than pushing his brother's weight. In a way it felt surreal, the snow hid the dead, covered corpses so that finding them became hard work. It also hid the grizzly remnants of the engagement. Sure, there were caved in roofs and shattered walls, but the white blanket masked those who had been squashed underneath.

Once before he had seen what an avalanche could do to a body; when they had recovered the victim's remains not one of the rescuers had been able to say if it had been man or beast. Maybe the families would be luckier never to find their missing loved ones. Knowing a father or husband was dead was bad enough, but seeing how he died... Jesgar halted in the middle of Dunth Street, right in front of the bridge to Miller's Strip, and vomited.

In his mind he saw Ben's head snapping back from the impact. He doubted his brother had felt any pain, or rather, he hoped he hadn't. Ben was dead. Clearing his throat, he took up the handles of the wheelbarrow once more and resumed pushing. The footing atop the bridge was bad, so much slush that he slipped more than once. One of these stumbles dislodged the snow upon Ben's head, and the shafts became visible once more, grim reminders of what had killed his brother. The Chanastardhians, Jesgar realized with a start, had only perpetrated the deed. His brother's idiotic stubbornness had killed him in the end. Had Ben listened, he would still be alive.

The grief was still there, but now he looked at his older brother's corpse differently. Sadness mixed with anger. Not at the Chanastardhians, but at Ben. With furious strength he pushed on.

Up here, on the northern shore of the Dunth, things looked less bleak than in the south. The Chanastardhian slingthrowers hadn't reached as far as Trann Street to begin with, and whereas the Merchant District and the slums had suffered the assault, the situation here almost seemed normal. Of course, none of the businesses were open, and carts with wounded clogged the street, but every building stood intact, no splintered roofs, no missing walls, and not a single mother wailing over losing her children to the rocks that had torn their homes apart. There were some mourners, men and women who had lost somebody in the defense, but unlike their fellow citizens in the south they only had to grieve for those who had taken up arms and actually fought the invaders.

Jesgar scowled and pushed past a man, a trader by the look of it, who held on to his children, trying to not let them see the mangled corpse of a woman who could have only been his wife. The family didn't even glance his way. A few yards down the street he regretted the expression he wore. He had not meant to offend or signify annoyance; he almost turned to apologize, and then realized nobody had noticed. Everybody was enveloped in their own grief.

Now that he had reached the paved roads near the cemetery, flashes of memories came back. Nothing definite, only the slight feeling he had been here before. This, according to Kildanor, was true, not that he remembered any of it. He had felt remorse for something he had done while in thrall to another when it had first been revealed to him, now he felt nothing. Why should he? Whatever he had done had happened while another had pulled the strings. That the entire affair sounded pretty much like what this Drangar Ralgon had done two years ago, with the exception that he hadn't butchered anybody, was the only thing he felt slightly queasy about. Kildanor and Ralgon probably had figured out the connection already.

Still, he realized as he approached the cemetery gates, the issue took his mind off Ben's death, the corpse he was pushing through the city was reminder enough. His brother was dead. What was expected of him now? Ben had taken over the smithy when their da had died. Would he be forced to do the same? It felt somewhat disrespectful to think of the future while the body hadn't yet been cremated, and still, it felt right. He had shed his tears. At least he thought he had on top of the wall, using Ben's maul to beat his killers to pulp. Never before had he mourned for anyone, mainly because nobody he cared about had died until now. He didn't even remember his father. By the time he had understood what death really meant, the man Ben had spoken of as "da" had been dead for most of his life. So, no, he knew not what it was like to grieve. Had Ben seen him atop the wall, beating back attacker after attacker?

Had he approved? Was he even now sitting in the Halls of the Gods feasting and toasting to his brave little brother?

Jesgar didn't feel valorous at all, he had beaten the brains out of many Chanastardhians, sure, but none of that really mattered. His brother was dead, and he would inherit the smithy and all the duties that came with it.

"I'll take care of her," he promised the motionless corpse. A smile crept onto his face as he imagined what Ben's reaction to these words would have been like.

"Maire can work the forge, runt. She'll do a far better job of taking care of herself than you ever could," Ben would have said. In a way he thought he heard his brother's voice. "Remember your first horseshoe? You're no smith." In Jesgar's mind Ben sounded less temperamental than he had ever been in life. "Go do what you feel is right, follow your path and not the path you don't want to travel. Make your own footsteps."

"Even in death your brother is very stubborn," a voice beside him rumbled, pulling Jesgar out of his reverie.

He blinked and looked at the speaker. All Deathmasks looked alike, that much he knew, but in a way, he felt this one was actually smiling at him from beneath the brass covering the face. "Excuse me?" he finally managed to say.

"You heard me and him, there is nothing left to say on the matter," the priest of Jainagath said with a brief bow. "If you wait here, I'll take care of the body." The Deathmask motioned to the chapel, and after a moment's hesitation he went inside, leaving the cleric with his brother.

Maire had said everything had been arranged, whatever that meant. As the door shut behind him, he remembered he had forgotten to tell the priest to proceed at once. He turned, opened the portal again and found the yard empty. The Deathmask must have known what had to be done. With so many dead and winter embracing the land quickly, it seemed likely that any high and formal funerals would be delayed until such time as the weather was more agreeable. That didn't delay the actual burying of the ashes, though.

The chapel, he noticed with surprise, was not what he had expected. There were a few skulls carved into the mantelpiece and the posts of what he guessed had to be the bed, but aside from that it looked more like a library of sorts, or a study. The room—he couldn't tell if there were more beside this one—wasn't exactly cold, neither was it as warm as he expected of a living space. He had been in barns warmer than this place. Determined not to poke his nose into things that were none of his business, Jesgar sat on the single hard chair and waited.

Soon he found himself staring at the skulls. Why was there a fireplace if it wasn't used? The friezes seemed to shift, as he inspected them, taking on features he had seen on his brother. One was laughing, another frowning, yet another glared, they depicted the range of emotion Bennath Garinad had displayed in all the years he had known him. That one grinned, like Ben had when Jesgar had thrown a snowball straight into the face of the neighbor's dog. It was a proud grin. Despite the emptiness he felt as he thought of his brother's lifeless body, the skull-faces brought forth all the memories he had of Ben. The hole his death had torn inside was slowly filled.

Jesgar smiled, wept, laughed, and scrunched his face in chagrin. The skulls seemed to say that all would turn out well, and to his surprise he believed them. In his heart, without even realizing he had done so, he had detached himself from the smithy long before now, but a part had always stayed there, would always stay there. And now, with Ben gone, the part that had left his home behind knew it was all right to go. The memories would remain, Ben would remain, in his heart, and that was really the only place they were meant to endure for as long as he, Jesgar, lived. When death found him, he would join his brother in the Halls of the Gods, and there they would celebrate. Until then, Ben lived in his heart.

At that moment, he understood that his grumpy, loving older brother would always be with him, he remembered something Ben must have said when he had been but a child. Ben had wanted his ashes be joined with their father's, in the forge. That their father had been with them all these years, whenever they worked the bellows or heated iron, he hadn't even been aware of. And Ben wanted the same.

Rubbing tears from his eyes, he looked at the mantelpiece

again, there were only carved skulls, staring blindly.

The door creaked open and the Deathmask entered. "It is done," the priest said. Whether he meant the cremation or the final understanding that his brother would always be with him, Jesgar didn't know. It didn't matter. "The stone will be engraved," the Deathmask continued. "Here, you know what he wanted you to do."

Jesgar nodded, tears again welling in his eyes. He took the urn, nodded once more, and then left.

Outside, already a few yards down the next street, he remembered the wheelbarrow. A few heartbeats later, urn secured on it, he pushed the contraption southward, home.

By the time he reached Hill's Road the last vestiges of doubt had vanished. His responsibility was, first of all, his own wellbeing. He was no warrior, even if the fight on the wall had demonstrated he could do battle if forced into it. The blacksmith's craft certainly wasn't for him either. He would do what he enjoyed, Maire would understand, and his brother approved. Spying, much like thieving, was mainly the boredom of observation and only in part exhilaration, but this small part was enough. He would remain the Baron's spy and go where his lord wanted him to go. In his mind he already saw himself wandering the places of power, not so much lurking about but mingling with the mighty, pretending he was someone else. Scales, it had worked in the enemy camp, it was bound to work elsewhere.

When he reached the smithy, by now the nearby buildings had been cleared of debris and casualties, the sound of the bellows and the roaring fire beckoned him. His brother's urn in hand, Jesgar entered the stiflingly hot workshop. Inside Maire was busy shoveling more coals into the fire. She wore Ben's old leather apron. The thing was far too big, despite the worn yet sturdy material having been bunched at the waist. She was working as hard as she would have on any other day.

She must have felt the draft, for she turned, wiped a sweaty strand of hair from her face, and regarded him. The way she stood, her pose, in a way she had taken her husband's posture and made it her own. Sure, she was hardly as tall as Ben, and the apron looked rather silly on her wiry frame, but she exuded a confidence and strength he had rarely noticed before. She pointed at the urn, her eyes still boring into his. "You know what to do?"

He nodded. Of course he knew, yet he was unsure whether Ben wanted him or her to pour the ashes into the forge. She must have sensed his hesitation for she walked to his side, folded her arms, and turned her head to regard him. "Your brother did the same for your father," she said. "Some stupid Garinad man-thing if you ask me, but that's what he would've wanted." Up close he saw that she was not finished grieving, the rivulets of sweat that washed the soot off her forehead were mixed with tears that still ran all too freely.

"You should go and see the Deathmask, and his fireplace," he said. Then, to lighten the mood, "Should children bearing our name ever walk this place we'll let this stupid male tradition slip away, eh?" He tried to wink, but ended up blinking fiercely. "Bloody smoke," he mumbled, wiping a sleeve across his face. If Maire noticed his weeping, she didn't mention it. Her hand was on his back, and she gently pushed him toward the roaring flames. Fumbling, he reached for the lid, pulled it off, and was about to empty the urn's contents into the fire, when Maire stopped him. He threw a questioning look at her.

"Together," she answered, eyes pleading. Without a thought, Jesgar nodded. She had been Ben's wife for almost as long as he had been his brother; the two had lived as a couple for as long as he could remember. Traditions were there to be changed, and if Ben was too stubborn to recognize her right to perform this last honor, he had better stay quiet.

Both of them held the urn in their hands. Jesgar glanced over to Maire, and saw her lips moving. The roar of the fire was too loud for him to hear what she was saying. It mattered not. His words, when they finally left his mouth, were as quiet as hers; he wasn't even sure he was actually speaking them. Then, in unison, when the flames had died down leaving enough of an opening, they tilted the urn, and Ben's ashes joined those of his father.

For a long while they stood in front of the forge, watching

the coals burn. The glow intensified and lessened, spreading from the center into the farthest spots. It looked as if it was searching for something. Jesgar liked the idea of it looking for Ben's ashes; it was a nice image. Once or twice Maire and he shared the duty of working the bellows, fanning the heat on. Then, unsure when he had put on his own barely used apron, they worked.

Sparks flew, hammers sang, and the bellows roared. How long they remained thus he couldn't tell, but it was well past dusk when they left. On their way out, Maire nudged him companionably and said, "Do me, you, and most importantly Ben's memory a favor."

He looked at her. The sadness in her face had been replaced by exhaustion, and there was a sparkle in her eyes, mischievous, yes, mixed with the last remnants of grief, if he were to guess. A smile crept onto his lips, unbidden, for he knew what she would say. "Aye?" Jesgar asked.

"Don't ever do any work in any smithy again, at least not with the hammer and anvil," Maire said with a smirk. "Hungry?"

"Scales, yes!" he replied. Casting one last look at the forge his brother had worked at for so many years, he followed her inside. Ben was dead, but life went on.

# CHAPTER 16

## Third of Cold, 1475 K.C.

Heavy snowfall had brought their journey to a dreary halt, and though warm, Drangar felt as if the cave walls were closing in on him. Aside from Kildanor and, strangely enough, the woman he would rather have met when he was bathed and clothed rather than splattered with blood from a good score of Chanastardhians, no one exchanged more than a few halting words with him. Solitude, he was used to it. At least his garments were dry, and the air remained breathable. He hadn't found the natural chimney yet, but one had to be there, somewhere. Touching his head ever so often, he felt tufts of hair clustering about the pate, and even the previously bald spots were slowly sprouting again. The same was happening to his eyebrows and beard. Lacking a mirror, he imagined his head looked less a nightmare now than he had a week ago. Not that this boosted his confidence whenever she came over to strike up a conversation. What did she see in him anyway?

Again, he ran his hand across his stubbly head and wondered why she even joined him. He certainly wasn't attractive, not like this, and women of her age usually went for looks instead of personality any day of the year. He scoffed. Right now, he was lacking in both areas. Maybe he had lacked them all his life?

When he closed his eyes, he saw the Fiend, restless, pacing, waiting for its chance. The thought of having torn apart a human being with his bare hands made him jerk awake at night. This vision replaced the vision of butchering the monster that turned into Hesmera, not that the new dream was any better. In the twisted way nightmares worked, Drangar was certain that sooner or later he would be tearing Hesmera apart. If the others were disturbed by his restless sleep, they didn't mention it. Not even Kildanor.

He didn't blame them; the Chanastardhians relied on rumors but generally kept to themselves, and Sir Úistan's people were busy staying clear of him. Sometimes, when she sat with him, he thought he could detect concern in her eyes. Yesterday she had almost broken the somewhat comfortable silence. She had tucked her curly hair behind her ear, bitten her lips, taken a deep breath, and in the end remained silent. Drangar was grateful for that. He didn't know what to say, what to speak of. Things had been simpler back then, before Dunthiochagh. He didn't even know her name.

The spot where he had chosen to put his gear was away from the others. One of the recesses branching off from the main chamber gave him the solitude he wanted. He chuckled, shaking his head. He wanted solitude; he didn't need it. But with so many people around, he felt uncomfortable. Ignoring the fact that he was drawn to her, he enjoyed her company. She made him feel at peace, made him forget that there was something within him that loved tearing through people, that loved bathing in blood. Had his situation not been as grim as it was, he might have asked Kildanor for advice. Courting had never been one of his strengths; Scales, it had taken him months before he had uttered the first words to Hesmera. The Scythe—how he hated that title now—being afraid of women had been a permanent joke with his mates. Not that he had ever been afraid of women, just a woman he really liked. Hesmera had had it, and this one had it also, the one thing he felt drawn to, a depth in her eyes hinting at the depths of her heart and soul. Even cultured Neena Cahill had carelessness in her eyes, a naiveté shining within, that made him shy away. Maybe this was because he'd seen all his dreams and hopes shatter before his eyes before he had ever had time to reach for them. In a way this flame-headed warrior had the same look about her, a kinship he was drawn to.

A kinship he dared not share again. He wouldn't endanger her like he had unknowingly endangered Hesmera. He would rid himself of the Fiend, and get the Sons off his back. Then maybe, if she would have him, he might be able to love himself, and her.

The sound of the whetstone running down steel surprised him. He hadn't been aware of unsheathing the sword. All the techniques of prayer and meditation the Sons had taught him were nothing compared to the calm that engulfed him when sharpening a blade. A few Chanastardhians looked his way, suspicious. He didn't blame them, had he been in their place he would have felt the same. The covert glances from Sir Úistan's retainers were different. Here suspicion had grown into worry, a fact that bothered him because he knew some of them. Now, going about their businesses, they avoided coming any closer than necessary.

As far as he could tell, they tried to maintain a vague resemblance of normalcy. Someone had carved dice from a chunk of wood, and the main attraction of the cave was a game of chance. No one had invited him, but he didn't mind, preferring the solitude. It was safer that way.

The stone ran down the blade automatically, he went through the motions with a precision born of years and years of routine. His eyes took in the scene before him. There were the dicers, Lord Cahill inspecting the snow-shut entrance, Kildanor looking his way, the Chanastardhian woman Cirrain, and her. Did he want to know her name? In the warband it had been easy finding out Hesmera's, everybody knew each other, here with people avoiding him it was more difficult. He could ask her, but that would open an entirely new bag of problems. Under normal circumstances he would have gone and asked her, talked to her, but his life was anything but normal. He tore his eyes away as she brushed her hair back with both hands.

"Can we talk?" the Chosen's voice startled him.

"Hmm?"

Kildanor sat next to him. "The Fiend you mentioned," he began, looking thoughtful.

"Hmm."

"Is it there now?" Drangar thought he detected some genuine

worry in the Chosen's voice. "Why did you come back?"

He arched a sparse brow, looking at Kildanor. "Like I had a choice in the matter. At first you thought Lesganagh or some other god returned me to life, eh?" Drangar scoffed. "I never asked for any of this."

"So, you don't know how or why you came back?"

"Other than to make my life even more miserable?" he asked, trying to keep the sarcasm down. "No."

"And the Fiend? Is it there?"

"I try not to think about it."

At first, Kildanor regarded him silently, and then he said, "Still, I need to understand…"

"You and me both, I think."

"So is…"

"Yes, it is there, all the fucking time," he interrupted. "I feel the bugger lurking, waiting. You shouldn't have brought me along on this." He nodded to House Cahill's men-at-arms. "They thought me strange to begin with, what with the eating and all. Now they think I'm a monster. Maybe I am."

"But you said it yourself, you were not in command," protested Kildanor.

"So, if a captain orders warriors to butcher innocents, the soldiers are not to blame?"

"The soldiers have a choice, you did not!"

"Is that supposed to make me feel better? I remember seeing my hands in that woman's stomach, around her spine, tearing her apart," he growled. "Do you really think I enjoy these images? Sure, every one of us"—he made a waving motion with the whetstone—"has killed. I imagine there are some torturers who'd applaud my creativity, even if I have done nothing. It's all I can do to stay calm and not allow the Fiend to gain the upper hand."

"What is he?"

"Damned if I know, mate." A sad chuckle escaped his lips. "Never gave me a name, nor did I see a face. Aside from the cat beasts you called demons. Fought them to regain control."

"What really bothers me is that you obeyed me when I told you to clear the way," said Kildanor.

"Aye, I saw that." He looked at the Chosen and saw the man blinking in disbelief. "Not that the bastard told me his intentions."

"What?" Worry was now plainly in Kildanor's face. "So, you had no hand whatsoever in that decision?"

"None. I regained control when that thing kept running into the shield wall," Drangar said. "I could see through my eyes then, like windows, so to speak. The massacre in the house, the killings as it, I, walked for the shield wall, I saw it and could do nothing."

The Chosen swallowed, face devoid of blood. "This being controlling you obeyed me?"

Drangar snorted in derision. "Well, I certainly did not order anything to go and clear the way." His hand was halfway up his head when he remembered there was no hair to rake through. Closing his eyes, he tried to recall anything he might have missed. The search, he felt, came close to that part of his mind where the Fiend lurked, sequestered for now. If any minute memories remained, they would return unbidden, much like the other flashes, just like the nightmares.

A hand on his shoulder brought him back to the cave. "Don't look for places you don't want to see," Kildanor said.

"I never saw them in the first place," he retorted. "It's more a matter of steering clear of this thing in my head." The Chosen looked doubtful. "It's there, waiting. Bastard's always waiting." In a way he felt reminded of the argument that the two, or was it three, disembodied voices had when he'd been in the dark place. *The time has not come!* His unseen protector had yelled at the shining lights that had tried to reach him. What time? It made no sense. *The time has not come!* Had the Fiend been waiting, lurking inside of him all his life? No. Or had it? Nothing made sense, and this Chosen was no help either. "I have to go to the places I don't want to go to," he finally said.

"The Eye of Traksor?" Kildanor asked.

"Aye, if anyone can tell me what the Scales is going on, it will be them," Drangar replied. Why did it feel as if the Fiend was squirming?

"What about Gwen?"

"What about who?" he asked, confused. There was a concerned look in Kildanor's eyes, now replaced by mirth.

The Chosen snorted. "Oh, man, you don't even know her name. She's been trying to talk to you for days now, and you've been trying not to ogle her too much."

"Her name's Gwen?" Now she had a name. It made things more complicated.

"Why the long face?" Kildanor prompted. "It's obvious she likes you. She's been trying to get to learn more about you. You should be happy."

His head snapped around. "Why?"

"Because in all this darkness you have one light shining for you, at you."

"She doesn't know me." He resumed running the whetstone down the blade.

"I wonder if you know yourself." Drangar tried to shut out the warrior's voice, in vain. "Why wallow in the darkness? If you don't let any sort of light into your life, you will be trapped. Trust me, I know of these things."

"You have no one in the back of your mind," he hissed. "That thing, I can feel it. It's waiting, waiting. I don't want what happened to Hesmera happen to her."

"And who says it will?"

"What if what you say really happens? What if she and I fall in love? Lovers quarrel. What if the Fiend uses this anger to slip in and regain control with me waking from it only after she is torn to pieces? I don't want to live with that, be it with her or anyone else."

For a moment it seemed as if Kildanor struggled for words, and then, "She has a name."

"And my saying it, can't it make things more difficult?" He shook his head. "I don't want to hurt anyone!"

"When you knew that it was not yourself who had killed Hesmera, you found it easy to forgive yourself and begin to live again," the Chosen retorted. "What makes this different?"

"I..." He fell silent. "The..." he began anew, and again the words failed him. "When..." It was useless. He didn't know what to say.

"There is no difference, other than you knowing how to avoid it happening again, or at least reining it in." One look told him Kildanor believed what he was saying. "Why not take strength from a person willing to give it? What are you afraid of? Rejection?" Drangar shook his head. "Being understood?" Again, a denial. "Being loved?" This time he hesitated. "You wonder if anyone can love you. Not if you don't find it in you to accept you aren't responsible for the things this Fiend does. Not if you can't love yourself. Aye, as long as you are incapable of loving yourself you won't be able to truly live and be loved in return."

"But Sir Úistan," Drangar argued.

"What of him?"

"He and his people, they saw what I…"

"No, not what you did, what it did!" Kildanor snapped. "He knows you saved his family, got burned because of that. He doesn't understand how one who so selflessly rescued his wife and daughter could rip through a score of people, leaving their bodies scattered."

"But we…"

"Well, we know what is controlling you, not why, but it wasn't your mind and heart doing these things, or?" It was hard to look Lesganagh's warrior in the eye. Drangar knew he was right; at least it felt like he was speaking the truth.

He tried again. "But we…"

"Don't know what it really is?" the Chosen finished for him. "Well, we can always ask the old coot Coimharrin again." That brought a slight smile to his face. "So you remember, eh?" It was hard to forget the Upholder.

"Managed to put some confidence in me the last time."

"No." The reply surprised him.

"No?"

"He just confirmed the truth, you did the rest."

"Could you please ask Lord Cahill to join us?" he said.

"Why not ask him yourself? Worried?" Kildanor stood and smacked his head. "Well then, just this once I'll fight your battles. All right?" Drangar nodded his thanks.

The look Sir Úistan gave him was far from benevolent. Neither was it wicked or angry. If he were to chance a guess, he would have called it reserved, suspicious maybe. That Lord Cahill had come at all made him hope he could talk to the man. Without preamble, Sir Úistan motioned him to remain seated. Then, arms crossed in front of his chest, the noble stood before him, waiting.

Drangar hated looking up at him, but knew the concerns Sir Úistan harbored were based on what had occurred in Ondalan. "Milord," he began. "I wish I could explain what happened. I can't, not really." The nobleman's brows bunched in a frown. Ignoring his discomfort as much as possible, he continued, "I know it is hard to believe, but I was not in command of either my body or my senses."

"And you expect me to trust your word?"

"Your daughter trusted me when I told her of what really happened the night Hesmera died," he retorted, unsure whether he sounded too hostile, or too apologetic. A glance at Kildanor showed no reaction; so far, he was walking the right path. He just hoped the Chosen would intervene should he make a mistake.

"Aye, she did at that."

"I still cannot remember the incident in our house in Cherkont that day, there are only my nightmares and what I was shown by the apparition." Before Lord Cahill could reply, he said, "I remember parts of what happened in Ondalan, although only through a veil, as a spectator if you will. If my body was a wagon, know that I did not steer." An almost imperceptible nod by Kildanor showed the Chosen approved of this slight alteration of the tale. There was no point telling the noble all that was going on.

"You're telling me someone else did all that?"

"Yes."

"Why should I accept this story of yours?"

"Because it's the truth." The answer sounded weak even to his ears, and it was. The nobleman's expression didn't change, the furrows on his brow became more pronounced. "Why would I lie?" Drangar asked. "If Upholder Coimharrin verified my tale, how could I still be lying?"

That brought a change to Lord Cahill's face. It seemed minute, yet he felt he had finally made progress. Maybe the nobleman's set opinion was wavering. "You did save my family."

He glanced at Kildanor who gave an encouraging nod. "On the field I was a killer, but I was never uncaring," he said. "Their faces still haunt me."

"So, who is pulling your strings?" Sir Úistan voiced the same question he had worried about for three days. His shrug, he hoped, was viewed as desolate, not casual. There was nothing casual about the entire situation. "You don't know either." Thankfully Lord Cahill understood his gesture the way it was meant.

"We made some guesses, milord," Kildanor intervened.

Sir Úistan turned as if he only now remembered the Chosen was still with them. "Have you now? And what conclusion have you reached?"

"None, unfortunately," said Drangar.

"I thought as much."

"Nothing conclusive anyway," Kildanor added. "There's only one thing we do know, or at least think we know."

"And what is that?"

"Blind anger opens the door for whatever was controlling him." The Chosen nodded in his direction, and the stare Lord Cahill gave him was as intense as those he had received as a child.

"Is that true?" the nobleman asked.

"Aye, we think so," he said. "In the turret room with your wife and Neena, it was different. My need to protect the women kept the fury in check." He thought a moment, and added, "I couldn't allow the bastard to take my last links to Hesmera." Saying her name was less painful than it had been a month ago. It was still there, dull, sometimes throbbing, but it was bearable now.

"You didn't break out of that bubble alone then?" Lord Cahill asked.

He looked from one man to the other, and saw the same question plain on the Chosen's face. "No," he replied.

"You never mentioned that," Kildanor prompted.

"I never made the connection until now. Never really made the connection."

"So as long as we don't royally piss you off, you'll be all right?" Sir Úistan asked.

"I should think so."

"I want you to look me in the eyes and repeat what you just said," the nobleman insisted.

"Why?" asked Drangar. "You're no Upholder; you can't see the truth like they do."

Cahill's grin was as threatening as it was confident. "No, but I am a damn good judge of character, and while my mind reels with what happened in Ondalan, I struggle with what I knew of you," he said. "I want to know if my gut is right."

There was no mirth in the man's voice, just plain, sharp steel, and Drangar knew Sir Úistan already believed him. He looked the nobleman straight in the eyes and said, "I was not in control in the village, and as long as I remain calm, in control, something like this will not happen again."

Lord Cahill turned to Kildanor and said, "You know, all of this would be even less frightening if he didn't keep sharpening his blades all the time."

Drangar looked at his hands, astonished. He hadn't noticed he was still whetting the sword. How long had he been doing it? The Chosen's laugh, thankfully, broke the tension. No wonder everyone saw him as a mad killer! A quick inspection showed the weapon was as sturdy as ever, but when he drew his belt knife, he saw the breadth was less than it had been even a week ago. And the edge was so fine and sharp he had no doubt it could split a hair. "It calms me," he offered weakly.

Kildanor snorted. "Try knitting."

At this Sir Úistan boomed with laughter so irresistible that Drangar couldn't help but join in. In a way he would have welcomed sitting there with thread and needles instead of a whetstone and a pair of blades; at least he would lose the image of a single-minded killer.

Their mirth drew attention, and soon he was the center of ridicule as the Chosen's suggestion was absorbed and refined by Lord Cahill's retainers. The Chanastardhians, having been with them only for a short period, had in all likelihood noticed his obsessive sharpening and joined in the surging laughter. Being ridiculed felt good. For far too long his life had been in the shadows and, unlike the children of his past, the people here in the cave laughed with him, not at him.

Consciously, Drangar sheathed his sword and put the sharpening stone away. Then, wiping tears from his eyes, he looked at Kildanor and said, "You wouldn't happen to have some needles and thread with you, would you?"

For a moment the Chosen retained his calm, then the combined laughter of Danastaerians and Chanastardhians shook the cave once more. He was laughing so hard he barely noticed the companionable slap on the shoulder Lord Cahill gave him. A look up at the noble showed a man from whose back a tremendous weight had been lifted. Sir Úistan gave him a brief nod then walked away, still laughing.

When he saw her, Gwen he corrected himself, pass Lord Cahill on his way back to the main cave, he almost felt his eyes pop out of their sockets. The good humor abated, but a quick look at Kildanor and the Chosen's encouraging smile helped him keep his calm and retain some mirth. As she drew closer, he discerned a bundle in her right hand. Now, with only a few feet separating them, Drangar understood why she was grinning like a lunatic. The bundle was a pair of needles and yarn.

"Thought you might enjoy it," Gwen said.

He spoke the first thing that came to his mind. "Drangar, Drangar Ralgon."

"I know," she replied, handing him the bundle.

"And he, let me assure you, knows nothing of knitting," Kildanor interrupted. Drangar was glad the Chosen had done so, because he felt rather silly being so tongue-tied. All he could do was to stare, Gwen's bundle, still in her hand, hovered inches from his face.

"I guess I can teach him," she said. "Whatever little I know of knitting." At first Drangar, and apparently everyone but Gwen, Anne Cirrain and Kildanor, thought this was a splendid finale to a good joke. Laughter rumbled through the cave once more, but when she remained standing before him, serious but for the smile on her lips, he understood she meant it. Uncertain he looked at the Chosen who mouthed something that could have only been an encouragement. He smiled and nodded, still too afraid to speak, worried that the only thing he would be able to force out of his mouth other than his name would be incoherent babbling. That he hadn't behaved thusly when meeting Hesmera didn't bother him at all.

Soon the others realized Gwen was serious also, and the laughter died down. And although many eyes were still on them, first and foremost those of Lord Cahill and the Cirrain woman, life inside the cave returned to its normalcy. Kildanor still stood at the place he had occupied since joining him, unmoving. Something in the wistful look he cast at Gwen and him gave him pause.

The Chosen said, "Damn, you cannot imagine how lucky you are. Both of you." Then he turned and left.

Gwen said something. He hardly heard her. All he did was stare at her, feeling like a boy just come of age on the first day of spring. "What?" he asked, feeling as if he was already losing himself in her blue eyes.

There was a sharp pain in his arm, drawing his attention away from her. "I said that I will teach you how to knit," Gwen repeated sternly, yet even though his attention was on the hole left in his tunic by a needle he could tell she was smiling. The bundle waved before his eyes. "This is what you have to focus on, understood?"

Later, when the roll of the dice and the cheers of the warriors bathed the cavern with sound, Drangar realized, for the first time, how truly difficult knitting really was. But even though he struggled to get fingers, needles, and thread into a coherent working unit, he was glad, for Gwen was teaching him. Soon any thought of sharpening a blade had gone. Needle and thread were enough. It really was a struggle, but her company, patience and humor kept him trying.

And somewhere in the back of his mind, Drangar felt the Fiend seething with impotent rage. He knew the peace he now felt wouldn't last, couldn't last. But he also knew that with Gwen at his side he stood a much better chance of remaining in control of his body.

# CHAPTER 17

"She seems to enjoy herself," Paddy commented, as they watched Drangar Ralgon struggle through the first, tedious row of stitches.

Anne would have liked to say the younger woman didn't know what she was doing, but the fact of it was that Gwen had very well proved she was able to make up her own mind, and keep her head on her shoulders. Every warrior helping in the ambush spoke highly of the girl—woman, she reminded herself. Even her cousin praised Gwen's levelheadedness. Still, the rumors of Ralgon tearing through Ondalan's conquerors persisted. Had it been one or two people talking, she would have dismissed it, but it seemed as if every one of Sir Úistan's retainers told the same story. Anne knew in her heart that this person was trouble. The feeling had none of the impulsive trappings of jealousy; she knew there was nothing about this maniac she considered attractive. No, her gut had warned her about the blood-caked man even before Lord Cahill's retainers had talked about the trail of corpses he had left in his wake. That he had later buried them in cairns hardly changed the fact that he was a man not to be trusted or relied upon.

"Jealous?" Paddy teased; that much was obvious from the tone of his voice.

"Bullshit," she retorted. "He's dangerous."

"Obsessive, crazy, somehow more than a man," Paddy added. "Aye, he is that."

"He isn't good for her."

Beside her Paddy straightened. They both had lounged near the fire, somewhat separated, as the odors inside the cavern grew rather rank. Not even the burning wood, which thankfully was dry enough to only give off a minimum of smoke, could dispel the stench of dozens of unwashed bodies. The straw they had found in another part of the cave complex prevented the horses from flooding the place, but the animals' urine added to the vile aroma. He turned to stare at her. "And who made you Lawspeaker?"

"All he's been doing for the past few days, when he wasn't ogling her, was to whet his blades," she retorted. "Given how he was when we first saw him, that pretty much says killer, doesn't it?"

"You look, but never really see, cousin," he said, shaking his head. What was that all about? Of course, she saw things. Her face must have displayed her anger because Paddy chuckled.

"What?" she snapped.

"Nothing," he replied, still smirking.

Now she felt fury rise. In the past, whenever Paddy had mocked her, it had been with good reason; she was the last person to deny that. But with this butcher, how could he be so blind? "What are you laughing at? I'm right, he is dangerous!"

"Dangerous, maybe," he answered. "They used to call him Scythe."

"It's no wonder, given the way he dealt with Kirrich's warriors." She vaguely remembered tavern-tales of a mercenary who had supposedly been blessed by Lesganagh. "And?"

"Have you ever looked at his eyes?" Paddy asked.

"Padraigh Cirrain, what the fuck are you talking about?"

He put on his mocking face, lips curling in disdain. Gods, how she hated him doing that! "You can see it, even now," he said, nodding in Ralgon's direction.

She gazed at the man's struggle with needles and yarn. "What about it? Knitting is a pain, I know, I've tried."

"Godsdamnit, you are as perceptive as a mole," he groaned. "Even now, see! There! He laughs, but the mirth never really reaches his eyes."

Was she really that dense? All she saw was a man she knew was a killer trying to knit. "There's nothing wrong with him," she retorted.

"His eyes, woman!" He smacked the back of her head. Their familiarity was such that she hardly noticed. Then, after scrutinizing the scene for a while, she thought she saw what Paddy was referring to. There was hurt, fear, and something Anne couldn't quite pin down. Even as he tried to listen and learn, and Gwen seemed to make every sort of effort to stay near him and touch him, it looked as if he was shirking away, if not physically, then at least emotionally.

"Gods," she whispered.

"As perceptive as a mole," Paddy repeated. "Even our allies see the way he suffers. They still worry, so do I for that matter. And who pray wouldn't? You, oh warleader, are so vigilant, see a threat in every bloody thing, but you have no idea what the people around you feel, do you? Scales, is your head made of bricks, or are you so involved with your own bullshit that you don't see what others are going through?"

This statement gave her pause. She considered. Of course, she knew what Alayn or Natheira were going through, and then she remembered the row a few weeks prior to their departure. Natheira had quarreled with her husband; supposedly he had been cheating on her. Everyone had proclaimed they had seen it coming, that Natheira had been moody and distraught for a while. The only person who apparently had not noticed the other woman's temper had been she. Was she really so self-involved she hardly noticed the troubles of those around her?

"He's been trying to ease his mind," Paddy said, breaking the silence. She looked at him, and he continued, "I don't know how many have noticed, but there's a calm in his eyes whenever he runs the whetstone down a blade." She followed his gaze to the odd couple sitting engrossed at the other side of the cave. Ralgon was smiling, and for the briefest of moments the worried, haunted look vanished. Then as he turned to face Gwen, something like longing flashed in his eyes, and his mood turned somber again. "One thing's for sure," her cousin muttered. "I wouldn't want to tread in his boots, even for a heartbeat. Whatever is troubling him, whatever is struggling inside of him to get out, no matter how stunning your squire is, I wouldn't want to be in his place."

Anne watched them a moment longer, realizing for the first time how little she knew of the world and the people living in it. Was that because of her stubbornness, she wondered. Her sisters were both ladies and warriors, aristocratic even when they drove a spear through an enemy, but she, she was more akin to Paddy and Dubhan, both in demeanor and attitude. Or so she had thought. Obviously, her cousin was more apt at reading people than she had ever been. What about her father? Was he as self-involved as she? Had she inherited this trait from him?

A sudden desire to walk overcame her. With a grunt she stood. Paddy made to rise as well. She shook her head. "Stay. I need to be alone for a spell." Without waiting on his reply, she left.

In the best of times the cave was cramped. Now, with her tenth round along the walls, Anne felt caged. She was on the return trip to where her walk had started, passing some of Lord Cahill's men-at-arms once again. For the first few circuits they had watched her with interest. Interest soon turned to routine, and now they were once more engrossed in their game of dice. She knew some of them by name, yet she was in no mood to strike up a conversation.

Was she really as ignorant as Paddy had put to her? She knew she paid attention to the people around her. Everyone knew she cared for them, didn't they? Again, she passed Dubhan who sat forlornly on a ledge near the fire. He cradled something in his hands, eyes fixed on empty air.

She looked into the horses' cave. All quiet there. The Danastaerian horse master, Bhaidin, knew his job, and aside from the a few bite marks there had been little trouble with the animals. Surprising, she thought. There were at least three stallions in this cramped herd, but with the rationing of feed and Bhaidin's force of personality—not to mention his whip—even Paddy's Landslide was behaving.

Again, she passed the dicers, approached Dubhan once more, and stopped, realizing her cousin was right; she paid little attention to individuals. Her sudden halt had drawn a few surprised looks, and then everything went on as before. Her old weapons-master didn't notice her as she approached to take a peek at the thing he held. It was a toy horse, lovingly detailed. Someone had gone through the trouble to accentuate mane and tail with knife strokes so fine it appeared to be running against the wind. His hands, Anne realized for the first time, were covered with scars, most of which had not been made by an errant sword. Little nicks dominated the landscape of his palms. He had carved the toy! Why hadn't she known about this before?

The answer was as painful as it was simple: because she was locked in her own world, too focused on issues most people never concerned themselves with. She knew what kind of wine Lord Gallinnor preferred, and how many bales of wool went to Herascor each year. Scales, she even knew the names of every noble House, from those who merely lorded over the small bors, to all those residing in the cors. But although she lived for the fight alongside House Cirrain's warriors, she lived apart from them. She didn't even know if Dubhan had family.

He must have noticed her, for he turned and gave her a toothy grin. "Lassie, what you staring at?" he asked, sounding as cheerful as ever.

Now, conscious of her lack of awareness toward others, Anne waited with her response. Dubhan maintained his grin for a moment longer then glanced at the carving once more. "Won't do yet, eyes need to be livelier," he muttered and drew a pouch from his pack. She thought she detected a note of sadness in his eyes as he opened the case and selected one of the knives arrayed within. Fascinated, she watched her old teacher at blade-work so different from his usual craft. There was a fierceness about him whittling away she had never seen in him before.

Suddenly he stopped and looked up at her. "Something you want of me, lassie?"

Embarrassed, and unsure of what to say, she replied, "If it stays this way we'll soon be drowning in dung."

His eyes narrowed and he scratched his whiskers with the knife hilt. "Girl, I've known you since you were pissing your pants," he said with the gentle gruffness that had enchanted her ever since she was a child. "Spill it!"

"I…" She stopped, ashamed.

"Come on, never knew you being lost for words."

"I didn't know you did…" Again, she faltered.

"This?" He held up both knife and horse. "Oh, well, sure you don't remember, made you that little knight doll when you were wee." He cleared his throat. "Well, actually your da asked me to make the thing. Said you were very happy."

Her face must have shown her wonder. "I didn't know."

"You got all them lordly things to worry about, or so your ma and grandma always insisted on. After you were four or so your ma ordered us to return you to the Hall should you show up at our place again. You loved it."

"Our place?" she echoed dully. Just how long had Dubhan known her? She had always enjoyed his easy familiarity without realizing there was more to it than that he was her da's best warrior and oldest living friend.

"Of course, you were fast friends with our lass, Briga" he explained. Then, after a brief pause, he added, "Oh, you don't remember Briga, how could you, you were barely five when she left us." The look on his face explained better than any dozen words what he really meant. And she hadn't known, did not remember. "Always had lots of fun, Briga and you. Always scampered off to cause mayhem." Dubhan looked from her to the horse and fell silent.

"I'm sorry," she whispered.

"Don't be, lassie," he replied, his voice hoarse. "Been a score of years since she left, how could you remember? Your ma always insisted on you being raised a lady. As if!" He forced a laugh. "You never were lady-stuff to begin with. We knew it, your da knew it, and somewhere deep down your ma must've felt it also." He held the horse up. "Her birthday, today," Dubhan explained. "She was spring's child."

Yes, they had always been comrades, she and the warriors, but it had never been a deep friendship. Even though she was outside the grasp of her mother the line had been drawn early. Not that she had been aware of it in the first place. In a way she was as remote as her ma.

Seeing Dubhan this sad struck a chord within her, and on

impulse she knelt next to her old teacher and embraced him. She didn't know what else to do. His sobs, however, told her the gesture was appreciated.

The moment of intimacy, a thing she had until now never considered doing—not even with her father, in fact she hadn't thought an ox of a man like Dubhan capable of feeling thus—was shattered by a commotion from the cave mouth. In her arms Dubhan straightened, one of his strong arms left her side, likely to wipe his face clean of tears. Anne pulled back. It was awkward, holding anyone like that. All her life she had been taught her position, leader, warrior, never a confidante or friend, not even to her parents.

As she turned to see what the noise was all about, the dicers abandoned their game and streamed forward. Even Gwen and Ralgon, who had been finishing the row they had begun. Everyone, it seemed, was heading for the exit. Comforting Dubhan had drawn her attention away from her surroundings, and for a moment she worried that this could be seen as weakness, but when a group led by Connar passed her, their glances spoke of companionship, not scorn.

Daylight shimmered into the cavern, and those in the fore were already busy digging, pressing blocks of cutout hard snow into the hands of those behind them. Even through the small opening she could tell the snowstorm had ended.

"Not a bloody day too soon," someone muttered beside her.

She turned and saw Ralgon, face somber, in his hands still wool and needles, with Gwen standing beside him. For a moment she was tempted to order her squire to join the workers, but then recalled what Paddy had said. Ralgon seemed less grim, and having him calm would work wonders on everyone else's morale, hers included. Instead, she gave Gwen a brief nod, and headed to join the line of people piling snow inside the cave. To her surprise the ones in the front, chopping out blocks of snow, were the Lords Kildanor and Cahill. They were spurring each other on, and with this game of trading well-meant barbs and insults they encouraged those behind them to work just as hard.

She joined the line and the teasing, though here in the back, it was mostly grunting. It seemed that every other heartbeat a block of packed snow was thrust into her hands, and in moments she had lost all feeling in her fingers. During a short respite someone thrust a pair of gloves into her shaking hands, and when she looked up at her benefactor, she saw it was Ralgon. She hadn't thought this killer was capable of such kindness.

Ralgon caught her look, gave a curt nod, and went on, handing out gloves to everyone in line. How and where he had got the garments was a mystery easily solved when she put them on. They didn't fit, and from the chuckles of consternation along the line she knew that none of the others matched either. A quick glance about was all she had before the next block was thrust into her still freezing but now thankfully covered hands. It was enough to show that every pack had been opened. And, to her surprise, Gwen passed out gloves on the other side of the line. Obviously Ralgon didn't care much about privacy when it came to getting a job done. Neither the Danastaerians nor her own people disagreed, although there were a few good-natured mutterings.

Then, as more snow piled into the cave, she spotted the unequal pair repacking the upended containers. Obviously Ralgon thought it best to move out as quickly as possible. Anne found it hard to disagree. At the beginning of the line, as the insults between Sir Úistan and the Chosen gained in volume, the speed of the barbs matched the pace of the snow removal. More sunlight streamed in, a quick glance to her right revealed a huge pile of melting snow. Just how much farther was there to dig? But the more important question was: how deep was the snow on the way to Dunthiochagh?

By the time the trench was finished, sunset was near. Trench was an apt name for the corridor they had dug. The wind had piled most snow against the mountains, and here, according to the Danastaerian Dewayn, the Shadowpeaks did not suffer from the Phoenix Wizard broken enchantment. Had the cavern been farther west, they would most likely have drowned. Frozen hands, Anne decided, were preferable to that.

An exhausted Kildanor stumbled her way. "Gods, I need

new hands," he mumbled through chattering teeth.

From behind him she heard Lord Cahill quip, "Or some Broggainh, is that too much to ask for?"

"How's that going to help my hands?" Kildanor asked.

"It don't, but it'll help you forget 'em while we chisel them off of you," Cahill retorted. How the two kept their spirits this high, Anne didn't understand, her hands had never felt colder, even with the gloves. "Oh, I see you have packed and saddled the horses, Ralgon."

"Also made some tea, milord," sounded a voice from deeper inside the cave. "Well, hot water with some leafs, no idea what it will taste like, but at least it's hot."

"And not porridge," the Chosen added.

"Well done, son," Cahill grunted. "You there, lass, ladle it out if you please, and then we'll finally be gone from this dismal place."

"Don't like stables, milord?" Kildanor muttered.

"Not anymore."

"Can't blame you. We could put our hands in the dung, though, mighty warm that shit."

"Kildanor, with all due respect, your brain's in your hands and frozen right alongside your fingers."

Some of the others groaned, while others snorted, even Anne couldn't hide her amusement. The only person unaffected by the banter was Ralgon, who proceeded to lead the horses out. Strangely enough, he seemed to be helped by his own charger. Why such a man owned a white stallion, obviously a horse meant for battle, was beyond her. She pictured the blood spraying the animal's coat and wondered how in the gods' names the man had kept the fur clean.

Gwen interrupted her musings by holding out a steaming mug that must already have passed through a good dozen hands. Anne drank greedily. It was, as Ralgon had predicted, mostly water, but it was hot and she had to restrain herself from putting her hands into the kettle standing on the stones beside the fire.

Next, a bottle of strong-smelling liquor was thrust into her hands, accompanied by Lord Cahill's firm command to drink, which she did without wondering what the contents really were. A moment later, hacking and coughing as if her lungs were on fire, she regretted that decision. Beside her, Kildanor, bottle in hand, gave her an encouraging wink. "Broggagh's beloved that is," he explained. "Triple stilled, made from all sorts of grain. Good, eh? Makes you realize you live."

She wanted to tell him they had similar brandy in the highlands, but her throat still burned. So, the only reply she could think of was a glare, which made the Chosen laugh all the louder.

"Pass it along, man!" someone yelled, and the Chosen, unfazed by the man's tone, handed the bottle to the nearest person.

It was Paddy. He took a sip, shuddered, and passed the container on. "Good stuff," he said a coughing breath later.

The only one of her warriors who seemingly had no problem with the brew was Dubhan. Those who had drunk their share of tea and Broggainh were ushered out, and, although the air had cleared considerably with the opening, the first breath she took outside seemed fresher than anything she had tasted before. That her clothes smelled rank bothered her little, the past few days had forced her to lose even the last of her inhibitions. People, Genice had remarked on the second day, died of cold, never of odor.

Then, finally, they were in the saddle, and riding single file, trotted off toward Dunthiochagh. Anne breathed a silent prayer, thanking the gods. She couldn't see her companions' faces, but from their mutterings she knew they were giving thanks as well. Even grim Drangar Ralgon, his voice harsher than most, grumbled his gratitude. Somehow, though, it seemed halfhearted, as if he wasn't really sure he had anything to be thankful for.

# CHAPTER 18

The snowstorm had not halted activity within the Palace. Rhea had spent most of the time with Coimharrin. The old Upholder didn't mind the company, even if it meant feeding an extra mouth. Payment for services rendered upon a finished deal was quite good, depending on the deal, and as such Coimharrin's larder had been well filled. But when rationing had begun a few weeks ago, he had donated most foodstuffs to the city at large, so Rhea grew quite aware of the strain she put on her colleague. Still, the Upholder insisted her mouth wasn't just there for him to fill, but also for him to talk to. His daughter Morwyn, as fine company as she was, was unable to reminisce about the past. Rhea filled that void, and on the second evening after the Chanastardhians had retreated, the two priests had shared a bottle of mead and their memories of Haldain. At first Morwyn had resented it, but the more anecdotes he told the more she began to enjoy herself.

Now, Rhea stood in the inner bailey, blinking against the bright glare of the sun reflected in the all-present snow. The lull the storm had created over the city had passed, and now warriors and craftsmen milled about the courtyard in seeming chaos. Here and there wardens and other supervisors directed people who acted as if they already knew what to do and obeyed with grunts and the occasional grumble.

As she watched, columns of workers, armed with shovels, filed past her out of the enclosed space. Their bearing hinted at warriors sent to tasks well beneath them, and she recalled her father mentioning the nature of idle hands and what would happen if people trained for battle were left with nothing to do.

In all likelihood Baron Duasonh had given the order, though it could have been Nerran. Her interest waned as quickly as the cold seeped through her coat, and she hurried into the Palace where things seemed just as chaotic.

The entrance hall was a bustle of bodies and voices going this way and that. She recognized the Caretaker who had ended Gail's life. The woman looked as if she had barely slept and still wore the clothes of three days ago. She must have noticed her, for she halted running a blood-caked hand through her equally dirty hair and nodded her head in greeting. Rhea replied in kind, wondering again how insistent Eanaigh's priests usually were when it came to somebody else's hygiene, but themselves being so blatantly careless even when dealing with their own patients. Briog had mentioned something about the goddess's protection, that a Caretaker could neither receive nor transmit a disease while taking care of the sick and wounded. Ironically enough, this explanation had been followed by Briog catching a cold. She smiled at the memory.

Then she saw Nerran. He looked older. His eyes were sunken, his hair unkempt, and his clothes had the same shoddy look to them as the healer's. Normally he would have been stomping his feet and bellowing at people, giving orders in his own special way. Now his indomitable spirit seemed almost buried by weariness. There was no zest in any of his commands, he merely pointed and nodded, barely saying a word. Why he was directing the effort and not one of Duasonh's lackeys she did not know. Maybe there was too much to be done and too few commanders.

"Ah, Princess," the Paladin said, some of his spirit returning to his voice, when she approached him. "Enjoyed a good few days of sleep?"

Guilt reared its head, and although some of her seeking refuge from the world after seeing Gail die a second time was a good enough excuse, she knew he was right. Taking shelter with Coimharrin had been running away from the pain. Instead, like Nerran and the others, she should have faced the matter head on. "I'm sorry," she said, aware of how lame the reply sounded. "After seeing a spike driven into Gail's heart, I needed to be alone."

Nerran, again, looked very tired. "I understand, lass. Nothing wrong with that. Still, you should have informed me." In all the turmoil, she had forgotten. He was many things to all of the Riders, voice of reason, boot of reason if need be, conscience, confidante, friend, but above all of that he was their leader. When she remained silent, he continued, "Everyone loses somebody in war, lass. You, above all the others, should know that, and know how to handle it."

She bobbed her head. He was right. They had been in so many engagements, so many battles, yet they had made it out of most unscathed. Sure, a broken limb or a cut down comrade every once in a while, but never before had they lost so many.

Nerran regarded her steadily, and then, as if he had read her thoughts, he said, "You did the right thing there, ordering the charge. There were bound to be casualties, and still it was the best thing to do. If you hadn't ordered it, the bastards would have taken the city."

"No victory is free," she mumbled, quoting the one phrase she hadn't truly understood until now.

"Aye, that is it."

"What can I do?"

"Uphold some stuff, I daresay," he replied, his eyes flickering a little with the old fire. Her confusion must have shown, because he added, "Get on your horse, patrol the streets, see that nobody steals. Gavyn and a few others are already out there, supporting the watch, badly undermanned the lot. Bust some heads if you have to."

"And you? You look tired."

"I am bloody tired, wish someone would take charge around here, but Cumaill's up in his rooms with some engineers already busy expanding our defenses."

"Best to be prepared for their return, eh?"

"Aye, they will return, and every week we are able to reinforce the defenses is a month we can withstand them."

"One lucky shot ruptured our line," she said, feeling once more the weight of responsibility settling on her shoulders. She had caused Gail's, Kyleigh's, Edmonh's and so many other deaths.

"Well, you can't prepare against chance, but with so much rubble in Shadowpass we have a decent supply of ammunition for the 'throwers. Now, off with you."

Again, the old cockiness returned to his voice, and for a moment a smirk played across his lips. It vanished almost instantly as he ordered a couple of servants to fetch fresh linen for bandages. Rhea caught the woman Caretaker nodding her thanks to Nerran. Then he cast a brief look at her, and said, "What the Scales are you waiting for, Princess? A Royal decree? Get your ass out of here!"

The salute she gave came almost instinctively. He slapped her rear as she turned and hurried away, and she heard him grumbling "daft nobility" as she reached the door.

At first the watchmen's justice shocked her when they executed a fleeing looter without a trial. But as the day ended and night began to darken the streets, she was doing the same thing. Mere theft would have resulted in a formal hearing and judging at a court, but looting a partially destroyed house was a different matter, and Baron Duasonh's standing order was to prevent it at all costs. By dusk she had killed half a dozen scavengers. It mattered not that some of them actually seemed in dire need of food and clothing; with Eanaigh's temple under new leadership these vagrants could have asked, and received, either of these from the Caretakers. Despair was no excuse, and justice was equal. That others she killed belonged to the freeborn craftsmen and merchants who did not need what they had stolen made the killing even more satisfying, for it showed the people that here justice struck down everyone, and position made no difference.

As an Upholder, Rhea had seen it all before, noblemen ignoring Lawspeakers and getting away with it. Scales, the recent change in Eanaigh's church had revealed the depth of corruption even within the clergy. She wondered if the same held true for Lliania's church. The goddess did not interfere; she didn't have to, for in the end, on the Bailey Majestic, Her Scales would judge everyone. Unfortunately, this was little comfort to all of those who suffered under the heels of people who used and abused them at their leisure. The Scales of Justice never stopped people who just didn't give a damn, even if their souls were destined to be spittoons and the like. She shuddered at the thought, and then drove her blade into the back of another looter, a richly dressed man. In a way she enjoyed this way of meeting out justice, it was refreshingly simple, as laws in general were supposed to be.

How long ago the dusk-gong had rung? She had no idea. It didn't matter; too much time had she spent in complacency while Nerran and many others had remained awake, busy with righting the city. The only thing she could do was to follow their example and make up for her mistake. She pulled the cloak tight; it was getting colder again. Fog wafted through the streets. This near to the river she was surprised it hadn't happened earlier. Now she found herself spotting shapes inside the banks of mist, and her sword remained unsheathed, its blade bare across her legs, ready to attack or defend.

She wasn't spooked easily, but this near to where so many people had died half a week ago souls, against all common knowledge, could still linger. It was a rare soul Jainagath forgot, the god was far too thorough, but as Coimharrin had related with the story of Caitrin Ralchanh's son, it was not impossible. Why Cat had lingered for so long was an entirely different matter, it merely proved spirits roamed the world, eluding the Death-God's guiding hand.

Another reason for the readied weapon was that now, under cover of darkness, more ruthless denizens stalked the night. The few patrols of watchmen she passed also had their weapons in hand. Some carried lamps, but in the fog the illumination was almost useless.

The horse she sat on was new, they hadn't bonded, and even though the beast was steady, she missed Talaen. What was this animal's name? She couldn't recall, wasn't even sure the stable hand had told her. The gelding was bigger, heavier, and its horseshoes clacked on the cobblestones so loudly that she was certain any looter could hear her from half a mile away. Before her lay the Hill's Road-Dunth Street intersection. The fog was even thicker here, and since the attack had destroyed nothing this far north, she decided to head back south. There were no half-ruined houses to loot in this area. Halmond Street and the western slums had taken most of the punishment.

The gelding turned on the slightest pressure of her thigh, surprising her with its agility. Maybe she would keep it. She didn't know just yet, and there were more important things to worry about.

Down Hill's Road they went.

"With all this fog and the bloody cold, one could truly slice the air," she muttered. "Don't you agree?" Most of the Riders spoke to their horses, and she was no exception. The talks she and Talaen had held never seemed one-sided; the mare had responded, neighing or snorting in accordance. This horse remained calm, but she could detect the swivel of its ears, as if it was paying attention. Maybe this one was her new companion after all. "Bloody cold," she said. She tightened her cloak once more, and then straightened.

The clacking of horseshoes had faded, and they were standing in the fog, unmoving. She saw the gelding's ears twitching, alert. Had the horse sensed something she had missed? A snort brought forth a billowing cloud of mist that mingled with the rest of the haze. Off to her right something crashed to the ground. Her gloved hand clenched around the sword's grip, and her steed stamped the cobble nervously. The meow that followed sent a wave of relief through her, and the charger relaxed as well.

Then, just as she was about to spur on, a figure coalesced in the white in front of her. Rhea had no other word for it. One moment the street was empty, the next the mists took on the shape of a person. Again, she gripped the sword, defense foremost on her mind. The horse must have sensed her anxiety even though it did not shy away from the apparition. Some part of her mind not occupied with this being of vapor wondered why the gelding didn't react to the hazy figure. The thing stood motionless, a tall, human-shaped pillar of smoke.

She had heard of spirits—who hadn't?—restless souls that had eluded Jainagath, but never before had she seen one. Not that she had given the tales of old midwives and grizzled veterans much thought. Now, here before her, a spirit had formed.

Maybe, she hoped, it was Gail come to impart some knowledge. Some ghosts were malevolent, come to haunt the living until some past wrong had being righted. Was it one of those she had killed three days ago? The fight had been just, but maybe one of her victims thought his death unfair.

Now the gelding sensed something was wrong. It nickered softly. A pat on its neck reassured the animal. The misty figure remained still, as if waiting on something.

"Hello?" Rhea called out, trying not to sound too alarmed. It wouldn't do to have more people join her observing a swirling mass of fog.

To her surprise the spirit lifted a smoke-filled arm, beckoning her close. It didn't seem hostile, but as long as one stood outside the marshland it looked harmless, she reasoned. Some of the tales the older folk told spoke of the vindictiveness of vengeful souls, and she was not about to put her trust in someone who eluded the will of the Gods.

Again, it waved its hand, maybe even tapping what could have passed for a foot. An impatient ghost? Never before had she heard of such a thing. Once a soul had eluded Jainagath successfully it was free to roam, until a Deathmask brought it down. "Come." The word sounded so faint that she doubted she had truly heard it. "Princess, please," the voice, as fleeting and insubstantial as the fog, pleaded, using the unloved title with a reverence she hadn't encountered in decades.

"What are you?" Rhea asked.

"Please," the form repeated. At least she thought it was the ghost talking. A quick look about showed she was alone.

Reluctantly she dismounted, taking care that her bare sword did not nick the gelding. For a moment the charger seemed unsure, neighing softly. She patted its flank then let go of the reins. The animal remained. Slowly, she stepped closer.

A yard away from the apparition, Rhea thought she was able to discern features in the pillar of fog. A woman, she noted, surprised. And there was something about her features she recognized, just barely. "What do you want?" she asked. "And how come you know me?"

"Look closer," the spirit said. And she did. The mist seemed to solidify, at least for an instant. But that heartbeat sufficed. She barely remembered the face, had hardly seen the woman back at court. Rhea had been younger than she, and of royal blood. But the features of Amhlaidh Ralchanh, her father's Justiciar, were unmistakable. "You must help him, I beg you, Princess."

Then the image was gone.

Rhea stood, staring at the spot which only moments before had held the image of Caitrin Ralchanh. Whom she was supposed to help was plain. The why and how were different matters.

# CHAPTER 19

Gaedhor had been right in his assessment that something was wrong in the Eye of Traksor. Sequestered, Lloreanthoran had been unable to talk to either the Knight Protector or Priest High Darlontor. Not to mention that he had heard no news regarding the woman Kevonna.

The cell they had given him truly deserved the name. A stark place, its only amenities were a straw-mattress bed and a small iron oven providing a minimum of heat. He was a prisoner in all but name.

How had it come to this? The Lightbringer had assured him the Sons of Traksor held the key to finding the instruments of dread the Aerant C'lain had held for millennia. Why then did the very same people incarcerate him? Twice a day the addled leader—there was no other way to describe Darlontor—paid him a visit, brought food and books. Twice a day the door was unlocked and shut again. It was for his protection, the Priest High claimed, but if the measures protected anyone it was the human.

The Eye of Traksor wasn't dead to the spiritworld; it just was incomparably harder to enter the realm of smoke. He still shuddered at the memory of icicle lances perforating his soul. His one journey outside his body had yielded information that put his situation into perspective. The Sons were divided, with each faction suspiciously guarding their territory as it was. He couldn't guess what had shattered the unity, and even the few attempts to get answers from Darlontor had resulted in nothing but determined silence and a shake of the head.

What was the human waiting for?

Much like the spiritworld, his magic seemed hampered, similar to what had happened in Machlon. It was as if all possibility, all chance had been torn away from this spot of land and replaced with fact. How this came to be, he had no idea. Gaedhor had never explained it, and lacking anyone to provide solutions he had stopped speculating.

The books brought to him were bare of any useful information, although the repeated mention of Traksor's last battle in the foothills of the Kumeen Mountains at least indicated the Tomes of Darkness and the Stone of Blood could be found there. But even this assumption was anything but definite. In a place like this, formed from solid fact, he would have expected to find accurate answers.

Lesganagh's Orb stood high above the trees when a key rattled inside the door's lock. He looked up from the book, another pointless piece of propaganda that yielded as much information as its predecessors. Feeding time was in the morning and evening so this interruption came as a surprise. The straw-mattress offered a better seat than the floor and so he occupied his usual position facing the exit.

Prepared for anything, he waited for the unexpected visitor to enter, and was surprised to see Darlontor, the man's face haunted.

"Come to entertain your guest?" His voice was laced with sarcasm, stressing the last word, putting as much venom into it as possible.

"I apologize," the other replied, closing the door.

"A little late for that. How long have you kept me here? Two weeks? Longer?" His kind enjoyed seeing an opponent squirm, and though he detested the jovial brutality of his race, seeing the Priest High's reaction gave him a moment of pleasure. He'd had days to ponder the conundrum of his imprisonment. For so long, anger had warred with the sense of urgency to stop the demonic threat that it had lost its fire. In the end, like in Graigh D'nar, he had accepted captivity as merely another turn his life had taken.

"I need your help," Darlontor said.

An amused snort escaped before he could compose himself. "I came here to offer it, and you locked me away. Now you ask me for the same."

"I did what I thought necessary."

"For whom?" The pleasure of seeing the human squirm returned once again.

"The order is divided, and your presence here might have tipped the balance toward an irreversible situation."

Lloreanthoran put the book away and waited.

Clenching and relaxing his hands, the Son of Traksor's leader's eyes darted about the room. Was it really that hard for him to speak the truth? Finally, he said, "We have always been protectors, not warriors, living under the guise of religion to perform our duty. Some of us believe we need to be more aggressive, striking at the heart of the enemy."

"So, you do know where to find them?" he interrupted.

"Yes and no." The answer was evasive. "But even if we struck, victory could not be assured."

"It never is." He sensed there was more to it than that, would have probed and prodded, but Darlontor seemed on the verge of breaking and he had no intention of pushing the man over the edge.

"Another faction has bought into the illusion of us having been appointed by the Lord of Sun and War. They see it their sacred duty to blaze through anyone and anything that opposes us." The Priest High paused, balled hands into fists and then looked him straight in the eye. "You want the information where to find the demonologists' stronghold even though you will most likely fail to retrieve that which you seek?"

"Failure is not an option."

"You failed to escape this room," Darlontor pointed out.

"The enemy's fortress is worse." He spread his arms, gesturing at the entire compound surrounding them.

"How can I beat this magic? It is magic, isn't it?"

Nodding, the human replied, "We'll teach you."

Lloreanthoran was about to ask when they would start when Darlontor added, "After you have done something for me."

"And what is that?"

"I need you to find someone, my nephew. He is in the Kumeens."

His eyes became slits as he regarded his host. "You're joking. I know how every attempt to penetrate the mountain range ended in failure. How do you expect me to succeed when, as you so aptly pointed out, I couldn't even escape this prison?" It was lunacy. "You want to kill me here and now, try, but stop playing games."

"You must understand the enemy, and for that you need to walk their lands. Only then can you do what is necessary. Only then will you be ready for the lessons."

"And what if I fail?"

"You won't."

"What makes you so certain I won't?" How was it possible that Darlontor sounded both so close to despair and yet so determined?

"You managed to wander in spiritform through this place. You have the determination. You will succeed."

The task, and its promised reward, felt like another attempt at procrastination. Why was Darlontor so eager to prevent him from gaining the necessary knowledge? He was of half a mind to ask. There had to be another reason beyond the splintering of the order. "Why the delay?"

The question was met with silence. Regarding the human, he tried to discern the truth. He was no priest of Lliania, neither could he work the same magic Gaedhor had used to verify his words. Magic, as he knew it, was nudging chance and possibility, not creating fact. Standing, he closed the distance between them. "Why all the secrecy? I am on your side." Though with all that was going on here he was unsure what the Sons' side really was.

"How fast can you be in the Kumeen foothills?" Darlontor asked, evading the question.

"Less than half a day's flight," he said, jaw muscles clenching in frustration.

"I'll locate him, and if we're lucky, you two will have returned by sundown tomorrow."

"How can you find someone in an area that doesn't even allow the Librarians sight?"

"You'll learn soon enough."

It was maddening. First the isolation, and now the rescue mission. Did he really need their help? What if the Lightbringer had erred? The memory of her presence erased that doubt immediately. No, she hadn't made a mistake. If she said these humans could help, they could. But why did he have to prove his quality to a group that was suffering from internal strife? None of the books he had read indicated this kind of division. According to the notes in Ma'tallon and the sparse literature he had been allowed to read here, the Sons of Traksor were a group dedicated to duty and protecting each other. How, and more importantly when, had this changed?

"So, I will leave in the morning?" he asked.

"Aye, the door will be unlocked, but please remain in this room. We cannot risk having your presence made public."

"As if keeping a supposedly empty cell locked for days does not arouse suspicion," Lloreanthoran said acidly.

"Not in this part of the Eye," Darlontor replied then added, "I will supply you with more books to peruse."

He didn't bother to hide his scorn. "I'll do as you ask."

Oblivious to the steel in his voice, the Priest High's lips twitched in a quickly subdued, grateful smile. "The tomes will be with you momentarily." Then Darlontor left, closing the door.

For a few heartbeats he waited for the key to scrape the lock once again, and when that didn't happen, he returned to his seat and picked up the discarded book.

Sooner or later, he decided, he would find out what was going on in the Eye of Traksor.

It was sooner, for Kevonna brought the books to him. The sword-priestess still looked old and wrinkly, but the substance that had been missing from her the day they first met had returned. Her greeting was a brief bob of the head, and then she kicked the door shut, her arms loaded with rolls of parchment and books. "Help an old woman, will you?" she said, her voice still sounding as brittle as before.

There were no infirm in Graigh D'nar. Even Julathaen, by far the oldest elf Lloreanthoran knew, was still as quick of mind as of body, and even though the Chief Librarian had been old, Kevonna seemed older still. He shrugged, stood, and took the load off her arms.

"Thank you," she wheezed, sitting down on the bed. "Too much work for an old warhorse such as me. Hope you don't mind; these bones aren't what they used to be."

Was this an act? Even with her tottering, Gaedhor had not moved a finger to help her. "Where is Darlontor? Why have you come? You were near death when last I saw you. How have you recovered so quickly? And why were you in that shape to begin with?" he blurted out, asking questions in random order.

"Darl is trying to track his nephew. I volunteered to take the books to you. Good eating. And burning the candle from both ends and the middle," Kevonna said, a sparkle of mischief in her eyes. All he could do was to stare at her. It was obvious she wasn't as fragile as she pretended to be. "And before you lob any more queries my way," she added, leafing through the parchments and retrieving one, "read this."

Stunned, he took the offered document.

Its contents were shocking, a revelation as to why the Sons of Traksor were in such a sad state. He finished and looked at her. "Are you saying this division occurred a mere fourteen years ago with the escape of this boy?"

"In part, yes," Kevonna replied. "Though I haven't been able to ferret out everything there is to know."

"So, this man is as much a threat as the demonologists?"

"More so, I think."

"Then why was he allowed to live in the first place?"

She gave a cryptic smile and said, "That is the essence of why there is no unity. I have my suspicions but none of them are of use to us. We thought we could change destiny. We failed. Some view him as the bigger danger, others think Danachamain and his ilk are worse, and still others are paralyzed with indecision."

"And you?"

"Darlontor is a good man, he just lost his purpose."

"And his nephew?"

"Dalgor? He might well be the answer to our problems." She closed her eyes and took a deep breath. Then she looked at him again. "Only as a unit can we succeed in countering the threat. Only the entire order can help you on your quest. Dalgor is the strongest mage we have; ruthless he may be, but he gets the job done, and he will be able to bridge the gaps between the factions. His uncle knows that, but he is too caught up in his own fears to relay his thoughts adequately. He meant no disrespect. He's merely cautious."

"And Gaedhor?"

"We sent him off again, accompanied by a score of warriors. He is to organize the evacuation of Machlon and every other settlement, bringing the people here where they will be protected."

Now he understood. "That is why you need me to find Dalgor! With three factions the refugees will not be protected at all. They'll be caught in the middle."

"We cannot do it ourselves. Dalgor is alive, that much we know, but our magic stands out like a beacon in the Kumeens. Any rescue effort has to come from an outsider."

"But I thought only your magic could defeat the demons and their creations."

"Aye, but the rescue requires stealth, and none of us can be stealthy there. Your skills will be feeble, but better weak and sneaky than strong and loud."

He looked at the parchment and up again. "This was not meant for my eyes, was it?"

Again, the mischievous sparkle returned to her eyes. "I said it before, Darlontor is a good man, but in his need for secrecy he can be a bit overprotective. I find it better to have an ally who knows what is at stake."

"Then why not go after this Ralchanh?" he repeated.

"Because now we have no way to reach him without interfering with matters in which we have no right to meddle." She rose far more quickly than she had hobbled into the room. "I'll leave you to your studies. The gods speed you along tomorrow. And safe return." She strode out, the pace belying her age.

When the door fell shut again, he dove for the books. Soon the task ahead was all but a distant nudge in his mind, the writings drawing him in further and further.

# CHAPTER 20

"You spoke with him?" The question was out before Kevonna had closed the door behind her.

Guiltily Darlontor looked up from his desk, his left hand opening the drawer while the right shoved the crudely drawn pictures inside. Was that a hint of understanding lighting her eyes? She may have guessed at the origin of the pictures, but he knew no one else was aware he still owned them. "Aye," he said, pushing the drawer shut.

Her kind smile couldn't hide the steel in her voice. "You had to send someone for Dalgor. Arawn might have succeeded, but then you'd soon have open rebellion on your hands." He saw no trace that her magic had almost killed her, only the slight tremor in her hand as she stroked her braid. "You need to be our leader, not merely act the part. And you need to face the truth, and soon at that."

Did she know? He caught himself before blurting out the question. "The truth is that Danachamain has returned from the dead." Would she add the obvious? That Drangar had also returned to life? He waited. One breath, two. When Kevonna remained silent he spoke on. "In all likelihood he has already reached the Kumeens."

"The recent attacks indicate he has. With your permission," she added sardonically as she sat on the one cushioned chair opposite the fireplace. Did she intentionally take his favorite place? In his mind's eye he saw the little boy sitting there, hunched over the drawing-board, a stash of papers piled to his right, tongue stuck out in concentration, his hand a flurry of motion, drawing, always drawing.

"I asked 'What took you so long to order the evacuation?'"
Kevonna's voice tore down the memory. Why were they returning now? There were more important things to do.

"I had to insure that Arawn would assist us in the effort to
keep the peace here and send some of his own with Gaedhor as
well," he replied, eyes still glued to the chair. Had she intentionally pulled it up at a similar angle? Was that what she meant
when pushing him to face the truth?

"And that took three weeks?"

He shook his head. "No, most of that time was spent arguing over what should be done, finding out if what the elf said
was the truth, and finding Dalgor."

"How did he survive there anyway?"

"He is the best we have. I traced him from Dunthiochagh to
Pudlain and Crossads and from there to Mtain Geer. Seems he
considered his options first."

"Would you have ordered him killed had he returned
immediately?" Kevonna asked. He had searched for the answer
to this question ever since decreeing the death penalty void.

Now he knew. "No." The shake of the head was brief.

"The idiocy had to stop anyway."

"Gryffor disagrees," he said with heavy heart.

"How has he been able to hide his zeal?" Did she know that
the way she folded her legs now was the same as...? No! He
would not go down this road!

"We were blind."

Kevonna pursed her lips. "Don't you mean that you, yourself were?" Was she testing him even now?

"You should supply our guest with more books, give him
some substance, but let him think it was on your initiative."

"Devious," she said, crinkling her nose. Rising, she locked
eyes with him and didn't let go until she reached the door.
Then, halfway across the threshold, she said, "You still love her,
don't you?"

Openmouthed he stared at the door as it fell shut. She knew!
Gods, she knew. She had known all these years and never acted
upon this knowledge. Squeezing his eyes shut, he banished the
unsettling thought. He still had to find Dalgor's exact location.

Whatever Kevonna planned had to wait.

Maybe she wouldn't do anything. Maybe her revelation was only meant as moral support. No! He had to find Dalgor.

The knock was loud. In this troubled time Kevonna and his few remaining supporters usually just entered without bothering to announce their presence, Gryffor hadn't come to his study in months, which left Arawn or one of his.

"Enter," Darlontor said, wiping away the last of Dalgor's blood. As he tossed the rag into the fire the door opened revealing Arawn.

The swordpriest's head bobbed briefly in greeting. Then, kicking the door shut, he folded his arms on his chest and regarded him. "They held another of their ceremonies."

Darlontor knew whom he meant and remained silent. His spell had been taxing, the land surrounding the Kumeens now fully under the sway of Danachamain's followers had taken most of his strength.

"Gryffor even pretends he is a Sunmaster."

Forcing down the weariness, he looked at Arawn. "What?"

"Has himself decked out in robes and one of the ceremonial staffs. The gods only know where he found that thing." Ever the warleader, Arawn headed for the nearest chair and sat without waiting for Darlontor's invitation.

"When did he start buying into the myth?" He hadn't meant for his thoughts to be spoken aloud but his sluggish mind registered the error only after the fact.

"The elders should never have started the nonsense in the first place." Arawn scoffed. "A landholding arm of any church, how ridiculous." Then he grew serious. "We all saw what fanaticism did in Danastaer, that and ambition. Maybe he buys into his own story; maybe he just wants to replace you."

Darlontor scowled at him. "As if you don't covet my position."

"Me? In your boots? Scales no." Again, the scoff. "Never wanted to be the leader. All I have ever wanted is to end the threat. Guardians"—he spoke the word with fierce derision as if there was no worse term—"waiting for an enemy to attack."

"It was what Traksor's followers wanted." Now that he

thought about it, now that Arawn forced him to consider the fact, he realized that the declared goal was perhaps not as lofty as he had always considered.

His doubt must have shown for Arawn said, "You see the foolishness as well, don't you? We live the lie the elders hammered into our brains. Just think on it. Lesganagh's Servant gave Tral of House Kassor the means to end the demonic threat. The prince dies, and those he has gathered to his cause vow to be there should the demons rise again. None of them knew how to wield Lesganagh's weapons. Scales, we understand more. How do you think they must have felt?"

His reply stuck in his throat. There was nothing he could say to deny the basic truth Arawn was saying. Had he not been so caught up in his own misery he might have had the same thoughts. "What do you want me to say?" he asked, his voice sounding defeated even to his ears.

"Drangar is irrelevant." The other snorted. "Scales, if we could dispose of Gryffor we might even be able to send his idiot followers against the Kumeens first, weakening their defenses."

"There will be no more..."

"I did not say we should kill the fool," Arawn interrupted. "Though you have to admit the idea has its merits. The elders vowed to fight the demons, knowing they could not win a direct assault. We know more than they did."

Shaking his head, Darlontor said, "We still know too little, and some of what I do understand frightens me."

A cocked eyebrow, followed by a skeptical look was the reply he expected. "Frightens you?" Again, Arawn snorted. "You scare too easily."

"Have you ever taken a look through the books? And I don't mean what Traksor and others have developed out of the existing material, but the source itself?" When the swordpriest merely shook his head, he continued. "The parchment shows..." How could he make Arawn understand? He knew there were few enough souls who bothered to look at the original manuscripts. Their magical knowledge was taken from the adapted works; the other books were disturbing to look at. What he had seen three decades ago had only underscored the concept of defense.

To go against the enemy, to fight them on their own ground required weapons, magic that would change them, transform them into the very thing they were meant to face.

"The parchment shows what?"

Was his revulsion that apparent? Disgust and fear so plain on his face? There was no way around it. Arawn had to see for himself. He pulled his badge of office, the gold amulet bearing Tral Kassor's seal, from beneath his tunic, unhooked the chain and held it out. "Very few people ever asked for it, and for good reason. Must have driven…" He paused. Gryffor had spent a lot of time in that part of the hidden library, translating, studying the magic Lesganagh's Servant had given them. Had the knowledge frightened the man into insanity? Was that the reason for Gryffor's madness?

"In the back of the room there is a shelf made of fir." He waited until Arawn indicated that he knew which one he was talking about. The other shelves were oak, not very subtle, he knew, but as old as the Eye of Traksor was, eclectic furniture had become normal. "Behind it you find a slot, a lock. This is its key." Arawn reached out to take the amulet. "I warn you, it is not for the fainthearted."

A grim smile creased the other's lips. "Never was one of them. Thanks for trusting me with this."

"All you ever had to do was ask; every council member has the right to look at the originals."

The shrug was a warrior's dismissal of the situation. "Why bother with the old when the new suffices?"

Anxiety over Arawn's reaction to the gift of Lesganagh subsided only slowly. Darlontor, despite the need for sleep, found himself pacing in front of the fireplace. How the elders had managed to tear what little knowledge they could from the malignant books was something he had considered when he had first ascended to the council. Back then the last of the original followers of Traksor had passed away and translation, no, adaption had stopped. Some things were best left untouched. He had sampled the tomes, same as Kevonna and Gryffor, in the hopes of gleaning information that might help them perform their duties. And though he had been able to put the nightmares behind, the lingering threat that lurked behind the fir bookshelf always cast a shadow whenever he used bloodmagic.

Dalgor had been to the hidden library as well, but if his nephew had been disturbed by his findings, he had not shown it. Maybe the gruesome books had driven Gryffor into his zealous rage? He had never bothered with the question of where the books had come from. The Servant had brought them, Traksor had used them to fight Turuuk, and in the end the prince had paid for his success with his life.

A subdued knock on the door interrupted his pacing. It was dark now. Arawn had spent some time in the dread place. "Enter," Darlontor said.

The swordpriest was pale. Gone was the determined glare, he thought he detected even a hint of terror in the other's stance. "You're right," Arawn finally said, leaning against the heavy door. "What little I could understand was enough to make me sick." A deep breath, and then, "What language is that?"

"Not ours, that much is certain. Seems similar though." He paused, motioning to a chair. "Sit." It wasn't a command, but the swordpriest barely looked his way as he slumped down. "Ever read something from the dark years? The time before man and elf existed together peacefully?"

Arawn shook his head.

"Neither have I. In a way it seems as if there wasn't much to say in the first place." He walked to his chair behind the desk and settled down. Folding his hands on his lap, he continued. "I spoke to a Librarian once. He told me the most curious thing: that our history began a few hundred years ago, as if we had just appeared out of nowhere." Arawn blinked and stared at him. "Look at our language, bastardized Elven, nothing more. Did we learn from the elves?" He shrugged. "Does it matter? And if we learned from them, whom did they learn it from? The gods? Or whoever came before them? If the language inside these books is the language of the gods, then we are better off without them."

On that the swordpriest seemed to agree for he nodded his head almost imperceptibly. "They aren't written in ink, are they." It was more of a statement than a question.

"No."

"Gods. Think Gryffor believes them to be the words of the gods?"

"I don't know what Gryffor believes. All I know is that we use only our own life force to feed our magic. Whoever wrote these books did not. I'm not even sure the so-called Servant was any such thing."

"Is that how you tracked Dalgor?"

"Aye, there is a spell I deciphered, adapted. It allows me to find someone by tracing their blood."

"That's how you knew where Drangar would be." It was a statement, a question, and even an insinuation. Or was it just his imagination playing paranoid tricks on him?

Darlontor remained silent. The truth would be told on Lliania's Scales, not a moment earlier.

# CHAPTER 21

## Fourth of Cold, 1475 K.C.

The books Kevonna had given him made Lloreanthoran's skin crawl. It all felt familiar. The castings with lifeblood, something he had suspected from the moment Gaedhor had wiped his hands clean, roused the same feeling of helpless submission he'd had once before, with the Lightbringer. His strength of will sufficed to beat down the despair. Ancient fiery tales told to misbehaving children summoned the same fear, primal, instinctual. Lloreanthoran recalled his own misery as a child when his parents had told him the story of the bloodyman waiting for him. He shuddered.

Why this tale of woe—of the cruel lord who punished those who misbehaved—worried him even now he couldn't explain. He doubted any elf could.

The details were sparse, whether accidentally or on purpose to mislead outsiders, he could not tell. Maybe the Sons' chroniclers like Traghnalach's Librarians wrote different versions of history. In the end it hardly mattered. The volumes hinted at enough that he was able to form an opinion, one that caused a new wave of discomfort.

Bloodmagic was stronger, yet it also was a perversion of nature. Where his magic played with past and future memories of one element or another, nudging things to create the desired effect, a person's lifeblood hammered chance into oblivion, creating fact. And, apparently, it was the only way to defeat the demons' servants. Fire had to be fought with fire. He recalled reading that during the Demon War Lesganagh's priests had summoned demons to battle the slaughtering hordes.

Again, the unnatural urge to cower arose.

Why did these things frighten him so? He had fought drag-ons, defeated Phoenix Wizards. None of those had ever pro-voked this primal fear. Animals reacted that way sometimes. The mouse scuttled away when the hawk's shadow crossed its path. Prey ran and hid from predator. He was no animal!

Would Julathaen have known what to make of this? Maybe. Working his magic here in the Eye of Traksor was nigh impos-sible, and now he knew why. The entire structure had been torn from the bowels of the earth, shaped by bloodmagic, a scar of fact. Yes, he had managed to explore the place in spiritform, but breaching the Veil of Dreams was more difficult than traveling in the spiritworld. Was it wise to communicate with the old elf? He looked out the window.

The horizon showed the first hints of dawn. A sliver of grey separated the black night sky from the skeletal fingers of Gathran's trees. There was no time. Soon Darlontor would tell him where he would find this human, Dalgor. He had a vague idea of what might be asked of him, and had it been easy he might have considered expending his energies on contacting Graigh D'nar. But if Dalgor were as versed in bloodmagic as Darlontor had hinted at and he was in trouble, he would need all of his strength to find the man.

Snow covered the circular bailey; winter had arrived, and smoth-ered the last vestiges of autumn under its white blanket. To the west clouds loomed, promising even more snow. After nigh a century in his people's otherworldly prison, he was happy to see a real winter. Seasons barely had meaning in Graigh D'nar; there the artificial weather patterns would be as alien to people here as nature's unpredictability would be to those born on the other side.

The Eye of Traksor stood some sixty miles east of the Kumeen foothills, by horse a trip of maybe two days; on foot it took considerably longer. But magic provided more than one way of travel. Darlontor had warned him of the dangers of tele-porting into any area that the shadow of Kumeen Mountains touched, and with that mode of travel out of the question, flying was the only decent alternative. Unhindered, he left the Eye; the instant his feet touched ground outside the fortress, the dreadful sense of finality was gone. The thought of falling came automatically; then he added the slight possibility of floating and voluntary movement, magic did the rest. In a matter of heartbeats the Eye, its plinth, and the Sons of Traksor's almost elven intrigue was far behind. Lloreanthoran soared over the whitened forest, twigs and boughs looking as pitiful and forlorn as black and white stick figures.

Soon the cold air began to sting. Cursing himself, he imagined a warm blanket covering him. Again, the mere possibility, no matter how improbable, was sufficient to create a sense of warmth about him. The chill was still there, but the layer he had created kept the worst of the cold at bay. A sense of loss spread inside him, as it always did when out in the snow. Everyone who beheld the covered world experienced it sooner or later; it was both the knowledge that all things would eventually be buried, and the feeling of peace gone for even this shelter of ice would fade in spring.

He had known jungle dwellers from near the Veil of Fire who, despite never having seen snow before, still felt the same loss. Even squirrels somehow knew winter was a time of death, Bright-Eyes had confirmed as much. But only those who lived and died felt it. The dwarves cared little, and the dragons even less. Then again, neither of those races was alive in the same sense as elf or human or squirrel.

Steeling himself against this melancholy, he soared west. The Kumeen Mountains, already a looming great white wall when seen from the Eye of Traksor, grew more ominous by the heartbeat. Frosted trees flashed past; he made out a few huts, a village, but these signs of civilization faded the closer he got. Soon the white foothills were all that he saw, sparsely forested, with granite crags and peaks that stood defiant against the grey of the clouds.

How had Darlontor managed to locate Dalgor in the first place? Every source claimed observation of the mountains was impossible. Maybe it wasn't? Maybe bloodmagic could pierce the shroud of nothingness the demonologists had pulled over the peaks? Maybe, and this thought caused his focus to slip for a moment, Darlontor could have rescued his nephew himself, but wanted to put Lloreanthoran to the test yet again? As ripe with intrigue as the Eye was, maybe the Priest High's absence would spell inevitable doom for the entire order? In a way there was no difference between the two people, both were far too selfish.

"Bloody humans," he muttered. Not that his kind was any better. Still, it felt good to curse someone else.

And just how was he going to find this Dalgor character? He had been given no conclusive information; what he had been told was as vague as everything else he had found out in the past three weeks. "Below the tree line, near a spring," was not really that precise. The Kumeens were riddled with springs, rivulets that in the end fed the Tallon. Under normal circumstances he would have probed the area in spiritform, but that—as was scrying and teleportation—was out of the question. Just how, he wondered, had the demonologists managed to seal off an entire mountain range? How much blood had they shed?

The answer forced itself upon his consciousness a moment later. Suddenly, without warning, the flow of magic seemed dull, muffled. It felt like it had in the Eye, only stronger, so much stronger. His flight became erratic; he banished the random musings, focusing solely on remaining in the air. Even the warming sheath about him vanished; he had no mind left for it. With stunning speed, the cold lashed out. Wind, which moments before had merely been an annoying howl, now dug its icy fingers into his flesh, piercing the meager layers of cloth. Just how strong was the bloodmagic in this place?

No sooner had the question formed in Lloreanthoran's mind than the sense of wrongness slammed into his soul. It was similar to the Aerant C'lain, this feeling of perversion so much stronger than the Eye of Traksor. But whereas the mindstorm had wreaked its own terror on his spirit, thus dulling the lack of anything natural, the all-encompassing peril seemed to leap up from the ground and permeate the air itself. Not even the encounter with the bloodbeast had prepared him for this!

Again, the ever-present atrocity to the natural order tugged at his already fraying grasp on magic. Had his teeth not been frozen in grimace, he would have snarled, cursed, instead he gave a mental shout and struggled to land safely. The last few yards were a desperate tumble. His link to all possibility gone, fact enveloped him. Powdery snow, barely enough to cushion his impact, rose in a cloud as he slammed into the ground. Certainty surrounded him, a grim bloodstained smothering cloak. The pain of impact was nothing compared to his despair. How could he pierce that? How could he defeat this, if the elements themselves believed it to be right?

Already he felt this decisiveness crawl through his clothes. Forcing down the agony, he rose, closed his eyes, shut wind and chill out, focused on magic as he knew and loved it. There! He sensed a drop of water frozen in the air somewhere beyond the reaches of this dread domain. It wasn't alone; there were more of its kind, all still unsoiled by the unbending will of the Kumeens. As they floated down, they changed, robbed of the possibility to ever be anything else than a snowflake or another drop of water. It wasn't so, he knew that, but they did not. Up, high in the clouds, magic was still unsoiled. Now all he had to do was reach out, and touch nature once more.

Then, like a flash of lightning, a realization struck him. "No!" Lloreanthoran whispered. "Gods, no!" he muttered through split lips. Was the elven realm beyond the Veil of Dreams becoming like this as well? The certainty of events dragged life out of his people. If Julathaen learned of this, the old mage would have every reason to call for a return. For if his people did not, they might become part of the same rigidness the soil here already belonged to.

With clenched teeth he punched through the muddle that formed the barrier between potential and certainty. It was as if a shaft of colors suddenly pierced the clouds above and the gloom around him. Like a breath of fresh air after a long rest in some sewer, he inhaled magic. Now, that he knew where to look for possibility, he felt confident he could master the perils of this land. The only thing to do now was to find Dalgor.

He had erred. His confidence evaporated when a deformed monstrosity reared its ugly head above a low rise. How this bloodbeast had come into being mattered little, his link to magic was too weak to leave the ground.

With bared fangs this symbol for the perversion of the land loped toward him. It had been decades since he had cast any battlespell, but the years spent fighting off Phoenix Wizards had honed his skills to such a degree that his reaction was almost instinctive. Before he knew what he was doing, Lloreanthoran had already searched the ground for a suitable pebble. This close to the mountains they were abundant. With a flick of his hand he launched the small stone at the charging monster. He hardly thought about the words, and spoke them in quick succession.

Nothing happened. The pebble still flew toward the salivating maw, unchanged. "Gods!" the elf breathed. Not only had he to remind the rock of what it had once been, no, he also had to remind the stone that it was a stone and had the potential to be something else!

The pebble struck the bloodbeast's head, lodged itself in its teeth, and still the thing came on. Lloreanthoran worked feverishly, summoning to his mind the roll of mountains, the things that could happen to its pieces. A small rock could become sand, or part of a house or castle, a child might play with it. The rock reacted, slowly, urging him to double his efforts. Again, he cast the spell. Scant feet from him, the magic finally worked, and the creature's head exploded in a shower of gore, in its place, if only for a heartbeat, lingered a chunk of rock as big as boar.

As he watched the rock shrink back to its original size, something disturbingly strange happened. The blood, still pumping out of the severed neck, almost took on a life of its own. It flowed freely, gathered into a puddle, and then vanished without a trace into the hard-packed ground, leaving behind nothing but carcass and furry splinters of bones, and churned but clean snow.

Even if winter had not covered the land, he would have felt cold. What had the demonologists done? Was the land a sponge, leaching blood to the last drop? He dimly recalled Julathaen expressing his regret for children; it hadn't made sense then, and although he still lacked detailed knowledge of what had happened all those centuries ago—that story had also been recorded in the Tomes of Darkness—suspicion dawned on him. Coupled with what he had gleaned from the books Kevonna had provided and the almost complete absence of possibility here, it could only mean one thing: to open the portal to the realm of demons his ancestors had made use of the biggest source of potential available. They had sacrificed lives, young lives.

If Danachamain had stumbled upon this information and made the lesser sacrifice of an adult, the door would have been considerably smaller. Lust for power was the greatest motivator for many people, human or elf, and many would find the death of others a simple price to pay. The countless wars of his kind alone were ample proof for that. What if the Stone of Blood was just a tool of murder, a sacrificial altar to the dark masters who went before? And what if the archdemon Turuuk had, in his brief time on this world during the Demon War, managed to infect this entire area with the qualities of the Stone? "One gigantic altar," he muttered as he came to this dreadful conclusion.

It was far worse than he and Julathaen had suspected. The state of turmoil among the Sons of Traksor and their subdued, secretive behavior made even less sense now. What prevented them from striking at the heart of evil? He recalled reading about Lesganagh's priests summoning demons of their own to battle the invaders. How much blood had these other fiends shed to be victorious? How much blood would the Sons need to win? The thought alone brought a new sense of dread. But what were Danachamain's followers waiting for? By now the gathered blood, great potential or not, surely sufficed. Unless... Cold dread ran down his back. He glanced at the mountains, the Kumeens' forlorn silhouette dim against the grey horizon. "They haven't spilled much blood yet," he whispered. "What are they waiting for?"

He already knew part of the answer, but his rational mind fought against the still lingering horror of having watched the formless ashes pile higher and gain shape. The chant seemed to reemerge from within the wind howling around him. "Rise,

Danachamain! Arise!" the air sang. The images rose from a part
of his memory his instincts had fervently tried to erase, blot
out due to the terror they still held. "Rise, Danachamain!" He
had seen it—him—peeling out of a whirlwind of ashes. It had
almost driven him mad to see how an impassive, naked figure
had formed in the middle of the Aerant C'lain. When this being
had turned its eyeless gaze his way he had fled. That much he
remembered of his time fleeing through Gathran, but little else.

He found himself kneeling before the monstrosity's corpse with
snow already piled up to his hips, his hands clawing the white
frost. Perceiving the lack of feeling in his limbs, he realized
he must have been this way for a while, thinking, reliving the
nightmare of which he had regained memory. Imbedded now
in his mind was a dread of what the future held. Not only were
the artifacts in the hands of Danachamain's followers, no, they
also had prepared for his eventual rebirth, and what could only
be a massive sacrifice to open not a door but a massive gate that
would unleash the demons.

All of them.

Somehow the inconvenience of frostbite felt insignificant
compared to this threat. Then, starting, he shook his head,
clearing his mind of the horror. He had to stay alert, not become
entangled in visions of the future.

Now calmer, Lloreanthoran focused his thoughts, reached
out to the untainted regions of sky, the spot he had drawn on
before. The link came quickly, and, although it was hardly as
strong as anything outside this zone of utter rigidity, he managed to cast a spell that re-heated his body. Then, when his
extremities slowly regained feeling, he began to consider his
options.

Dalgor was still alive; maybe that was wishful thinking on
Darlontor's part, maybe the truth. Whatever the case, he had
agreed to find him. If the Son of Traksor had made it this far
and still lived, he probably was beset by bloodbeasts and worse.
How the human stayed ahead of these creatures was something
he would tackle once he located Dalgor.

For the first time, he studied the dried out, frozen horror.

It was huge, even with the massive head scattered about. The fur, just like the head, looked remotely familiar; he just couldn't pinpoint the species. It seemed as if aspects of wolf—the jaws had definitely belonged to a wolf—had been mixed with those of a goat, the beast's feet were cloven. How Danachamain's followers had created this amalgam he didn't want to know, the fact that they had done it was upsetting enough. There would be more, of that he was certain.

The magic warming him flickered, faded, and then returned, albeit weaker. If he had to fend off more of these monsters, he would lack the time to reestablish connection and tease out the potential of every rock used as a missile. He didn't even know whether this memory remained inside the pebbles once established. Groping around the bone shards, he found his previous weapon. A flick of the wrist and the little rock flew away.

He focused, willed the stone to remember.

For a moment it felt as if the fragment had a hard time growing back to its former size. A further nudge brought the desired effect. So, it was possible to circumvent the certainty of the land! His confidence rose. There was a way to wield magic in this gods-forsaken region.

Rejoicing, Lloreanthoran began to gather and attune pebbles. Then he resumed his journey, on foot.

# CHAPTER 22

## Fifth of Cold, 1475 K.C.

The sky had cleared, but winter did not relinquish its grasp. Lloreanthoran's connection to magic was fractured. This land dampened not only his spirit but also the natural order of things. Nothing in the Kumeens was as it should have been. And still there was no sign of Dalgor's passing.

He hadn't slept since he'd crossed the invisible border. Normally he would have rested to regain strength, but that was impossible here; he dreaded what would happen once his guard was down. Neither had he eaten, afraid that the corruption of nature had also taken hold of what little wildlife he saw. Granted, none of the animals looked as if a mad god had jumbled pieces together, but who was to tell the hard fact that permeated the land hadn't also changed the rest.

Had Darlontor sent him on this fool's errand to be rid of him? For the past day the question had resurfaced time and again, and he still had no answer.

That Darlontor had not told him the whole truth he now accepted as fact. Yet he couldn't deny the concern in the human's eyes when he had spoken of Dalgor. Maybe he should have just plunged into the man's mind and retrieved the knowledge. A truly elven act, at least according to the fools who considered the killing of others sport.

Now, as he rounded another bend, wind's icy breath covering his face in another layer of hoar, he wondered if this lack of morals was what was needed for his mission.

A noise from up ahead!

Unsure how far away whatever he heard was, Lloreanthoran

inched closer to the next outcrop. Humans would have perished long ago, had they been in his place, but courtesy of the bit of magic at his command, the cold only stung.

He squinted, peered around the corner just as another rumble filled the air.

A skeleton of a man, gaunt, his clothes seemingly keeping his body erect, stood on a ledge some fifty yards to the west.

"Come on, you bastards!" the man shouted. "Let's finish it!" To his surprise, the stranger, in a move that belied his fragile condition, hurled a fist-sized rock at something Lloreanthoran could not see. Then, his eyes still on the stick figure, he saw how the man stabbed something into his palm and howled syllables that made his skin crawl. The stone shattered in mid-air, each splinter in turn grew in size until an entire barrage of fist-sized chunks disappeared from sight.

The pained scream that followed showed the stranger knew what he was doing.

"Is that all you want to throw at me?" the man shouted.

As reply a cloud of vapor—he had no idea how such a thing was possible in the frigid air—rushed toward the stranger, threatened to engulf him. "Lesganagh, aid me!" the man shouted, bit his tongue, and spat bloody saliva at the mist just as it encircled him.

Never before had Lloreanthoran seen the use of blood-magic. He had felt the effects, had been feeling them ever since entering this dreadful domain. But this was different. The spell proved effective in countering the fog, which vanished in an instant. And even though the stranger was victorious, the land demanded its toll. The stranger stooped a little, gasping. "You will not win!" he wheezed.

And for a moment he seemed to be right. Whatever had assaulted him had stopped. He watched the human stagger his way, blindly. His first impression was supported by the fact that there truly was not much substance left on the man. Bloodless, almost lifeless, the coat and trousers he wore might have fitted once. Now they simultaneously seemed to keep him standing and drag him down.

This had to be Dalgor.

He stepped into view, and instantly the man was on guard, though it looked more like he staggered to a halt, drawing a rasping breath. "Stand aside monster," he said, his accent similar to that of the Sons of Traksor. "Stand aside!"

"Dalgor?" he asked instead.

"Bastards are in my mind as well!" the man who obviously was the one he was looking for snarled. "You will not take me alive! Like Traksor I will gladly die and take you with me!"

For a moment he wondered if Dalgor was addressing him, and then he saw shapes detach themselves from the gloom of the nearby cliff. The bloodbeasts he had seen before seemed pathetic compared to what came for them now. The human raised his right hand—bandaged as he now saw—and removed the stained cloth. Underneath, revealed by the light as a repeatedly slashed cut, was a wound that with the removal of the bandage bled freely. He knew what Dalgor was doing, had seen it just moments earlier. The other hand was cut as well, and even from the man's lips trickled red spittle. Neither of the wounds gushed, but from the looks of both palms this Son of Traksor had been forcing magic for a while now.

What then followed was something Lloreanthoran had never seen before.

Dalgor closed his eyes, hummed, bloodied saliva running down his bearded chin. The air about them pulsed, boiled. A great rushing boom followed, as something solidified before them. A geyser of magma materialized, surged forward, and engulfed the two aberrations. Not knowing what to observe, his eyes flicked back and forth, from the burning mass of lava tearing into the shrieking monsters, to the hiss and sizzle of blood evaporating from the man's chin and palms.

No sooner had the enemy fallen than Dalgor turned about and faced him, the shine in his eyes less mad than before. In the heat and rush of air that followed, the backwash of the explosion had dislodged the elf's hood, and now Dalgor knew what he was facing. "Your magic is useless here," He snapped. "Best you bloody your hands and do what needs be done." Then, after casting a look back to the stone encased monsters, he added, "This place is a violation of nature, if you want to survive, play by their rules."

Stunned by the man's ferocity, Lloreanthoran remained silent. Their rules? The demons' rules? "Are you saying?" he finally stammered.

"Aye, and since you don't look like you just arrived, I suggest you stop fooling yourself."

"I came to find you."

"So you did," Dalgor replied, taking him by the arm, careless of the wound in his palm, and steering him away. "Been running for weeks now, the land changes, been in the fucking mountains most of the time. What enters, no matter whom, they intend to keep. More blood to feed their accursed lakes." He poked his free thumb in the direction of the cliffs and the cooling lava. "They hound you."

"Who are they?"

Dalgor gave him a scornful scowl. "Those who wait on Turuuk's return," he spat. "Followers of Danachamain." The swirling ashes, the chants and... the figure of soot that had risen from the chaos. "Get a move on, who knows what they throw at us next."

When dusk reached them, they were still trying to find a way down. Stumbling, blinded by snow, Lloreanthoran had, under Dalgor's derisive explanations, finally begun to grasp the immensity of the threat. Twice the human had managed to kill the perversions the land threw at them; it was a miracle the blood loss hadn't weakened him more. In clipped, terse, panting sentences Dalgor had tried to explain how to force magic with a minimum of harm done to the body, and from the explanation he had gathered this man's magic was an amalgam of what elves used and the old, the dark way.

His mind reeled at the idea of breaking the bonds of possibility. Everything he had ever done was just within the realm of what might happen; Dalgor's approach, though not as draining and violent as that which the ancients had used, was still alien and frightening. His mind balked at the prospect of breaking his skin and sacrificing his own life force to invoke, to create things that could never be.

Now, with the sun low in the west, Dalgor was searching for a cave in which to rest.

Looking around, his heart filled with doubt and despair about what the night would bring, Lloreanthoran asked, "How can we find a safe spot if the entire land is poised against us?"

The human gifted him with the arrogant smirk he had already grown used to, and replied, "You fool it."

"You fool the land?" Suddenly he felt similar to the young apprentice he had been quite long ago. All this was so worrying, so frightening, and understanding came haltingly.

"No wonder your people retreated," Dalgor grunted.

Lloreanthoran was so taken aback at the venom lacing Dalgor's voice that he forgot to put the human into place. He just opened his mouth, staring.

"Gods, you are dense!" This time Dalgor laughed. "It was a jest." From such a thin man, he would have expected a weak blow, but when the comradely slap on the shoulder landed, the elf staggered back.

Forcing himself to recover the last shreds of dignity, he straightened, found his footing on the treacherous slope, and stood, regarding the other. "Explain if you please."

"The land's changed, given enough time it could be returned to what it was, but only once the bastards are gone. But with enough focus you can convince it to reshape itself to a normal cave," Dalgor explained.

"So why can't you leave?" he asked.

A snort, and then, "With focus I mean meditation. Can't move much when you're trying to make a mountain listen to you, even a sliver of a mountain."

This mirrored his own experience, and shone light on some of the things that had bothered him since coming here. "How do you know they won't attack again?"

"They like to play, like cats," the Son of Traksor said as he settled on the snowy ground. "Always give the prey the illusion of a chance, wear it down until it just gives up."

He was tempted to ask why Dalgor hadn't already given up, but thought better of it. There was no point antagonizing him. He watched his unlikely companion close his eyes and

wondered what he could do to assist. Rest was more than welcome. He thought of slipping into spiritform to watch what
Dalgor was doing, and had almost thrust his mind out of his
body when he remembered the pain walking around in the
Eye had brought. Seeing Dalgor fend off wave after wave of the
aberrations, had shown just how powerful forcing magic really
was. Maybe there was some truth in the human's words. Maybe
he would have to adapt to survive.

Turning away from the meditating mage, he drew his dagger and was just about to pierce his skin, when a stalling hand
landed on his arm. "Don't!" Dalgor hissed. "If you do this the
land will remember, and then we may have to fight once more."

Sheathing the weapon, Lloreanthoran looked at him. "I
need to learn so we can get out of here."

Dalgor sat back down. "Plenty of time to learn tomorrow,
trust me. I thought your kind never bothered with such minor
concerns as the passing of time."

Just how much had the Priest High kept from him? Of course,
he hadn't doubted for a moment that Darlontor had his secrets.
But he had never imagined a human being this disrespectful.
This mage made him feel like a snot-nosed learner. He wanted
to learn, to help, and was ignored at every turn. If Dalgor was so
good at what he was doing, why then had Darlontor requested
his help?

He stood, glowering at the meditating figure, pondering
what to do and how to proceed, when, to his continued astonishment, the rock face before Dalgor trembled, fissured, and
finally revealed the entrance to a cavern. A triumphant smirk
on his lips, the human rose and bowed mockingly, gesturing
for him to enter first.

He struggled to keep from lashing out, even as he stooped
to leave the snowy night air behind. Looking back, he saw his
companion follow, and wondered briefly if the man really was
as coldly determined as he seemed. For one who had struggled to escape this hostile environment for almost a month, he
appeared as rigid in thought and body as anyone at the onset of
a journey. What exactly had Dalgor been doing here in the first
place? Surely, he would have known that heading deep into this

territory could only result in death, if one was lucky. There was so much he did not understand about the motivations of either the Sons of Traksor or humanity in general. And of all foreigners, Dalgor seemed the most determined.

Inside, with dry rock surrounding them, the mage regarded him, a slight smile—one less derisive, at least—playing around his lips. "Food's hard to come by when all life is drained away." He breathed deeply, calmly, closed his eyes, not in concentration but in honest relief. "Gods, how I hate this," he sighed. His eyes opened once again, and for the first time Lloreanthoran noticed a deep weariness lurking within. "You want to learn how to fuck the land before it fucks you?" Not waiting for an answer, Dalgor continued, "Great, guess we both could do with some heat. Just focus, beat the rock into submission, and force it to heat up, understood?"

It sounded easy, coming from Dalgor's lips, but the truth was it wasn't. Under the human's tutelage, which was stern most of the time, Lloreanthoran finally managed to raise first a stalagmite from the ground, and then heat the cone. By the time he was done, Dalgor was cutting fresh strips of cloth from his tattered cloak. The old bloody bandages he stuffed into a pocket, explaining, "Blood's blood, don't waste a single drop of it." He patted an empty-looking wineskin. "Every one of us keeps a bottle of his own blood with him at all times, just in case."

"How do you keep it liquid? Won't it congeal?"

"Herbs, fresh whiteleaf works best. Up here the flask is useless; the cold freezes it. Besides, I used most of it when trying to get through the thrice cursed mountains."

"Through the mountains?"

Dalgor nodded. "Aye, wanted to get to the bastards' hole, wanted to do some good before I die." He spoke of his death so calmly Lloreanthoran wondered if he had heard correctly. "Oh, don't look at me like that," muttered the human sleepily. "We all die, and because of what some idiots did, we all have to pay for their mistake. I just wanted not to waste my blood on the cobblestones."

"Why do you have to die?" he asked, but in the light of the stalagmite he saw Dalgor had fallen asleep.

# CHAPTER 23

Their return to Dunthiochagh had taken longer than expected. To his surprise, Kildanor found out he was not the only Lesganagh worshiper in the band, and at dawn and dusk the score or so Chanastardhian faithful, among them Anne, prayed for the sun to clear their path. The others made offerings to Broggagh the Weatherlord. He joined them afterward, but it seemed neither deity heard their pleas, for the snow did not melt. The lack of a fresh snowfall was enough of a blessing; at least they proclaimed so when they finally reached the North Gate.

The city was unusually quiet. Few warbands were about, and those who were, escorted wagons loaded with building materials southward. After Cahill's loud proclamation of who they were, entrance had been granted with no further challenge, and Kildanor could hardly blame the guards for not recognizing him. He was as unkempt as the others; the grime of more than a week had given his skin a patina not unlike that of a beggar. The others looked no less filthy, and he dreaded the moment that four walls and a roof would surround him again, for then the stink could not escape anymore. A bath, the thought was foremost on his mind.

Having fulfilled his duty, the Chosen said his goodbyes to Cahill's retainers. After Cahill had discovered that the carts laden with iron ingots had made it safely to the city, he was in a better mood than he had been in days. He thanked Kildanor with the promise to consider marrying his daughter to Cumaill. Provided Neena agreed. In the places where riding side by side had been possible, they had done so, talking politics.

At least he would have some good news to tell the Baron.

The Chanastardhian turncoats accompanied Kildanor. Their astonished looks, as they took in Duthiochagh, told him most of them had never been inside such a big city. Chirnath, the province from which they hailed, wasn't much more than a few villages spread over a handful of valleys surrounded by mountains. Anne Cirrain had told him as much. She, looking far less impressed by the houses and storefronts hemming them in on each side, had been to Herascor, and Harail. The others had rarely traveled far from their homes.

"I thought there isn't much to it," muttered Anne's cousin, Padraigh.

"Just that bloody wall south of the river, eh?" the old warrior, Dubhan, retorted.

Their leader turned in her saddle, snorting. "As if you aren't impressed." Kildanor had noted the change Anne Cirrain was going through. She was less aloof than when they had first met, and reminded him a little of Cumaill. That, in his opinion, was a good thing.

"It stinks," Natheira remarked.

"It ain't the city, lassie," Dubhan said. "It's you."

"But the one who reeks like a pigsty is you," the huntress snapped, much to everyone's amusement.

The ruckus of their laughter caused some neighbors to open their doors and windows to watch the bedraggled looking band pass by. He looked about and saw that many people wore mourning white, far too many. This had nothing to do with the melancholy roused by the coming of winter, he realized. Even the Chanastardhians must have grasped the import of it, for they fell silent.

Their path had kept them out of sight of the Dunth's southern shore and the enemy camp. Mireynh had not taken the city; it was far too calm for that. Kildanor wanted to ask the carpenter, Bacán, whose shop they were just passing, but instead of the man he only saw his young wife, also in mourning white. What was her name again?

He didn't recall, although he had shared wine with them at their wedding. Too many names and too many faces, three

lifetimes of people filled his memory. Who was he to be surprised at that he'd forgotten somebody's name? It happened all
too often with those he met only sporadically. Besides, he told
himself, as filthy as he was, the carpenter's wife wouldn't recognize him.

Anne Cirrain touched his arm. He hadn't noticed her spurring her horse close to Dawntreader. The wide road allowed a
handful of riders abreast, but through sheer force of habit they
had been riding double file. "Seems you've won."

"At what cost?" he replied. Even with General Kerral's warriors, most of the defenders had been citizens. Sure, most knew
how to handle a weapon, but how many of them had ever truly
seen combat? Most people died only after the whole affair was
done. Wounds, despite the healing hands of the Caretakers, had
the nasty habit of infecting before any healer ever saw the victim. A nick to the skin, seen as a mere scratch by the wounded,
could fester and kill just as any sword blow to the head could.
There were never enough Caretakers, and despite the priests
of Eanaigh's claim to treat everyone equally, the fact was that
those of import were preferred over a villein forced into battle
by his lord, or the carpenter who fought to keep his wife safe. It
didn't matter if Lliania weighed the souls in the Bailey Majestic,
most people didn't give a damn about the afterlife; their wellbeing while they lived was what mattered.

Maybe growing up in enlightened Kalduuhn affected his
outlook on things, even after decades of living in Danastaer,
or maybe it was just the thought of decent people dying while
the dregs of humanity claimed rulership and shat on those
whom they saw beneath them. It mattered little if nobles like
Cumaill and Sir Úistan tried to make a difference. This was not
Kalduuhn and no towering city rested above the rich people's
heads to remind them to stay honest. He resisted the temptation
to ride through the Noble's Quarter, saw no point in checking if
the aristocracy had also unpacked their mourning whites.

"Where's the lassie?" Dubhan's voice broke the silence.

Kildanor, torn from his musings, looked back at the double
column. "Who?" he asked.

"My squire," he heard Anne say. "Gwennaith." Then she

added, in reply to the warrior's question, "She'll join us later. Told me she wanted to accompany Ralgon."

The bond the unlikely pair had formed during the past days had not gone unnoticed, and even though Lady Cirrain—he forced himself to think of her as nobility instead of the comrade Anne had been for the past days—viewed the budding relationship with worry, he found the calm Ralgon displayed when with the young woman a welcome change from the man's usual brooding. Explaining the details of the mystery and disquiet surrounding the mercenary was something he was loath to do. For now, Drangar was at peace, and whatever was lurking in the back of his mind remained silent, and for that he was thankful. "Don't worry," he told Anne. "She'll be safe."

That the noblewoman was not convinced was obvious. She shook her head, as if dismissing the thought, and said, "She's of age, her choice."

"Aye," Paddy, who rode behind them, piped in. "Remember how moon-eyed you were at her age."

"Bet his broodiness works on lots of women," Dubhan added. The Chosen glanced over to gauge Anne's reaction. Dubhan's booming laughter was cut short by her glare. He saw that she was only half serious when he caught her sticking her tongue out at the warrior. It was a small gesture, but refreshing nonetheless.

The Palace, with its mismatched walls and haphazardly added towers, came into view as they passed Beggar's Alley. He could only imagine what sort of impression it made on the Chanastardhians; he guessed their reaction was like his when he had first seen the edifice. Much like a well-loved cloak, it had been patched and expanded over the years, yet the walls, as the refugees would find out very soon, were sturdy and once more in good repair.

People were leaving and entering; the drawbridge, some smidges of snow still lacing the rim, must have been lowered since before the blizzard. Even the barbican was pulled out of the way. Either, he guessed, the enemy had granted Dunthiochagh a respite, or they had retreated to sit out the long months of winter. He doubted the war had been won; Chanastardh's troops were too many for that miracle to have occurred.

A mutter from one of the warriors down the line caused the others to suppress their laughter. Kildanor guessed they were making fun of the Palace's appearance. He didn't blame them.

As they passed into the outer bailey, however, those whispered remarks ceased. The Palace had that effect on newcomers. Decades of improvement had left the original manor surrounded by two squares of battlements that looked shabby only on the outside, lulling observers into thinking the fortress weak. No slingthrower had ever bested the walls, and from the appreciative whistles sounding behind him, the Chosen could tell Cumaill's guests had realized their error in judgment.

He had given his name to the Warden of the Guard when the woman had challenged them crossing the bridge. Now, as they passed into the Inner Bailey, he heard Nerran's distinctive bellow among the muttering of soldiers, the hammering of steel, and the sharpening of weapons.

"Fuck me! You're one louse away from being competition to the gutter-mutts!"

The tension the Chanastardhians must have felt was released in a combined, albeit uncertain chuckle.

"And you, mighty Paladin, should hand your tongue to the maids to get it cleaned!" he replied.

"Paladin?" Anne echoed in a whisper.

"Did that once, hasn't helped," Nerran retorted, stomping across the slushy courtyard. He stopped, taking Dawntreader's rein. "Gods, is that your stench or his?" he asked the horse.

"Mate, may I present the Lady Anneijhan of House Cirrain?" Kildanor interrupted the Paladin's well-meant tirade.

Nerran looked over to the noblewoman. "I don't know." He gave her a knowing wink. "Best present her when she is presentable. Don't you agree, milady? So far you'd be more suited for latrine duty than a reception."

By Anne's silence Kildanor could tell she was confused by the Paladin's rudeness. He didn't blame her; Nerran had this effect on most. "I apologize..." he began and was interrupted by the aging Paladin.

"What he means is he should have shown you the bathhouse

before any of you dragged your rank bodies here." The statement brought forth a murmur of agreement.

"Well, there you have it, lad; come back when you don't reek like manure anymore." Nerran sketched a bow, pinching his nose shut, and then retreated.

He had never seen his friend this rude. Something was bothering him immensely. Then, for the first time, he noticed the Paladin wearing much stained mourning whites as well. Was he drunk? How many of his Riders had he lost? He looked about, and saw that scores of warriors, while practicing with their weapons, wore white. Just how many had died?

"Him? A Paladin?" Anne asked, shock plain in her voice. "A drunk, nothing more."

"He's grieving," her cousin, Padraigh, said. "See with your heart as well as your eyes."

"I was told a Paladin of Lesganagh always was courteous, honorable, and honest."

Kildanor looked at her, and for a moment didn't know what to say. Could it be true that beneath the surface the woman was that naïve? He had seen priests leading a sermon while the vomit stains were still drying in their beards; he had seen a King sodomize a boy of eight years. Then he remembered. Her grandfather had been a Paladin. Maybe she had known him, and he had told her stories, naturally glossing over the parts where he'd done the church's bidding, no matter how ruthless it had been.

He was about to put her head straight, when Dubhan growled, "Lassie, you're old enough to realize that stories are always glorious, no matter how much pissing and shitting and bleeding actually happened. Scales, you do the damn thing yourself. So, this Paladin is drunk. Who gives a damn? Think that will spoil the memory of your grandda?"

For a moment she was silent, looking as if some realization was plunging straight to her heart. Then, after closing her eyes and taking a deep breath, she said, "We turned and deserted, what honor is left for us if not that of the past?" Hadn't she made her peace with the situation? Apparently, the conflict within was far from being resolved.

"Had we remained you would've been imprisoned to force your da into submission, with the rest of us getting to know the business-end of an axe," Dubhan snapped. "You know it same as we do, lass. Stop rolling those things round in your head; Wadram decided to secede, and if we don't honor our lord's decision, then who the fuck are we supposed to honor at all?" He spat in disgust. Kildanor was tempted to voice his opinion as well, but this talk had to remain the Chanastardhians'. An outsider would only cause dissent. "Be reasonable, lass. Think! There's much to be done as is. We need to get home safely, and fight the buggers."

"The buggers," snapped Anne, "are our countrymen!"

"Aye, the same bastards who had no qualms shooting down retreating allies," Padraigh interjected. "I saw your concern. You didn't like it, and now you complain about losing face?

"Lass, you're a warrior, worth ten times as much as any of those bastards obeying Mireynh's orders. Why the Scales does this bug you so much?"

Because now it was truly sinking in that House Cirrain was firmly set on a path of desertion, Kildanor realized. "Maybe," he said into the ensuing quiet, "you should discuss this privately." Other warriors were already ogling them, and some of their looks, now that they realized Chanastardhians accompanied him, were all but hostile. He couldn't blame them.

"Nonsense," Dubhan spat. "This has been brewing for too long already. Always you concern yourself with our motto, but never with the heart of the godsdamned matter."

"You said it yourself, Mireynh isn't worth fighting for," Padraigh added. Both men were right, and judging by the struggle Anne's face displayed, she had reached the same conclusion, but still doubted its validity.

"Come on, lass," Dubhan said calmingly. "You're smarter than that. Think!"

"He's right," a woman's voice added.

They turned and saw Upholder Rheanna standing in front of them. She also wore mourning white. Of course, none of the Chanastardhians knew she was a priestess of Lliania. To them she was only another dark-haired stranger interfering in their affairs. "Lady Cirrain, may I introduce to you Rheanna, Upholder of Lliania," he said before anyone could hurl insults at Rhea for meddling in things that were none of her concern. From the ongoing silence he guessed their tempers were at least somewhat calmed.

"What the Scales do you know about..." Natheira snapped, but Rhea interrupted.

"Justice and what is right? A whole lot, judging people and making deals helps; so does insight into Lliania's will."

"What about honor?" Kildanor asked slyly.

"Honor is nothing if not ruled by common sense." The reply was just as cunning.

"If I don't get off this animal now, my saddle sores will marry my breeches," another Chanastardhian, Connar he thought the name was, muttered. The tension broke.

"Honor's nothing if common sense doesn't rule, lass."

Anne shot Dubhan a vicious look, and then nodded. Maybe, Kildanor hoped, Rhea's decree had finally silenced the argument inside her head. And the Chanastardhians still did not know about the dwarf. He stifled a groan as he dismounted. There was more than enough talking and arguing to be done. He nodded his thanks to Rhea who indicated for him to follow her. A stable hand took Dawntreader's rein and he hurried after the Upholder.

She halted in a far corner of the Inner Bailey, and turned to regard him as he approached. A few steps away, Kildanor felt a cramp clutching at his legs. Stopping, he straightened and began to massage muscles that hadn't hurt that much in ages. "Scales!" he swore, the word hissing through clenched teeth.

"You need to ride with us, Sunsword," Rhea commented his pain. He looked up, wishing for a moment his glare could kill. She chuckled.

"Two bloody days for half a day's ride. Bloody snow! I'm not used to this anymore."

"Stop complaining," she said, snickering. "Before you ask, the Chanastardhians assaulted the walls a day after you left."

He nodded. "I know, the turncoats told us."

"What they didn't know is that they retreated, gave up the

siege once Duasonh's Wizardess took down their foothold on the wall."

"She did?" he asked, the pain forgotten.

"Aye, wiped the wall clean." Her voice had taken on a mournful note. "We're still searching for our people. Snow has the nasty habit of covering everything."

"They'll be dead by now," he said, realizing why so many wore white. Not only for those who had been found, but also for those who hadn't. "Scales," he swore. "How many?"

"Hundreds." She drew a deep breath and let go of it in a billowing cloud. "That, however, is not why I need to talk to you," she continued.

"Hmm?" He wondered who of the Riders had not survived.

"The dead are dead, Sunsword," she snapped. "Concentrate on the here and now."

It took a moment, and then he was able to focus on Rhea. "Speak, I'm listening."

"What do you know of Drangar Ralgon? Is there anything strange going on with him?" she asked. But before he could reply, she added, "I know of his regeneration, and Coimharrin told me about the murder he hadn't committed, said that somebody else had taken control of Ralgon's body to kill the woman. What I need to know is if there is more to this."

"Why?" Maybe it was a bad habit, maybe it was something else, but being questioned by a woman he barely knew, even if she was an Upholder, was odd.

"Let's just say I am familiar with his family," she replied, evading a proper answer.

Like the deity who's Chosen he was, Kildanor had no patience for Chiath, either verbal or physical dancing was against his nature. He brushed the answer away with a curt swipe of the hand. "Cut the bullshit, will you? Why do you want to know about Drangar?" For a moment he wondered if using the mercenary's first name reflected the friendship he felt for the man, but even if it did, it mattered not.

"Coimharrin told me about a woman's spirit supposedly taking him into the past," Rheanna went on, unperturbed.

This caught his attention. "Speak on."

"I…" she paused. "This is crazy! Forget it."

"Believe me," he said, trying to sound amused and failing. "Nothing is too crazy where Drangar is concerned."

She nodded. "Well then, what would you say if I told you I was asked to help him."

"All right? That's nothing unusual, I dare say. He still has some people who care about him living here."

The look she gave him was indicator enough that she was not amused by the comment. "No shit, really?" Her voice dripped with sarcasm.

It had already been a long day, and his legs hurt. "I've no time for games, Rhea, just tell me what's going on, will you? I want a hot bath, and to be out of these boots!"

"Why would he need my help? And why would the ghost of his dead mother appear to me and ask me for it?"

All Kildanor could do was stand and stare.

# CHAPTER 24

This morning he had worked the bellows with Maire to help prepare the forge for a new day's work. Now, Jesgar stood in the Baron's study, waiting. The atmosphere in the Palace had barely changed since the Chanastardhians' retreat. Some drunks in the Tankard yesterday evening had proclaimed that it was doomed from the beginning. One look at the braggarts had shown these men had never seen combat. He had, and wished he hadn't.

Baron Duasonh, he could tell by the man's tone, was also aware of how close things had been. The Baron wore his bandaged arm with pride. Rumor had it an enemy's spear had pierced his shield. Since none of the defenders had come away unscathed, Jesgar believed the gossip.

Since Ben's cremation he had stayed with Maire, had been granted a few days leave to help her return operation of the smithy to normal. The house was crowded. Pientic, the wheelwright two houses down the street, had been sheltering some refugees. But enemy stones had destroyed the craftsman's house, and Maire had offered to take them in with her. Their home wasn't big enough to house a score of folks, most of the space was dedicated to smithy and storage, and now there were people everywhere. One couldn't put a foot down without stepping on somebody else's toes. And on top of all of that, Pientic's oldest daughter followed him wherever he went. In another lifetime he would have welcomed the attention, the lass was pretty enough, but now, even with his grief gone, chasing skirts felt trivial. The Baron had cancelled his leave, and it felt like a blessing.

Entering the study had ended the joy. Aside from Lord Duasonh, two very familiar faces greeted him with resigned nods. Upholder Coimharrin seemed angry, maybe even a bit disturbed; Librarian Megan scratched her cheek, which, he had come to learn, was a sign of disappointment. For the most part the two priests ignored him, listening to the Baron who was pacing back and forth, despite the obvious discomfort. All Jesgar could do was wait and listen.

"You have until Seed, at the latest. No, actually it'd be better if you got him ready mid-Thaw, this way he'll be on his way to Herascor by the end of the year."

"Do you think I have nothing better to do than teach your pet spy?" Coimharrin asked. Gone was the doddering old fool he had met when first introduced to the man. There was steel in the priest's voice.

Duasonh paused and regarded Coimharrin. "He is not my pet spy, Upholder. And, no, I do not think you have anything better to do, because if we don't kill this threat at its roots, we will have the Chanastardhians again laying siege to the city once their crops are planted."

"And what do you want him to do once he's there? Kill Drammoch and his High Advisor?"

"That's the general idea," Duasonh said.

Jesgar swallowed, felt his knees grow weak, but none of them so much as glanced his way. They wanted him to infiltrate the royal palace in Herascor and assassinate the two most powerful men in this part of the world? Not that he knew that many other parts of the world. Had Duasonh lost his mind? He couldn't just walk in there; he would have to behave like he belonged there, play a nobleman's part and mingle with the Chanastardhian elite. He, a simple lad from the street.

"The boy can hardly keep his mind on matters when reading a book," Librarian Megan said in her brittle voice. "How the Scales shall we teach him when most of the stuff runs off of his mind like it is made of wax paper?"

That was not true. He wanted to protest, say how much he had learned in the few weeks he had spent with the priests, but so far, he had not been given permission to speak. And, surely, the Baron hadn't invited him to hear his opinion.

"Is that so?" Duasonh asked. "I was told otherwise."

"Oh," Megan said.

"I told you, the boy was just playing the fool," Coimharrin said, his doddering old man act resurfacing. Jesgar would have given an arm and a leg to be able to deceive people like the Upholder did.

"So what?" Megan countered. "So maybe he can act the imbecile, it won't help him in Herascor. I tell you, he will be lost like a lamb among the wolves. My church can fill his mind with knowledge of Chanastardhian nobility, but where could he learn their etiquette?" He looked at the Baron. "No offense, milord, but this pigsty of yours is no royal court, and with your servants and other members your house is a well-mannered tavern, at best."

Coimharrin sniggered. Even the Baron struggled to suppress a smile. "Pigsty, I like that," the Upholder said.

Lord Duasonh must have noticed Jesgar's urge to speak, because he gave a brief nod, allowing him to proceed. "I managed to get by fine in the enemy's camp."

"Son," Coimharrin said, turning to face him. "An armed encampment has as many similarities to a royal court as a pound of iron does with a dove's feather."

Librarian Megan bobbed her head in agreement. "You've never seen a real court. Harail, even under that fool Lerainh, had a court that truly made us here look like bumbling drunkards, and Harail is nothing compared to Herascor."

"He will learn," Duasonh said.

"The Cirrain woman!" Jesgar exclaimed, finally understanding the Baron's plan.

Coimharrin winked at him while Megan shook her head. "There is work to be done, Lord Baron," she said. "His mind needs to be razor-sharp. So far he is a blunt instrument and looks the part." She glanced at the Upholder who nodded. "We have work to do." To Jesgar, she said, "You come with us, and don't expect to participate in the Returning. Winter will last a whole lot longer for you."

They had tested his wits? Gods, how many ways did those

old geezers know to challenge his mind? Following the two priests, he wondered if he should have written off spying and thieving as a bad idea and instead stayed in the smithy.

To his surprise, the two priests led him to the audience chamber. He had expected to trudge through the slush and receive his training in one temple or the other. Instead he was caught completely off guard when they entered the well-lit hall. Its furniture had been removed, rushes covered the floor, and every candle and torch was alight. His confusion was complete when he spotted a trio of musicians on the dais. On each side of the cleared center, about ten yards apart, stood two chairs, and in the center of the room waited a man of middling age.

"What is this?" Jesgar spurted.

Coimharrin chuckled. Even stone-faced Megan snorted in amusement. Neither answered. The pair parted, and sat.

"This, young man," the middle-aged man said, "is a ballroom. I am Cadwan, your teacher." Jesgar swallowed, dreading to ask what kind of teacher Cadwan was. The man supplied the answer a heartbeat later. "You, young friend, will be taught dance and behavior at court. Not the tavern brawling you are probably used to. I have taught the finest squires and ladies of Kalduuhnean society, learned the graceful steps of elven dance and am quite familiar with what makes events at the Royal Court of Herascor such splendid affairs." Jesgar didn't bother to stifle his groan. "There, there, young friend, it isn't as bad as you might think."

He wasn't so sure of that, especially when he saw the amused faces of Coimharrin and Megan. The Upholder seemed a tad preoccupied still, but he was obviously enjoying this.

"And while you strut about and worry which foot is which..." Megan said.

"He will not strut, milady Librarian," Cadwan said indignantly. "He will glide, float about the floor."

"Well," Megan continued. "While you do that you will learn. We will teach your mind while he teaches your feet."

"Not to mention his heart, dear lady."

Megan scoffed. "You have to be able to do small talk while

dancing. Once you mastered that, we… no, never mind, master this first, the rest will follow."

"You may groan now, boy," Coimharrin added with a cackle.

By evening he was surprised no one had ever gutted the fop Cadwan. Aside from his prissy, stuck-up voice, the constant corrections, given with a courtesy and elegance that made him feel less a man with every passing breath, grated on his nerves. To top it off, he had had to recite all the noble Houses of Chanastardh. He had forgotten most of them already. Whenever he had made a mistake, it mattered little whether it was academic or dancing, the music stopped and the dance was repeated in its entirety.

Even now, as he headed to his small quarters in the keep, he rehearsed the steps, while another part tried to piece all the House names together. Somehow, during the day, the part of him still concerned with how pathetic he must look had quit whining. He didn't give much of a damn anymore. His feet ached, and still he went through the motions, what the servants and whoever passed his way thought didn't matter. Finally, with a dancer's flourish, he dropped onto his bed and passed out.

Someone was tugging at his shoulder, yanking it hard enough to wake him. By the feeling of wool on his skin, Jesgar knew he was naked. He had no memory of how or when he had undressed. Again, the tugging.

"Oi! Boyo, get up!" a voice hissed.

With a start he was fully awake, and he knew to whom the coarse, harsh voice belonged. He sat up. "What're you doing here?" His mouth felt as if it was filled with dust. Hacking his throat clear, he tried again. "What are you doing here?"

"My work ain't done," the former thieves' guild member said. "You still have a lot to learn and my head ain't outa the noose yet."

Pain shot through his muscles as he sat up, wiping the grime from his eyes. The room was still a smudge of darkness. "I'd a week's worth of dancing lessons today, leave me alone."

"No rest for the spy, boyo. Never. Get used to it."

Groaning, he mumbled, "What do you want?" How the

Scales could his arms ache when he had been hopping like a peacock all day? And why was he undressed? Hadn't he just dropped into bed? Shocked, understanding dawned. "Have you…?" he let the question hang in the air. Not that he was shy. The Gods knew how many women he had had, but he preferred to see their faces while they saw his body.

"Relax," the thief said, chuckling. "Nothing I haven't seen before." The pause that followed implied much, but then she continued, "One of the servants did you the honors."

Her explanation solved little. Then again, he realized, it hardly mattered. "What do you want?" he repeated.

"You'll sleep when your soul's weighed by her Scales; until then, you'll learn."

"More learning?" he groaned. As if the steps to numerous courtly dances and inane facts about Chanastardhian history and heraldry and nobility didn't suffice.

"Well, one can never know enough, especially when your life depends on it."

In the room's murk he could barely make out the end of his bed, yet he had a feeling the thief, he still didn't know her name, was smiling. "So, what now? Want me to dance a jig on hot coals?" he asked, not keeping the acid from his voice. Why bother with courtesy when this woman knew none?

"Not today," she replied, the grating in her speech changed little. "Get this done, and I will tell you my name and you can sleep through until dawn. Fail and you will have another session in the barracks. We've improved them."

"Get what done?" The blankets had fallen into his lap and now he felt the biting cold. He shivered, tried to keep his teeth from chattering.

"Deck out in nightwork-gear." He fumbled for his tinderbox. Her hand stopped him. Surprised, he registered how soft her palm and fingers were. "No! You will get dressed in the dark."

"What's the point?"

"Aside from a thing you get poked with?" It was an old joke, but the cold certainty in her voice made him realize the thief was no one to be trifled with. He heard her take a deep breath and release it slowly. "Well, then. The point is that you might not want to draw attention to your nightwork. Especially when you're in a well-guarded mansion. You will dress quietly, and when you're done, I will tell you the rest. Understood?"

"Aye."

"Good boy," she replied. "Now, get dressed!" Arguing was pointless, so he began to search for his clothes.

The cell had been his for a day maybe, and unlike his room back home, he was utterly unfamiliar with it and where his stuff was. Thankfully he had done similar things back home when he had sneaked out without Ben knowing, so he knew by touch what his nightwork-clothes felt like. It was much harder, however, to find the bloody things in the first place. Again and again, he bumped into furniture. He suppressed the hisses and complaints such bruising usually provoked, while the thief talked.

"You may find yourself inside a place, as a guest, and there mayn't be time for you to get to know your quarters. Understand, boyo?"

"Aye," he whispered, keeping the glee from his voice. He had discovered a wicker trunk. Gently pushing the lid up, he discovered that his clothes had indeed been put here.

"Always know where your stuff's at!"

His "aye" sounded muffled as he pulled the black shirt over his head.

"You may sleep in a room with others, no bloody idea what kind of shit those Chanastardhians are into. If you do, you'll have to be as quiet as the dead." He didn't bother to reply. Instead, he slipped into his trousers. "Always make sure you know where guards'll be posted, and when they patrol. Evading the bastards will be easier." As if he didn't know that already. Who did this woman think she was? Or who he was for that matter? He was the Hand, and had done so many break-ins that he had stopped marking them on his board.

She must have somehow sensed his resentment, because she said, "Listen, butch! You have no fucking idea what a well patrolled mansion or palace is like. Don't think that this sort of thing is easy just because you were able to get in here unnoticed when a traitor ran the show. The guards back in Jathain's day were drunken fools most of the time." He slipped into the soft-soled black boots. "Have you really bothered to inspect this place since the bastard was sent packing? Probably not. No, not the dagger." He stopped in mid-motion, the belt with the sheathed weapon still lose in his hands. "Lose the poker, you won't be killing anyone." He did as she asked. "Here take this." She crossed the distance between them, as surefooted as a cat. An object was thrust into his gloved hands, and for a moment he had no idea what it was. It felt soft, yet solid at the same time. "Bunched leather, should you be detected or feel the need to murder someone, hit 'em, they know the rules."

Rules? What rules?

"Now, are you ready?"

"Aye," he replied, wondering what he should be ready for.

"Good. Your job is to reach the Baron's study and retrieve a letter from the Earl of Bullshit."

"The what?" he asked.

"Names don't matter, so we made up one," she said. "Find the letter and return here. Unseen and unheard, of course. If you are discovered, stop that person before alarm can be raised. You do that by being quick and tapping the leather to the guard's throat. They know what to do. Dispose of any body, naturally, without drawing attention. Understood?"

"Yes, but how do I get to the study from here?"

"You need to commit the layout of every area to mind. You obviously haven't done so," she said derisively. "Not my bloody problem. Now go!"

The dismissal could not have been more obvious. Intent on proving his worth, Jesgar inched to the door. The only thing he heard was the soft rustle of his own clothes and his breathing. Outside, all was quiet.

A gentle tug loosened the bolt and the door swung open. A quick prayer to thank the gods the bugger's hinges were well oiled. Then, following a darting glance to either side, he stepped into the corridor. The scant illumination, only every fifth sconce held a burning torch, indicated how deep into the night it really was. Had it been earlier the corridors would have been well lit.

Now there was just enough light to guide people to the privy without bumping into walls. The gloom suited him just fine.

Jesgar crept along one way, to the right, staying alert for any sound. He always went right, had learned early in his life that sentinels usually patrolled in this direction. Maybe it was in honor of the path of Lesganagh's glowing orb across the sky, or maybe coincidence. It didn't matter. In this twilight he would still be able to spot anyone approaching. A door he passed stood slightly ajar, light spilling into the corridor.

He chanced a look inside, and saw a Caretaker checking on someone lying in their bed. The priest was so preoccupied with his patient he barely looked up. To prevent his shadow from falling into the room—there was a torch opposite the door—he moved to the other wall, stepping lightly on the rushes covering the floor. Once there, he hugged the stone and crept into the illumination of the flickering firebrand, and was gone.

Crisscrossing the corridor, he kept out of the light if possible, alert for any sound or movement from beyond the shut doors. A noise from up ahead made him stop.

Two voices, low but still audible.

Keeping to the shadows he approached the speakers. Two men, warriors he reckoned if the jingle of mail was any indicator. The corridor ended at a corner, he noticed. A torch embedded into the far wall illuminated the cross-section, and in its light stood the pair of guards. He couldn't hear what they were saying. What he could tell, though, was they were sharing a bottle between them, passing it back and forth for a swallow each. They spoke easily, not the drink-slurred speech of the sentinels he had encountered when first breaking into the Palace, but the well restrained, disciplined talk of people who knew what they were doing. One of them hammered the stopper back into the bottle, the other complained loudly about the earthenware container not being able to keep things warm. Then they were off, heading the other way.

Jesgar breathed a silent sigh of relief, waited until the jingling sound of armor was muted enough, and then, keeping safe distance, he followed. The corridor fanned out into a semicircle and continued straight ahead. He had never been to this part of the Palace, and suppressing his curiosity about the assorted doors, went on into the passageway. The ringing of chain was still audible, but no one else seemed about this time of night. Down a flight of stairs, past a privy that badly needed cleaning, up to an intersection he went, careful not to disturb any of the rushes too noisily. Reaching the crossway, he hesitated, held his breath, and listened. Which way had the guards gone? His gut told him they had gone right, but the lack of illumination in that direction told him otherwise.

He needed a familiar spot, the kitchen would do, also the main audience chamber. Where the Scales was he? The left-hand corridor and the one up ahead were as sparsely lit as the one he stood in. There! The rustle of feet on rushes and the jingle of mail came from the left. That the Palace was this big he became aware of only now; getting in before had been easy. The job then had taken half as long, but getting the general lay of the Palace was easier when one operated from the main entrance. Compared to the labyrinth these lower levels presented, the frontal approach was simple. How was he to know all the chambers and corridors? Had he stayed in the barracks, getting in would have been a joke.

Angrily grinding his teeth, Jesgar followed the guards who, by now, were out of earshot. Caution, he reminded himself, slowing his pace to the inaudible crawl he had adopted before. There was still enough of a chance that some other inhabitant would take a late-night piss, and then the mission would have failed. He would have failed not only the thief who was training him, but also the Baron. Sure, it was just for practice that he sneaked through the Palace, but the way the lessons had picked up momentum, he reckoned failure meant even more and tougher training.

Just outside a torch's flicker he halted, spotting the two guardsmen. Or rather, one of them, the other was nowhere to be seen. The single warrior leaned against a wall next to a door, scrutinizing the nails on his right hand. Obviously, he was waiting on his comrade. His left foot tapped the stone floor, disturbing the rushes. Now he heard the soldier whisper, "Come on, you bastard."

From behind the door the other one hissed something Jesgar did not understand.

"I need to take a piss, hurry up, will ya?"

The portal opened and the other's head poked out. "I got some dried apples, mate, let's go!" Lord Duasonh certainly wouldn't mind a few filched apples, Jesgar thought as he watched the pair close the door and head right.

The pantry!

When they were gone, he headed for the door. It indeed was the pantry, although he didn't remember this entrance; no wonder, really, considering how big the room was. It had awed him the first time he'd been here. So much space would have housed a big family. The only thing he now needed was the door to the kitchen. Finding his way from there was much easier.

It was dawn when he finally entered the Baron's study. The guards had certainly improved without Jathain's misguiding hand, and it had taken him until now to get up the stairs. Now, as he eased open the door, Jesgar discovered the room was occupied.

She sat in the Baron's chair, feet propped up on the bare desktop. Her face was still hidden in the shadows, and it remained thus as she straightened to greet him.

"Took you long enough, boyo," she whispered. He entered, feeling more humbled than ever before. The door shut behind him, and she spoke on, addressing someone else. "There's more work to be done, milord. I apologize for his clumsiness."

He felt his eyes widen as he stared at her. Then, slowly, he turned and found Baron Duasonh standing behind him. Astonished, he almost forgot to bow, thankfully his instinct took over and he greeted his ruler as was proper. "My lord."

"Easy, son." To the woman thief the Baron said, "At least he didn't raise any alarm."

"Aye, he did not do that."

"Can he do it?" the Baron asked. He felt like hiding somewhere dark as Duasonh regarded him. "Can you do it?"

Jesgar looked at the thief. The sun had barely banished the gloom of predawn, but the light was enough to illuminate her face. Had the scar around her neck not marred her, she would have been perfect. Still, even with the scrunched-up skin, burned and maimed by the hangman's noose, she was striking. No wonder her voice was hoarse all the time. How she had survived the hanging was something he would have to ask her later. For now, he could just stare.

She showed no shame, no embarrassment, didn't even move to hide the scar. "Well?" she asked, cocking an eyebrow.

"Uh. What?"

The Baron smacked his head. "Stop playing dumb, son!"

"I need to learn more."

Her smile put the sun to shame, lighting up the room. "No sleep for you, not much anyway. Unless you can sleep on your feet, that is."

Jesgar groaned. This winter would indeed be long.

# CHAPTER 25

Despite Sir Úistan's assurance that everything was all right, Drangar knew it was time to leave Cahill Manor. He could feel the suspicious stares from people who had, until Ondalan, liked him. The whispers had spread quickly through the household, and even Neena seemed afraid of him, though she put on a brave face. She had argued his case to her father, despite him asking her not to, but the conversation had lasted merely as long as it had taken for Drangar to realize that nothing here was his to pack.

All through this Gwen had stayed with him. Why she stood by him, he didn't understand, but was glad for her presence all the same. Aside from Kildanor, she was the only person among the returnees who had no prejudice against him. He didn't comprehend her reasons, or the Chosen's for that matter, had he been in their place he probably would have kept a safe distance as well.

The nightmares had returned. They were different now. Scenes from Ondalan mixed with those of Little Creek and Cherkont Street. One night he had roused the entire camp with his screams. To his surprise they had abated after Gwen had sat down next to him. She had said she would make sure the dreams were kept at bay. They had been, but now she looked weary, and he wanted to tell her it wasn't her duty to ensure that he slept well. He had broached the subject a day ago, only to have her scowl, and then smile at him and tell him what she did was none of his concern. That smile of hers could have started wars, and ended them, and he found himself unable to fight her determination.

The slush on Trade Road wasn't bad; he imagined there were other, worse places where the hard-packed dirt turned into so much mud. Was Cherkont Street paved? He couldn't remember. For now, the two of them led their horses by the reins, silent. Drangar had known little of small talk to begin with, even before Hesmera, and he didn't want to burden Gwen with his troubles. She accepted his silence.

The glances they traded roused something inside him he had considered dead and gone for more than two years now. Was it love? He sure couldn't tell. "It's nicer in summer," he said, feeling foolish. Her smile stopped him from saying more. Was this for real? Could she really like him for himself, and not consider what he had done?

When they entered Beggar's Alley, Gwen broke the quiet. "Tell me about her."

Stiffening, he stopped, looked at her and saw only interest in her eyes. "She died. I killed her."

Eyebrows knit together, she said, "I wanted to know who she was, not how and why she died."

He stood there searching her face for any hint of pity, and saw none. What was there to tell? He had tried so long and hard to forget the past, and the only thing he had managed to put aside was the person, not what he had seen when waking from the stupor. Little things, like the twinkle of her eyes, were always overshadowed by the image of her remains lying on the floor like puzzle pieces scattered by an angry child. "I..." he began, and then swallowed the lump building in his throat. How could he describe her?

Gwen's look hadn't changed; her brows were still knitted as if in deep thought, now her lips pursed. So unlike Hesmera. She had always been so... "Carefree," he said. "Lived each day to its fullest. Fought that way also. Cunning, clever, even vicious at times. Strong anchor in a shield wall; I was never much of a team player. She could have been a leader; she never told me why she preferred the ranks, but I guess she enjoyed making fools out of the warleaders far too much to give that up and become a figure of ridicule herself. Flowers, not the tamed kind people have in gardens, no, she liked them wild, just as she was.

But I think there was a part of her that wanted to be a lady. I didn't even know she was a friend to Neena and Leonore. Of course she was no courtier material; when she was angry she cursed like the worst lout you can imagine." He paused, looked down to his free arm, and saw Gwen's hand on his elbow.

"Come," she said, "Let's visit her." Then, "Best you lead, since I'd likely end up in a tavern or worse." Her apologetic grin was infectious, and he couldn't help but smile back. "There, that wasn't so hard, now, was it?"

She was right. He felt lighter, somehow. Not like what he had felt when seeing her grave. No, this was different. As if the sun had finally broken the cloud cover and shone onto the wet grass. "All right," Drangar said, and they turned back the way they had just come.

Despite the cold, the cemetery was busy. It appeared as if Dunthiochagh's nobility had also lost some members. Or maybe it was just one House honoring a singular death. He couldn't tell. Leaving the horses tied to one of the poles at the front, they passed the gate and some of the mourners, thankfully ignored by the peacocks milling about the yard in front of the small chapel. Most of them, like everywhere else, were...

"Pretentious buggers," Gwen interrupted, completing his thought. "And take that hood off, you aren't disfigured. Why hide your face?"

He looked at her as he pulled the cloth back. The cold was tolerable, and a slight breeze tickled what little hair had already grown back. His face must have displayed his surprise and wonder, for Gwen smiled at him. "If a ship's done for, you sink it. If it's still serviceable, you fix it."

"Um" was the only thing he could think of.

"Don't worry about what they think," she said, poking a thumb at the people dressed in mourning white. "As for me, if I were disgusted by the state of your scalp, don't you think I would have told you by now?" Gwen had her hand in the crook of his arm, her grip light yet firm. She squeezed, his concern lessened. "Men," he heard her hiss "can be so godsdamned dense!" He regarded her, speechless. What was happening here? "So, are you gonna take us to her or should I fetch some shovel and dirt so you can grow roots?"

Her cockiness made him feel elated and foolish at the same time. Even with Hesmera he hadn't felt like this.

They walked on.

Reaching the mound, Gwen held him back as she regarded the snow-covered hill and sarcophagus. "Damn," she said.

"House Cahill had that built," he explained, the shame of having fled rising once more.

It must have reflected in his voice, for Gwen pulled him to face her, and said, "Who wouldn't have?"

"What?" Drangar asked dumbly, not quite understanding what she was talking about.

"Who would have stayed? Oh, don't look at me like that. Her death was talked about, and Sir Úistan's retainers heard more than most, what with her being friend to the two ladies. They also spoke about your confession, how you told them you don't remember anything."

He opened his mouth to reply, but she put a gloved hand to his lips. "Shhh, I talk, you listen, all right?" He could only nod. "You're cute when you have that look," she said, grinning. Then, more seriously, she continued. "What would anyone in your situation have done? I pieced it together from the bits Lord Cahill's men told me, and waking up without knowing what one did and seeing this horrible picture, who wouldn't have run? That's something everyone can relate to. When I broke my ma's favorite vase I hid as well."

He wanted to say that breaking a piece of pottery and chopping a person to thumb sized bits were two completely different things, but she pressed her hand even stronger to his mouth, as if she knew he was going to argue. "I talk, remember?" she said, her voice now stern. "What you did was natural, running that is. Forgive yourself; I'm sure she has."

Her glove smelled of horse and a touch of lavender. Drangar waited, expected her to say more, and the more moments passed, the stronger he felt the truth in her words. "Why do you do this?" he finally managed to say.

She gave him a look of pure astonishment. Then the

mischievous twinkle returned to her eyes. "Because somebody has to," she said. He felt she wanted to say more, but was somewhat relieved when she remained silent. His gaze was transfixed, caught by her blue eyes that wouldn't leave him. "And because I like you," she finally whispered.

How much he had longed for her to speak those words, Drangar realized when his breath caught in his throat. He wanted to reply, tell her the same kind words, but how could she love him when he was nothing but turmoil and bloodshed?

His concern must have shown, for she frowned, the radiance gone from her eyes. "You don't get it, do you?"

Crestfallen, his mind awash in a mix of feelings, Drangar looked at her, terrified she would turn from him, and afraid to stand alone. He needed her. How and why, those were things he couldn't explain, didn't want to explain. He looked at Gwen, saw her anguish—was that a vague hint of rejection?—and took her hands into his. "I... please..." It seemed her eyes were pleading along with his words, as if she urged him to open up. "How..."

She yanked her right from his left and delivered a stinging blow to his cheek. "Gods, you are so fucked up it's a wonder you manage to dress yourself in the morning. You swore her you'd avenge her." She pointed at the mound. "Yet you crawl back into your uncertainty whenever some shit or other happens!"

He couldn't hold back any longer. "I tore your countrymen apart! These hands were buried in a woman's belly, gripping her spine and ripping her in two!"

Her look was unchanged, maybe even a little more resolved. "Was that you? Because, frankly, I cannot imagine that the man standing here before me would do any of these things." A triumphant smirk lit up her face as he struggled for a reply.

"Well?" Gwen said. She was right, and knew it; Drangar bowed his head in defeat. "I did not spend my nights by your side to see you bumble around. So those responsible are not in your sight right now. Who gives a shit? If faced with no wind, you get the godsdamned oars out and row. Understand?" Fury was plain on her face. "I have seen your looks—well, everyone has seen them—so just say it. You already know I like you. And I am old enough to make my own choices, so bugger the rest of them if they think I'm crazy. I like you, you idiot!"

"I like you, too," he blurted out before any other thought had formed. The doubts and worries were drowned in feelings of happiness enveloping him.

"There," Gwen said, triumphantly. "That wasn't so bad, now, was it?"

Now they were holding hands, and he looked into eyes full of conviction and hope. "No."

Her smile broadened. "Tell me of her."

The dusk-gong rang across Dunthiochagh as they left the cemetery. Their cloaks had stopped keeping the cold at bay a long time ago, so Drangar had suggested they retire to some tavern. Gwen had refused, saying he needed to get this memory out in the open next to Hesmera's grave. She had been right, and he was glad they had stayed. Now, though, he yearned for a steaming mug of tea and a roaring fire to drive the chill from his bones. Gwen simply nodded at his stammered suggestion; she was too busy keeping her teeth from shattering each other. He looked at her, envied how robust this young woman truly was, and tried to smile. The pain stopped him from trying too hard.

A nearby tavern, a place too shabby for this noble neighborhood, really, drew them in. Once inside he understood why this business had survived in the noble's district, although for the moment it hardly mattered. They hunkered down on a pillowed bench near the fire, and for a long while they remained silent, unmoving, their feet propped up on the fireplace's lip. Someone came, asked a question neither he nor Gwen heard. A blanket was put around their shoulders.

When a lass fed more logs to the flame, he realized how close together the two of them sat. Had they started out this way? He couldn't recall. Now her head lay on his shoulder, one hand draped on his lap. Her breathing was even, relaxed, she was so calm he dared not move, afraid to wake her. Inside his boots he wiggled his toes; thankfully the cold had done no harm other than freeze them half to death.

"Think the publican will mind if I get out of these boots?"

Gwen asked, surprising him. She hadn't been asleep after all. "My feet are killing me."

He turned his head, scanning the taproom. There were a few guests with socked feet propped on their tables. By the look of them, he guessed they were nobles who used this place to escape the tediousness of home. Now that his senses were once more alert, he realized that the shoddy exterior was just a smokescreen. The interior could have served as an example of how a well lived in and loved home should look like. In a way it spoke of comfort without being either loud or oppressive. The oak furniture, its wide chairs sporting comfortable pillows on everything but the armrests, was almost black with patina, aged and maintained so well that it shone like polished obsidian. Even the bar, which certainly had seen years if not decades of use, kept up the appearance. This wasn't the Tankard, although from the notches in some of the tables he could tell that the place had seen its share of brawls. "No," he finally said, as Gwen wriggled around in an attempt to snuggle closer. "They won't mind."

"Good," she said and let go of him. As she bent forward to untie her boots, he noticed her absence immediately. It felt strange, being attracted to Gwen; it was unlike anything he had ever felt before. No, he told himself, not unlike anything he had felt before. But she couldn't and didn't want to be compared to Hesmera. Yet, whereas his mind had always been in turmoil, even when Hesmera was alive, he felt at peace now.

"Gods, this is glorious," she said and looked at him. "What are you smiling about like a mooncalf?"

"This," Drangar said. "You."

"You hardly know me," she replied, though he could tell by the tone of her voice she was holding back. Could it really be love? Could love really be that simple? "But, aye, I feel the same. Dunno what I looked like, snuggled against you, but I guess my smile was as wide as yours."

He was about to caress her hair when he saw his gloves still bore the bloodstains of Ondalan. No, he thought grimly, pulling them off and tossing them into the fire, he would not sully this moment by running bloodied gloves through her hair.

Gwen must have caught what he was doing and chuckled. "Hair's already red, aye?" She tried to maintain an air of seriousness as he gaped at her, struggling with his own mirth.

"Are you for real?" Drangar asked. She grimaced, and then pinched him. "Guess so," he said, still feeling young and more foolish than he ever had before.

"I'm sorry, milady," a voice interrupted.

They both turned to the publican. "Aye?" Gwen asked.

"Please be so kind and put on a pair of fresh socks." Drangar saw she was about to snap a reply, when the middle-aged man added, "We'll provide them for you and your companion. They've been washed, handmade by my wife."

"Certainly," Gwen said.

"Companion, eh?" Drangar said when the man had left. Did he look like someone's companion?

Gwen giggled. "Better than slave, I'd say."

"Aye. What about..." The publican's return silenced him. Drangar removed his boots and socks and wiggled his toes once more. Satisfied that they were all unharmed, he was about to pull on the socks when he realized just how long they had been on the road. The smell was unbearable and he tossed his socks after the gloves, taking Gwen's off her and sent them burning as well. "Better wash them now," he hissed, "before they kick us out." He waved over the serving girl. "Is there some place we can wash our feet?" he asked when the lass stood near them, wrinkling her nose.

"Certainly, sir," she answered. "Follow me." She led the way to a far door hidden behind a heavy curtain, into a room that reminded him of a bathhouse. Obviously, they were not the only ones ever to enter this tavern in need of a wash. "Want to take a bath?" the lass asked. She must have seen his discomfort—from the way Gwen was shifting she must have felt ill at ease as well—and added, "We have tubs separated from each other."

Drangar's sigh of relief was almost as loud as Gwen's. He looked at the girl who shrugged as if it was all the same to her, and said, "That would be great." He dared not contemplate their odor.

"Please wait," the girl said and hurried out once more.

Next to him, Gwen whistled softly. "I'll be damned. Look at the floor," she said.

He did, and immediately understood the cause of her surprise. The floor was solid stone, yet their feet didn't freeze. In fact, they were comfortably warm. He went back to the door and peeked out into the taproom. It sported the same stone floor.

"How do they do that?" Gwen asked from behind.

Somewhere in the back of his mind a memory stirred to life. It was one of those things he had tried to banish from his head, something he had learned as a child. The Eye of Traksor also had floors that were warm in the winter, and as... Darlontor had once explained, men who had known the elven way of building had designed the entire keep. Fires burned below, the heated air running through clay pipes underneath the floor, thus warming the stones. One winter, when he was maybe ten, he had gone exploring the depths of the Eye, and had stumbled into the scalding hot heating-room. There had been a handful of workers down there, stripped to their loincloths, feeding wood into ovens twice as wide as a man was tall. He had rarely seen such architecture outside of Kalduuhn. That the founder of this inn had gone to the lengths of building his livelihood this way impressed him.

"Elven design," he said.

"You think so?" She was still squatting, inspecting the almost seamless stone floor.

"Aye; must've cost a fortune to build, neither the Palace nor Cahill Manor has such a thing."

Gwen looked up at him, obviously astonished. He saw she wanted to ask something when the serving girl re-entered, carrying soaps and blankets. "Sorry, had to throw some mint-leaves on the fire," she said meekly, obviously embarrassed by mentioning the need of masking their smell.

"We have to apologize," Gwen said.

"Long road you traveled?" the girl asked, putting down the pile on one of the stools lining the wall. She then went and pulled away two curtains Drangar had thought were covering windows. Instead he saw two chambers of equal size beyond, each containing nothing more than a stone bathtub and a pair of spigots embedded into the wall.

"Yes," he said absentmindedly, wondering if the interior had been removed from somewhere and rebuilt here. "Bloody long road." Gwen snorted.

"Left's hot, right's cold," the lass explained. "Pull the plug when you're done."

Almost as an afterthought, Drangar remembered one important detail. "How much will this cost?" His purse held some money, but this luxury certainly would not come cheap.

The girl faced him, frowning in obvious consternation.

Gwen intervened, saying, "Money is, of course, not an issue." She briefly glared at him, and then added, "Money is never an issue."

"Enjoy your baths," the lass said, and left.

"We would not have come here were we unable to pay," Gwen said, her voice almost as stern as it had been when she lectured him before. "This place caters to the rich, and money with them is never an issue."

"But..."

"You have some plunder, right?" she interrupted him. He shook his head, appalled at the thought of taking money from the torn corpses. Plunder was a warrior's reward, true, and as mercenary he had taken his share from the dead. But the thought of taking anything from the Fiend's victims had been too much for him to bear.

"I have a few..."

"No worries; I killed some rich bugger, so we do have enough. Provided they accept Eagles that is. Oh, don't look at me like that. There's no love lost between most Chanastardhian nobility and me. My da is a pirate at heart as much as my great-grandda was one, and how we got our position was most likely through bribes." He realized he hardly knew anything about her, and all this time she had listened to his woes. In a way he was glad she spoke of herself now. "Landed gentry, indeed," she spat. "So, I figured, if I am to desert, I might as well bugger the bastards good. No quarter, no ransom, other than what they carry in their pockets." She grinned savagely, and for a moment

Drangar could picture her on a galley, captaining the wolves of the sea. "Now," she said sternly, "get behind that wall." She pointed to the other partition, and added, "No peeking." By the twinkle in her eyes, he knew she was serious but also enjoyed his company. To reinforce her statement, she pulled the curtain shut behind her.

Not that he had considered doing anything, being near her was enough. Her presence had calmed the Fiend so much, the monster rarely made itself heard. He went to his compartment, undressed, and began fiddling with the spigots. Operating the damn things was easy; getting the bathwater to an agreeable temperature was not. From the hissed curses he could tell Gwen faced the same problem. Two years of washing in a spring had made his body sensitive; the lukewarm water felt like boiling oil.

The relaxed sigh coming from the other side told him Gwen was finally settled in the tub. Years ago, he would have enjoyed soaking in a good bath; now things were different. Drangar immediately went to business. He realized quickly that scrubbing his body whilst sitting was uncomfortable at best, so he stood and lathered himself in soap. The beginnings of a new beard were sprouting on his chin. No steady, continuous, all covering growth, but tufts of hair scattered all over the place. His scalp wasn't in much better shape. How could she like him? He was a caricature of a man, and without a mirror he imagined himself looking more like cabbage with patches of mildew growing haphazardly. Looking about he discovered a cupboard and mirror next to the curtain. Another lathering, and then he left the tub, and headed for the piece of furniture.

On his way there, he wrapped himself in a towel, took one of the stools, and finally settled in front of the looking glass. Even in the gentle illumination he could tell that the image of the cabbage hadn't been so far off. There were patches of skin still bare, while other spots already showed traces of his original hair color. No, not cabbage, he decided, rather a child's doll that had seen one too many games of tug. The belt knife was with the rest of his gear, in the stable; he had refrained from sharpening any blade since the caves, and now when he needed a shave, his knife was not around. Drangar was about to ask Gwen, when another thought crossed his mind. If this place was indeed as elitist as it appeared to be, the mirror was not only there to provide vain people with a place to brush their hair.

A moment later he held a razor in his hand. It had been ages since he had held one of these, the buggers always made him uncomfortable. Why this was so, he had no idea; the blade certainly was as sharp as his knife. Rummaging about the cupboard, he discovered a bowl, a massive brush and block of soap. For so many years he had shaved without soap, and he wouldn't change now.

He returned to the cooling bathtub, remembered the lass's remark about a plug, and knelt, his hands searching for the stopper. As the water gurgled away, he briefly contemplated filling the bowl with the slush, but decided against it. If he could help it, Gwen would never see that utterly raw side of him. Instead, he filled the bowl with cold water from the spigot and headed back to the mirror.

Shaving was much simpler and faster with half his face still looking like a newborn's rear, although the scraping of the blade irritated his skin so much, he looked flushed without having exerted himself. Finished, Drangar regarded himself, wondering if he should also get rid of the hair on his scalp.

He was just about to guide the razor across his temple—a rather lonely patch of hair was growing there—when he heard Gwen's voice. "You know, just leave it be, won't be that bald for long, I reckon. Give it some time to heal."

Her head was poking out from behind the curtain, and by the look of it, she had been standing there for a while. Face and hair were already somewhat dry, and from her expression she liked what she saw, despite his patchy hair. "And if it doesn't?" he asked, feeling rather more self-conscious than he had in years.

"Then you can always get a wig." When he glared at her, she stuck out her tongue and retreated behind the curtain, laughing.

"Wig, my ass!" he growled.

"I could picture you as a blonde." He snorted. A blonde, yeah, right! "Where will you live?" Gwen asked, her voice losing all humor, sounding far more serious.

"Dunno. Thought about going to my house." Truth was, the thought had come before, but he had always been afraid to go because of the memories connected to the place. "Not sure that is such a wise idea, though." When Gwen remained silent, he spoke on. "The house is still mine, but why should I go there?"

"Because you also were at her grave, making your feelings known to her," she said.

"I told you, not her. She's..."

"I know," Gwen interrupted. "I know. But do you think I asked you to tell me about her just so that I would know? No woman enjoys hearing about her predecessor; trust me. So why did I ask you? There at the graveyard? I figured you never told her how much she really meant to you, saying 'I love you' is easy. Saying you know someone and care for someone very deeply, that is hard."

"So, you think I should go?"

"I think," she said, her hand snaking out from behind the curtain, searching, "you need to decide. I am not your decision-maker; that honor goes solely to you. Pass me a towel, will you?"

# CHAPTER 26

Aside from the progression of souls when they died, Rhea knew little of spirits. She had already consulted a Deathmask, and Jainagath's priest had yielded little extra knowledge. "Yes," he had said, "some souls remain, evading the god at the time of dying." Not that this answered why Cat's spirit had come to her. Neither did it explain why the spirit had chosen her to guard her son.

For two days, her search for answers had been cut down to a bare minimum. Aside from the Deathmask, she had been unable to look deeper into the matter; Nerran's erratic mood swings, his constant drinking and general disarray had made her into the practical leader of the Riders, and—she hated the thought—she felt obligated to wet-nurse Nerran. The Paladin was in pieces; the loss of so many friends, while hard on all survivors had struck him strongest. It saddened her to see the confident man stumble about the Palace, his mourning whites getting filthier with each sobbing breath. Regret, another part of grieving, seemed to weigh Nerran down, and he lamented his failures to whomever he met. She could pull him out of a brawl with imaginary foes one moment, and he would stagger off to find more booze the next. Just now she contemplated sending him to the dungeons and locking him up.

"And you knows wut?" slurred the Paladin to a servant who visibly struggled not to turn away. "She's got that nose that crinkles whenever she's pissed off about something. Should've seen the guys she whacked when they pissed her off." He was talking about Gail. "And that bitch had to drive the life outta her. Would've lived she would." The servant tried to distance himself from Nerran, but the Paladin had him by the shoulder. "Finest Caretaker I ever knew, and she had no flatulence about her. Not like that cocksucker Danaissan."

How many times had she dragged him away from annoying servants and townsfolk? And it had only been two days. It seemed Nerran had decided to ignore sleep. That his body was handling this extreme punishment of booze and tears was a miracle.

"My Lord Nerran," the concerned man pleaded, "I need to get back to my duties."

"Yer a servant, aye, lad? Then go'n serve me some more mead," Nerran slurred, straightened, and burped. Saliva bubbled from his lips and mixed with the liquid already gathered in his beard and tunic.

It was best, Rhea thought, to beat him senseless and wait until he regained some of his dignity. Then, deciding this might actually be in everyone's best interest, she took her sheathed sword from her belt. The servant caught her intent, and moved himself and Nerran into position for her to strike.

The Paladin thudded to the floor like a sack of grain. "Thank you, milady," the servant said.

"Don't thank me just yet," she said. "You're going to help me get him out of the way."

Admittedly, Nerran, like every Rider, was in splendid shape, yet he was a bulky man, and it took the help of two more retainers, off-duty guards, to carry him to a cell. Rhea had decided he shouldn't burden anyone by vomiting on carpets or quilts. The dungeons already smelled like piss and vomit, so Nerran's being ill would hardly add to the place's sewer stench. "Leave the door unlocked," she ordered the head Warden when they returned to the guardroom.

Finally she had the chance to consult with Coimharrin, who might not be that well versed in spirit-lore, but had known Amhlaidh and Caitrin Ralchanh and might be able to explain what the Scales was going on.

Upholder Coimharrin was busy. In Lliania's Court he was passing judgment on various looters and other unseemly elements that had tried to use the battle's aftermath to fatten their pockets. Rhea entered as her colleague ordered someone hanged. As was his habit, something she had learned to loathe and love at one time or another, he played the scatterbrained fool, luring people into traps of their own making. The next culprit that a guard brought in explained his actions in the most eloquent manner while Coimharrin fiddled with a string that was sticking out from his linen tunic.

"Indeed, your honor, I was at the place, but my intent was not to steal; I wanted to help."

"Huh? What?" Coimharrin said absentmindedly.

"I wanted to help the survivors of said house."

"Which house was that?" Now the Upholder scanned his desk for something. Rhea reckoned it to be a knife.

"The house in question. The place where these brutes arrested me!" the accused snarled.

"Oh, right. Anyone got a knife? This bugger is bugging me." Coimharrin held up his sleeve. His daughter helped him out. Satisfied, he said, "Thanks, dear. Now then, you say you wanted to help the poor souls in that house, right?"

"Yes! There were people trapped and I wanted to help!"

"Who was trapped?"

"The owner and his family!"

"When were you arrested?"

"This morn."

"Oh, right, says so right here." He fiddled with a paper lying in front of him.

"So, I came to help."

"Whom? Names please." Now Coimharrin began to clean his fingernails.

"I don't know, I heard them yelling!" The thief, Rhea had no doubt about what he really was, played innocent, and had to be very naïve and uninformed not to know the Upholder's tactics. None of the good criminals ever got caught, or, if they did, they knew better than to join Coimharrin in his game of subterfuge. They admitted their guilt, paid a hefty fine, and were then let go. Normally these kinds of people did not get caught with their hands dirty of one crime or another; although—Lliania knew—their hands were usually awash in dirt and blood. This fellow seemed blissfully unaware of whom he was trying to con, and she enjoyed seeing him twitch on the line, with Coimharrin's hook already firmly embedded.

"So, let me get this straight: you heard survivors in Blaithan's Jewelry four days after the place had been hit by a slingthrower-stone? Right?" The accused nodded, somewhat dumbfounded. "Right, then. How many did you rescue?"

"None, your honor. I was interrupted."

"Yes, yes. Can I have some more tea, dear?" He took the refilled mug from his daughter's hands, leaned back, and sipped. "Needs more honey." Turning back to the out-of-luck thief, he said, "So, you rescued none. How can you explain the golden torque and the rings in your pocket?"

"I had bought them for my wife."

"From Blaithan's?"

"I... err... aye."

"Would the honorable Etgal Blaithan step forward please?" Rhea knew Coimharrin enjoyed the look of panic on the thief's face as much as she did. A middle-aged man, stooped from hours and hours of hunching over his work, his little remaining hair grey, stood and approached the dais. "Warden, please show him the items. Take your time and inspect them, dear sir. Since you're dead I guess you have all the time in the world."

The audience, there was always an audience when Coimharrin held court, chuckled, and she caught herself smirking as well. When things had quieted down, her fellow priest asked, "Now then, did you create these items for..." He turned to the culprit. "What's your name again?" Rhea knew he was playing for laughs. The audience response was as expected.

"Tannan, sir. Tannan of Ondalan."

"Hard times, eh, what with your home in ruins, eh? So, did you make them for this young man?"

"No, sir."

"Son, if you want to rob a place and claim you wanted to rescue inhabitants, just make sure they aren't with relatives in a different part of town. Even if that's not enough." He pointed at the jewelry. "An attempted alibi is something that's pretty pointless when any possible survivor would have died from the cold already, and well, you know, having the plundered goods in your pockets and being caught waist high in the ruins." He gave a sigh. "Why do I even bother? Tannan, can you fight?"

The man's eyes grew wide. "No, sir."

"Then you'll learn. You are to serve Dunthiochagh." He surprised Rhea with the sentence. Normally, thieves were given one choice: left or right hand, if they were lucky. If criminals were treated this leniently, how would others learn a lesson? Politics again interfered with justice, and some claimed this was a necessary evil, but to her, seeing Coimharrin play to the Baron's tune was something right out of her nightmares.

In Haldain, her home, watching the bloodied swords that had cut down her parents, she had learned the worth of true justice. Those who had killed her family had been pardoned, for political reasons, to forge alliances, to further trade. Justiciar Ralchanh, she had later learned, had been forced to rule such compromises. Now here, there certainly was need to bolster the warbands, for come spring Chanastardh would return. Did necessity overrule common sense? She thought not, and although he made a show of passing this judgment, she knew neither did Coimharrin. Yes, he had sanctioned the ruling spoken by Cat's son, Drangar Ralgon, and it had some merit—without it there surely would have been fewer healers available, and the casualties would have increased—but pardoning every criminal because there was a need for bodies to toss against an enemy seemed insane. Who knew whether this crook would do worse in the future? Aside from a few the gods truly had chosen, who knew their will? Rhea would have liked to claim she was one of them, maybe her sense of justice, the gift of Lliania, was such a mark, or maybe she had it all wrong and Coimharrin was the one who heard the goddess clearly. She didn't know.

Ahead her fellow priest ended this day's court by waving his hand in a shooing motion. She caught his eye right before he turned his back to the petitioners. He whispered something to Morwyn who nodded, and then left. Rhea decided to wait, passing judgment was tiring business, and she knew firsthand how important a few moments of peace and quiet were afterwards.

The last culprit, Tannan, passed her, smirking. To her it was obvious that this man had neither learned his lesson nor intended to follow Coimharrin's ruling. Had her fellow Upholder actually bothered to detect the man's honesty? If he did and had not followed up on this, he truly was just dancing to Duasonh's tune. If the pardoned folks were willing to fight, she saw no harm in the verdict; these people would do their best. Yet she felt Tannan did not belong to those who honored a judge's words.

The decision to interfere came quickly, and before Tannan had passed the door, she stepped up to him, took him by the arm and held him back. "A word with you," she said, making sure he knew this was not an invitation to polite small talk.

"What do you want?" The looter sounded more annoyed than worried. Why shouldn't he? After all he had been freed.

"Tell me," Rhea said, "will you stand fast on the wall when the Chanastardhians return?"

He must have detected her authority, because he stiffened and looked about nervously. Rhea waited, silently reciting the Prayer of Truths, asking Lliania to grant her the power to tell sincerity from lie. Thankfully Tannan remained silent a moment longer, staring at her dumbfounded. Then, as she felt the goddess's gentle touch, the image of a black and white painted scale manifesting itself in her mind's eye, Tannan answered. "Sure. The bastards will fall before my sword," he said with bravado. Had Lliania not touched her, she would have believed him. But the Prayer of Truths unerringly showed the difference between word and thought. It couldn't tell more than the subjective validity of a statement, but with a blatant lie, such as this one, the outcome was definite. Her mind's scale moved, the black-enameled bowl swung downward, and Rhea knew this man spoke false. "Left or right?" she asked, looking the man straight in the eye.

"What?" he said, panic in his eyes.

"Choose, left or right!" she repeated.

"I... err... I am innocent!" The bowl stayed down, yet another lie revealed. The bastard knew what he did was wrong and still continued.

"Fine, both then. Live off the scraps people toss you," she said calmly, determinedly.

Morwyn must have watched the exchange, because she now hurried over, her feet pattering on the stone floor. "The city needs warriors," she said.

"The city needs people who are willing to fight," Rhea retorted. "This one here will not keep his word." Years of combat, either practice or actual battle, had honed her reflexes, her muscles were as corded as those of Briog or Fynbar, and all it took was a jerked hand to bring the now struggling Tannan to the floor. "You are judged and sentenced by me, Upholder Rheanna. With the authority imparted on me by Lady Justice I pronounce you guilty. Since you neither speak the truth about the deed and a possible, unharmed future, nor refuse to choose which hand, you will lose both," she said, summoning her most official voice. Another tug, her right leg stopping Tannan's own step back, and the criminal was on the floor. "Put your arms on the bench!" She kicked him in the flank, waited, and when he didn't comply repeated the process.

Finally, he relented, put his arms on the stone, his hands dangling freely in the air. "Move and you die," Rhea warned as she drew her sword. Morwyn surprised her when she put her booted foot into Tannan's lower back, keeping the thief down. She had never seen Coimharrin's daughter participate in any judging, but should have known better. Of course, Morwyn knew the rules. Rhea nodded her thanks, and then, with practiced ease, swung the blade down, cutting off the man's hands. Immediately the weapon clattered to the floor and she was down on her knees, tying off the wrists so Tannan of Ondalan would not bleed to death.

Morwyn surprised her again when she said, "I'll fetch water and a rag; nails are by the door, if you want to display his hands." Traditionally a criminal's hand was exhibited on the market square, but since Dunthiochagh had more than one, most hands were nailed on Old Bridge's central flagpole, a wooden beam whose lower section was usually covered by the booths lining the crossing.

Rhea hardly heard the thief's wails, the battle's noise too fresh still in her mind to notice. She tightened the thongs that stemmed the blood flow, and considered. "I'll do it later, first I need to…"

The door behind them banged open. "What the Scales are you doing?" Coimharrin roared.

"Tannan of Ondalan, you are free to go," she said.

Morwyn took her boot off the man's rear and bent to help him up. He struggled to his feet, still crying in pain. "Go to the temple," she said, leading the whimpering man out.

Only when the criminal had left did Rhea turn to look at the aging Upholder. She waited until the door was firmly shut and Morwyn on her way to fetch water and rags, then said, "I could ask you the same thing."

"What do you mean?" Coimharrin looked tired, but the state of one's mind was, in her eyes, no excuse for not paying attention to a culprit's statements.

"You did not invoke the Prayer of Truth to see if this man would actually fight." When her colleague remained silent, she went on, "Politics are not our business; justice is! And even if Dunthiochagh's ranks are depleted, Lliania knows how many people you let go because of Baron Duasonh's need for warriors. This man wasn't going to join, and had you asked for insight into his words you would have seen it." She took a deep breath, waiting for him to reply. Then, when he stayed still, she said, "I don't think Cumaill would appreciate you letting people go without checking the validity of their word."

"This is my court," he said feebly.

"And I have no right to interfere, aye, normally that would hold true. But first and foremost, this is Lliania's Court, and we her instruments." She relented, seeing his weariness. "Listen, if you want me to step in for a while so you can get some rest, say the word."

For a moment it seemed as if Coimharrin would weep, then he pulled himself together and nodded. "That'd be nice; all this shit is getting to me. Little sleep because of settlements that were demanded in the middle of the night. One would think the buggers have no sense at all."

Maybe they hadn't, Rhea thought, but didn't voice her opinion. "Well, then. I'll start tomorrow."

"You didn't come here to chop off people's hands though, did you?" the old Upholder said when they had settled on a bench in the kitchen.

Rhea shook her head. "No, I need to ask you something."

"Advice from a geezer like me?" Coimharrin chuckled. "After you've shown me what it means to be a judge?"

She couldn't help but feel embarrassed. He was her senior by a few decades, had also been her mentor ever since she had fled Haldain. Now she was the one putting his head straight. The reversal of roles made her uncomfortable. It wasn't that he had lost his touch, not really, she reminded herself. No, it was that she had gained more insight. Maybe, had she been as tired as he, she would have made the same mistakes. Weariness did strange things to people, made them commit adultery, or gamble on when all reason told one to stop. She had felt the same when Gail had been brought into the stinking tanner's shop. She had wanted her to live, but now, with decent sleep having refreshed her mind, she knew the Caretaker's decision had been sensible. "Justice takes no sides," she said, unsure, at the moment, whether she meant Coimharrin or the world in general.

"True enough," he replied. "Now tell that to the Kings and Lords. But I reckon you didn't come here to discuss the Lady's dogma." So at least he agreed, which, she thought, was good enough. "Come, child, let's talk."

To call Coimharrin's kitchen comfortable was stretching the word. Rhea had rarely seen a place more raw than this. It served its purpose, although, she considered, there may have been something to living under such bare conditions. The room's only homely area was in front of the hearth and its adjoining cupboards, Morwyn's domain. Yet the Upholder's daughter appeared to be remiss in her duties, for the clutter of pots and bowls spread across table was so high she could barely see the aged wood.

"So, what brings you here?"

While Coimharrin unceremoniously pushed away some of

the leftovers, dumping a few wooden bowls and mugs off the other side, Rhea spoke. "Have you ever seen a spirit?"

The Upholder stopped in mid-push and regarded her. "Sober you mean, eh?" She nodded. He shook his head. "No, never, and I'm grateful for that. Spirits are nasty business. Buggers always want you to avenge them or protect something." He discovered an apple amidst the clutter and broke it in two, offering her one part. "So, you weren't drunk and truly saw a spirit, hmm?"

"Aye, two nights ago, in the fog." She nibbled the apple, found it was still good, and ate in earnest.

Coimharrin seemed more interested in the fruit's uneven structure, for he studied it intensely. Finally, he said, "Why come to me with this? Isn't that something Deathmasks could more easily explain?"

"Already spoke to one. Didn't yield any new insight, and for more answers I would have had to summon a soul and ask questions. Too high a price attached to that," she said. "I like my memories just fine."

A sagely bob of the head, and then a bite from the apple. He was ever the showman, even around her. "Too true, besides they are creepy, at times. Although, I had a nice little chat with one a week ago or so," he mumbled, chewing. "Oh, don't look at me like that. He was a good Chiath player." He swallowed. "So, what did this spirit want?"

"You're not gonna ask who it was?"

"Gods, your face! Priceless," he chuckled, biting into the apple again. "All right, who was it?"

"Cat Ralchanh."

Coimharrin stopped chewing, all mirth gone from his face. "You sure?"

"Aye, I barely remember her, but her father's features were etched into its face."

"Much like this Drangar fellow?"

She nodded.

"So, what did Cat want from you?"

"She wanted me to protect him."

"Ralgon?"

"Yes, but she didn't say from whom or what."

"The buggers never do, least that's what I've been told. Cryptic messages and all that nonsense. Maybe I should ask my Deathmask acquaintance about that." Scratching his beard, Coimharrin regarded her. Not many liked the old man's scrutiny and Rhea was no exception. But there was something in his look that indicated he was thinking, rather than reading her.

At times like this, she knew, it was best to leave him to his musings, and instead of wasting time staring at the pile of dirty pots and bowls, Rhea got up and began clearing the table in earnest. Most of her life she had done just that, busying herself, the indulgent past long forgotten. Just how many bowls and pots did he own, she wondered when she discovered the sink filled with even older pots. With a groan she set about clearing this mess first, and for the first time in many years did she hear her prissy aunt's scolding voice echo through her mind. A princess was not supposed to do such menial tasks. That may have been true in her father's palace. Here, in a world where no one gave a damn about her noble blood, things like this were normal. And necessary, she thought glumly, withdrawing a pot so moldy it almost seemed alive.

"All of this," Coimharrin said a while later, "is somehow related to this Drangar chap having been used as someone else's puppet. He killed his wife-to-be, you know."

"So, what shall I do?" she asked, scraping the last of the pans clean.

"Unless you want Cat's restless spirit haunting you for the rest of your life, I see no other option than to do what she asks of you."

"Why me?"

"Dunno. Maybe because I am too old to be of use to anyone when it comes to fighting."

"Think there will be fighting?"

Coimharrin cackled. "Silly girl, you heard what happened at the Cahill's, didn't you?"

She had, and nodded to the wall she was still facing.

"Then trust me, there will be violence involved. Also, he swore to get to the bottom of his lover's death, and with his reputation, when he does it will not be nice and clean." Somewhere underneath all the dirty kitchenware had been a bowl with apples untouched by mold. Another crack sounded from behind her. "Apple?"

"No thank you," Rhea said mechanically. The old man apparently enjoyed teasing her with the overripe fruit. And she would get no answer from him about why Cat Ralchanh wanted her to help her son. Maybe his long silence had been to goad her into cleaning. She didn't mind, part of her still thinking she had to make up for the years of bossing servants about when she was just a child.

The kitchen door opened and Morwyn announced herself with a shout of surprise. "You didn't have to do all that," she exclaimed, embarrassment plain in her voice.

"I needed to pass the time," Rhea said.

"Father keeps me busy with errands. I'm sorry."

Finally, the pan was clean. Her turn around was accompanied with a sigh of relief, and the stretching of cramped muscles. She needed a massage. "Don't apologize," Rhea said, looking sternly at Coimharrin. The Upholder seemed utterly unconcerned with the situation.

A little while later, he looked up, his face devoid of any hint of shame. "What?"

"Nothing, father," Morwyn intervened, throwing her a look that quelled any sarcastic remark. And Rhea really felt like setting the old man straight. "Lord Cahill's returned," Morwyn added. The time as Coimharrin's daughter must have taught her well how to avert conflict due to her father's eccentricity.

It worked, Rhea noted, because this news meant she was able to speak to someone who was closer to Drangar Ralgon. Kildanor had spent far more time with Cat's son than anyone else, and maybe he would be able to shed some light on the spirit's request. Nerran, had he not been so drunk, would have laughed at her, saying that hope was usually misplaced if not downright silly. Coming from a man who had dedicated his life to restoring Lesganagh's faith in the aftermath of the Dawnslaughter, such a comment could safely be ignored.

# CHAPTER 27

Cherkont Street hadn't changed. Even under the cover of snow Drangar recognized the houses. He remembered who had occupied the buildings lining the street; whether his neighbors still lived he didn't know. Hiljarr surprised him. The stallion flicked his ears, whinnying softly. Obviously, the horse recalled as well.

Gwen gave a reassuring nod when he glanced her way. She was right. He had to take this last step if he wanted to make peace with the past, put Hesmera's death behind. The closer they got, the more nervous he grew. What if someone other than Jasseira lived there now? How could he explain to a stranger they occupied his property? It was his house; that much the city records had proven. What the files did not show was who was paying the taxes. Rob had provided the information weeks ago, but until now Drangar had stalled his return here.

Again, he looked at Gwen. In gloom of the night, with few guttering torches placed haphazardly along the street, she looked serene, an anchor of calm. How was it she was so blessed with insight at such a young age? He was reluctant to pry, afraid she might shun him, scorn him for meddling in things that were not his business. Not that he regretted telling her about Hesmera, or what troubled him. She had listened, passed no judgment. And she had encouraged him to return to where his torment had begun. She had fanned the spark that had lain dormant for so long.

Suddenly Hiljarr stopped. Drangar looked about and saw they had arrived. He would have passed the house if not for the horse, and he scolded himself for being so absorbed in his thoughts that it had taken the charger to remind him where he had lived. "Smart horse," Gwen commented with a smile. He hoped she didn't mind his silence. "Want me to come along?"

"I don't know," he admitted. Did he want her to join him? No, not want. He needed her with him. The thought felt both strange and right, and he wondered if it was really his heart that needed her, or if he was just this insecure. Someone had taken good care of the place, he noted. The roof sported new thatch, and even the shutters wore a fresh coat of paint. Her hand was on his arm, squeezing gently. He looked at her, and worried once more he might harm her as well. Ondalan had revealed what happened when he lost control. Even now he felt the Fiend lurking, laughing in the back of his mind. "I won't let harm come to you," he muttered, realizing too late that he had spoken out loud.

Gwen smiled, squeezing his arm once more. "Let's go. Time to cut down your fears."

The pole with its iron hoop he had planted into the ground was still there. When the horses' reins were secured, he knew he could no longer postpone the inevitable. For a brief moment, just before they came to a halt in front of the door, he felt the reassuring pressure of Gwen's hand come to rest on his forearm once more. Then, as he raised his left hand to sound the knocker, she let go. He knew he had to do this alone, face the last of his demons, and still the absence of her touch made him pause.

"Come on," she reminded him, her voice teasing yet stern. How was it possible that a woman so young possessed so much wisdom? Right now, it mattered little, but he decided to find out in the future, hoping things would resolve themselves once he got his answers from the Sons of Traksor. The surge of rage he felt the instant this thought crossed his mind halted his hand in mid-air. For a moment it felt as if the terror hidden in the back of his mind howled in triumph. Then, as he saw his fist clench and unclench before his eyes, he felt Gwen's touch. The fury receded.

Taking a deep breath, Drangar took hold of the brass ring and knocked. Her hand was gently squeezing, the contact made him feel more confident then when they had entered Cherkont Street. "Thank you," he said. She smiled.

He wanted to say more, felt there was more that needed be said, but the sound of a bolt sliding back checked his words. The door opened and he peered into the face of none other than Jasseira. Two years hadn't changed her much, although she looked tired, and her hair was cropped short. For a moment it seemed as if she didn't recognize him. He couldn't blame her, the past years had changed him, and with his hair in patches he doubted many of his old friends would be able to identify him. "What?" Jasseira asked. Then, he was just about to reintroduce himself, her eyes widened with surprise. "Drang?" she asked. Whether it was concern, joy or anger tainting her voice, he couldn't tell.

"Aye, Jass," he said.

She scrutinized him, most likely weighing the options of what she was to do. "Tell me one thing."

"It's a long and bloody complicated story." Gods, how many times would he have to retell this tale? "The short version is that I did not kill her."

"Why did you disappear?"

"Because I thought I had to."

"You swear on Jainagath's balls you did not?" she said, squinting at him. He didn't blame her for being suspicious. Everyone else had been, himself included.

"On Jainagath's balls."

Jass waited on the god's reaction. When nothing happened, she nodded, a flicker of relief flashed in her eyes, yet the rawness remained. "Those your horses?" In the dark one barely saw the steeds' outlines, only their snorting was audible. "Take them to the stable. You know the way." Jass closed the door once more but did not lock it.

It was the middle of the night when Drangar had finally explained the events surrounding Hesmera's death in every detail. Jass was more inquisitive than anyone else he had spoken to. Even Gwen, who knew most of it already, had, after an initial interest, nodded off, snoring fitfully in a chair near the fireplace.

Not much had changed, although Jass had merely given a brief tour, showing them into the common room quickly. Here nothing looked the same. There was a carpet on the dark wooden floor. The panels covering the wattle and daub had been replaced, and the patina of the floor showed much use, but also that the wood had been replaced. Jass had made the place her own. He didn't blame her, would have done the same had he been in her stead.

Jass looked thoughtful. She was nursing a mug of ale in one hand, her left; the sling around her sword arm reminded him of the battle that had happened here while he had been fighting like a blood mad demon. Until now he had done most of the talking, and was utterly sick of it. "I should write a scroll about it so I don't have to ever tell this tale again," he said, leaning back on his chair.

"Do you think many could read it?" Jass asked. "Not everyone has been reared in a monastery."

Drangar snorted. "Monastery, right! Bunch of murderous bastards, if you ask me."

"You need to find out why."

"Thanks for telling me the obvious." He hadn't mentioned the mindless rage that had taken hold of him in Ondalan; it had nothing to do with Hesmera's death. And he couldn't stand another pair of eyes viewing him as some monster that had been spat into the world to bring carnage.

"So, you'll head to Kalduuhn next?"

"In Thaw, going earlier would be suicide."

"Until then?"

He shrugged. "No idea. Practice, maybe train with some warriors. It's not really a plan at all, never considered what I'd do until the roads are clear again."

"Threatens to be a bitch of a winter," Jass said.

He remained silent, small talk had never been one of his strengths, and she knew that. Yet the crackling of the fire reminded him how little there was to say now that his tale had been told.

"Who's she?" Jass finally broke the quiet.

Gwen had shifted on the chair, the mane of hair covering

half her face. In the cave he had tried not to watch, not to stare while she slept. Now, he couldn't get enough sight of her. Peaceful, he found no other word. Not only her features, but also her pose. Did he have the same look when he slept? Somehow, he doubted it. "Chanastardhian noble, Gwennaith of House Keelan," he said.

"You love her?"

He scoffed. "What?"

"You keep looking at her. I've eyes, you know."

"I hardly know her." Had he really?

"She's good for you."

"What makes you say that?"

"Even with Hesmera you were restless, and with all the shit you've been through recently I would have thought you'd be even more so. Yet here you sit, calm, the first I've ever really seen you this way." When had Jass become so perceptive? Had she always been this way and he just hadn't noticed?

Drangar remained silent. Then, finally, he said, "I don't want her to be in danger."

"She's already in danger, idiot. What do you think will happen to her if her people take the city next year? She's a fugitive already." Jass cocked an eyebrow. "There's more you haven't been telling me isn't there?"

He hesitated, then nodded. "Aye."

"Wanna talk about it?"

He shook his head. "No, not really."

"As you…"

"Things are happening around me, with me, and I can't explain them," he interrupted her.

"What things?"

"Remember what we joked about back in the Watch?"

"You being blessed by Lesganagh?"

"Aye."

"Given how you went about fixing things that needed be fixed between people, I'd have said Lliania favored you."

Cursed sense of justice, he thought. "Well, you always made fun of me when Hesmera told another war story."

"No one believed what she said, not really."

"They were true, nonetheless." Now he had her attention. Jass sat up straight, regarding him. "I don't know who or what blessed me, though it feels more and more like a curse."

Then he told her about Ondalan, and the helplessness of being trapped in his own body, able to only watch as he tore through the enemy warriors. When he had finished, Jass remained silent, while Gwen stirred on her seat, saying, "We need to find out what the Scales is going on with you."

How long she had been listening? He hadn't realized she was awake until now. She already knew most of it, but not in its entirety. He felt her stand and move next to him, putting a hand on his shoulder. "We'll get through this," she said with such conviction that all worry and doubt momentarily vanished.

"Listen to her, Drang," Jass said, managing a weak smile. "Gods, I'm tired," she yawned a moment later. "I made the attic habitable, it's just a hole, really, but you can billet there." To Gwen she said, "There's an extra cot in my room, you can sleep there if you want to." She threw a meaningful glance at him, winking.

Gwen squeezed his shoulder. "Thank you, yes."

He didn't begrudge her the privacy; it was enough to know she was there. Some things in the house, Drangar noticed, hadn't changed at all. Jass barred the fireplace with an iron grille that prevented sparks from leaping onto the carpet, thus keeping the place warm throughout the night. They took the two lamps illuminating the room upstairs. The women held the lamps, lit his way into the attic and helped him arrange some blankets amidst wicker chests and baskets, and waited until he had lain down. Then they left him in darkness. There were a few muffled sentences spoken below, and then silence, and he tried to sleep.

*Sleep doesn't come to him, not in this place. It is dark again. The same oppressive absence of light he has been in before. Voices sing, but he can't make out the words. Screams. Is he dreaming, he wonders? A light appears in the distance, and he walks toward it. Does it come closer? Is he making any progress? He can't tell.*

*A figure peels itself out of the gloom, falls into step beside him.*

*He doesn't see its face. It speaks words he can't hear. Where is he?*

*This is unlike any nightmare he has ever had before.*

*His feet tread liquid. The light reflects starry into the dark, and still he can't see what the liquid is. Growls echo from walls unseen. Feral and baleful they surround him. Shafts of radiance break the void, but instead of being reflected by whatever he steps through, the liquid remains unseen.*

*Danger lurks close; he can feel it.*

*This time no sword leaps into his hand. There are no dancers, no music, and no monstrosity feasting on her body. No hands clutch at his legs; and still he fears this more than what has gone before. He tries to speak. No sound reaches his ears, not even the distorted bit of his voice usually going around one's head.*

*The light draws close. Or is it he who is closing in? Mechanically he puts one foot before the other, heading for the light. The growl becomes purr. It is meant to calm, yet panic surges up in him. Now, inside the radiance he sees flashes, mere fragments of what lies beyond. The web like fence of light seems more fragile now, more distinct. A face, if it can be called that, surges into sight and drops away.*

*A moment passes.*

*Memories rise.*

*He looks to his feet, naked in the flow of... blood.*

*He remembers. Helpless, so helpless, unable to intervene, unable to control his hands, arms, feet, only able to watch in horror as his body tears them apart.*

*Run! Obeying the command, he turns and flees. The web of light is only a step behind, inexorably closing in on him. Blood splashes up his legs, coating everything. Faces surge toward him. Hesmera, the Chanastardhians, the villagers, they all look worried, afraid. They fear him. He runs on, passes them, but they reappear to silently curse him.*

No!

Yes.

*He has only been a witness, and in her case not even that. His body is his, no one else's.*

*Laughter.*

*The faces are gone.*

*Frightened he looks back, stumbles, and splashes into the river of blood. Now he struggles to stay afloat, find safe footing to escape. This is not what he wants. He never wanted this... death.*

No!

Yes.

*An altar. A screaming woman. She swears revenge. Hair surrounds her head like a bloodstained halo, the petals of a flower, shredded and dipped in gore.* "No!" *she screams.*

*Again, the feral, lack-of-comfort purr. Yes.*

*And still he drowns. His mouth fills. He knows the taste. Gods, how sorry he is to know that taste. Splashed onto him from numerous battles, unnumbered victims.*

*A hand plunges down beside him. Claws wrap around his legs, tugging. The stranger's hand takes his, and pulls...*

Drangar woke with a start, a scream half-formed in his throat. Slowly the light that surrounded him registered in his mind. A dream, he told himself. Yet it felt as real as those about Hesmera. His old house's attic. Warm, despite the lack of blankets. And why was a light shining?

Out of the glare a face solidified. Gentle blue eyes looked down at him. Her hand stroked his cheek, while the other held one of his.

"Hush," Gwen said gently. She had cradled his head on her lap. "I'll protect you." Again, she caressed his cheek. "Sleep. Rest. I'll watch over you."

He wanted to tell her how much he appreciated her being here, but she silenced him with a gentle yet stern look and the shake of her head. "Sleep, I won't leave you."

Cradled in her lap Drangar felt safe for the first time in many days. He looked at Gwen, basking in her radiance. Then darkness, and sleep.

# CHAPTER 28

Dalgor couldn't look any more famished. No, Lloreanthoran decided, not famished. The sorcerer looked starved, almost indistinguishable from a corpse. And still the human kept running and fighting. He had used bloodmagic sparingly, but Dalgor's hands and arms were in tatters nonetheless. Both of them were sporting numerous bandages, and his clothes hung in ruin about them. How Dalgor stayed alive, the elf didn't know, didn't want to know. The fuel that powered the human's magic was life itself, a type of magic he had thought extinct when his ancestors had beaten the masters into exile. At the same time, after two days of desperately trying to harness magic the way he was used to, he began to realize—and dread—that the human's magic was the only chance they had in defeating these mountains.

The Kumeens were alive. There was no other term. Even when heading toward the rising sun, the ground warped, turned and twisted in a way he could not understand, altering their course ever so slightly yet steadily back to the forbidding cliffs. His magic had been of some use. He had killed two more monsters. Compared to the scores Dalgor had destroyed he felt like an acolyte.

"You have got to learn," the human panted as they huddled underneath a ledge, momentarily out of sight. No place in this area was outside the enemy's awareness. The mountain was their enemy. Dalgor uttered a frustrated growl, initially his arguments had been angry, but now his display of frustration was only mewling. "Listen, I am too weak to get anyone out of this place. I can teach you. If you don't use it, we both will die and not one soul will be the wiser. They'll all think the

Kumeens merely a cursed area, not the blood-sponge it really is." He paused, struggling for breath.

The human was right, but the utter rape of the natural order was a line he had always been unwilling to cross.

Dalgor must have sensed his struggle, for he said, "Listen, I do not kill others to work magic. Never have and never will. It shall be your will getting done what must be done, because if you don't, those bastards will get us, and, believe me, you don't want to be part of their menagerie!"

Failure, a word the elf had always dreaded, and if he were to deny this option, he would fail not only his people, but the entire world. If the monstrosities they had battled were just the vanguard, what kind of creature would they unleash next? And what if the fiend Danachamain would make his threat come true? He shuddered at the thought, no matter how vague the memories of his last few moments inside the Aerant C'lain truly were. With great reluctance he said, "Teach me."

There was very little Dalgor could tell him about the theory of bloodmagic, and Lloreanthoran felt the young Son of Traksor knew just as little. What he learned was both dangerous and frightening. Rage, it seemed, was one of the components, if used uncontrolled, however, that fury would consume the spellhurler. Spellhurler he called himself, not mage or wizard. A warrior whose weapons were both kinds of magic as well as the sword, but in the past two days he had not seen Dalgor use a blade in battle. The scabbard hung untouched at his side, the sword nothing but dead weight.

"Remember," Dalgor told him as he drew his own dagger and set the edge to his palm, "the land here drinks your blood. Don't ever let a drop of it touch the ground."

Lloreanthoran remembered the lifeless monstrosity, how its blood had been drained. "What then?"

For a moment he thought the Swordpriest had dozed off. Given the wounds he had inflicted on himself, the human truly needed rest, and he expected at any moment his companion would succumb to the call of sleep. Dalgor blinked, shook his head, and regarded him. "You force the world into the shape you desire," he said. "The type of magic you employ is based on memory, possibility; this type is brought into existence by sheer will." He paused as if he was gathering his waning senses, and then continued, "A drop suffices, mostly, sometimes you need more, but whatever you do, don't lose control over your emotions."

"Why?"

A broad gesture, encompassing the rugged terrain around them, a grim smile, then Dalgor said, "This place is an example of what will happen if you lose your grip. The land doesn't need blood to change its shape, yet more of it makes things even easier. Whoever worked magic here either did this on purpose, or lost all control. If your focus slips, or your emotions run amok, the magic will demand more and more and more until there's nothing left."

"So, there is no special need to cut myself?" he asked, reluctant to prick his skin.

"If you think you can control the amount of life force necessary to power spells without seeing how much blood they consume," Dalgor replied acidly, "no."

The problem to such an approach was evident. No being could gauge just how much of his life was still left, otherwise a battle crazed combatant withdrew before it was too late. He understood. "What kind of emotion is best?"

"Any kind of anger will do, but the best is that which is so deeply ingrained that one thought of it could make you lose your temper." The patter of feet on snow interrupted Dalgor. "Here they come again."

"You want me to…"

"No, fool, I want us to die, now get started!"

Whirling around, Lloreanthoran's first instinct was to draw once more on the possibility of events. The monster, a grotesque mix of goat, wolf, and eagle, came into view, its deformed head poking around the nearest bend. There was no time to concentrate. In this soiled land it had become more and more difficult to use magic his way, so he summoned the most enraging memory. Lilanthias, Aureenal, Bright-Eyes, each death senseless, hurtful. The edge of the dagger cut into his palm. A glance back at Dalgor, a last silent plea for support, showed the Son of

Traksor had fainted. He was on his own.

He looked at his palm, and saw the drop of blood forming. It wasn't much, yet he felt the soil beneath slavering, almost screaming for the red, life-giving liquid. The creature's eagle-wolf head echoed the silent howl. Lilanthias, the name echoed through his mind, the image of his daughter's last moments in this world, maimed beyond recognition, his hand wielding the blade that ended those few pain-filled moments.

Rage surged up in him. The drop of blood on his palm sang, and he felt a power unlike any he had ever wielded. This was not the same as the gathering of wizards who had built the bridge into the false realm beyond the Veil of Dreams. No, this was a snarling, growling, slavering beast ready to do his bidding, whether it was toppling a mountain or tearing apart the winged, horned perversion that now charged him. Its wings beat in an attempt to become airborne, the seven malformed feet pounded the greyish snow, while the eagle's beak, filled with razor-sharp teeth, stretched to its limit in an unearthly howl. Closer and closer the monster came. And the hurt and pain inside Lloreanthoran surged and soared ever to new heights. The drop of blood pulsed, almost burning his skin.

The curse that spewed from his lips was the embodiment of his anger, his frustration at losing everything he had held dear. He flicked his wrist, hurling the pulsing drop of life at this perversion, which, at this moment, stood for everything he loathed and regretted.

As the pulsing, hammering bead of blood sped toward the monstrosity, he felt at once drained yet filled with power. The blood loss didn't weaken him, yet it was enough for the nightmarish creature still hurtling for them.

It screeched, twisted for but an instant. It warped in on itself, its innards blossoming for the blink of an eye while the feathered fur was drawn inside. Then with a frightening absence of sound, the thing splattered about the cliffside only to vanish completely.

Lloreanthoran stared. Weeks ago, he would have thought such devastation impossible. Not even the oldest pebble ground to its size through millennia, from the tallest peak to its current state, could cause this kind of destruction. Behind him Dalgor stirred. How the human managed to chuckle was beyond him, but the cough that followed shortly afterwards was evidence enough that Dalgor's humor was only temporary and the situation just as dire as it had been. He turned and regarded the hacking man.

"What was that?" he asked.

"That, elf, was you pissed off, I'd say." The coughing was briefly interrupted by another gasping chuckle. "Pretty frightening, eh?"

He nodded, feeling slightly shamed by this man who had not even seen forty summers. He had wrought death before, certainly, but this feeling, the power he had summoned through his lifeblood was different. "Is it always this… strong?"

Dalgor shook his head. "No, the change wrought on the land amplifies it. Outside it's still powerful, but not like this." He coughed again. "Now, we need to get out of here. There'll be more of them coming." A scream reverberated from the mountains. "And soon. They really don't like trespassers." The trace of wry humor was unmistakable, and he wondered how Dalgor managed to summon this mirth.

"They?" Lloreanthoran asked.

"Did you think I came here just to enjoy the scenery?" the human scoffed. "I wanted my death to have meaning, but now staying alive is far more important. Don't ask. Still, the way you wield this magic gives me an idea."

Somehow, even with Dalgor as weak as he was, their roles had been reversed. The human, who would never grow as old and learned as he, had become the mentor, and he the student. He had forgotten what it felt like to be the learner, and now, in the shadow of this gods-forsaken mountain, he waited for a plan that would help them escape.

"Even with bloodmagic we can't teleport," Dalgor said.

"Then how shall we get out of here?" He saw the human's smile, and suddenly understood what he had in mind. The land, hills, cliffs, everything changed to prevent their escape. If going atop the snowy rocks did not work, and teleportation was prevented as well, the only alternative was to go through the soil. Dalgor must have watched him, for his coughing chuckle began anew.

"I see you can answer the question yourself."

Feeling less silly, he nodded. "Aye," he said. "A tunnel leading due east. We burn our path through stone and earth."

"Indeed. Think you can do it?"

He regarded the human. There was no mockery in his eyes, only concern. For what, he couldn't tell, but felt certain that it had something to do with what Dalgor had discovered in the depths of the Kumeens. Resisting the temptation to boldly declare he was capable, Lloreanthoran didn't answer. Instead, he pondered the task ahead. The Swordpriest wouldn't say how long he had gone without food, and though elves needed less nourishment, he knew that sooner rather than later they both would starve. Whatever decision he made, it had to be soon.

A straight line, a tunnel that could resist the changes the terrain wrought on itself to prevent their escape. It had to be similar to the passageway his people had used a century ago, a magical pipe, ignorant of the world around it. Alone, with only the magic he had known and used all his life, this would have been impossible. Now, with this new dangerous power at his command, he felt confident he could force reality to change according to his desire.

Dalgor shivered in his cloak. He hardly noticed the huddled form, absentmindedly blasted another two attacking beasts into oblivion, and then, finally, felt ready to create the tunnel. By now, Dalgor was so weak that he had to strap the human to his back, but the load was so light he moved with ease. Or maybe it was the cold, and his body welcomed the extra insulation provided by this other layer of flesh.

He didn't know how much blood it would take to create and maintain the magical pipe. Still, he reckoned it required more than the lone drop a prick of his dagger yielded. With Dalgor secure on his back, Lloreanthoran turned east, the dagger in his right hand. With reluctant strokes, he cut first one then a second line across his left palm. The cold had already dulled most sensation; he hardly felt the wounds. Blood welled up instantly, and as his stiff fingers barely obeyed, he cupped his hand, thus preventing even a single drop from falling to the ground. He summoned the magic; it was so strong that for a moment he feared it would rip his hand apart. The chant he and the other mages had used when creating the bridge rose from frost-torn lips. He whispered and hummed as best he could, yet the power merely wafted and pulsed. He was about to lose hope, the blood in his cupped hand congealing faster with every breath, when he heard Dalgor growl into his ear.

"Punch through it!"

The voice snapped him out of his daze; his reluctance had almost ruined their escape. From behind he heard the thudding of a many-hoofed creature. Now or never, he thought grimly, and punched, sent his mind's eye forward. Pulsing, snarling, flashing, the magical energies surged through the frozen soil, obliterating everything in their path. Aware of the approaching threat, he diverted a sliver of magic to tear through the monstrosity. Then, with the tunnel glowing in front, a steady, straight line unperturbed of the earth and stone that roiled about it, he hurried in.

They had barely passed the threshold, when from behind the mountains began to rumble. "Gods; hurry!" Dalgor urged, and trusting him, he sprinted forward. The roaring of stones behind grew louder. He almost felt pebbles striking the space where his feet had been just moments earlier. The mountain was trying to bury them! And still he ran.

Up ahead he saw how his spell faltered. A glance at his palm showed the clot. More blood, he thought, fumbling for his dagger. Blade in hand, he didn't pay attention to the cut, he just put the edge into his cupped hand and gave a quick jab. One brief glance to confirm the now freely flowing liquid did not spill onto the ground—he felt earth and stone closing in on them from all sides—then focused on the passage. The pipe drilled forward once more, and Lloreanthoran followed. Was there light at the end? He couldn't be sure, couldn't tell if it was his magic or real daylight.

"Close the passage behind us!" Dalgor hissed.

He grunted, angry with himself for being so stupid. His anger surged into the un-clotted liquid in his cupped hand, lashed out behind him, and sealed the pipe. An idea blossomed in his panicked mind. Up! Out of the foothills, into the air, away from the mass of treacherous soil! Ahead of him, he saw the magical tunnel change. The pipe curved up ever so slightly.

Running, he had to keep running.

Again, the blood clotted in his hand, and again he had to slash the dagger across his palm to bring the red liquid forth. The tunnel wavered briefly, then steadied again as he summoned the magic and forced it into shape. He wondered, how far they had come. For a while now the human had lain limply against his back, silent. Lloreanthoran wanted to ask Dalgor how to alter magic once cast but was reluctant to wake him, if he were still alive. If the Son of Traksor wasn't... He dared not consider the thought.

Despite his brash behavior, he liked Dalgor. There was a fierce determination about the man, a mind so focused on his goal that nothing seemed able to stop him. The pipe had arched away from the land, but with the shimmering walls surrounding them he was unable to tell where exactly they were. He smiled wryly, feeling foolish. He was no learner, had used magic centuries before any of the humans alive had had their grandparents soil the world. Why did he need Dalgor's advice? If he couldn't figure out how to alter the magic, it probably wasn't worth considering anyway.

There was still some blood left on his throbbing palm. Soon he would have to cut again, but now, with the power that remained, he shifted part of his focus away from maintaining the tunnel, used a fraction of the energy pulsing in his hand to alter the spot he was standing on. He stopped, mind lost in concentration. What had Dalgor said? One forced the magic to do one's bidding, and force it he did.

The floor, if it could be called that, wavered, thinned until it glimmered opaquely. He willed it to become translucent, glasslike. The milky yellow surface swirled, eddied, until it lost all color, and finally he was able to peer through onto the ground below. It seemed not so distant, and, doubting his eyes, he told the magic to display things as they truly were. Trees, looking like tufts of grass, dotted the land. How far up were they? There! That speck, not more than a flea in size, was a deer. Or was it one of the abominations that had hunted them these past days? Nothing normal was alive in the Kumeen foothills. The smear closed in on some shrub, just another spot of dirt really, and was joined by another, smaller flea. None of them displayed the sort of instinctive violence he had observed with the bloodbeast. It had to be a deer.

"Down," he whispered. The pipe obeyed.

Too late he remembered he had used the last drop of blood to get a clear view of what lay beneath him. Now, with the tunnel losing all coherence, the slight angle he had wanted to achieve turned into a yawning abyss. The pull of the ground demanded its long due toll, and they plunged. Lloreanthoran struggled with his knife's hilt; his cloak tangled his arms, his sight blurred by the biting, rushing wind. He had to prick his skin, draw more blood to slow their fall.

His hand closed on the weapon, when the weight on his back shifted. The roar of air rushing past them had woken the human. Dalgor snarled, spat curses; he felt the Son's arms wriggle in their bonds. Then he heard his companion's ragged breathing in his ear.

"The gods know I have nothing more to give," the human wheezed. "Forget the blade, elf. Bite your lip, your tongue, I don't care what, draw blood now and use it or we won't draw anything else ever again!"

He was about to hammer his teeth into his tongue, when he realized they were free of the blood-drinking lands of the Kumeen Mountains. Here, magic worked the way he was used to, the kind of magic he had utilized for centuries. It was difficult to switch from one way of casting spells to the other; and, as the ground filled his horizon, he briefly wondered if biting his tongue wasn't really easier. He felt the draw of this most ancient source of power, could imagine, albeit briefly, how the slavers of old must have felt. The blood beckoned still, the call of magic so wild and ferocious.

Then he thought of the creatures this same magic had warped into being, and the glory of it all dissipated like the distance that lay between them and the ground. No! He would not use this magic unless he had to, and now, maybe an eye blink away from the ground, he summoned forth the possibility of a storm cushioning their fall.

It wasn't the same surge of power, it couldn't have been, but it was so very familiar, and comforting, like an old, well-worn pair of shoes. They touched ground roughly. Dalgor, still panicking, struggled to free himself of the bonds, while Lloreanthoran stumbled, banged his knees on the frozen earth, slid a few feet and finally came to a stop with his face mashed against a boulder.

It was, as he had guessed, a place outside the Kumeen's influence, and thankfully winter's sadness wasn't the only thing in the air anymore.

# CHAPTER 29

## Sixth of Cold, 1475 K.C.

Drangar woke with a stiff neck. In fact, most of his body felt like he had slept on uneven ground. He sat up, groaning. For a moment he knew not where he was, and then, with someone else hissing curses behind him, it all came back. Dunthiochagh, his house, the nightmare, Gwen watching him through the night. He remembered her illuminated face. She must have brought a lantern, and he began groping about in the dark. Once or twice he touched her, where he dared not ponder, but her pained groans stopped. His head had been on her lap, and she had sat behind him. Had she slept that way also?

He found the lamp, its metal cool to the touch. No light there, he thought glumly. Trying to spark the flame back to life here in the attic was an arsonist's dream come true, so he dismissed the idea of rekindling the flame. Would they have to wait on Jass to leave this place? Gwen now complained noisily about her own stupidity, and he was glad the dark hid his smile. This woman could swear with the best of the worst, he thought, once again glad she had come last night.

The creaking of hinges, and a slight beam of light lancing into the attic interrupted his musings. "Are you two decent?" Jasseira asked.

"What the fuck do you think we did?" Gwen growled. "Ouch! Bloody baskets! What do you keep in here anyway? Cursed thing poked me in the back all night!" Drangar now saw the awkward position she must have slept in. Sometime during the night, she must have shifted a pair of wicker baskets off their perch, and instead of waking she had slept amidst a jumble of old pans and pots. He snorted.

Gwen's glare was the exact opposite of the benign face he had grown to… like. "What's so godsdamned funny, huh?"

He opened his mouth to reply, but Gwen snarled on, "Don't laugh, if it hadn't been for you thrashing and screaming and me coming here to see if I could help, I wouldn't be in this position! Now get me out of here!" He did as she asked, and when their noses touched, she said, "You owe me a massage, Ralgon!" Now it was Jess's turn to snort. "What?" Gwen turned on her, wincing. "Damn!"

"Nothing," Jass said. He saw she was struggling to hide her laughter. "Get out of there, I'll clear this later."

They scrambled down the ladder, Gwen wincing and complaining with every single step. Judging from the mess she had bedded herself on, it must have been a very painful night, and he felt bad that she had found it necessary to come and look after him. "I'm sorry," he said as he touched ground once more.

"What for?" Gwen asked, her face a twisted mask of agony. "Not your fault you have bad dreams." Grimacing, she tiptoed and, to his utter surprise, kissed his cheek. "Better? Good. Now I hope for your sake and mine you know how to get all those kinks out of my body."

He must have stood there, dumbfounded, for a while, because suddenly both women laughed, although Gwen's mirth was cut short by another pained groan. He smiled awkwardly.

"You can use my bed for the massage," Jass said. "I'll heat water and stuff." Then she headed down the stairs to the kitchen, adding, "Only for massages, understood?"

"Of course," he said loud and firmly.

Gwen winced as she tried to lift her right arm above her head. "As if I could do anything else," she said, grimacing.

Never before, or so Drangar thought, had he touched a woman's skin so gently, tenderly, and at this first instant when his hands glided across Gwen's bare back, he felt content, at peace. Was there also a trace of lust? He didn't think so, and as he traced her spine, fingers applying only the minutest of pressure, he marveled at the paleness of her skin. She lay still, arms above her head, her tunic on the floor. He stared at her, smiling.

"Don't ogle, massage, oaf," she teased, her nose crinkled as she turned her head to look at him.

"I'm sorry," he stuttered. Why did he feel so calm around her? With Hesmera it had always been passionate, a fierce lustful struggle. He couldn't remember if he had ever massaged her back. Thankfully he had been to bathing houses before, and knew what he was supposed to do, although it took time to discover the cramped muscles, force them to relax.

Gwen never complained as he tried to guess his way along, and once he had felt his way about and developed a rhythm with his hands, she half moaned half sighed in pleasure. That she had stayed still surprised him. On the road, in the cave, they had always been surrounded by others whose presence had kept them physically apart, and had she not come to him he doubted he would have ever approached, much less talked to her. Some muscle, hardened by her less than comfortable choice of bed, refused to budge when he slid his palms across. Drangar hesitated, afraid he might hurt her. She looked so fragile. Even after hearing how she had killed her countrymen, he thought her tender.

She opened her eyes and caught his, peering across her shoulder. "I'm not made of paper, just get it over with."

"As you wish, milady," he replied.

She chuckled, and then uttered something between a howl and a groan, as he kneaded her flesh. "Yes!" she hissed.

There was a knock on the door. "You two done?" Jass asked loudly, her voice muffled by the door.

Drangar felt like a child caught with his hand in a sweet-cake-jar. He stood, stumbled across something Jass, never a tidy person, had left lying on the floor, saying, "Almost."

"Good, there's someone here to talk to you."

"Oh," he said, and looked back at Gwen who was just rising off the bed. He averted his face when he caught her glare.

"No peeking," she admonished sweetly. Seeing her smile like this would have made him blush even had he not already been drawn to her. She giggled; heat rushed into his face. He whirled around, tore open the door, and hurried out, Gwen's laughter ringing after him. And to his ears, this expression of humor was gilded with affection.

The door slammed shut behind him and he looked into Jass's astonished face. The warrior-woman was already half-way down the stairs, her body now opposite the bedroom. She cocked an eyebrow, regarded him for several heartbeats, and then shook her head and walked the rest of the way. "You're in love, Drang," she stated matter-of-factly as she passed into the kitchen.

Was he? It felt different than what he'd had with Hesmera. Affection, yes, very much so, he cared for Gwen. Just thinking her name made him beam like a madman. Her smile, he would fight the world to see her smile. Had he felt something similar when he had courted Hesmera? He didn't know, and it didn't matter. Gwen and Hesmera were as different as two people could be, although they shared the swearing and cursing habit.

Still feeling flustered, he entered the common room, and almost wished he hadn't done so when he saw who was waiting for him. Not that he disliked Kildanor, but the Chosen had seen the Fiend unleashed in Ondalan. Still, the memory of the destruction, the way he had killed the Chanastardhians, shoved all the pleasant thoughts of Gwen right out of his mind. It also reminded him of the nightmare. Why did he always remember what those horrible dreams were about? He was just glad none of them involved her.

The woman accompanying the Chosen he had met once before. What was her name? Rheanna, yes. She had returned his sword. The Upholder looked at him, and the same strange expression he had seen once before spread on her face again. She had already hinted at some familiarity, but he couldn't remember ever meeting her before.

"Good morning," Drangar grumbled. No, he wasn't angry, just concerned the Chosen would once again talk about demons. Right now, he wanted no part of that.

Kildanor moved to say something, but Upholder Rheanna spoke first. "Does the name Ralchanh mean anything to you?"

Had he not been wide-awake before, the mentioning of his

mother's family name would have woken him instantly. His surprise must have shown, for the priestess of Lliania gave a triumphant nod to the Chosen. "What of it?" he asked.

"Do you remember your mother?"

"She got pregnant with me and died in childbed."

"Do you know anything about her?" the Upholder prodded.

"She got pregnant with a bastard son and died, what else is there to know?" Drangar snarled. "What is this? A trial for not using my birthmother's name? Didn't know it was a crime."

"Mate, we're here to help," Kildanor said calmly.

"Help me with what? Not letting me find peace?" He heard Gwen descending, and felt his emotions warring within. Anger and affection—he dared not call it love—struggled. The latter won when she touched his side. He couldn't help but smile. Why did she have this effect on him? "Very well," he relented. "What is it about my birthmother?" Just having Gwen standing by his side was enough.

"Your mother was Caitrin Ralchanh, daughter to Amhlaidh Ralchanh, Justiciar to the Royal Court of Haldain."

"Great, so what?" This revelation meant nothing.

"You said you traveled into the past, led by a ghost who showed you what really happened that day two and a half years ago in this very house." He had the glum feeling that the little peace he had just found was about to be rent asunder. "I'm no artist, and my memory of your mother is vague, at best, she was older than me, and we traveled in different circles," the Upholder continued. She retrieved a parchment from her shirt, unfolded it and held it up to him. "Did your spirit guide look anything like this?"

Drangar felt himself staring at the picture. His knees buckled and he slumped to the floor, his eyes still on the crude drawing in the Upholder's hand. The portrait depicted a young woman, her face untouched by the ravages of time and still it bore the same features as the spirit he had seen. He had suspected then, by the way the woman had spoken, her gentle familiarity, her reproachful advice, that she could have been his mother, but until now he had not been sure.

"You have her eyes," Gwen remarked from behind him.

Her hand now rested on his shoulder. Stunned he looked up at her, oddly aware of how close her face was. She still smelled of the herbs and soaps from the bath, flowers with some mint. Their eyes met and for the briefest of moments he forgot they weren't alone. All that mattered was she. The Upholder cleared her throat and broke the spell, and they turned away from each other. Drangar caught a little blush creeping into Gwen's face, and was aware his face was reddening as well.

"This is my mother?" he said, trying to downplay the moment of intimacy.

"As I remember her, aye," the priestess replied.

"How old was she?" Gwen asked. He still felt her hand on his shoulder, her scent surrounding him.

Upholder Rheanna stared into the distance for a few heartbeats then said, "She was nineteen when I last saw her."

"It matters not," Drangar muttered. "She's dead now."

"And that, mate, is where you err," Kildanor interrupted. His voice sounded friendly, but he detected the steel underneath the joviality.

"She is dead, isn't she?" Jass asked. She had put a tray filled with mugs on the table and now leaned against the wall.

He nodded. "Aye, why else would she appear as a spirit and show me what really happened in the past?"

"But," Upholder Rheanna added, "things aren't as simple as that. Her soul should have gone to the Bailey Majestic, unless she decided to remain." He understood, and saw the flaw in his own thinking. "Left behind souls are stationary, bound to the place they died. Where were you born?"

"Kalduuhn."

"So why did she come to you here?" Gwen voiced the question roiling in his mind. It truly made no sense.

"More importantly; why did we find a mummified dog in your cell, when the same animal had been seen alive a mere day before?" Kildanor added. He had almost forgotten Dog, and the advising voice that had repeatedly told him not to forget. "Not to mention that the Wizardess saw a woman overlaid by a snarling dog screaming at something she couldn't see," the Chosen went on.

Drangar stiffened. "What? She never told me."

"Because all of us forgot," Kildanor said. "There was so much going on at the time with the pinnacle of strangeness of you having returned to life that we simply forgot. We had the war to worry about, so the entire affair with her seeing a dog overlaying a woman in the spiritworld was lost amidst everything else." The Chosen shook his head, "I should have connected the dots then, but in a way, I wanted to believe you were a sign that Lesganagh was on our side."

"Are you saying his mother was a dog?" Jass asked, a trace of hysteria ringing in her voice. Gwen snorted.

"No," Rheanna said. "His mother's spirit, Cat's spirit—her nickname was Cat—had somehow managed to manifest or root itself in the animal."

"Why didn't Dog... she... my mother tell me?" Drangar asked, feeling silly the moment the words left his mouth.

"Would you have believed her?" Kildanor said.

No, he realized, he wouldn't have, but remained silent. All of this became stranger by the breath, his mother guiding him into the past, watching over him as his sheepdog. The nightmares, Hesmera's death, the blood raging fiend in his mind, how did this all make sense?

His confusion must have shown, for Kildanor said, "I promised you we would get to the bottom of this, and I stand by my word. When you leave for Kalduuhn I ride with you."

"I never made a promise to you, Ralchanh," the Upholder said formally.

"Ralgon," he corrected, sounding much weaker than when he usually corrected anyone who used his old name.

"Ralchanh," Rheanna insisted. "As I said, I never made a promise to you, but your mother's spirit asked me to help you, and so I will."

He stared at her, stunned. What the Scales was she talking about? Dog was dead, his mother's spirit gone. Why else would the animal have died? And why, if his mother's soul still walked the world, did she talk to some Upholder? "What is your connection to her that she would task you with this?"

"She was part of the household I was born into."

It was Gwen who grasped the significance of Rheanna's words, for she drew a deep breath and whistled softly. He had never much bothered with priesthoods and all that, so he looked up quizzically, first at Gwen and then at Rheanna. "She's of royal blood," Gwen explained. "A Justiciar is assigned to a royal court."

Drangar shrugged. "Long way from home, princess," he muttered, receiving a stinging slap from the woman at his side. In a way he knew he deserved this, knew he was reverting to the sullen man he had been for more than two years, but he couldn't help it. All these revelations, added to the fiendish threat inside his mind, were too much. He shrugged, said "Sorry" and stood. He turned away from this assembly, and not even Gwen's scent reached his mind or heart. He felt an emptiness growing within, darker and more desperate than anything he had ever felt before, heard the Fiend's triumphant call and cared not. Spirits, demons, breaking a magical cage that had almost killed him once more, tearing apart human beings with his bare hands, he wanted nothing of that. A bottomless pit seemed to open beneath him and he felt himself falling, falling. It didn't matter. Nothing mattered…

Except that a soft but strong hand somehow reached through the blackness, grasped him before he could pull away, tugged him back. "Stay," Gwen said. "Don't run, please."

"And why shouldn't I?" he asked, not suppressing the frustration he felt. "It seems as if I have not a bit of control over my life. Spirits, ghosts, magic—Scales!—even being brought back from the dead, I never asked for any of this. I never wanted any of this." Drangar felt himself sink to his knees. "How can I keep my oath if those behind her death are already dead as well?"

"The Sons of Traksor?" Kildanor asked.

He looked at the Chosen, furiously wiping the tears from his eyes. "No, the bastards who did this to me! The bastards who made me kill her."

"Do you think they put this fiend in you?" Kildanor regarded him steadily, frowning.

He thought briefly then shook his head. "No, the rage was there before I ever set foot in Dunthiochagh. The sword, remember?" Gwen's hands rested on his shoulders now.

"As long as you haven't gotten to the bottom of this, Ralchanh," Upholder Rheanna said, "the attacks will eventually continue. No soul will be safe with you, but there is more to it; otherwise, why would your mother ask me to protect you? I will not deny a dead woman's wish, so when you go to Kalduuhn I will accompany you."

"So will I," Gwen said, squeezing his shoulders.

"Drangar, if you want to find peace you must go to the Eye of Traksor and ask all those uncomfortable questions. You must find out why you are who you are," the Chosen said, pouring a mug of tea. "Drink."

He took the mug and sipped. Someone kissed his cheek. Gwen. Her scent was unmistakable. "We'll get through this."

He hoped she was right.

Why were things so difficult? Yes, he had dreamed of being a hero, a shining warrior to rescue kings and queens. He had been young then, and still a ward of the Sons of Traksor. A bastard as it turned out later. They had put those thoughts into his mind, told him what honor meant. And then they had spat in his face, and he had run.

He wanted to run now; the instinct was strong, so strong. All he hoped for was that it would end once the truth was out, once Darlontor, Dalgor and all the others had confessed their crimes and had been made to pay. What if things had gone differently? What if Darlontor had never cursed him? What if he had grown up still thinking himself the Priest High's son? Would his life have been different? Would he still be haunted by nightmares, taunted by demons, feel so helpless?

What did it matter that he now knew his mother's name and her ancestry? Nothing had changed. Nothing at all. All he wanted was peace, to live a life as far removed from all the wars and conflicts that had dominated his existence for so long. That, if nothing else, was the one true thing he had told Kerral back at his hut. The joy he had once known when fighting was gone, dead like so many other things he had once held dear. And he wasn't even sure this was a good thing. Sometimes the only thing that brought justice was a decisive stroke of a sword. As strange as this thought was, Drangar felt a kernel of truth in it. After all, when he had passed judgment on the bastard Eanaighist Danaissan, he had done more good in the big picture of Dunthiochagh's defense.

Maybe knowing his grandda had been one of Lliania's Justiciars wasn't such a bad thing. Maybe he had inherited his own sense of justice from a long dead man. Was that his road, to walk the path of the Lawgiver? He chuckled. Only the gods knew that answer. And besides, how could he pass judgment when he had committed so many crimes himself. He refused to take the easy way out, would not argue that the slaughter of an entire village had been a just thing. That angle hadn't worked in Ondalan; the Chanastardhians had not tortured their prisoners, and tearing through them had not been a just act. It was what it was. Nothing more, nothing less, and he had to atone for it, even if it hadn't been his mind that guided the savagery. At the very least he would drive out that monster lurking in his mind.

Drangar stared at the flames dancing in the fireplace. He was sitting in the room in which he had killed Hesmera. No, he reminded himself forcefully. This was the room in which Hesmera had been killed, by his hand, certainly, but not by him. The difference was all. He had not killed her, never could have killed her. His feet moved as if to shift straw away from the flames, a habit he had acquired years ago, drawing rushes away from the fire. Here, in this house, he realized when his boots only made a muffled scrape on the carpet, the fireplace was bricked heavily; a span of stones prevented most sparks from ever reaching the floor.

Gwen entered. He already could tell it was she by the way she walked. She stopped by the table and waited. Most likely, she was regarding him. Why she was attracted to him he could only guess; the tufts of hair surely made him look more like an abused paintbrush than a human being. He closed his eyes and tried to ease the tension in his neck.

"You need to stop worrying," she said. Was he that obvious, that predictable? "You brood over every godsdamned detail. Sometimes there is no ulterior motive, you know?" She crossed the few feet that separated them and put her hands on his shoulders. "Sometimes things just are."

He half turned, the first syllable of his reply ready to roll off his lips, but she shushed him into silence. "I like you, understood? There doesn't have to be a reason for everything." Her hand caressed his scalp. "Besides, it does grow back, not that it matters. Some men, you know, are so concerned with their grooming you can see them searching for a mirror wherever they are. But they never look themselves in the eye; if they did, they'd realize they're empty inside." Her red tresses surrounded her face like a halo. "With you, well, let's just say you'll never have to worry about people thinking you shallow." She tweaked his nose, stuck out her tongue, and walked away.

He smiled, then snorted, then laughed. Gods, it felt good to laugh. The nightmares certainly would not go away, but Gwen was there to calm him. Not everything he had seen in Ondalan was bad. He turned, and saw her looking at him. Again, she stuck her tongue out, saying, "Don't worry, we'll get to the bottom of this. You are not alone."

# CHAPTER 30

A century of negligence had changed the Elven Road through Gathran. Not many had dared following the straight paved lines that bisected the forest from east to west and south to north. At its center lay Honas Graigh, and humans, being the superstitious lot that they were, believed dead elves haunted the place still. Some stretches of road were still clear of shrubs and ferns and moss, but they were rare, becoming fewer each year.

Lightbringer walked through such a space right now, and wondered how the elves would act once when they had returned and reassumed command of their capital. She hoped the issue could be controlled without their endless deliberations; the humans had adopted this most irritating trait, bickering and politics had halted what should have been a simple procedure. Had the fools acted when they'd had the chance, things would not have been as bad. Instead of driving home their advantage, the idiots had sat back and enjoyed their success, swearing oaths and promising each other to be ever watchful. Why had none of them ever pursued the foe and finished them off? She had given them the tools, and the advice to use them guardedly. She had also told them to strike without mercy, without regret. And the simpletons had let their pride get the better of them. With their leader dead, they had not carried on the war. They had watched and done nothing. Where their endless elaborating and politicking had brought stability to one region, it had condemned another to ruin.

Now she had to intervene, again, and longed for the day when sentience would not vanish after power and ambition had beckoned. The human prince had understood, and had left his family and title behind to do what had to be done. One visionary was never enough, though, and he was usually dead before he could see his dream vanish in the mists of ambition and greed. Maybe this was what the elders had meant. Maybe she could teach herself how to use magic differently. Maybe...

She punctured her skin, drawing a drop of blood. Gods, how could elves and humans change when the one who had taught them, who aided them, had never truly changed at all? She was the addict who preached abstinence, the ultimate hypocrite. Yes, if she were to fight and defeat the forces her brother was gathering, she would have to abandon the old ways. Completely.

Blood, so pure and powerful, its tang hitting her nose even though there was only one drop on her hand. Her reaction came instinctively, leeching her will even before she realized what she was doing. "No!" she hissed through clenched fangs, resisting the urge to abuse only because she could. Nature battled thought, reason, and she recalled the multitude of lives she had taken to feed her magic. Until this moment Lightbringer had never counted, never considered how many souls she had sacrificed to bludgeon magic to her will. Millennia of death, rivers, no, oceans of blood, whole cities worth of people drained of every last drop of this purest, most powerful liquid in the world.

Old habits reaffirmed themselves even as she sought the faces of at least some of her victims. The drop in her hand became two, three, four, a tiny rivulet. How could she battle instinct, her nature, for so many years? Nearby patches of snow melted, so strong was the draw of her subconscious. If she relented now, it would kill her, and all her work would come undone.

No!

There was still too much to be done. Her work was never truly finished. Unless...

The elves had banished her kind with her help. She had given them magic, but it had been her power, her disregard for life that had sealed the gap, barred the door, and it had been blood that had barred it twice after that. Only blood could kill them, but its magic didn't have to be wasted, smashed into shape by blunt determination. Wasn't that what she had taught the human prince?

So many were dead because she was afraid to change. Then, as if struck by lightning, Lightbringer recalled a face, her last victim, lured like all the others by her call. The girl's frightened eyes had been wide; terror amplified the old magic, the more of it the better. Even now she felt her fear of failure mounting. No! She refused to fail, refused to submit to the instincts edged into her being when the world was young and elves were like cattle.

No! She was Lightbringer, Firebringer; she had shaped this world almost as much as had the gods. She would not fail!

Gritting her fangs, she pushed, shoved, and fought the part of her that sat, like a petulant child, on the old knowledge. And the more she struggled, the more faces she remembered. First by pairs, and then dozens, and then scores, male and female, young and old, terror etched into bloodless faces, staring accusingly at her until the flames enveloped them. Magic she had wrought for the betterment of others, at the cost of others. No! Never again! The rivulet of blood, now nothing more than a trickle, then a single drop, pulsed in her hand, demanded more just as her instincts raged for more. But more was not needed, had never been needed. She had passed this knowledge on to the human prince, but like all advice had never heeded it herself.

In her hand she held more than enough power, for now. It sufficed to warm her, dress her more appropriately, and draw forth from the slush roots she could eat. The knowledge was there, had always been there, but her subconscious had refused to admit it. Even now, when her mind registered that she could work magic without copious amounts of blood, the part of her that still was steeped in forgotten-thought and hated tradition rebelled, wanting ever more. Just a hare, or an owl, it would have been so simple. No!

Now that she knew she could, she refused to allow instinct to wrest control from her. She neither knew nor cared if the ancestors approved. A patch of sun shown in the cloudy sky, its light lanced down to touch her. She made the circle with her thumbs and index fingers, and for the first time in ages said, "I hail thee, Lesganagh, father." Whether the Lord of Sun and War heard she didn't know; she was no priestess. What she did feel, though, was her spirit calming. Was that what she should have done from the start? She chuckled, raised her face to the glowing orb and basked in its newfound glory. He had made the world, but not without help, and she knew that neither could she fight alone the threat from beyond the Veil of Shadow.

# CHAPTER 31

## Seventh of Cold, 1475 K.C.

So far, the Baron Duasonh had proven to be a good host. Anne and her people were quartered in one of the barracks, and although guards accompanied them on the rare occasions they did go out, they had no reason to complain. Even Paddy and Dubhan were happy. The food was decent—there even had been some mead—and the building was heated. Despite this, Anne wondered why Duasonh had not yet spoken to her. Her recent inquiries had all yielded the same answer: the Baron was busy.

She sat on a windowsill. The glass panes were iced from without and within, offering no good view of the outer bailey. Not that it mattered; this place was much like home where, even in deepest winter, warriors trained. She heard the wardens shout at freshly levied troops, barking orders as if their own lives depended on it. Which, she guessed, they did, given that this was only a respite until the new year, when Mireynh's forces would lay a real siege to the city.

Here near the outside, a biting chill emanated from the brickwork, the air was much colder, and she enjoyed it. Back home life, even in summer, had never been cuddly, and though she liked a hot bath as much as the next person, the heat spreading from the iron ovens on each side of the barracks was too much for her. She missed the mountains, her mountains, and worried how her father was faring, wondering still why he had broken with Herascor, and if Chirnath valley was crowded with Royal troops.

She realized she had been staring at the frosted glass; the

moisture from her breath crystallized as yet another layer of ice. "Bugger that move." "You touch it, you move it!" She glanced over her left shoulder. Dubhan and Paddy were playing Chiath. Like every other table—just how many tables did they allow the troops in the barracks anyway?—it had been shifted to the walls; beds now formed a mound in the building's center. Warmth at night was good, but no one in House Cirrain would be caught dead sitting comfortably and warmly by a fire for longer than it took to eat a meal. They were all so used to the chill that some—she noted Natheira and Connar arm wrestling by another window, dressed only in their shirts—wore their coats only when it became very cold. "What doesn't chill you, makes you stronger" was a saying coined by one of her ancestors. It had stuck, and every generation kept inventing new madness to prove they were hardier.

The far door banged open, and she felt the cold wind against her legs and face. In any civilized place people would have started complaining the moment the breeze hit the room, shouting, "Close the door!" Dubhan and Paddy shouted, "Leave the damn thing open!" Then Paddy added, "Guess you should roll your legs down, cousin."

A guard stood on the threshold, waiting. Unlike her folk, this man wore a heavy woolen cloak, and tried to inch closer to the far oven without actually intruding. "Lord Baron Duasonh will see the Lady Cirrain now," the man said, and then scowled, obviously wondering if he should close the door. He shut it, anxiously looked around as if expecting them to complain, when nothing happened, he relaxed visibly. "Lady Cirrain?" he asked, probably expecting her to be dressed according to rank.

She jumped off the sill and rolled down her trouser legs. "I heard you," Anne said, wondering if Cumaill Duasonh expected her to wear any specific wardrobe. If so, he was bound to be disappointed. She slipped into her boots, buckled her sword belt, and threw a white traveling cloak on her shoulders. The cloak was standard in winter, allowing for an extra layer of stealth in snowy terrain. Every man- or woman-at-arms in House Cirrain owned one, and though they had left most unnecessary things behind, these garments were as much a part of their marching gear as weapons, shield, and armor. It kept enough of the cold at bay, but the warrior, who now had reached the oven, would probably complain about the chill within moments. Not that the Danastaerians were weak, but they were not used to the biting cold of her home.

The look the man gave her when she approached was one of confusion mixed with surprise. They left the barracks and once they reached the inner bailey, he pulled his cloak tighter and asked, "Aren't you cold, Lady?"

She shook her head. She had felt worse.

Unlike other royal houses, Dunthiochagh's Palace bore little resemblance to an abode of kings; she had noted that much upon arrival. It was a fortress, most likely had never been anything but a fortress. None of them had been allowed to walk the ramparts, but if the gatehouses were indicator of the thickness, the stone that had gone into building and patching the walls could have built a small town. The keep, which she had until now only seen looming across the inner curtain wall, was as much patchwork as the palisades surrounding it. Bits and pieces had been added over numerous years, but it retained much of its original shape. It looked decidedly plain, had nothing of Harail's charm, and promised as much subtlety as a mailed fist pounding into one's face.

Anne liked it. It reminded her of home, and the feeling grew when she entered. Of course it was chaos, organized and disciplined, but chaos nonetheless. Even the servants had scabbarded knives at their belts. She saw few children which she found only fitting. The retainers' families were probably lodged in the added buildings, or dwelled within the city. A pair of warriors, Swords mostly, seemed to guarded every door and passageway, but there were also some Pikes. They passed several corridors, and on more than one occasion she saw Wardens inspecting their charges, making them stand at attention, and barking orders when necessary.

Soon she lost track of where they were heading. Obviously, her guide was not leading her to any reception hall. The lack of pomp reinforced her impression that Baron Duasonh had no patience for courtly affairs. "What's your name?"

The man-at-arms glanced back at her but remained silent. His reaction was nothing new, for although they were treated with the necessary courtesy, the Baron's warriors barely hid their resentment. She and her people were, after all, Chanastardhians, and still viewed as the enemy, even though they had deserted and were the Baron's guests. She couldn't begrudge them their reservations, would've acted the same had roles been reversed.

They stopped in front of a nondescript door, guarded as all the others, but in this corridor the sentinels were more alert. "Wait," the warrior told her, nodded to his comrades, and walked off.

For the first few moments the sentinels' unease was palpable. She answered their scrutiny with calm. These types were familiar. They bore scars, none too recent though, and their hardened features softened a little when she gave them a lopsided grin. "Rough day, eh?"

"Boring more like," the taller of the two said.

"I know how that feels," she said, leaning against the wall opposite the door.

The two shared a glance then the other said, "What do you know of guard duty?" She regarded him; his temples were touched by grey but the rest of his hair still showed a rich chestnut brown. Unlike her people, these southerners preferred to shave their beards. Beards hid scars; the guard's shaved chin displayed his proudly. "Well?" he asked, apparently in a better mood than the one who had brought her here.

"Done my share of standing and waiting," she said.

"Right," the taller fellow said. His chin bare but unscarred. He scratched his thinning hair. "Like you high-ups do that sort of thing."

Was he goading her? The past weeks had worn her pride down, but now her temper rose. It took her a moment to rein her anger in, and then she said, "How many battles have you been in?"

Grey-temples chuckled, and slapped his comrade's shoulder. "Come on, tell her."

Baldy frowned. "Well, how many have you fought?" he

asked instead, an obvious attempt to save face. Anne had seen it all before, men who struggled to maintain their bluster. She decided to not offend him.

"Not many." Then pride got the better of her and she added, "In the last year anyway."

"Oh," Baldy said, crestfallen, while the other guffawed.

She was about to add to her statement, when the door opened and the Chosen, Kildanor, poked his head out. "Ah, Lady Cirrain, come in."

Giving the two a warrior's salute, she entered, wondering whom else she would meet inside. Once over the threshold she paused, surprised at the smallness of the room. Somehow, given the size of the Palace, she had expected more than this little study. It wasn't much bigger than her own chamber back home, and the shelves and massive table gave the room a more intimate feeling than the Royal study Mireynh had occupied in Harail. Her gaze wandered from the stuffed bookracks across a map of Danastaer to the impressive desk behind which sat a man in well-worn tunic. He looked at her and in his eyes she saw a fierce will not unlike her father's. She bowed. "My Lord Baron."

A nod, and then Cumaill Duasonh returned to the parchment spread before him.

She waited. Kildanor shifted uncomfortably, then walked past her and settled on one of the chairs at their side of the desk. Duasonh looked up briefly, regarded the Chosen, and then continued to read. Anne considered taking a seat as well, but remained standing. Her warrior's upbringing, determination and pride dictated that she impress the Baron. A yawn escaped the Chosen's lips, causing Duasonh to once again raise his head and scowl in irritation.

Only the crackling of fire in the hearth, and the occasional rustle of paper disturbed the silence. And still she remained standing, wondering when her host would deem it time to talk to her.

Finally, Duasonh spoke. "Who is the High Advisor?" He raised his head and regarded her. "Well?"

"I don't know." She had never heard the title officially,

though there had been rumors of a man in whom Drammoch confided more than anyone. She said so.

"Could he be the reason your father seceded?"

"I don't know," she answered truthfully. Until Jesgar Garinad had revealed House Cirrain's warband had been put under guard, none of them had known of the events back home. "I haven't heard from home since our departure."

"What do you know of crystals?"

She regarded the Baron, surprised. "Other than that, they are shiny rocks dug from the earth? Not..." She hesitated; remembering a story her grandda had told her when she was young.

"There is more, I take it?" Duasonh asked. Somehow the master of Dunthiochagh had managed to draw all her attention; she barely noticed Kildanor had also turned to look at her.

"Yes, no, I don't know, Lord Baron."

"Well, girl, spill it."

"Nothing but a fiery tale, really."

"Most fiery tales have a kernel of truth," Kildanor said, "believe me."

She regarded the Chosen, blinking. "Well, it is a tale of the dwarves, nothing but superstition, really, for no one has ever met a dwarf."

"Not entirely true," Duasonh said.

"Well, the northmen claim they speak to them and work with them, but they are a bunch of liars and bandits."

"If they are such, why then has your father allied your House with them?" the Baron asked.

Her da fought with the highlanders against Herascor? "That can't be true," she blurted out, upon which Duasonh held out one of the parchments he had been studying.

"This is a translation of a coded message we intercepted. Go ahead, read it."

Anne took the paper and what she read stunned her. "This can't be true," she stuttered. "We kept the barbarians at bay for generations. There's so much bad blood between us, we would never come to terms."

"Why then encode the message?" Duasonh regarded her.

"Why then put you under guard?"

She had pondered the same thing for a while now, and would never have considered the possibility of an alliance between House Cirrain and the northmen. "I don't know."

"What about this fiery tale?" the Chosen asked. The worry in his eyes was obvious. "What about crystals?"

"It has been a long time," she replied. "It was said that the smiths, the warriors of stone came to aid the gods in the old days, and that the enemy they fought burned their crops."

"Stones have crops?" Duasonh and Kildanor exclaimed.

"Aye," she said, looking from one to the other. "But not like we know them, not wheat, oat, barley. No, the dwarves grow their food from the rocks that are their shelter, and the oldest enemy destroyed it."

"They eat crystals?" Duasonh sounded incredulous.

"That's what the fiery tales say. If you ask me a bunch of nonsense." The Chosen cleared his throat and the Baron grimaced. "You're joking, right? You can't be serious."

"Well, a whole lot of refugees saw one. And he—it—told them that they are killing the crystals."

"Who is they?" she asked.

"Why did the highlanders fight you?" the Baron said.

"They raid our lands and mines whenever we..." She fell silent, wondering if the barbarians' claims were also true.

"Whenever you what?" Duasonh insisted

"Whenever we dug too deep, milord," Anne said, realizing her voice had risen in pitch. "They say we have no right; that we intrude on sacred lands."

"What else do you know of the northmen?" Kildanor asked.

"Nothing more than rumors and what a few prisoners revealed. They claim to be allies of the dwarves."

"Thank you," Duasonh said, holding out his hand until she returned the parchment. "That'll be all."

"What about us? Are we prisoners?" she asked.

"Aren't we all? It's winter and we are all trapped, but you are free to travel home if you want to try."

"So, what shall we do?"

The Baron opened his mouth to reply, when Kildanor rose

and stepped to his side. Whispered words were passed back and forth, and finally the Baron said, "You know the customs of Herascor, do you not?"

"A little, milord."

"And you know how to dance, right?"

Where were these questions going? "Aye."

"Are you also familiar with the goings-on at the Royal Court?"

"Somewhat."

"Good, then I have a favor to ask you in return for my hospitality," Duasonh said.

# CHAPTER 32

## Fifteenth of Cold, 1475 K.C.

The last thing Ealisaid recalled with all its painful clarity was plummeting down and hitting a shingled roof. Everything else was a haze of agony, dulled but not relieved by colorful dreams in which knives and needles and blood red arms had entered her body. She opened her eyes, expecting to find herself in the Bailey Majestic before Lliania's Scales surrounded by hundreds of other souls awaiting or dreading judgment.

The light was dim, not what she had thought it would be. The goddess's priests always said the light of truth shone into everyone's heart before they were admitted to the Scales, but if the light of truth was this gloomy, what good was it?

"She's waking," someone said.

Waking in the Bailey Majestic seemed wrong. No one woke there, one just stepped off Jainagath's Chariot. No, she decided, this was not the afterlife. A shape blocked out the vestiges of illumination and it took her a moment to realize it was a man. Or woman? She wasn't sure.

"Praise Eanaigh," the shape said.

Ealisaid blinked, tried to focus on the speaker. Slowly the shadow coalesced into a person. Judging by the symbol that hung about the man's neck, he was a Caretaker, a healer. She tried to speak, but no word escaped her lips. Her throat was parched, aching, and the only sound she brought forth was a croak. Someone else held cold metal to her lips. She drank, greedily, not tasting the liquid, only partly aware that it was bittersweet. The ache in her throat lessened. Her eyes grew heavy. The light dimmed even further.

The next time she woke the gloom had been replaced by slightly brighter light. Somewhere outside her vision two people spoke. One, a man, said, "Don't go starting with this being another miracle." His voice seemed familiar, but when she tried to remember whose it was, the room began to spin.

"What else could it be?" the other man asked.

A derisive snort. "Why then do we have so many dead?"

"The goddess wanted her to live."

"Bullshit! Think, man! You attended her for an entire day; the others had their hands full with scores of wounded and dying. If you want a miracle, fine, then consider your focus on her at the exclusion of everyone else the miracle." A short pause followed. Then the man—somewhere in the blur of her mind a name drifted to the surface—said, "You did good here, Braigh, and certainly with Eanaigh's blessings, but it's still your work that saved her."

"Yes, yes, whatever. Oh, she's awake."

"About bloody time, too, I need her to poke around some-one's head."

An exasperated exhale. "What? Kildanor you can't be serious! She is in no condition to do anything. The wounds are still mending. Any strenuous activity would kill her. You know that, so why the Scales do you propose such a thing? She almost died here!" The last was whispered in a false pretense of confidentiality.

"I can hear you," she said. Her voice sounded raw, unused, and not like hers at all. Ealisaid wanted to say more, but the pain in her throat returned, not as strong as before, though it spread into her chest. She whimpered.

"Drink, Lady Wizard," Caretaker Braigh said. Or was he High Priest now? She couldn't remember. A cool-rimmed mug was put to her lips, and her mouth filled with the same taste as before. Again the light dimmed, and before she drifted off into darkness, she wondered how they kept her fed.

The pain in her throat and chest had gone. Breathing was easier now, although she hazily recalled it had been quite painful. Light, the room she lay in was bright, glaring. She opened her eyes, blinked to clear her vision, and beheld a small chapel. Corn motifs adorned the walls; this chamber was dedicated to Eanaigh. Better than a cell, she mused; the thought made her smile, but only briefly. Her muscles moved sluggishly and felt leathery, as if her face was glued into place.

"Don't move too much, it's still healing," a woman said from somewhere in the room.

"What happened?" Ealisaid asked. This time, her voice sounded a little better. Shingles, she recalled them closing in on her, and crossbow bolts speeding toward her before that, piercing her while she cleared the wall of the enemy.

"You're lucky to be alive," the woman said. "High Priest Braigh was able to save you." She sensed a slight pause, as if the speaker wanted to say more but stopped herself.

"But?" She tried to move her head toward the speaker, already dreading what she might say. A fraction of an inch was all she managed before being restrained.

"Don't, not everything is yet healed." The speaker stepped into view, dimming the light. It was another Caretaker, which made sense considering where she was.

"You said I was lucky to be alive. What's wrong?"

"Don't excite yourself, you must stay calm," urged the priestess. "Please."

As if she could remain calm without knowing what had happened. Her first anxious impulse was to sit up and glare at the Caretaker. Restraints and the pain surging through her body stopped her. "What the Scales is wrong with me?" she growled, fighting against her rising dizziness.

"You mustn't excite yourself!"

"The more you tell me to calm down and the less you tell me about my condition," she spat at the Caretaker, "the more upset I will become, and trust me, you don't want to piss me off. Understood?"

Now, as the Caretaker nodded fearfully, she saw her companion was barely of age, a novice of Eanaigh, nothing more, and she regretted losing her temper. The pain in her chest and neck reinforced that regret. She wanted to apologize, but the girl spoke first. "You fell; scraped down the shingles, face first. High Priest Braigh was able to restore your body, but not your appearance, I'm afraid."

Had the pain not been threatening to drag her back into darkness, Ealisaid would have despaired. Now, with the agony coursing through her body like molten lead, she realized her need to look good was as immature as her old belief that the Phoenix Wizards would last forever. So, she would not find a companion who would be drawn to her attractive face. It didn't matter. "What's your name?" she asked.

"Mella." The novice still looked concerned, came closer and inspected something beyond Ealisaid's line of sight. Her young face had grown graver when she came back into view. Immediately she left her field of vision, heading away. A bell rang. A moment later footsteps approached.

"What is it?" Ealisaid asked, worried her outburst had worsened her condition.

Mella didn't reply. Instead the girl addressed whoever had arrived. "Send for the High Priest!" she ordered. Then the footsteps hurried off. Again, Mella came into view, concern plain on her young face. "I'm just a learner, and the High Priest tended your injuries. He knows what to do."

"Is it bad?" she asked, worried that her own temper had reopened her wounds.

"I... I'm not sure."

The girl's hesitation did not sound promising, and even though the pain felt no different, she reined in her emotions. There was nothing to do anyway, so she waited.

The High Priest's arrival roused her from the half-dazed slumber. She opened her eyes, saw him inspecting her, and feared the frown on his face meant her condition had worsened. Before she could ask, Braigh spoke. Had she met him before? Ealisaid did not remember. "You were lucky."

"I don't feel lucky," she replied.

He launched into an explanation she barely understood,

and somewhere in the middle she realized this was how non-Wizards must feel whenever she told them about magic. There was a puncture somewhere, and ophain had been poured into her veins, for she had been unable to swallow. She had slept for two weeks; they had worried she'd never wake again. It was a—Braigh visibly refrained from using the word "miracle"—marvel she had survived at all. Her wounds had been numerous, and just how they had managed to sew her shut had surely been under the auspicious blessing of Eanaigh herself. Why the goddess had wanted her to live was something Ealisaid pondered while the High Priest spoke. She had brought death to so many, and wouldn't have begrudged the Lady of Health and Fertility had she deemed her unworthy of living. Yet here she was, listening to the babble of a priest who was obviously overwhelmed by her recovery. Briefly she remembered Drangar Ralgon who had returned from the dead. Was he the reason that Braigh refused to speak of a miracle? What had the Caretaker just said? She dragged her mind back to the chapel and asked.

"I said that you will walk with a limp, and that the break in your shoulder has healed, but you will never again have the full range of motion with that arm," Braigh replied.

"Which arm?"

"You landed on the right side. Collarbones, shoulder joint, most of the bones in that section were shattered. I had to open you to set them."

Thankfully she was already lying; otherwise Ealisaid would have slumped back in shock. "How much have I lost?" she asked. Then added, "Of my motion, of course."

"That remains to be seen, I suggest you stay in bed another week or so before we check your capabilities."

"A week? What about the Chanastardhians?"

"They've retreated for now; winter has come at last and they lost the taste for the escalade."

"I heard you speak to the Chosen."

"Ah, yes, that would have been earlier this morning."

"What did he want from me?"

"I honestly don't know, milady. Things are still rather busy, and my new duties keep me occupied." He didn't look as sad as he sounded. Weary, certainly, but High Priest Braigh seemed to be at peace with himself.

She looked at Mella. "Can you send for the Chosen?" The acolyte waited until her superior approved then hurried out.

"You must not put too much strain on yourself. It will slow the healing."

The pain in her neck prevented her from nodding. "I understand, but if the Chosen needs my help it has to be important."

Braigh gave her a wry grin. "I guess you are right." After having observed her from a distance, he now stooped closer, gently poking and prodding. It hurt, which, he explained, was a sign that the body was healing. When he touched her shoulder, she whimpered. He nodded sagely. "You'll be short of breath, maybe forever. I don't rightly know. It was the first time I ever operated on a lung." His monologue was interrupted by a knock on the door. "Enter," he said.

In came a woman clad in a heavy, oversized winter cloak. Ealisaid made out few features. Her face looked as if black paint was running down, forming an uneven mask of rivulets. The smell that accompanied the arrival was a mixture of wet wool and fire. "This is as thin as I can make it, your grace," the woman said, producing a wooden box from beneath the folds of her cloak. "If you want them any thinner, I suggest you try a glassblower, though I don't know if one could manage."

Braigh took the container and pried open the lid. His face lit up when he looked at the contents. "This work is worthy of the Garinad name," he exclaimed, smiling broadly. Then his face saddened. "Again, I want to express my regret at your husband's death."

The smith shrugged. "People die in war; there is nothing to feel sorry about. It happened." Was she related to the Baron's spy? "How will you get liquid through it? I tried, but more spilled than went the way it was supposed." Then Braigh must have looked at her skeptically, for she added, "I had to see if it worked, didn't I? Wouldn't want this just to be a fancy looking wire. My husband's good name would be smeared if I didn't deliver the promised item."

"I have some ideas," the High Priest replied. "You can make more of these, if needed?"

"Certainly."

"I'll send the money as soon as I return to the temple. Eanaigh's blessings with you."

"And with you." The reply seemed more of a reflex than an honest courtesy, at least to her ears, but when Braigh's face came into view again, she saw the priest hadn't noticed. He was far too excited about the hollow needle in his hand.

"This," he proclaimed proudly, "will make things so much easier." He then launched into a passionate explanation, of which she again understood very little, and finished by saying, "Cases like yours can be treated now without poking massive holes into one's veins to administer the ophain. Maybe the elves knew of this, but like most of their knowledge, they took it with them."

She wondered if the elves had bothered with this type of healing, and recalled something she had picked up once from one of the old Wizards. "Elves," he had said with a rheumy voice, "are curious buggers. They value life, but only until they tire of it and find something new to play with." The quote had stuck. Thankfully the pain in her face prevented a smile at the Eanaighist. In all likelihood no elf would have come to help her, as broken as she was.

The door opened. "You wanted to see me?" the newcomer asked. She recognized the Chosen, though she barely saw him.

"Aye, well, actually it was the Lady Ealisaid. She's awake now, but I doubt she is in any shape to help you."

"She can talk?"

"Yes," Ealisaid answered, sparing herself a new rush of the healer's speech, into which the High Priest would have otherwise launched. The pain in her throat and jaw forced her to add, "Although it is difficult."

"Great," Kildanor said. "Braigh, may I speak to her in private?" Since the priest had his back to her, she couldn't see the Eanaighist's reaction. The Chosen however, had, and added, "I will call you should something divine or miraculous happen, all right? Good! Now go." He gripped Braigh by the shoulders and steered him out. When the door was firmly locked, he muttered, "Little bugger worries I'll desecrate his precious chapel." He chuckled. "Idiot."

"He did heal me," she interjected.

"Aye, that he did." He stepped into view, and she saw he had changed since the last time they had met. His cheeks seemed narrower, he had grown a beard, and the dark smudges beneath his eyes told of long nights and little sleep. "Cumaill demanded that you be fixed. A whole bunch of others died while he poked knives and needles into you."

"Spare me the details," she said.

He regarded her.

"So, what do you want me to do?"

"Things have come up, really strange things and I need to know what they mean."

She tried to squint at him but abandoned the effort because of the pain. "You're aware of my condition, are you not?" Now she saw how worried the Chosen looked. The last time he had looked like this was in the aftermath of the events at Cahill Manor. "There's been another magical attack on Ralgon?" she guessed.

"In a way."

She wondered if she still had brows she could raise in mock surprise, not that the pain allowed it. "You want the help of a bedridden woman and the best you can come up with is 'in a way'? Boatload of help that is."

"It's complicated."

Instead of laughing, she coughed. "Isn't it always?"

The Chosen's tale of what had happened in Ondalan sounded very much like the fiery tales she had heard as a child. Of outside forces trying to gain control over an innocent to further their needs. Kildanor relayed to her how he had slipped into spiritform to observe what was happening, and that he had seen Ralgon's struggle against these demons. "He has good days and bad, and his nights are plagued by dreams filled with demons chasing him. Sometimes the girl's presence helps; sometimes even she can barely calm him."

Ealisaid felt drowsy, and only the past vision's horror they had shared when entering the spiritworld in what seemed ages ago kept her awake. She also remembered the overlapping images of Ralgon's dog and the woman, and wondered if they were all connected. "So, what do you want me to do? Dig into his mind?"

"Aye, maybe you can figure out what is going on inside of him. Gwen told me that every day is a struggle. He tries not to let his temper flare, is afraid that 'the Fiend,' as he calls it, will surge forward and take over again."

"He defeated it in Ondalan, didn't he?"

"He did."

"So, what prevents him from doing it again?"

"I think his mind is so buggered up, with no real foe to fight he is simply lost."

"And you think that if we know what is going on it will help him? I might be able to tell if this Fiend is truly a different entity, but even if that is so, it won't help him much."

Kildanor sighed, nodded, and said, "Aye, and with us being snowed in, we can't head south until Thaw."

"Why south?"

"Because," he explained, "that is where the bastard who cast the spells in Cahill Manor came from. He hopes to get answers and his revenge there."

"Revenge?"

"Justice maybe, not that it matters right now. He had enough unpleasant memories of his dead lover; now he has seen his hands tear apart enemies."

"I thought you were speaking figuratively!"

"No, quite literally, in two deaths his sword wasn't used. He just tore through the poor bastards."

"He must feel terrible."

"Only when he isn't knitting," Kildanor said, a smile playing around his lips.

"Knitting?"

"Scarves mainly, or one long scarf. He made everyone nervous sharpening his weapons all the time. Looked like a madman sitting there all grim and calm, whetstone in one hand, blade in the other. It was meant as a joke, but the lass, Gwen, had taken a liking to him and actually showed him how to knit. I'm told he barely sharpens his weapons anymore, but knits stitch after stitch. Next, they'll teach him how to sew, I reckon."

"Thaw is... what?"

"Two months from now. The time to travel safely that is."

"Well, I hope my wounds have healed by then."

"You can't do it now?" the Chosen asked.

Again, her laugh turned into a cough. "I need to be calm, and with half my bones broken and all of my body in pain you really think I can be calm? Sure, I could drink some ophain, but that would make me too calm." She stifled a yawn, afraid it would tear the scars in her face. "Speaking of which, I'm tired. But I wouldn't mind talking with you sometime later."

He gave her a brief, understanding nod, and then left. She was grateful that he didn't mention the way her face looked; sooner or later she would have to gaze into a mirror, but until then the illusion that she was merely ill was a good one. The moment the door fell shut behind Kildanor, it opened again. "You must be exhausted," Mella said. "The High Priest has other business to attend to, but he asked me to give you your medicines." A cup was lifted to her lips. "Here, drink." She swallowed the bitter liquid, and moments later her eyes fluttered shut.

# CHAPTER 33

"You can't go," Cumaill insisted. "The Chanastardhians will return come spring, and I need you here to fight."

They had danced this dance several times now, and Kildanor was more determined than ever to accompany Drangar when he left. He still didn't know what the shared vision of demons manipulating the mercenary meant, but was certain it wasn't a good portent. He didn't need Ealisaid's help to know what he had seen, and even if the rent bodies could have been explained in another way, the blood hissing into vapor to heal Ralgon only reinforced the notion that demons had somehow gained a foothold in the man's mind. Worst of all, the struggles were still going on. Both Gwennaith Keelan and the guardswoman Jasseira had confirmed Ralgon's reoccurring, sweat-soaked nightmares and his single-minded pursuit of retaining his calm. He hadn't seen the man in days, but the women were deeply troubled. Aside from supporting Drangar, the trip south might help him shed light on why his brothers had become slaves to the demons. Maybe he would even get the chance to complete the Chosen once again. "I have to," he finally told Duasonh.

"Bullshit! What good will you do for him?"

He had no ready answer. How could one explain instinct? He knew in his gut that going to Kalduuhn was the right thing, didn't even bother to contact the other Chosen at Dragoncrest. Should he remind Cumaill that his gut feeling had revealed Jathain as a traitor? If he hadn't hired Jesgar Garinad in the first place, Dunthiochagh would surely have been in Chanastardhian hands by now. He looked at Duasonh and for the first time saw there was uncertainty in the Baron's eyes. This, he realized, had nothing to do with his leaving as much as Cumaill needing someone to share the burden with. "I'm not your wife, mate," he said. "So why don't you just tell me what the Scales you really want from me."

"I don't need a new wife! It's just that..."

"What? Kerral giving you trouble?" The rogue general had proven himself remarkably well, a disciplined warlord, even if he was pigheaded on occasion.

"No," the Baron replied sullenly.

Kildanor sighed. He had feared that this moment would come. Cumaill was tired, had pushed himself far too hard over the past weeks. This whining was his weariness talking. By now the damage done by enemy slingthrowers had been repaired to the point where the houses were habitable once more; the dead had been burned. Scales, even the publicans and innkeepers had finally accepted the billeting of Kerral's warriors, and still Cumaill kept pushing himself. He had assumed control without any emissaries to rely on, had basically dismissed Kildanor from his duties, and with Braigh busy with church matters and Nerran still looking for solace at the bottom of a mug, there was no one to shoulder part of the burden.

"Don't worry," he said soothingly. "I'll see what can be done."

Duasonh was too tired to answer. He left the Baron slumped in his chair, and went to search any of the surviving Riders. With luck, one of them would know where their leader was drinking himself senseless. That Nerran had fallen so far still confused him. Sure, the Riders had suffered casualties, but it wasn't the first time the group had lost more than half their number. He couldn't fathom what had driven the jovial, determined Paladin to hide in a bottle.

He found Fynbar in a heated argument with one of the stable hands. "No, these boxes are reserved for us, and even if we lack the numbers right now, this is our space, the Riders' space, so get those horses out of here," said Fynbar.

"The General Kerral ordered them stabled here, and until the Baron countermands this..."

"He gave this place to us," the Rider interrupted. At times

Kildanor wondered whether the other Eanaighist priests should take the Caretaker-Riders as an example. "So, get those animals out of here now!" Fynbar's hand wandered to his sword's hilt, and the readiness for violence convinced Kildanor such an example was not that wise. He intervened.

"Sunsword!" Fynbar exclaimed when he approached. "Great! Talk some sense into this man, please."

"No, I talk some sense into you, Caretaker." He stressed the title.

"What?" stuttered Fynbar. The stable hand gave a sigh of relief.

"How many horses do you have right now?" Kildanor asked.

"Fifteen, but…"

"No buts! How many Riders?" This was Nerran's job, and he had come to find him, not haggle with one of the Paladin's followers.

"A dozen."

"Good, so you don't need all that space anyway, do you?"

"No," Fynbar agreed. "But…"

"Again a 'but,'" Kildanor interrupted. "I don't like the word when it's used to question my authority. Do you understand or shall I express myself more simply?"

"No, sir."

"Good. Now, is there any chance you will have more Riders in the foreseeable future?"

"I don't know, sir." The fighting had beaten the youthful spirit out of Fynbar, and now it showed. He looked as weary as anyone who had fought on the walls. Kildanor understood he was merely trying to maintain some semblance of order, to keep the illusion of brotherhood that surrounded the Riders. With Nerran in his cups and Upholder Rheanna busy with other things, Fynbar was the one attempting to keep up the morale of his crew. He understood the importance of what the young man was trying to achieve, it was commendable, but the heart of the matter was that horses needed to be stabled. With some of the places on the other side of the Dunth in ruins, Horse and Lance needed to shelter their steeds, and this was as good a place as any. Maybe Fynbar saw the validity of the argument, maybe he didn't. It hardly mattered. The Riders' pride would suffer no great blow by relinquishing their stables; Nerran's drunkenness was an entirely different issue.

"The horses stay," Kildanor decided. Then he pulled the Rider to the side. "A word," he said. When he thought they were out of earshot, he spoke anew. "Listen, son, I understand what you are doing, and why you're doing it. The thing of it is that you aren't a senior Rider; barely blooded, that's what you are. Where's Briog?"

"I don't know," Fynbar answered. "Most of them stabled their horses and then went off."

"I saw some of them here yesterday."

"Oh, they do return, but the spirit's gone." Kildanor wasn't sure the young man meant general morale, or Nerran.

"So, you had casualties; it's war."

"That's what we kept telling Nerran, but when he saw Gail's corpse, he lost it." His face must have shown his unvoiced question, and Fynbar added, "They were lovers. She was pregnant."

"Oh, fuck me!" Now he understood the Paladin's grief. Nerran had lost his family during the Dawnslaughter three decades ago, the night when Eanaigh's priesthood in Danastaer had hunted and killed every priest or follower of Lesganagh they could safely lay hands on. Nerran had barely come of age and had witnessed his parents' death. None had known that he and Caretaker Gail had been lovers. It surely explained the priestess's easygoing nature, and the ferocity of Nerran's reaction. "Why did she fight?" he asked.

"She refused to be excluded, said she was a Rider and had her duty to us."

"And the others?"

"They're fed up with everything right now, too many dead, Nerran's spirit is broken." Fynbar's voice trailed off.

"Where is he?"

"Some dive. No idea."

"You gather the others, who was Nerran's second?"

The young Rider gave a sad laugh. "Gail."

"And who else, of those still alive?"

"Rhea."

"Good, I fetch the Princess, and you gather the rest, and then get Nerran, understood?"

"Whatever for?"

"Has Gail received a proper burial?"

"No."

"Then we start from there," the Chosen said, and turned around, calling for Dawntreader.

Recently he had heard Lliania's Court was now called Coimharrin's Court, but Kildanor doubted the old Upholder enjoyed his new celebrity. The new, unofficial name did nothing to improve the temple's appearance. While the lingering snow-covered thatched roofs with a coat of white, and poured off the shingled ones on occasion, the prevailing unkemptness of Coimharrin's Court seeped into the snow as well. It looked grey, and he would have bet money that the priest would claim it fitting, since justice was neither black nor white, only was.

He found Rhea passing judgments in the temple's only chamber of note. Coimharrin was nowhere to be seen, which suited him fine. Even from a distance she looked impressive, regal, and the ruling she was passing as he entered was as cold and impartial as any he had ever seen. Cumaill wouldn't like it, he was certain of that. The Baron hadn't liked what Ralgon had done to Danaissan, saying it was unwise to alienate the Eanaighists, and what Rheanna did was just as painful as nails driven through a man's knees.

"Rigall of Camlanh, for the rape and murder of two women you are sentenced to death by gelding. The execution will take place on Old Bridge, today," she said.

Someone near him whispered, "I still can't believe he is being punished at all."

"Wouldn't have happened back home, aye, but then again, our Lawspeaker receives sacks of money to turn a blind eye on some things," another replied.

"Think it's true what they say? That his son is pleading with the Baron right now?" a woman added.

"Heard Lord Duasonh is a decent man, won't let a bastard

like Rigall off the hook, even if it means he'll lose the support of someone as wealthy as him."

Kildanor was certain Cumaill wouldn't pardon the crime, but since his friend was swamped with work there was little risk of him hearing of the case. Money, he regretfully admitted, motivated many people to go against their beliefs, and with so many more mouths to feed, and warriors rightfully demanding their pay, who could blame any ruler for turning a blind eye? The terrible howl rising from the front showed that at least one person was not tempted by money. Rhea was an Upholder to his liking.

She must have seen him, for she adjourned, and approached when the throng of people had left. "Come to see Coimharrin?" she asked. "Caught a cold last week, and is still in bed."

"No, I came to speak with you."

"Then speak." To the four guardsmen dragging away a screaming and protesting Rigall of Camlanh, she said, "Proceed now, no point in waiting. Let it be a warning to others."

"The Riders need you," he began.

"The Riders need someone who looks after them, even in battle. I failed."

"Nerran is drunk most of the time, and the others are spread all across town. You did what was necessary, and no one blames you."

"No, but whenever they look at me, I'm reminded of the deaths I caused."

"You did what was necessary, and that isn't pretty most of the time. Your actions helped us keep the wall."

"How do you know what my orders did?" she snapped. "You weren't there. And the Chanastardhians retook that portion fast enough afterwards."

"Did you know of Gail's pregnancy?"

She shook her head. "Only Nerran knew."

"So why do you hide from your responsibility?"

"I don't..." she trailed off. "My work here..."

"So, you think doing Coimharrin's job will make up for a correct decision that you deem a mistake? Bullshit!"

"I got people under my command killed!"

"You don't want people to die in war? Don't go to war then."
He knew how she felt, had felt the same when his brothers had
deserted the Chosen, and though he cared little about their
betrayal now, he understood what Rhea was going through.
"Listen, you did well. Your actions saved the city. If you hadn't
led the Riders into that shield wall, the enemy would have taken
the south."

"But…"

"All of you know the danger of riding into a shield wall,
right?" She nodded. "And still they followed you." Again, a nod.
Survivor's guilt, he thought. There was nothing he could do
about that. Only time would heal this wound. Rhea had buried
herself in someone else's work and tried to work through the
pain in her own way, he realized that. He also knew Nerran and
she had to honor Gail and the other dead with a proper funeral.
The bodies had already been burned, but they still could show
their respect.

"We will meet at the cemetery east of here, and you will
come," he told her. In a way he was reluctant to visit the place
again, the Deathmask there had taken his anger at Ethain's and
Ganaedor's betrayal. From what Jesgar had told him about the
older Garinad's funeral, or at least the time the spy had spent
alone in front of the fireplace, he had been able to leave his
grief behind. It would help the surviving Riders, of that he was
certain.

"When?" Rhea asked.

"Now, the others are being gathered."

"What about Nerran?"

Of all of them, the Paladin needed to attend the most. "He'll
be there, even if I have to drag him by the ears." That made
her smile, and reminded him of the carefree girl he had met
years and years ago. Not much of the young Princess was left
now, and if he lived, he would see her grow old and attend her
funeral. How old was she, he wondered, did the math and was
once more reminded of all the people he had known who were
already so many ashes. In a few decades she would join those
who had gone to the Bailey Majestic before her.

"Have you heard of Ralgon?"

He was grateful for the change in topic, and told her what he knew. "At least he is reining this Fiend in," he finished the small report.

"He's no priest, so what good does all this meditation do a warrior? He needs to fight this, not contemplate it."

"You mean he should not wallow in self-pity?" Kildanor asked, forcing his mischievous smirk off his face. Thankfully, Rhea was looking the other way, inspecting the metal Scales dominating the hall.

"Aye, dwelling on things past rarely helps one living in the pre…" she trailed off, turned, and glared at him. "You bastard!" The insult was accompanied by a chuckle. "Guess I needed that."

"Sometimes we all need a kick in the head," Kildanor admitted. "Now, let's look for Nerran and kick him too."

They found the Paladin in the Tankard. By now the surviving Riders had been rounded up and accompanied them. With not much to do, many off-duty warriors were flocking to the tap-rooms. Most of them drank peacefully, but on more than one occasion in the past two weeks the Watch had been called to break up serious brawls. The Tankard, courtesy of its proximity to the western slums, was one of the worse dives, and Kildanor expected to find the place packed with drunks flinging insults and the sporadic mug. Instead the place seemed peaceful, almost deserted when they arrived.

The reason for this calm sat hunched over a table near the fireplace. Nerran looked up when the door opened. His face was puffy from mead and tears, and for a moment he appeared oblivious to who they were. Then, with a shuddering sigh, he turned his attention back to the bottle he was nursing. "Stay away," he grumbled.

He had never seen his friend so desolate. Then again, he had never heard the Paladin talk of raising children either. So much of Nerran's time had been dedicated to the Riders and the return of Lesganagh's faith to Danastaer, and gruffly advising Cumaill Duasonh on whatever matter struck his fancy. Maybe, he thought, Nerran had talked about a family, just not to him.

"No, we won't," Rhea said. She approached the Paladin, the other Riders following her. Some of them looked as haunted as she had, but no one had fallen as far as Nerran. Sure, they had lost friends, but it had always been Nerran who had spurred them on and kept the flame alive. Now this pillar had crumbled, and although Briog and Rhea were decent leaders, none of them could replace the man who sat drunkenly and forlornly before them.

"Piss off!" Nerran snarled.

"No, we all will go and honor the dead," Fynbar said.

"No bloody Deathmasks, they steal your thoughts."

"You need to…" Briog began.

"To what? All I need is to die."

They were too gentle with him, Kildanor realized. Nerran was not the kind of person who sugarcoated words; rather, he was as straightforward as an arrow. He made his way through the semicircle of Riders and took the bottle from Nerran's hands. "You will come with us, if not for yourself, do it to honor the dead. If Gail deserves anything, she deserves respect, and you bloody well aren't showing it by drinking yourself sillier than usual."

"Fuck you, Chosen! What do you know of loss? Oh, I forgot, you forgot what you felt, didn't you?" Nerran snorted. "I forgot you forgot, we all forget, don't we? If we go to the godsdamned Deathmasks, we forget. I don't want to forget. Buggers just take your memories."

"No," Rhea interrupted the tirade. "No, they don't take the memories."

"What do you know, Princess? Whom do you…?" He never finished the sentence. Rhea's hand flashed forward, and the slap echoed through the taproom.

"Don't you bloody dare," she snarled. "Now get your carcass out of here and to the nobles' cemetery, the only place suited for those we have lost."

"You killed…" again Nerran's insult was halted, this time by Briog. The Rider was even less gentle about hitting his leader.

"Shut your mouth," Briog said.

Outside, the first thing they did was dunk Nerran into a pile of snow for a few heartbeats. That woke him and drove some of the booze out. Then they marched to the cemetery. Initially, Kildanor had pondered the wisdom of attending the ceremony. He was no Rider, but the more Nerran sobered up the more he seemed to depend on him. The Paladin clung to him, his breath still reeking of mead and ale.

"How do you deal with it?" Nerran slurred.

"Deal with what?"

"All the death."

He shrugged. What could he say that was not filled with regret? No one, except his fellow Chosen, knew what it felt like to see loved ones grow old and die while one stayed young. That was the main reason that they all avoided relationships; there was no point. People one loved grew old, feeble, and died. It didn't matter if it was another Chosen, for the offspring would not be one of them. He had witnessed one such relationship and seen it end when the children themselves had become grand-parents while their own parents were as healthy as their now adult grandchildren. Utter misery, it was nothing more. Sure, physicality was something they all enjoyed, but emotional attachment? No. "We live on," he finally said.

"And?"

"And nothing, we live on, and that's that."

"Pretty bleak, eh?" Nerran coughed.

Kildanor remained silent, for what could he answer? There was nothing to add. Life as a Chosen was pretty bleak. It was not a new thought; he and Galen had discussed this decades ago. To be reminded of it now, by a drunken Paladin no less, was painful enough. "Aye," he finally said. "Pretty bleak."

They arrived at the cemetery. The Deathmask stood in front of the gate, unmoving, as if it had expected them.

"Let us begin," the priest of Jainagath said with a bow.

# CHAPTER 34

Ever since Dalgor's return, the fronts had hardened. The Eye was divided, but Darlontor's faction was the weakest. And he wasn't really sure what he defended. The elf had found Dalgor. In a way he was glad his nephew was alive, but his return had not mended the rifts. Arawn, Dalgor, and their supporters demanded the assault on the Kumeens, while Gryffor's faction kept celebrating the delusion of faith, demanding not only Drangar's death but also Dalgor's. They had struck against the recovering man and had lost. Now they huddled in their false chapel, praying, plotting. And in the middle were Darlontor's bunch of feeble old men and women. Soon Gaedhor would bring the refugees here, and when that happened, things were bound to get ugly.

His rank as Priest High was no help at all. Neither side listened to his call for unity. Maybe he had anticipated that his nephew's return would not heal the wounds, he did not remember, but now as always, it seemed, it was too late. Thank the gods, the elf was growing in power so quickly he now was feared by those willing to expand the arguments into full-fledged skirmishes. After a failed attempt on Dalgor's life, there had been brawls, even some wounded, Lloreanthoran's presence prevented either of the two sides from assaulting the other. Though he had no doubt that there would eventually be open warfare.

The few Sons loyal to Darlontor maintained a steady presence at the gatehouse, thus insuring that everyone could come and go as wanted. Their tenuous hold on the Eye's sole entrance, and their determination to only allow one side or the other to pass, kept them from solving their disagreements outside. Sooner or later, he knew, weapons and blood would be unleashed, and then any semblance of unity would irrevocably be clubbed to pieces. And there was nothing he could do.

Maybe he should have stopped the executions of failures when it all had started. Maybe he should have treated Dalgor more kindly. Maybe he should have been a better example to all the others. Maybe he should have tempered his anger with wisdom. The thoughts that had been nagging him for the better part of the past two years came back. Not that they had ever really left. Had he been honest with himself that… No! This was a road he would fight walking forever. The situation was not his fault.

Outside, in the courtyard, several Sons traded insults. A welcome distraction, he thought sarcastically. Everything that could keep his mind away from the error that had spawned all the others was welcome. Scales, Darlontor would have greeted a melee with higher spirits than the place his thoughts were leading him to.

He wished Cat had never left him. At least he would have had a loving face to turn to. What was the past if not an accumulation of regrets and missed opportunities? And there was so much he regretted.

Someone knocked on the door, yet another distraction he was glad for. That the door didn't open immediately told him who had come. The elf. No one else truly bothered anymore to wait for him to say "Enter!" which he did now.

The journey to the Kumeens had marked Lloreanthoran. Darlontor had no experience with elves—who in this day and age had?—but the wizard's finely chiseled features looked weary. Lloreanthoran, so he was told, usually sat in the library, reading, learning. And if he wasn't there, the mage tried to force magic with as little blood as possible. By now he expected the look of concern shrouding the elf's face.

"This can't go on," Lloreanthoran said instead of a greeting. Never before had he seen the wizard speak so frankly. "You should be preparing to fight."

He scoffed. "They are preparing to fight."

"They should fight the monsters that turned the Kumeens into an abomination of nature, not each other!"

"So, what would you have me do?"

"Talk to their leaders!"

"And then what? It will be the same as last time." He steeled his mind, unwilling to reveal too many feelings to this outsider. "I will speak with them, when I have something to say."

"We need to find the Tomes and the Stone."

"You've been to the Kumeens; do you really think they still need the Stone?"

"Aye, I've been to the mountains," Lloreanthoran replied. "And you know the danger is more imminent than ever before. So why the Scales do you sit here pondering past mistakes, when you should be leading the Sons of Traksor against these worshipers of demons?"

Darlontor stopped himself before he blurted out the reply that came to his mind. Instead he said, "Because the time is not yet right."

"And when will it be right?" the elf retorted. "When your people have killed each other?"

Darlontor felt a not-so-gentle push in his head. The bastard was trying to read his mind! The parry to Lloreanthoran's spirit-thrust came easily enough. "Don't you dare," he said, failing miserably to remain calm. "You are my guest."

"Yours, and Dalgor's, and Arawn's depending on the day. And before you start to attack me, or throw me out, I should remind you that my presence alone is what keeps order here. Yes, your magic is strong, for those who can use it anyway. I learned to wield it, and I studied magic long before the House of Kassor was even a glint in any god's eye. Why else do you think Arawn's people respect me?"

Darlontor noted the difference. They no longer were his people, but Arawn's. The elf looked as if he wanted to say more, but instead he stared wide-eyed at something behind him.

He whirled around and once more saw Cat's sad features as they vanished in a ray of sunlight. No! If he admitted this, then the floodgates would open and there would be nothing left but chaos. Again, he felt the push against his mind, and in this instant of concern that battled with forced ignorance, the elf slipped into his mind.

Darlontor unsheathed his dagger and pricked his skin, drawing blood. He focused now, intent on forcing the mage's mind from his own. This was no game of thrust and parry, but a battle of wills, of trying to block the mage from those memories he had locked in the deepest recesses of his mind. He glanced at Lloreanthoran, and saw that the elf hadn't even drawn blood to power the spell. His mind swung, bashed, snarled at the alien seeker within. Then, suddenly, the presence was gone. He looked at Lloreanthoran, and saw the astonishment. "You gods-damned bastard!" Lloreanthoran spat, and then turned and left.

He slumped against his desk. The elf knew, and had judged him accordingly.

# CHAPTER 35

## Twentieth of Cold, 1475 K.C.

Keeping everyone outside in the belief he was struggling against the Fiend had freed him from being constantly patronized by Kildanor and the two Upholders. Aside from Jass and Gwen, no one knew he was searching for a way to fight the thing lurking in the back of his mind. Though he hadn't had a good night's sleep for weeks now, he was determined to beat the thing that was painting his nightmares in blood. His nightmares, Gwen's presence kept them away, but snippets remained, even though she slept next to him all the time now. Jass had offered to move to the attic, but returning to his old bedroom was something he could not stomach. It was hard enough sitting in the room where Hesmera had died, and although Gwen and he had only shared a friendly caress on a few occasions, it felt wrong to sleep next to her in a room he had once shared with Hesmera.

Now, he was sitting in the snowy garden behind the house, trying to picture what he had felt when the Fiend had healed the cuts he had suffered in Ondalan. Maybe that was the true reason Darlontor had cursed him so many years ago. Maybe the old bastard had known he could turn blood into magic and had feared him for it. Or maybe he was just imagining things. It wouldn't have been the first time.

"You sure you want to do this?" Gwen asked.

He looked back at her as she lounged against the wall, and smiled. "If something goes wrong you can always hit me with that thing." He pointed at the staff next to her.

"Oh, don't worry, I'll club you good and true." She paused, scanning the area. "No sharp objects here, are there?"

"Aside from the needle? No." They had talked about this, more than once, all three of them, Gwen, Jass and himself, voicing their concerns, arguing fiercely. In the end the two women had agreed, but not before reminding him how stupid he was to tempt fate like this. "You're my anchor, remember?"

"Aye; and I'll beat the snot out of you if you forget!" Her smile was shadowed by the fierce glint in her eyes. He had no doubt she would keep her word.

He had pushed away so many things, had tried to forget so many memories of his youth. He had never seen any of the Sons use magic, although there had been rumors galore, whispers among the children. Like all of them he had attended the prayer-sessions, and they had bored him: the constant sitting and mumbling, the endless meditations. Had all this been designed to prepare the future Sons of Traksor for the magic they were to wield? In the past week or so of musing, he had concluded that it was so. How else would Dalgor the bully have been able to summon the fiery cage? A detail that had escaped him in Cahill Manor but remembered now was the bastard squeezing a hidden bag, squirting blood into his palm right before he had vanished. Blood had also hissed off his own body in Ondalan. Blood was the key, he was sure of it. The Fiend had used it to heal Drangar's body. How the bugger had gotten into him remained a mystery, but at least he now knew what supplied the strength. Kildanor had mentioned something similar. So, if the magic was within him, he should be able to use it.

The only thing that bothered him was what effect it would have on the monster in his mind.

They all had agreed that he should test his idea outside, with Gwen standing guard should anything unforeseen happen. She had even suggested chaining his legs so he would be unable to move, but obtaining such a length of chain would have aroused suspicion. No doubt someone was still keeping an eye on him, and while no one was actively watching the house, the purchase of a few yards of strong chain would have brought an audience he did not want to have.

Jass had some rope, though, and they had tied his legs with it. He hoped it was enough.

Ignoring the chill that penetrated his cloak, Drangar closed his eyes. The last time he had meditated was a decade ago, but the principle was easy enough. Steady breathing, sharp mind, ignoring the outside world, focusing on the world within. He had to find peace.

The cold woke him. That and Gwen's shaking. Drangar blinked, found he was lying on the ground, cuddled in his cloak. "Guess I never drew blood," he mumbled, grinning sheepishly. His legs were free and his hands were wrapped in rags. "Did you?" he asked, noting that Gwen wore gloves and an extra cloak.

"I couldn't wake you, and the gods know I tried."

"Guess I should always meditate before I sleep."

"You could have frozen to death!"

"How long was I out?"

She glanced west, toward the sinking sun. "You missed the noon-gong." He sat up, or tried to sit up. "Jass is still walking the ramparts," Gwen said by way of apology for having left him in the frosty air.

"Help me," he said through lips that were numbing more and more with each moment.

"I couldn't lift you then, what makes you think I can pull you up now?"

"I'll help."

"Right." Against her complaints they managed to get him standing, and then, leaning on her, he stumbled into the house's warmth. Once inside Gwen let go of him, and he slumped to the floor. "You're heavy."

"It's the clothes."

She snorted. "Stay here, I'll get some tea."

"As if I could go anywhere." He hadn't summoned magic, but at least he knew it was possible for him to sleep without nightmares. Then again, he pondered, he hadn't slept all that long. Maybe the bad dreams would have returned in time.

"I'm glad," Gwen said upon her return, a steaming mug in her hands.

"Hmm?" he asked, taking the tea from her.

"That it didn't work."

"Why's that?"

She flicked a strand of hair back and regarded him. Sometimes he still wondered what she saw in him. Sure, it was comforting, but he had never considered himself attractive. "What if learning to use blood as magic is what it wants?"

Sipping tea, he mulled over her worry. This was an aspect he hadn't thought about before. Maybe she was right. No, not maybe, in all likelihood she was right. Over the past two weeks he had come to appreciate her keen mind. She rarely let it show, preferring to remain a silent observer. It was at moments like this that Gwen displayed her intellect. But if she was right, what about his past? What about Darlontor's outburst? And just how long had he been carrying this Fiend in the back of his mind? If it had been there before he had come to the Eye of Traksor and had wanted him to use magic to gain more control, or rather wrest control from him completely, his... father's anger was understandable. No, he decided, this was nonsense. The Fiend must have lodged in his mind later, even if he could recall no such incident.

"What are you thinking?" Gwen interrupted his musings.

"Nothing," he said irritably.

"Your face does not say 'nothing,' dear," she said in an almost motherly tone.

"Stuff," Drangar muttered, sipped the tea again, and almost spilled it when Gwen slapped the back of his head.

"Gods, you're dense! Do you think I guard everyone's sleep? Or that I let any man come this close? Speak! Talk to me, you idiot!"

So far, he had barely told Gwen of his youth; the past seemed less pressing than the present. But as he spoke, he realized this was not true. Everything that had happened to him, every part of his pathetic life seemed to be linked, connected by something he couldn't identify. The easiest denominator probably was the demon, but even Gwen agreed that this was too simple a solution.

When he was done, Gwen said, "Guess the only way to get a decent answer is this Darlontor character."

"So, all we can do is wait." He scoffed. "Need a new scarf?" The look she gave him told him she had other things in mind. And suddenly he was afraid. No, he would not make love to her, he would not become awash in emotions that would make him lose control.

She must have deciphered his expression, and instead of the expected pout, she began to laugh. She laughed even harder when he felt himself blush. "Gods, you men think with your cocks more than your heads." She gasped for air. "No, I won't sleep with you. It's not what I had in mind. Sewers are cleaner than a man's mind when he's around a woman he likes." She scoffed. "No, we will practice. You need to hone your skills with the blade."

He gaped at her. A young squire telling him about weapon practice? He had been killing people when she was still wetting her father's trousers. "Are you serious?"

Her smirk dazzled and mocked him at the same time. "No, you idiot, I was joking, you are fine the way you are, and your swordsmanship is without equal," she said.

"But I..."

She interrupted. "You won't use magic, but you need a way to convince this Darlontor you will carve the answers out of him. Do you think you can convince anyone when you're howling like a madman, banging against shield walls like an enraged animal?" And then, "Yes, I spoke with Kildanor, briefly."

He exulted. She knew and did not care about this unwanted side of him. Hard, cold fact slammed him down once more. "What if I... I don't..." How could he tell her he feared for her safety? He didn't want to hurt her in any way, and battle brought anger, which in turn loosened the Fiend's bonds.

"You won't," she said simply.

Would she really be there to rein him back should the demon take over again? How would he know she was safe? Again, his face must have betrayed his fears, for she leaned down and caressed his scalp. The hair was growing back, and it felt as if he was covered in soft down, but the truth of it still was that he was loathe to have anyone see him like this. He jerked back, banging his head into the wall.

"How do I know that you won't hurt me?" she voiced the question herself. Smarting from the impact he gently bobbed his head. "Because," Gwen said, counting off her fingers. "I will not slip you a love potion." With a teasing smile she added, "I don't need help driving a man crazy." Then, "So far I've always been able to keep the nightmares at bay. And finally, you wouldn't hurt me." She stated this with such conviction that Drangar believed her.

"Besides, I won't train you," she added a moment later. "Dubhan will."

Dubhan was the oldest of House Cirrain's warriors, the arms master of the noble family, a gruff man who spoke his mind. That much he had gathered on their journey back from Ondalan. Drangar didn't doubt the Chanastardhian would treat him like any other recruit. Then he rolled his eyes. These people fought with sword and shield or spear and shield, and he liked neither option. Gwen didn't reveal how she had convinced the old weapons-master to agree to this plan. The more important question was when had she done so. They barely left the house under the pretense that he struggled with his nightmares. Jass, he decided, must be involved in this little plot of Gwen's, not that he minded. There was something oddly relaxing in holding a sword in his hands, and no amount of knitting could replace that.

Still, he was not sure this was the right way, feared that against Gwen's prediction he would hurt her. "I don't know," he admitted.

"That's why you won't have much of a choice in the matter," she replied happily. "Oh, don't give me that look. If things were up to you, you would sit and brood all day and toss and turn with bad dreams all night." Was he that obvious? "Isn't that what you were doing in your shepherd's hut? My da always says that if there's no wind, you just get out the oars and pull. Seems like you haven't rowed in ages." She was right and knew it, and Drangar couldn't help but submit to her logic. Were things so much different now, he wondered. No, not really. He had to do something rather than mope.

"Very well," he agreed. "Let's do it." Though, he still hated the thought of fighting with a shield.

Dubhan arrived shortly before the dusk-gong rang across the city. He followed Jass into the common room, grumbling and complaining in his thick northern accent. That he accompanied Jasseira supported Drangar's theory that the warrior woman had played the part of messenger between Gwen and the Cirrain retainer. "Bloody rain," Dubhan muttered. "Can't it just snow like in normal places? All this slush now, and fucking ice in the morning." He halted, regarded first Drangar then Gwen. "So, you two ain't lovers at all, eh?" he said.

Gwen looked at Jass. "You didn't tell him?"

"'Course she told me. Believed her, too, I did, but rumors are harder to kill than a Northman bastard," Dubhan answered. To Jasseira he said, "Nice house you got here."

Drangar waited on his friend to reply, and then decided any explanation would lead to more questions and leaned back in the chair. Jass must have thought the same thing, for she thanked the Chanastardhian. "Drang, I brought you a shield. Dubhan says you'll need one."

He groaned. Shields were good in a wall, but otherwise useless. A good arrow pierced it more often than not, and the point from a charging lancer couldn't be stopped anyway.

"You don't like shields?" Dubhan asked. "Tough luck, mate, you'll use it. Heroics only get you killed that much faster, shield to shield, that's how true men fight!"

"And still I live," he muttered. Whether any of the others had heard, he couldn't tell; they remained silent.

This was almost as soothing as sharpening a blade, Drangar thought as he slid into the chainmail. Jass had thrown away nothing, or next to nothing, and so his war-gear had been stored in one of the wicker baskets next to his bed. Ever the thorough warrior, she had oiled the metal yearly, preventing rust from settling and growing. Still, the heavy linen shirt and even more so the leather on top of it, were stiff from disuse. The leather creaked, as he whirled his arms about, testing its flexibility. Somehow, he couldn't explain the feeling, the layers of armor and padding gave him a confidence he thought long lost.

The chain went down to his knees, slit below the crotch for easier movement. His legs were clad in caergoult, the heavy wax-boiled leather so stiff from disuse that for a moment he worried about mobility.

Jass tossed him his boots. He caught and donned them. Unlike the riding boots he preferred to wear, the plate-reinforced leather was about as subtle as an anvil.

Gwen and Dubhan regarded him as he stalked down the stairs. There was nothing elegant about his movement, and Drangar felt as if each booted step made the stairs groan in protest. This was his gear, his armor, not the stuff Lord Cahill had given him for Ondalan. His movements were clumsy, and he wondered how he had ever managed to walk much less fight in this, or how anyone else could.

"Bloody infantryman, that's what you look like," the weapons-master said. "Bloody young infantryman at that."

With pleasure he noted that Gwen had not taken her eyes off him. But now was not the time to contemplate his feelings for her, or hers for him. Maybe when all this was over, but not now.

"Sorry about the shape of the leather," Jass said, obviously enjoying his awkward gait. "Should have oiled it."

"That you took care of the chain was more than I ever would have expected. Scales, you didn't even know I would return at all," he told her, buckling his sword belt. This stuff weighed more than a full-grown sheep. How he had ever managed to move in this, he did not know.

"Well, then, you dress like a warrior, mate. Let's see what you can do." Dubhan walked for the backdoor, adding, "And don't forget the shield."

How he hated shields, and strapping this monster to his left forearm only reinforced that emotion. "Bulky bugger," he grumbled. The thing was rectangular and as wide as the door. He had to twist sideways to get out. Behind him, Gwen and Jass giggled. That Gwen would giggle in such a girlish way he had anticipated; Jasseira's like display of amusement surprised him. The warrior woman had never struck him as the typical female prone to giggling, and she was being exactly that.

Outside, the Chanastardhian had taken up a defensive

position, his shield-protected flank facing Drangar. He barely remembered the moves, yet another thing of his past he had tried to forget. Dubhan braced against his shield, peering over its rim.

"Charge me!" the weapons-master ordered.

The Fiend remained quiet. Maybe his lack of anger kept it that way? Whatever the reason, he was here to train and his teacher had ordered him to charge. The weight of his armor bolstered his confidence; he drew his sword and obeyed. Leading with his shield, Drangar raced forward. He didn't hold back, thought Dubhan didn't want him to. A yard, then only two feet separated the two shields, and closing his eyes, he prepared for the impact. Less than a heartbeat later he was still running, aiming for the far thornleaf that separated this garden from the next.

He skidded to a stop, balancing to regain steady footing. From behind Dubhan growled, "No, you imbecile, no! You do not close your eyes! You never close your godsdamned eyes!" Drangar whirled around, equally embarrassed and angry with himself. "Do you think a proper enemy will close his eyes when you come charging at him? Might as well throw bones or dice instead, if everyone runs about blind," the Chanastardhian grumbled. Then, shaking his head dismissively, he turned to Gwen. "Been meaning to ask you something, lassie."

Drangar barely heard the younger woman's reply. Blood was pounding in his ears, and the Fiend's faint voice, barely audible before, was edging him on. He took a deep breath and forced himself to calm down. If any of the others had noticed the struggle, he couldn't tell.

"So, what shall I tell Anne?" Dubhan asked.

"My place is here," Gwen replied.

"In Dunthiochagh?"

Upon hearing that, Drangar looked up, hopeful. "No, too dry for my liking," Gwen said. The hope drained from him. Had he misread that a relationship was forming? In the back of his mind he thought he heard a shout of joy. What the Fiend exclaimed, he couldn't tell, but it clearly was happy with that development. Then she pointed at him. "Where he goes, I go." Her words were like music, and while Drangar caught himself grinning like an idiot, the Fiend snarled in anger. Why and how Gwen managed to keep the demon at bay, he didn't know, but that mattered little. She did.

"No," Gwen said. The roaring inside his skull made it impossible to follow the entirety of the conversation. "Of course I plan on returning home. Da will be pretty upset with me once word reaches him that I deserted."

"Most likely someone at the head of Drammoch's army will deliver that bit of news," Dubhan replied. He then turned to Drangar. "What are you smiling about, mate? Don't get mushy on the lass here, understood?" Behind the weapons-master's back, Gwen winked at him. He felt his grin broaden again. "What's so funny, eh? Get your shield up, rush me again!"

"Yes, sir!" he answered.

Dubhan braced for impact, and Drangar forced his eyes to stay open when the two shields connected. In the last instant, the Chanastardhian shifted ever so slightly. He saw the change, but with the ground as slippery as it was and his momentum, Drangar was unable to adjust.

Steel-reinforced wood grated on steel-reinforced wood, but only for a moment, and then Drangar was free again, the impact had barely slowed him down. He barreled into the brick wall of the house, the leading arm flattened between shield and armor.

The others laughed.

Again, the Fiend roared, raged, and he wasn't certain it was only the hidden demon. He turned, glaring, and something in his look made everyone, Gwen included, take a step back. Something similar had happened in Carlgh, at the Boar and Bustard. He had been so furious at the imbecile noble's disregard of courtesy and his threats against the serving girl then, and everyone had tried to escape his eyes. His attention was drawn to a window that reflected his image. He stopped, unable to believe what he saw. He blinked, and when his focus returned, he regarded the same face and the same eyes he had always seen when looking into a mirror. But for this one moment, this one instant before he had blinked, he had seen his eyes glow. "What the Scales," he muttered, turning to regard the others. "You all saw that, didn't you?"

Their stunned nods were all the reply he needed.

# CHAPTER 36

## Twenty-second of Cold, 1475 K.C.

Kildanor decided Cumaill looked better, as he watched his friend working behind the table. After having spent a long time in front of the Deathmask's fireplace, Nerran had emerged a new man and immediately begun to assist the Baron in running the city. Not only that, but the Paladin had convinced him to invite Úistan Cahill into the small group of advisors. With the Lord Cahill came his daughter, Neena, supposedly to assist in accounting, but it soon became clear that Sir Úistan had something else in mind for her. And Cumaill, to everyone's surprise, relished the lady's presence.

Maybe, Kildanor thought, all it took was a woman's touch. As the Cahills took on a large portion of the work, Nerran in turn was free to look for new Riders. The Chosen doubted the warband was still needed, and with Danaissan's stranglehold on Eanaigh's church gone normalcy was bound to return soon. But even he admitted that rebuilding the church of Lesganagh would take years, if not decades. So maybe the Paladin was right. It was unfortunate that the Librarians only recorded history, and not secrets of faith. Thus, the restoration would likely be hampered by lack of knowledge until some Sunpriests came and settled in Danastaer from one of the other kingdoms. That also was a day far in the future, for even though the imminent threat of the Eanaighists was gone, the horrors of the Dawnslaughter lived on in people's memory. Convincing any Sunpriest that the danger had passed, and making sure it did not return, would now be the new task for the Riders.

Cumaill rifled through a stack of Watch-reports from the past week. After Jathain's failed rebellion, the Baron had taken a keen interest in what went on in the city. The mug of heated wine remained a few inches from his mouth as he read. The Baron frowned, looked as if he only now realized the container was aloft in his hand, and set it down. "Didn't you say Drangar Ralgon was at his old house brooding?" he asked.

Kildanor cut a slice off the roasted ham as he said, "That's what I've been told, aye."

"Hmm, have a look at this." Cumaill passed the parchment to a servant who in turn held it out to him. "Wipe your hands before you touch that," reminded the Baron. Ever since Neena Cahill had taken the position of accountant, she had also taken a great interest in the Palace's records. One of the results was her justified complaint that no one had ever truly bothered to keep the records in pristine condition. It was true that none of them, not even Jathain when he had run the Watch, had bothered with tidiness. A man's world, Neena had remarked acidly on several occasions, claiming there even was a slice of sausage now firmly glued to two pieces of paper.

Consciously the Chosen wiped the grease from his hands. He hurried through the lines that described repeated complaints of neighbors about the noise of military exercises performed somewhere near Old Wall Street. The last such protest had prompted the nearby Watch commander to send some of his people to investigate what had proved to be the residents of Cherkont Street, always a place where retired warriors settled, participating in shield wall and weapons training. Chief among them these days were all the Chanastardhian turncoats and one Drangar Ralgon.

He looked up at Cumaill, saying, "You've got to be shitting me."

"Nay," the Baron burped after draining his mug. "The commander is a good man; he wouldn't fuck around with this."

"No, I know this Maelgwn. What I meant is that Ralgon is allegedly sitting around moping, while he is actually training to go to war." There was more to his worry, but so far none of those who had been to Ondalan had spoken about the slaughter.

Neither did Cumaill know of the demons that apparently vied for control over Drangar even when the man was calm.

"Good for him. Look at Nerran, a bout of depression can really mess with you, and I'd say this Ralgon fellow has more to be depressed about than Nerran."

Should he speak of the Fiend? Were circumstances different, he'd have confided in Cumaill a while ago, but the Baron already had enough on his mind. Food was more readily available, all the refugees and warriors had been billeted, yet troubles had only been postponed. The enemy was bound to return, if not in spring then certainly in summer. He wished he could share his concerns, would have voiced his worries under other circumstances. That Drangar practiced fighting was dangerous, not only to the man himself but to everyone with him.

"He's probably tired of all the attention. I don't blame him. More wine, please," Cumaill said, holding out his mug. A servant refilled it. "Do you have any idea how bloody annoying it was to have you and Braigh smothering me with attention when that assassin of Jathain's managed to cut me? Unbearable, I tell you! Would have done anything to get the two of you off my back." A long pull, and then he added, "We should ask them to do it elsewhere though, with all that has been going on, open military exercises can make some folk mighty uncomfortable."

"Better uncomfortable than dead, I'd say."

"There's that, of course." Then, "You still want to go south with Ralgon come spring?" Cumaill had been avoiding the topic ever since he had first made his decision known. It was bound to happen, but Kildanor was surprised that it had come out now. With Sir Úistan and Nerran having taken over some of the Baron's workload, his friend had more time to think.

"Aye, as much for Drangar's sake as my own," he said.

"His sake?" Cumaill cocked an eyebrow.

"Don't worry about it, it's..."

"Stop that nonsense," the Baron interrupted. "Too many strange things have been going on around this mercenary, and your decision to accompany him just adds to the mystery."

"Cumaill, listen..."

"No, you listen, there are things you have kept to yourself

and I respect that, but Ralgon's return from the dead, the brutal killing of his woman, his strange state when he was in our cells, you freeing him and talking of demons you saw. All this isn't something to be put away lightly. I demand you be honest with me. Why do you want to go to Kalduuhn with Drangar Ralgon?"

There was no way around it now. He took a deep breath, put aside the report and fixed Cumaill with his eyes. "The truth is that there is more to Drangar, something that is trying to take control. I've seen it, not only here but in Ondalan as well. In Ondalan, though, it wasn't just a struggle. The demon or demons had won."

Wide-eyed, the Baron asked, "What do you mean won?"

"Your plan would have failed had Sir Úistan not angered Drangar, but his anger only freed the demon to take over. That monster inside him took out the entire Chanastardhian force." For a moment he fell silent, remembering the bisected corpses, the man desperate enough to jump to his death before becoming a victim of the slaughter. "And the strangest thing of all is that I think I was able to direct that demon. Had I not intervened and reminded Drangar of the mission when he had Lord Cahill in his grip, we all would have died there."

Cumaill blinked, glanced at the servant whom Kildanor had completely forgotten, and said, "No word of this will leave the room, understood?" A short pause followed. Then, "Is it dangerous to let this go on?"

"Could be."

"And you're sure it wasn't Ralgon who did the killings?"

"Absolutely. You should have seen him, he was terrified."

"Is that the only reason that you want to accompany him to Kalduuhn? Wouldn't it be more prudent to help free Dragoncrest?"

Now came the tricky part. Cumaill knew him too well to overlook an evasion. He couldn't stop his discomfort showing. Dragoncrest was still besieged. More than a hundred enemy soldiers had erected an almost permanent camp at the fortress exit. The fact that this warband remained while the bulk of the Chanastardhian army had retreated to Harail was a clear indicator of what the High Advisor's true goal was. "I should, but aside from helping Drangar, there is something personal in Kalduuhn that needs my attention." Before the Baron could ask the obvious question, he continued, "Ralgon mentioned something about my brothers."

"I thought you bore no grudge against them anymore." Cumaill helped himself to another slice of ham.

"I don't, but Ethain and Ganaedor are still blood. Even if they sided with Danachamain and the demons they still are my brothers—and Chosen."

The Baron's fork halted in mid-air. "What?" he snapped.

This explanation should have come years ago, Kildanor knew that, but Chosen business was discussed with outsiders only on rare occasions. Normally he wouldn't have told Cumaill even this much, but in the past week the Cahill's influence, especially Neena's, had worked marvels to nudge his friend toward the throne. If Cumaill were to become King, he would know these things anyway. "Twenty-four were Chosen by Lesganagh, each one to be replaced at the death of another. My brothers and I were among them. Since the Demon War there have only been twenty-two. Figure out the rest yourself." Maybe he should have waited until they were alone, with servants waiting in two of the room's corners there was bound to be gossip, and soon. He doubted even Cumaill's order or any threat would confine the conversation to this room. Not that it truly mattered. The Chosen's duty, Kildanor feared, would all too soon become apparent. That the High Advisor was after the Hold and what it held was fairly obvious by now. He wondered if he should divulge the entirety of their mission, but was thankfully interrupted by Nerran barging in.

"Bloody bastard!" the Paladin roared.

"And a good morn to you, too," Kildanor said. Cumaill still seemed preoccupied with the revelation. "What bastard?"

"Kerral," Nerran grumbled, pulling a chair from the table and hunkering down. "Bastard thinks he runs the defenses."

Irritated, the Baron asked, "What's the matter?"

"Kerral; are you deaf?"

"Distracted. So, what is the problem?"

"He's gathering workers and shovels and picks."

"What for? Come on, mate, tell the whole story, don't let me drag it out of your nose bit by bit."

"He has this mad idea to divert part of the river to flood the southern plain," Nerran said.

Actually, Kildanor thought, the idea was brilliant. The General was thinking ahead, preparing for the Chanastardhians' return in spring. He remained silent, unwilling to get involved in this struggle of egos. Cumaill looked as surprised as he felt, but neither shared the Paladin's anger.

"You told the bastard he follows our orders." Was Nerran complaining about someone else taking on the challenge of preparing to defend the city? Or was he merely whining about not having thought of it first?

The Baron's words echoed his thoughts. "You were senseless most of this month, mate. I doubt Kerral meant to make a fool of you." Nerran was doing that all by himself throwing such a tantrum.

"So, you agree with his actions?" Maybe this still had to do with compensation for losing Gail, Kildanor thought.

"Sounds reasonable," Cumaill replied. "Even if he hasn't discussed his plans with me." The Baron sent him a pleading glance and he nodded briefly. He would back his friend, but this was a fight Cumaill had to fight alone. Nerran grieving was one thing, clinging to issues that had been diluted by his absence was another. And Cumaill had made it very plain that he ruled.

"What do you mean? I thought you and I were leading the defense." Did he truly complain that someone else had thought of a good plan?

The Baron must have felt the same, because he spoke very curtly. "General Kerral has proven himself a good leader, and willing to follow orders. If he has taken the initiative now there is nothing wrong with that. What are you so bitter about? Is it that someone else has a good idea, or are you afraid that everything will slip through your fingers?"

When Nerran remained silent, Cumaill went on, "Gail was a bright woman; she knew what she was risking. Scales, you knew what you two were risking by allowing her to join the

fight! You can't control every aspect of everyone's lives, especially in a battle. Next year Mireynh will show up with more
than two slingthrowers, and you damn well know it. If we
aren't prepared Dunthiochagh will fall, and Gail's death will
have been in vain. So, unless you have a better idea, I suggest
you drag your ass out there and make sure Kerral doesn't fuck
things up. Understood?"

For a moment Nerran stared at Duasonh, and Kildanor didn't
know whether this show of strength on the Paladin's part had
merely been an act, or yet another way for him to deal with his
repressed anger. Then, much to the Chosen's surprise, Nerran
bowed his head. "You're right. It's just that I don't want..."

"War's war, people die, you know how it is," Cumaill said.
A brief nod was Nerran's only response. "Would you have been
able to order Gail away from the fighting?"

The Paladin looked up, lips curved in a sad smile. "Fuck no!
She's as hardheaded as a bull. Err, she was." He stood abruptly.
"Should've paid more attention to the fireplace," he muttered
and stomped out again.

Chosen and Baron shared a knowing glance. The fireplace
was a feature almost unique to the nearby cemetery, but anyone
who went there could visit it, alone, and receive some manner
of peace. He had never bothered to ask the Deathmask about
it, the fireplace just was. Other cemeteries had similar ways to
help mourners deal with their pain, but the silent skulls on the
mantelpiece were impersonal.

"So, your brothers may still live?" Cumaill said into the
silence, picking up where they had left off.

"Not may, they live. And I think there is a connection."

The sycophants had finally recovered their limited wits and
were bombarding Cumaill with presents and demands even
before the Baron had reached the audience chamber. One of
the more obnoxious trade-representatives, a fool who blatantly
shoved a bag of something at Cumaill, was taken in by the
guard and introduced to the blunt end of etiquette. These people never seemed to learn. None of the Duasonhs had ever been
corrupted. Cumaill's great-grandda, rumor had it, had even

executed a score of courtiers as an example for the rest. Should there be a King Cumaill, Kildanor knew, those in Danastaer who put their interests above the wellbeing of the entire nation might well reap another hunting-season. He smiled at the notion. Cumaill didn't mind looking the other way when it was for the betterment of all, the kind of people who usually were scrubbing chamber pots or helping the tanners or equally distasteful jobs, but bribery and corruption were as bad as murder and rape.

He saw that Úistan and Neena Cahill were waiting in the audience chamber, let out a relieved whistle, and hurried away. Spending even a few moments with the sycophants made him feel unclean. Cumaill would understand.

His walk took him to Cherkont Street, and the noise of shields clashing reached him long before he entered the road. What surprised him was the mass of children who, instead of lobbing snowballs at each other, watched the lines of armed men bashing into each other. He recognized some of the colors present. Among the Dunthiochagh's crest depicted on many shields there were the coats of arms of a few Houses who had joined General Kerral's army, and here and there blank shields that most likely belonged to the retired warriors of the neighborhood. Some were lounging against nearby houses, taking a break from the hard work of fighting in a shield wall.

In the teeming mass it was difficult to make out any individual; the press of bodies was too tight. He didn't bother to count heads. There were too many of them, and more arrived still. Some of the newcomers weren't old enough to grow a beard, and others were old enough to be their grandparents. Maybe this militia business had something to it. He even saw one or two beggars carrying old battered shields, down on their luck like so many veterans who had spent their money on booze and whores and dice, and would lose it all before long. The one thing that did surprise him was the number of women present. Not that the sight of female warriors was uncommon, but here, by the look of it, were housewives straining with warriors in the same line, and making it look easy.

To his right, on a hastily erected platform stood the

Chanastardhian weapons-master, Dubhan, shouting orders at one group or another. There was no kindness in his voice. The otherwise jovial man was the drillwarden and as such he performed with excellence.

"Worrying about me?" someone said from behind.

Kildanor turned and saw Ralgon stretching his muscles. He hadn't recognized the former mercenary in the war-gear. Ralgon had taken his helmet off and was wiping his sweat-soaked brow with a gloved hand. "Yeah, I look different," he said.

He sounded different as well. Not as tortured as he had after Ondalan. And the patches of hair had formed into something that no longer resembled a holey quilt. "Didn't think you had it in you," Kildanor admitted.

"What?" Ralgon smiled. "Dressing up for war or practicing within a shield wall?"

"Either, both," he admitted. "Why didn't you...?"

"Tell you? You would've worried about my sanity, and I was tired of being treated like a crazy."

"Didn't think you had it in you."

"The discipline? Aye; neither did I, but it turns out this is exactly what I need."

They were interrupted by a shout. "Ralgon's group get back in here, let Keelan's group take a break!" Dubhan hollered. "Move it! Anne, take your lot back in as well, let the freeborn catch their breath!"

"We'll talk later," Kildanor said, but Drangar was already heading back to one of the now separating warbands. He watched as Gwennaith Keelan stepped away from the line, gave Ralgon a gentle pat on the armored arm, then strolled toward him. What was the relationship between the two? That Ralgon fancied the girl he already knew, but the thing seemed mutual enough. Maybe she really had a soothing influence. Why else had the man's behavior changed so drastically?

"Morning," Keelan said, taking off her helmet and wiping her brow. "Come to check on him?" she asked almost casually. So, there was something more going on.

Instead of asking her directly, he nodded and said, "Some

people complained about the noise you are making."

She scrutinized him for a moment then snorted. "Right. And the Watch has other things to do." The young squire was quick-witted. "You worry about him having another of those... episodes, don't you?"

"Episodes?" he said. Her look told him she would not accept anything short of the truth. "After Ondalan, can you blame me?" The entire Chanastardhian warband had heard about the massacre, and it would be a real miracle if Cahill's retainers hadn't spoken of it.

Keelan shook her head. "No, not really, and truth be told I was worried also. At first, that is. And so was he."

"True, but had he become angry it might have happened."

"He was afraid of himself, and what he had done, even if he knew it wasn't him."

"How did you manage to get him out of that mood?" Kildanor asked, realizing the instant the words left his mouth that he already knew the answer. Gwennaith Keelan was witty and gorgeous to boot, and she was a stranger.

The look she gave him was amused and belittling at the same time. "What can I say that you can't figure out for yourself? Drangar doesn't need something to worry him. He needs a purpose, something to occupy him."

"And fighting in a shield wall gives him that?"

Keelan nodded. "It gives his life order."

He understood. Ralgon had lived as a shepherd after the slaughter of Hesmera, a hermit by choice. The loneliness, combined with the paired need to understand and do penance, would have driven anyone mad; with the realization that he had not killed Hesmera, the guilt had been removed but the hermit had stayed. What Gwennaith had done was to drag this man out of his isolation and back into the world of the living. Pretty smart for such a young woman, he thought admiringly. The luxury of Cahill Manor had most likely reminded Ralgon of what he had fled from in his youth. What if being alone also weakened Ralgon's defenses against this Fiend? It was a possibility, although this did not explain where this otherworldly influence had come from in the first place.

He realized that Gwen Keelan was looking at him, waiting for a reply he had not yet made. "I should have thought of that," he said, hoping it sounded apologetic enough.

"Given the circumstances not many people would have," she said. "You had a war on your hands. Besides," she added with a smirk, "Lesganagh's followers are not necessarily the most empathetic." What was she hinting at? The Dawnslaughter had affected the other kingdoms not as harshly as Danastaer, and there still were a few active Suntemples in Chanastardh.

"I'm the daughter of a sailor, the granddaughter of a pirate," she said. His confusion, probably mixed with a little apprehension, must have shown. "The Lord of the Sea and Horses is whom I worship most. And the sea adapts; war and sun are usually quite straightforward, as are their followers." The conversation had taken yet another turn, and he saw more clearly why Drangar was attracted to her. Sure, at first it had only been the pretty face, but he was forced to admit that young Lady Keelan was charming and insightful. Now that he thought about it, he realized she was right, and he was not above admitting it.

"We are a very direct people," he said.

"Keelan!" Dubhan shouted. "Enough chitchat, get your group back into line! Ag Marranh, yours take a breather!"

"Try not to worry too much," the young woman said as a farewell. "He's in good hands."

He believed her.

# CHAPTER 37

## Sixth of Ice, 1475 K.C.

This was the coldest part of winter. The sky was clear, and for the past two days a chill, dry wind had gusted through the streets. Dubhan had agreed to call off the practice bouts until it grew warmer, though by now Drangar could tell the weapons-master was less than happy with the situation, claiming that lowlanders were a bunch of pampered bastards. A sentiment he only shared with the warriors of House Cirrain. How the highlanders endured this cold was beyond him, and he regretted agreeing to the sparring matches even as he shrugged into his chainmail. "This is no weather to go about banging swords at one another," he grumbled.

"Just don't lick your armor," Gwen teased.

"I'll try to restrain myself."

Over the past few weeks they had grown closer still, and he thought it evident that their relationship had outgrown the cordial formality that still reigned them. Then again, he could not shake the feeling he was not yet ready for anything physical. It wasn't Hesmera's spirit lingering near that prevented him pursuing Gwen more aggressively, far from it. He was at peace as things were, why mess them up with proclamations of love and tumbling in the blankets.

Sometimes, when she looked at him, he saw his yearning reflected in her eyes, but they both remained apart. He had repeatedly meant to broach the subject; the training, however, kept them occupied. Now was not the time. He smiled as he donned his coat. Things were good. Even the Fiend had not reared its ghastly face. Why then would he fuck all of this up? Certainly not for a bit of fleshy pleasures.

"What're you smiling about?" Gwen asked.

His first impulse was to say "nothing," but the change he had gone through thanks to her went deeper still. Four months ago, he would have surprised himself by saying, "I'm wondering when and if there will be a right time." Now, as he spoke the words, they came naturally.

She looked at him, and he again saw the longing. "We'll know. I hope," she added with a chuckle. So, she did feel the same. Drangar was elated. "But it's not now." She pulled his cloak taught, stood on tiptoe and kissed his cheek. "No matter how much I wish it were different."

He wanted to sweep her up, hold her tight, and his desire must have shown, for she tsked at him and left the room. She was right, now was not the time.

The layers of armor didn't feel that uncomfortable anymore, but outside with the wind freezing everything, the stiffness of leather and steel once more hampered him. His cloak didn't help either. Dubhan waited for him in the open, and he wore the same threadbare outfit he had worn when Drangar had first seen him. How the highlander could stand the biting cold was something Drangar did not want to consider. The mere thought of young warriors running up snow-covered slopes with barely a thread on their bodies sent shivers up his spine.

The weapons-master was accompanied by several of his countrymen, as skimpily dressed as the older fighter. "Hope you have your head protected," Dubhan greeted him.

"Aye," Drangar replied. Out here in the cold his stoicism returned, not that it mattered to the rough-cut warriors. He figured any additional word that allowed the chill to enter one's body was a word wasted.

They practiced with wooden swords, none of them willing to submit their warsteel to the rigors of the cold, and soon, despite his apprehension, Drangar began to enjoy himself. It surely was not the kind of exhilaration he had felt in years long gone; there was grace in this dance of sword or spear and shield against a warrior wielding the same. He had always thought the shield wall a stupid, useless thing if one was strong enough to break it. But nothing compared to the camaraderie of people acting as one singular being, bracing for the coming impact, straining to keep the enemy at bay. It was grueling work, certainly, but at the end of a day he felt good about himself and the warriors he stood in line with. There was no anger in the wall, only determination, and it taught him something he hadn't been aware of: that relying on others was not only possible, but also pleasurable. Sure, whenever the lads and lasses went for a pint or two to guzzle down the past day's weariness he withdrew, unwilling to touch alcohol; what further amazed him was the fact that they understood.

Now, as he practiced maneuvers with Dubhan, Padraigh and a few others whose names he could not recall due to exhaustion and cold, he felt the same kind of excitement he felt whenever he was with Gwen. These people accepted him. They did not treat him as an outcast anymore, and while none of them—he included—understood what kind of terror lurked in the back of his mind, they had all come to realize he was a decent enough person to sit and joke and talk with.

"Mind if I join?" someone asked from behind him. Drangar turned and saw Kerral.

For a moment he stood still and regarded the man. General Kerral, the title bothered him, the man bothered him. How had this lowly mercenary warleader become a warlord in his own right? In his hut he had made it very clear how he felt about his former friend. Brothers did not stab each other in the back yet Kerral had done just that, had betrayed him. Suddenly, without warning, the hurt at the duplicity rose back to the fore. He remembered how his one friend in Mireynh's army, his warleader, his captain had turned his back on him when all he had done was obey Mireynh's order. He had brought the treacherous son's head back and demanded his due reward. Kerral could have stood by him, should have stood by him, and supported him, because he had done the right, the just thing. Instead the bastard had howled with the wolves.

"Fine," Drangar growled.

Now they stood facing each other, shield to shield, staffs held as lances, pushing, stabbing. For a moment it looked as if Kerral wanted to speak, a forceful shove shut him up. Instead the older man shifted his shield so that Drangar slid past and stumbled in the slush. A heartbeat later, his balance regained, he turned to face Kerral once more. The others laughed. It wasn't the first burst of mirth, but this time it stung. Years and years back the children at the Eye had laughed at him, had laughed when the older boys, chief amongst them Dalgor, had kicked him about the courtyard. He had wanted to prove himself to them, show them he was their equal, and no matter where he lunged and swung, his blade had always connected with a shield or another sword.

Dalgor made him stumble, again. No, not the hated cousin, but the man he had called friend. Kerral, General Kerral. They had never sparred, he had never stood beside the man in a shield wall, but still they had been friends. General Traitor, Drangar wanted to spit.

He had brought back Mireynh's son, and the head of the bastard who had betrayed them. It wasn't his fault they'd been one and the same! Mireynh had been furious at his demand for due payment, but after all he had accomplished both missions.

Again, the shields ground against each other, and again he lashed out with the staff. Kerral leaned to the left as if anticipating his move. Was he using his knowledge of him against him? The counter-attack came before he had time to pull his weapon back. A slap to the helmet, nothing serious, but for a moment it numbed his senses.

Just like Dalgor had done in so many sparring bouts.

Drangar managed to bring his shield up in time to prevent another hit to the head, a hit that never came. Instead the other's staff smacked against his left leg. Unbalanced, he struggled to remain upright. Now even the grass underneath the snow was against him! He fell.

Again, laughter sounded, despite someone trying to calm the men standing around. Just like the children back then, they mocked. Just like his comrades who had scoffed at his demand for payment for two missions. Kerral had... no! Dalgor had laughed with the others. Kerral had done nothing. Nothing!

It had been unjust, wrong. No friend abandoned another, it was law, unwritten, but it needed no contract. Struggling to his feet, he faced Kerral once more.

Shields collided yet again.

They parted, Kerral panted. His breathing was calm, controlled. But inside, his emotions tumbled, roared. Warleader Kerral was now a warlord, respected. And still he fought like a whirr, as if he did not enjoy the easy life of all leaders? Drangar dropped the staff and picked up the wooden sword. It was time to show the bastard what true fighting meant. Barely acknowledging the fact that Kerral held on to his staff, he grumbled and approached again.

Shields slammed into each other, but only for a moment. Drangar was aiming for Kerral's head. The general danced out of reach. The momentum of his swing whirled him around, and again the ground rushed to meet him.

This time he was up on his feet and running in a heartbeat. As his shield hammered into Kerral's, he slashed right above its rim, aiming for the head yet again. Kerral ducked. Wood scraped metal. Somewhere in the back of his mind he heard someone shout. The voice ordered him to stab. And stab he did.

Kerral went to his knees, the shield rising at an angle to deflect the blow. Again, the call to stab came.

Drangar thrust again.

A general. How could such a treacherous bastard attain such a position? Whom had he stabbed in the back to claim that rank? The bastard did not deserve it.

Again, the shields crashed into each other. He would show them all who deserved the respect. Kerral should not hold such an honored title. If anyone deserved to be warlord, it was he, Drangar. He should have been the hero, for a hero Kerral was, if only to those who did not know him as Drangar did. He could have held the fraying army together as well, no, better than this thrice damned imbecile, this wretch, this traitor!

Bastard!

The call to stab sounded once more, urgent. Or was it stop?

Drangar stabbed, missing the enemy's head by a fraction. Kerral spoke. He did not hear. Once more, he drew the sword back. How much blood would a fighter yield? Another stab. The other's shield moved up, redirecting the blow.

Traitor!

He was torn from his feet, crashed into the packed snow. A face came into view. Who?

Gwen.

The Fiend had crawled into his mind again, and he had never even felt it. Now the monster roared out its anger, tried once more to break through the shadowy bars holding it at bay. How? Why?

People—his friends—pinned him down, shouting, but he heard none of their words. He almost would have—no, not him! The Fiend! It would have killed Kerral and the others. This time there was no Chosen who could have directed its rage. The cold penetrated cloak and armor, and still the others held him down.

He did not blame them.

"So, it's true," someone, Dubhan, muttered. The first coherent words he made out through the roaring in his mind.

"What was that?" another asked.

"Thank gods you were here, lass!" a third exclaimed.

At that Gwen's lips curled up in the hint of a smile. "Are you back?" she asked, her eyes boring into his.

He was; the Fiend had withdrawn not a moment too late. "Aye," Drangar said, wheezing. The highlanders stood, released him, and pulled him up right into Kerral's sight.

"You aren't blessed by Lesganagh, are you?" the general asked, shock still plain on his face.

His first instinct was to run, hide, weep, and bury himself in misery. A hand on his shoulder restrained him. "Don't," Gwen said. Her voice sounded soothing, but he heard the concern layered underneath.

She led him inside, the others crowding in after them. He thought he heard whispers, mouths yapping, repeating, and confirming rumors, claiming he was cursed. It was so like his nightmares Drangar glanced back at them. All he saw was somber faces. Shock was etched into their features. Even Kerral displayed none of the cockiness he had come to expect from the warrior.

"Sit!" Gwen's determined voice ordered.

He obeyed, slumping down onto a chair opposite the fireplace at the far end of the room. The others gathered around him, concern slowly replacing the masks of shock on their faces. Now Gwen pushed herself before the others, arms folded on her chest, stern determination lining her eyes. There was nothing gentle about her expression.

"What the Scales is your malfunction?" she snapped. "For weeks you were all right, and now this!"

"You take slights..." Kerral began.

"You call a friend's betrayal a slight?" he heard himself growl, wondering if it was he or the Fiend speaking.

"Calm yourself," Gwen said soothingly, yet there was steel in her voice. Over her shoulder she said, "Tell me what happened to make him resent you so much."

"He was in my warband, years ago. It was there he got the nickname, Scythe. He volunteered for breaking walls."

Astonished mutters rose around him. "Drangar's the Scythe?" "I heard it say he was blessed..." "No one survives charging a wall alone!"

"Shut up!" Gwen snapped. "Go on."

He tried to make out Kerral's face, read his expression. Someone stood before the fireplace, the bulk blocking the firelight. "We became friends. Not many folks befriend their warleader, thinking we're mean bastards or something, and despite his impossible successes they shunned Drangar. Sure, there were the rumors, about him being blessed and all that, but the others usually steered clear of him."

Silence engulfed him, until Gwen's hands cupped his cheeks and he found her face hovering before him. "Stop staring, start listening, understood?" He bobbed his head.

Kerral continued, retelling the tale from his point of view. How he had volunteered to bring Mireynh's son and the traitor's head back. "He did as promised," the warlord concluded. "Returning with Kirran Mireynh's head, turned out the little shit had sold us out." Some of the people attending chuckled. "It could have ended there, but Drangar had the cheek to demand payment for both missions accomplished, totally ignoring the fact that he had murdered our warlord's son." The laughter died down. "He stood there retrieving the bugger's head from a bloodstained bag and tossed it to Mireynh's feet."

"He had promised a reward for both!" Why couldn't they see that he had done the right thing?

"And here I thought Connar was stupid," Padraigh Cirrain muttered.

"You calling me stupid?"

Gwen answered his question by walking behind him and wrapping her arms around him. "Shut up, listen, and learn, dear," she whispered into his ear, her head resting on his shoulder. "You may have judged at Eanaigh's temple, but you are not objective here."

The Fiend receded. He hadn't noticed it crawling up.

"Aye," Kerral said, looking him in the eye. "He promised a reward for both, but do you think any father enjoys seeing his son dead? You could have thought that far ahead when you caught up with the little shit. It was not that you were wrong, mate, it never was! It was about you robbing Mireynh of the chance to pass judgment over his son. And you stood there so bloody self-righteous, demanding payment from a father whose son you murdered. He probably would have killed the bastard himself, but you took away those last moments, and were proud of it as well. It was never that I sided against you, but I heartily disagreed with your attitude."

Even the fire seemed muted. All he heard was his own breath rattling in his lungs. He had taken away a father's chance to face the facts, had, in a way, done to Mireynh what Darlontor had done to him. His cursed sense of justice. Unlike his grandda, he was no judge. He had done the right thing, but it would have been just as easy to subdue Kirran Mireynh and drag him back to his father.

Somewhere, in the back of his mind, he thought the Fiend was raging.

"You've been alone all your life, mate." Kerral's voice penetrated the silence. "Unloved, always had to prove yourself to yourself and others, striving to be recognized, but never recognizing that none of it mattered to the people who consider you a friend. Scales, you never understood why anyone cared, and how could you? Singled out, mocked, hurt every step of your way."

Drangar tried to focus on the man, blinked fiercely to clear the tears from his eyes. When had he begun to weep? When had Kerral become so… kind?

"I've never stopped being your friend, even after you turned and ran. If only you had allowed me to speak instead of screaming insults of betrayal and worse at me. Back in Carlgh you did the same thing. I thought you had changed, and you had, but not as much as I had hoped. You killed the oaf Haggrainh, not a bad thing, considering what I'd heard about him, but you did what was right and shat on the consequences. You did the world a favor, in both cases. In Haggrainh's case not even his uncle misses him, but what if there had been an investigation? What if the Lord Haggrainh had decided the villagers had paid you to kill the little shit?"

"Aye," muttered Padraigh. "Every story has two sides, and even if your view is the right one, the other might still be pissed off at you, or any other judge."

"So, you really killed Mireynh's son and asked for both rewards?" Aoibhan, the youngest of the Chanastardhians, asked.

The murder Drangar realized, seen from Mireynh's perspective, could not be considered justice, only spite. Kerral was right, had been right then, and he had lived with the impression of betrayal for years, holding a grudge where none had been warranted. "Aye," he finally said, bowing his head.

"Pretty ballsy," the young warrior said.

The others, even Kerral and Gwen, laughed, and he knew that they were laughing with him, not at him.

The warriors had left shortly after the dusk-gong; none had mentioned Lesganagh's non-blessing or his glowing eyes, and he was thankful for that. He heard Jass return but didn't move to greet her or introduce Kerral when she entered the common room. His wish to be left alone had not been granted, and he was in no mood to talk. There were enough disturbing memories running amok in his mind already, and any reminiscing would rouse more. Gwen must have sensed his mood for she was the one talking to Kerral, distracting him. How had they grown so close in such a short time, he wondered, and not for the first time. Yes, they lay together, but they weren't lovers. Already his affection for her had complicated things.

Undistracted, he had used the time to analyze how the Fiend had managed to take control. It had turned the resentment and painful memories of being mocked against him. Both feelings had opened a path the monster had sneaked along. It wasn't just outright anger the demon fed on, no, its talons clawed into any and every weakness. In time it might even use his yearning for Gwen as a means to take over. This he could not allow. Love was as strong a feeling as anger, drowning out reason. And if one thing was certain, it was that he needed his wits to get out of this. Even if he still had no idea what "this" was.

"And just who are you?" Jass asked.

Even with his back turned Drangar could see the image of Jasseira standing in the doorway, her stance tense yet relaxed. He had worked with her for enough months to know her habits, and though he would have loved to watch the scene unfold, he remained as he was, staring into the fire. Kerral's reaction was more difficult to picture, ten godsdamned years since they had been friends; the warleader was a general now, a warlord, who had led hundreds of warriors into battle and then on an organized flight to Dunthiochagh. His jealousy was dead, if it had ever truly existed. His... friend deserved to lead fighters; he could barely lead himself.

A chair scraped; then Kerral spoke. "Madam," he began. Drangar smirked, knowing full well Jass liked the formal blathering as much as he did. Her snort reassured him that some things remained the same.

"If it wasn't for little Gwen there'd be no lady here," Jass said, earning an exasperated drawing of breath from Gwen. The two had become close, yes, but Jasseira was the older and mocked the younger woman's status whenever she could. Not that Gwen cared one way or the other. The exchange was as much to their amusement as to confuse Kerral. "So, who the Scales are you?" Drangar almost said "my friend" but caught himself before the words spilled out. Instead he coughed. "You all right, Drang?"

"Jass, this is Kerral," Gwen said, he could just picture her impish smile. Now Kerral was probably glaring at her for forgetting his rank. "Err, General Kerral."

"Sir," the warrior woman said, her words probably accompanied by a nod. Jass wasn't the type to salute anyone in her home. He heard Kerral clear his throat, a habit he'd already acquired when the two of them first met, probably wondering what he was doing here living with two women.

Another chair was pulled back; Jass was settling in as well. Whatever the three of them spoke of, it was hushed enough for Drangar to hear little more than the occasional snippet. A while later the muted conversation subsided. Kerral cleared his throat once more.

Then, "Drangar," the warlord said, "we used to be friends; if it was up to me, we would never have stopped."

"You were a brother to me," he finally muttered. "I told you things I didn't even tell Hesmera. It hurt when you did not stand by me."

"Do we have to go through this again?" grumbled Gwen. "You insulted your leader before his troops. You made the mistake, accept it." Then, in a soothing voice, she added, "Sometimes it is wrong to do the right thing."

"Drang, had we just followed the evidence, we would have hunted you down, but we trusted our guts. Lliania knows right from wrong, and Her Scales will tell the truth. A man forced into treason by means of threat will still feast in the hall."

They were right.

"Mate," Kerral said, rising and walking over. "Hold on to the lass, she is good for you. I've never seen you this calm, so stop grinding every past slight, real, or imagined, through your mind. Start looking forward. Underneath all that doubt and misery is a person well worth knowing and calling friend. Make peace with yourself, it's the only way to survive."

He felt the warlord's hand on his shoulder, a slight squeeze. Then he was alone once more. Somewhere in his mind the Fiend was lurking, waiting. "I'm sorry," he whispered.

"Don't, mate," said Kerral from the door. "I understand."

He looked up and saw him smile as the door closed behind him. Into his view stepped Gwen. "You're lucky to have such friends," she said, leaned down and kissed his cheek.

# CHAPTER 38

## Tenth of Ice, 1475 K.C.

Who would have thought healing took such a long time? Ealisaid certainly had not, and although a servant had washed her daily and changed the sheets regularly, the bed had grown quite rank. She did not know why High Priest Braigh and not one of the other Caretakers was the one dressing her wounds and caring for her, nor did it matter. In a way it made her feel special, even when every other sense in her screamed she was anything but. The Baron visited her on occasion, and even Kildanor attended her at least once a week. But instead of merely sitting and chatting, Lesganagh's Chosen had prodded her with questions about forced magic, obviously thinking her an expert on the matter. Among the blind the lame was king. It had something to do with Drangar Ralgon, not that this revelation had been of any help. She had suggested that Ralgon was mentally ill, that two distinct personalities vied for control. And Braigh had thwarted even that theory when he had witnessed the brainstorming.

Over the past few days her strength had returned. So far, she had managed to sit up, had even walked to the privy, aided by Culain who spent every free moment with her to the point that she had ordered him to get some rest. Yesterday she had taken the first few unaided steps, only as far as the door, which wasn't far at all, but the three yards had felt like a mile. Thankfully Ysold had arrived in time to help her stumble back to bed. The girl had a knack for appearing just at the right moment, and Ealisaid suspected her pupil was learning much more on her own than she herself would have been able to teach. Maybe the Baron was right when he claimed that the lass was not tied down by years of conventional learning and could therefore start afresh. Upon returning from the Shadowpeaks she had been so confident, brimming with willful energy. Taking on the enemy had seemed so easy, until it hadn't been, until the bolts had shredded her flesh and the fall had broken almost every bone in her body. That Braigh had been able to save her at all, even though the term had been abused a lot lately, was nothing short of a miracle. To her surprise, even the Chosen agreed, though his exact description of her salvation had been more reminiscent of a butcher's shop, but still, it seemed as if Eanaigh wanted her to live.

She struggled to an upright position, and her body ached from the newly healed wounds. Braigh claimed she was as good as new except for the scarring, and Culain it seemed, was attending her more out of pity than desire. How bad was it? How badly disfigured was her face? Her limbs looked like cloths haphazardly sown together by a seizure-stricken seamstress; there was barely an inch that had not been lacerated or pierced by either bone or bolt. So far no one had allowed her a mirror, all claiming she had to remain calm in order to heal.

The last time she had seen her face it had been bandaged to the point that barely enough room remained for her eyes, nostrils, and mouth. Three days ago, a servant whom she had not seen before had entered and for the barest of moments the young man's gait had faltered. Judging by that reaction, she feared the worst.

Now she had her right leg over the rim of the bed, her foot dangling in the air. That motion alone caused pain to surge through her entire body, but she wanted, needed to make the trip to the door and back on her own. She refused to be an invalid for the rest of her life. The other foot swung next to the first. Her breath hissed through clenched teeth. Arms propped against the mattress, she began to push, every inch tripling her pain. The pampered side of her wanted to call for help, to curl up and cry until someone came, but the independent side hollered on, forcing her delicateness into submission. No one would help her if she did not help herself first.

Another inch, and another, she didn't care about the night-gown riding up her legs, had seen the network of scars so many times by now the sight did not stun her into immobility. Naked feet touched the ground, rushes pricking her soles. She was glad she felt anything, glad to be alive to feel. With a grunt she heaved out of bed.

Did Culain really just stay because of pity? The talk about character being more important than looks was nothing more than a threadbare curtain, because upon meeting someone a person was immediately judged by their appearance. And she and Culain had never had the chance to truly get to know each other. It had started with passion, had maybe grown into attach-ment, but since her fall this attachment seemed to be fraying, severing.

She reached the low shelf with the mirror on top and saw the reason why Culain and supposedly everyone else pitied her. Had she cuddled with a pair of scissors, the result might have looked the same. Gone was everything that had made it into her face. A mass of red and white scars turned her countenance into a relief of wind-torn dunes. She would have wept for the loss of her beauty only a few months ago. Now, having lived with the scars covering the rest of her body, she would have been surprised had she retained her looks. That she lived put things into perspective. She could have died, should have died, and yet survived. Maybe that was her destiny, to live. The Heir War had raged while she had slept—the last of the Phoenix Wizards gone. Maybe this was a sign that she had to carry on to rebuild the order.

Or maybe it was all just a tremendous joke the gods were giving form through her.

"You could use magic to cover it," someone said.

Ealisaid looked to her left, a slow process due to the scar-ring on her neck. It felt as if part of her cheek, of her face, had melted into her neck's skin, forming an inflexible leathery sur-face. The lean man she saw bore little resemblance to the broken wreck he had been in Cahill manor. "Ralgon," she said. "This is a surprise."

He nodded his head. "Heard about your problem. Caretaker said you weren't to be disturbed whenever I came to see you."

"I expect you didn't come to see how I was faring," she stated. There was no reason for the mercenary to look in on her because of gratitude. She hadn't done anything for him, except that one journey into the spiritworld.

Ralgon smiled wryly. "No, not really. I've seen enough broken bodies to last ten lifetimes; I avoid them when I can."

"Well, with that out of the way, what do you want?"

He scrutinized her, most likely trying to figure out how well she really was. Then he said, "If I had the money, I'd hire you." Money? What was he talking about? Her confusion must have shown despite the scars because he hurried on. "As soon as the worst of the frost's gone I intend to ride south and finish this business with the Sons of Traksor once and for all. They obviously are magic-users, at least some of them, and I'd like to even the battlefield, somewhat."

"You think I could help? I barely survived my first real battle," Ealisaid replied.

Ralgon took a deep breath, closing his eyes for a few heartbeats. Before his lids were completely shut, she thought she saw a glimmer. "I don't want you to fight, I just want you to be there to remind the bastards to play fair." He looked at her, his eyes plain once more. "I'm past the vengeance thing; it won't bring Hesmera back. Lliania will judge them when they enter the Bailey Majestic, and I don't need to hasten their crossing over. I just want this to be finished one way or another. I want answers, nothing more, nothing less, so I can start living again." He scoffed, looking at the ceiling. "Gods, who knows, I might even return and bash in a few Chanastardhian heads to help defend the city."

"Why me?" she asked.

His gaze caught hers. "That should be bloody obvious. I can't take the girl, she's a bit young for that sort of thing, and I can't think of anyone else capable of leveling a house or three. Can you?"

She found no fault in his reasoning, except, "I have to be here to help in the defense when they return."

Amusement turned to bemusement. "You're that eager to play pincushion again?" And before she could reply, he went on. "Mireynh is a canny bastard, he knows your weakness now, and you can be damned sure he'll use that knowledge next time around. So once his troops see you swooping at them, he will bring you down." He paused for a moment, and then said, "Unless…"

"Unless what?" The mercenary displayed the annoying habit of luring others to beg him to continue.

"Well, maybe—and there's no guaranteeing this—the Sons will be able to teach you some of their tricks so you won't get shot out of the sky again." He must have realized how eager she was to be of service to Dunthiochagh. Initially her fighting alongside the Baron's troops was nothing more than serving out a sentence, but now she wanted to fight. That and being tied to the bed for the better part of two months was enough to make her yearn for any morsel of knowledge others might have to share.

"Who says they will teach me?" she demanded. He shrugged, prompting her to keep talking. "And while we're at it, who says the Chanastardhians won't be back before whatever you plan to do in Kalduuhn is over?"

Again, a shrug. "There are no guarantees in life. But you've studied what remains of whatever that bastard summoned to cage me, and you damn well know he wasn't just another goon. That alone should suffice as argument for you to accompany me. Next time wouldn't you be better off knowing that when you fly above the enemy, they won't shoot you down?"

He could drive a point home; she had to give him that. And he knew he was right; his entire pose spoke of confidence. "How long have you thought on this?" Ealisaid asked.

Ralgon pointed to the window. "It's fucking cold outside, so there's not much else a body can do but think, eh?"

"Who else will accompany you?" She doubted he would travel alone, already suspected that Kildanor would travel south with the man. Now that she thought about it, she was certain the Chosen had a part in the venture. His reply verified her thought.

"The Chosen, one of Lliania's Upholders, Gwen," he said. "Who's she?"

Now Ralgon's eyes glowed with emotion. "My anchor," he answered as if this explained everything. And maybe it did, Ealisaid wasn't sure. "Think on it, we'll ride mid-Thaw, maybe earlier, depending on the weather." He was halfway out when he turned to face her once more. "And I guess I don't have to tell you that all that counts is one's personality." Was that an attempt at humor? If so, his look told her he realized just how badly it had come out. "Sorry," he said, almost meekly.

He looked so distressed she almost laughed, but earlier attempts had made her face hurt so bad that she forced the mirth down. "You're no jester, that's for sure," Ealisaid said instead. "But I will consider your request."

"That's all I can ask for." And a moment later he added, "Thank you." The look on his face betrayed the struggle he must have fought to utter even this pleasantry.

Undisturbed, Ealisaid worked through the pain. At first, she merely paced, and then, when her legs stopped aching, she began work on her arms. She had never considered herself much of an athlete, scorning physical activity when magic could achieve the same result, but now, with scarred tissue hampering even the slightest of movement, she was forced to give her body the workout it needed.

How long she went about stretching her arms, lifting first small items and then larger ones, she didn't know. Time had no meaning for her. She hardly allowed herself to rest.

When she was convinced her hands could grasp blocky objects once again, she started working on the fine manipulation of things. To an observer, she thought, her tapping fingers on the mattress or against the thumb of each hand probably looked ridiculous. The exercise was strangely relaxing. It bore similarities to meditation, a mantra of motion.

"Need some help?" She would have recognized Culain's voice amidst hundreds of others, and looked up, pleasantly surprised. A pained look crossed his face for the briefest of moments. "Caught you walking earlier," he said. "Didn't wanna disturb you, figured I'd come back later." The smile he gave her now was faltering but sincere.

"You don't have to do this," she said, realizing her speech was slurring.

"Do what?" Culain arched an eyebrow and entered.

"Come here because of pity." The change in his expression surprised her.

He stopped by the cupboard, arms folded across his chest, glaring. "And what, by Lliania's Scales, do you mean with that?" His voice quavered with barely suppressed anger.

"I..." She took a deep breath and began anew, "I look hideous; you don't have to comfort me."

Now he scoffed. "You're so full of shit, you know that?"

"What?" Pain lancing through her jaw at the exclamation. Holding her cheeks with both hands, she scrutinized his rough features and saw no disgust there.

"You heard me," he replied, almost gently.

"I understand if you want to leave me."

"Who said anything about that?"

Why would he stay? There was no reason now that she was ugly. She had never considered lying with someone as scarred as she was. Would she have wanted to be with him, had he taken such a fall? Until now she had never considered the alternative. The thought alone made her shiver. Would she still love him, if he were as deformed as she?

Ealisaid straightened. What was that? Had she just admitted she loved him? Did she?

"What's wrong? Shall I fetch a Caretaker?" Culain misjudged her reaction, probably thought she was in pain. Silently, with her eyes still fixed on her... lover, she shook her head. She loved him, and to her it would matter not had he been the one to suffer the injuries. Her expression must have caused him to worry even more. "What's wrong?" he urged again.

"I love you," she whispered.

"You do?" He looked both relieved and confused.

"Aye. And you?" Somehow, even though he hadn't replied yet, she felt certain she knew the answer. Still, she was afraid, wondering once more if he stayed only because of pity.

"You think I jump into bed with every pretty skirt?" he asked, scoffing. "You think I spend all my off-duty time here to watch over you just for fun?" He took a deep breath, and she feared he would still dismiss her. Instead, he raked his hands through his hair and smiled. "I was afraid to tell you how crazy I am about you; you were always so distant, even when we were together. I thought you merely used me to steady your spell-casting." There were tears running down his cheeks. "What the Scales do you think, eh?"

Before she was able to reply someone else entered, shattering the soul-sharing moment of intimacy. Kildanor stomped in, clearing his throat as if to announce himself, something his heavy footsteps had already accomplished. Culain stiffened, wiped the tears from his face and turned toward the Chosen. Ealisaid remained seated.

"A rare guest," she remarked.

Kildanor nodded a curt greeting then said, "I take it Ralgon's already asked you." He waited for a reply, and when she kept her silence, he went on. "I'm not in favor of you coming, not with your injuries, but it turns out we need you with us."

She scrutinized him. His usually calm demeanor wavered, as if something was troubling him. "What brought up this urgency?"

Closing his eyes, he briefly shook his head as if to dismiss a troubling thought. Then he said, "Dragoncrest is still under siege. The bastards reinforced the troops there, and the Chosen outside can't get past them."

"The Chosen outside?" It was Culain who raised the same question she was about to ask.

Kildanor glanced at him as if ready to dismiss a mere guardsman. Then, after a moment of consideration, he shrugged, muttering, "As if it really matters." More loudly he replied, "During our sortie in Harail some of us were killed and not replaced as quickly as we would have liked."

"I thought you were immortal," Culain stated.

"Not as such, no. We can die, by violence. There've been twenty-four since the Choosing, and when one dies, he is replaced; Lesganagh chooses someone new."

"And those who were chosen now cannot get to those inside Dragoncrest," Ealisaid said.

"Indeed, so before we cross into Kalduuhn we will send the Chanastardhians packing, reinforce Dragoncrest, and allow those outside to join up."

"Why Dragoncrest?" Again, her lover took the thought from her mind. Maybe this was what others spoke of when saying they formed a bond.

"Why not?" he said dismissively. He added, "What say you? Will you come and help clear the way?"

# CHAPTER 39

## Twelfth of Ice, 1475 K.C.

Nothing was eternal; time took its toll on everything. Mountains were worn down by rain and wind, the same wind toppled trees that in turn killed whatever was in their path at its moment of death. A circle as steady and as erratic as the world's movement around the sun. Had Lesganagh always intended it to be like this, Lightbringer wondered. No. She shook her head; he had not. Her kind was as close to the gods and immortality as the firelings and the dwarves, and all of them could be killed. Then again, the sunargh were Lesganagh's creatures while the other two had been here from the beginning.

She stared at the ruins of Honas Graigh, and remembered the time that she had helped build and strengthen the Aerant C'lain, thought-ward and prison to the elven work concerned with breaching the Veil of Shadows and opening a portal to her people's prison. Everything failed, but just like tree or mountain it had taken her a while to realize she had to abandon the old way. Teaching something different was easy; it only became difficult when one had to follow one's own lessons. Her journey had taken as long as the elven race had been around; it had begun long before she had freed them. Elsewhere their kingdoms still thrived, the ancient buildings and roads in good repair or being replaced by improved ones.

Here in Honas Graigh, the idiots had taken the easy way out, choosing exile over the struggle that accompanies change. The road bisecting Gathran Forest was in as good a state as the buildings here. Overgrown ruins dotted the landscape in every direction, barely resembling the splendor and achievements of a people not so different from her own. The human's wizard war had taken its toll on every country, but whereas the other nations had struggled on Gathran had hidden in the vastness behind the Veils. And by doing so, had left the door open for others to unearth what should have stayed buried.

The Aerant C'lain was quiet, the mindstorm gone. But so was the soulward. Naghturuu'klanagh's followers had paid the blood price, pitting terrified souls against those who had gone to their deaths voluntarily to keep the knowledge stored away from curious minds in this grave for thoughts. Now what had been designed as stronghold of protecting spirits was silent, empty, another ruin amidst this city of ghosts. She could have stopped it, had she known about it. But the threat would have remained, for within the blood-soaked Kumeen Mountains her magic, so powerful everywhere else, would have been only as strong as theirs.

A quick gesture, still a little clumsy, reminded the snow that it could have drifted elsewhere, thus clearing the entrance to the Aerant C'lain. Her fangs touched her lower lip as the upper one curled into a smile. She had used the past weeks to train. Forcing change still came easier to her than nudging the possibilities, and yet she was pleased with her progress. Even the combination, the forced nudge she had taught the human prince, worked as expected three times out of five. Had the idiot prince done as she had told him, Naghturuu'klanagh would have died. In a way she envied the humans their conscience, but it prevented most of them from truly achieving their goals.

Lightbringer stooped and entered the Aerant C'lain. The place was still, deserted, devoid of any presence benevolent or malevolent. Then again, most would consider her an evil spirit as well. It was all a matter of perspective; she had been unable to understand that for the longest time. No, not understand, for understand she did, she just had been unable to turn thought into reality.

Something rustled behind her. A quick, conscious act summoned a barrier, reminding the air what it felt like to be buffeted by a tornado. Then she turned, slowly.

The space was as empty as before.

Maybe...

She thrust her mind into the spiritworld, and took another look around. There, barely visible even to her well attuned eyes, in a corner, a young girl's ghostly head peeked into the Aerant C'lain, at least she thought it was a girl, with mankind she always had trouble telling when they turned adult. Yet, there was no hint of ghostly breasts, and her face lacked the lines that came with life, so she guessed this was a girl child. Now, upon seeing her, the young female's eyes widened, and she disappeared.

For a moment Lightbringer considered following her. In the end caution overruled curiosity and she returned to her body. The child had looked afraid. Maybe their paths would cross again, and if not, it hardly mattered.

What had brought her here she couldn't tell. Not really. She could have bypassed the city easily by not following the Elven Road, but in a way, she felt the need to remind herself of what might happen if her plans failed. How was it possible it had taken her so long to realize she couldn't remove herself from the world either, could not move beings across the world-spanning game board the gods had set up. She was another piece, not a player, and had to act the same as everyone else. And yet, somewhere deep within her, the old feeling of superiority burned brightly. Yes, she was different from the others that came after the first ones, but she was also the same.

"About time you realized it."

Despite its strange echo she recognized the voice. "Cat!" she exclaimed and whirled around. The same luminance that had surrounded the ancestors also made her glow.

"You know what needs to be done," the apparition declared with such force the last doubt vanished: Cat had ascended to be a Servant of the gods.

Yes, she knew, but older habits died even harder. Did she possess the strength of will to finish what should have been finished millennia ago? Cat must have sensed her doubts for when she spoke, she addressed this concern. "Others have always done your dirty work. You've manipulated everyone, from elves to man, by pulling strings that most of them did not see." The gods saw everything, and as their Servant Cat knew of her past meddling. "It's time to pull your own weight, Princess. Time to end what should have ended when you helped the elves win their freedom."

She knew Cat was right, had known the truth for a long time. Yet the various excuses in which she had wrapped herself had always buried the cold, hard truth. The followers of Tral Kassor were but a piece to the puzzle, but not the solution. That solution lay within herself and Cat's son. "I'll find him," she promised the spirit.

# CHAPTER 40

## Tenth of Thaw, 1475 K.C.

The cold had eased its grip almost on time with this last month of the year, and even though it had been his suggestion to ride as early as possible, the knot in Drangar's stomach did not lessen. Even Gwen's presence could not ease his mind, no matter how much he wished it.

Already they had passed Falcon's Creek, and by evening they would reach Silver Meadows. It had not been his choice to take this direction. In truth, he still resented Kildanor for demanding they first beat back the Chanastardhian troops that besieged Dragoncrest Castle. He didn't want to fight, had told the Chosen his concerns, but Lesganagh's warrior had remained adamant about freeing the fortress on the pillar before heading south and west for the Eye.

Gwen rode beside him, the Chosen a little farther down the column of riders. What had, in his mind, been a group of five had become a warband one hundred strong. Of those, only four would accompany him further south. The rest were to stay at Dragoncrest. And not only did the hooves turn the dirt road into a mud path, they had to halt every once in a while, because the two ox-carts regularly got stuck. Several times he had complained about the lack of progress, suggested leaving the carts behind and taking the horses cross-country, but the Chosen insisted they were to carry on along the road. Thankfully the ground was still frozen underneath the muck, so aside from an occasional lost horseshoe and the constant slurping, the only delay was the wagons.

Two days ago, they had come across a dozen naked corpses, Chanastardhians, Kildanor had suggested, and Gwen had explained that House Cirrain's warband had encountered a group of bowmen hailing from House Grendargh. Maybe they had ambushed the scouting party.

Drangar twisted in his saddle and scanned their surroundings, far more alert than he had been when the bastards had killed him in Shadow Valley. There! His eyes remained on an easterly spot where the setting sun reflected, if only briefly, off a piece of metal. Was someone following them? And if so, who was it? More Chanastardhians? Or Grendargh's haphazard warband? Or maybe it was yet another group, the ones that Dewayn and Morwen reported had shot enemy warriors from such a distance that it should have been impossible for them to take aim. If Mireynh was sending out scouting parties already, the possibility that he had reinforced the troops at Dragoncrest again was there, even if Kildanor claimed it wasn't so. The Chosen might possess extraordinary gifts, but he preferred eyes more than random claims any day of the year.

Magic was a different matter, even though Ealisaid still struggled with it, almost as if she was in the same position he had been in only weeks ago. Should he talk to her? More importantly, would she listen to him? When it came to advice, he was no authority on how anyone else should lead their lives. He decided to chance it. At worst, the scarred woman would scorn what little support he offered, and if not, she might actually get better. Just as he turned to look for her, Gwen squealed in delight. He looked at her, surprised to hear such a sound. She was staring west, her mouth hanging open.

"Dip me in fish oil and tie me to the mast," she said, the words merging into one another. Now others turned to regard her. It seemed as if none of them existed.

Drangar turned the direction she was looking and saw them. Judging by the shouts of surprise issued by the others the two elves who approached were something of a novelty, something they'd tell their children and grandchildren, if they survived that long. He had met elves before, back when he had been south, and all of them had been aloof buggers. Up here

the elves had abandoned Gathran, and though the elven kingdoms had stretched far and wide as evidenced by the roads that
crisscrossed the country at right angles, most of their kind were
hidden now. Not gone, but they shunned human company.
Sometimes, he thought, they were the smart ones. They had
even abandoned Ma'tallon, a city built for man and elf.

More and more riders stopped, gaping, and to Drangar's surprise it was Kildanor who rode toward them. Aye, the Chosen
had been alive during the Heir War and would have known
elves not only from storybooks. But the longer he watched the
exchange, the more he wondered what the Scales they were
talking about. By now almost the entire warband had halted,
with the exception of the carts and a few riders that continued
down the road. At the pace the wagons were going they'd catch
up with them soon enough.

Now Kildanor returned, the two elves following him. As
the pair came closer, he saw the bows, strings wound around
the staves, on their backs. This, he thought, explained who had
killed Chanastardhians from extreme range. The buggers' eyes
were better, and the bows probably attuned to their bodies.

The Chosen waved to him, and he nudged Hiljarr toward
the trio. The charger's sluggish reaction told him just how
annoyed the stallion was. Another gentle tightening of the legs
and Hiljarr finally trotted toward them.

"They're Chosen," Kildanor stated once he had crossed the
distance. "They've been busy trying to get to Dragoncrest."
The warrior looked mightily confused, and rightfully so. From
what Drangar knew Chosen had always been human, a pair
of elves joining the fold was indeed very odd. Or maybe, he
struggled to hide the smirk, the gods had finally decided it time
to start improving relations. With a dwarf showing up in the
Shadowpeaks it definitely was a possibility.

He gave a nod. So far, he had only given some measure of
deference to Baron Duasonh, and he would not change that
because of a bunch of elves. Instead he said, "Got horses?"

"We acquired some," one of them, a blond fellow with dark
eyes, said with an alien accent.

"So why not use them?" Kildanor made an exasperated

sound, and Drangar added, "Why are you so sure they are what they claim to be? They could just as well be..." He trailed off, not knowing what else to say. After all there wasn't really a sane reason for anyone to travel during winter. "Never mind, it's not like I have much to say anyway."

Later, it was growing dark and the silhouette of Falcon's Creek loomed in front of them; Gwen and everyone else had finally outgrown their excitement. Drangar was glad the constant chattering finally abated. The two elves were nothing new anymore, and the rising chill quelled all thought but the desire to reach the fortress.

"How come you aren't excited?" Gwen asked. He had never considered meeting an elf something special. There had been no reason to speak of the encounter, and people here would not have believed him. His answer didn't satisfy her. "You weren't the tiniest bit excited when you met one?" she persisted. Now that he thought about it, he did recall the younger man he had been, jaded already, but the world hadn't lost all its magic. "You're smiling," Gwen said; he could hear the grin in her voice.

"Aye," Drangar finally admitted. "It was something of a great thing, for about two sentences. Turned out the ones I met were real bastards, arrogant and all that. No idea if the ones here are much better. Frankly I don't wanna know." Seeing her astonished look, he added, "Thinking about how to go on from Dragoncrest."

It was best to head cross-country to Dunlan, and then follow the dirt road south. His memory of the area was hazy, mostly relying on knowledge he had gained from maps. Pudlain and then Crossads, and from there another long trek through Gathran. Then Machlon and finally the Eye. They were still a long way from the Kalduuhnean border yet he couldn't suppress the growing nervousness. What if Darlontor wasn't Priest High anymore? How much could five people achieve should the entire order decide his presence was just the invitation they needed to strike?

"Don't forget to smile." Gwen's voice pierced the wall his thoughts had once more erected. "You're not alone in this, you know."

He gave what he hoped was a confident grin; her grimace, however, told of his failure. "What if all we find down there is death? I don't wanna drag all of you with me." He knew he was reverting to the moody person he had been, struggled against it with the newfound confidence, and it took Gwen's gloved hand on his to reassure him. The look she gave him now as he smiled once more was encouraging.

"You said they worship Lesganagh, right?"

"Him and all the rest, I think."

"So why would they attack one who's under the protection of both a Chosen and an Upholder?"

He had never thought of it from that angle. "How can one so young be so wise?" he asked earnestly.

The grin that split her face almost made him blush. "I'm not, but among the blind the one-eyed is king." Then laughter bubbled up. He knew she was teasing, and she probably knew that he knew, which made it all the more amusing. He joined her, all tension released through one guffaw. A few heads turned to regard them, one of the warriors, a man named Maelon, shook his head.

"There might be Chanastardhians about, you know?"

"If there were, don't you think the buggers would have attacked long before we started laughing?" Drangar shot back, still chuckling. To Gwen he added, "Thank you."

"What for?"

"Just being there." The Fiend had retreated once more to the back of his conscience. The bastard was lured out whenever he felt lost, moody. Then, in lower tones he said, "Sometimes, when I worry, I think it is trying to take over."

"I know," Gwen replied. "I figured that out all by myself. It wasn't that hard, you know? Why the Scales do you think I carry on with cheering you up?"

"Thank you," he repeated, basking in the beam that lit up her face. She looked so lovely. Acting on impulse, he leaned over, pulled her close and kissed her. For a moment he was afraid she'd resist, but when her lips opened up and he felt her tongue brush his lips he knew she never would. Their eyes met as they kissed and again he saw his longing reflected in hers.

A long moment later they drew apart, yet Gwen kept staring at him, the smile even brighter than before.

"About bloody time," she said. He couldn't agree more.

The fortress at Silver Meadows predated the Heir War, and it looked the part. Drangar had never been this way before, but he recognized the old-fashioned style. No one built like this anymore. It was as massive as the one at Falcon's Creek, but the ramparts, towers, even the gatehouse bore an undeniable elven influence that had vanished in these parts after the Heir War. He had never been to an elven city, only the suicidal went to Honas Graigh, and though he had skirted Ma'tallon on his flight from the Eye he had never set foot inside. Here the elven influence was unmistakable.

"Damn!" Gwen hissed. "It's pretty."

For a moment all he could do was stare openmouthed at her. She turned and looked at him, her eyes declaring the question as loudly as if she had spoken it. He chuckled. "I've never heard you sound that…" He struggled to find the least offensive word.

"Well?" she prodded.

"Girlish is as good a word as any." If looks were capable of murder, he would have died right then and there. Instead, he felt himself blush. What was she doing to him? Trying to escape her gaze, he looked back at the fortress. It was pretty to look at. As means of an apology, he said so.

"Ha!" Gwen exclaimed. "Who's girlish now, eh?" The teasing in her voice was obvious, and he breathed a sigh of relief, unable to even consider her being angry with him. "I've never seen that kind of design before. Elvish isn't it?"

He nodded.

"Back home all is mortar and stones, and wood and nails, bleak, no artistry about it."

"Like most places up here nowadays, the Heir War and the Demon War after it fucked up a lot of old buildings."

"Even the slums in Dunthiochagh are more colorful than Herascor," she added.

Having never been to that city, Drangar remained silent. Chanastardh was a rough, practical land with no eye for architectural beauty. "Further south, where there are still elves, you see more of this."

Later that evening, in a well-heated hall, they sat near the fire-place, sharing a single blanket. So close did they sit that he felt her breathing, their arms and torsos touching. He wanted to wrap his arm around her, was sure she would not object, already he felt himself falling back into the gloom of his brooding. Unlike the kiss they had shared before the castle's gates it was Gwen who now took the initiative and snuggled closer to him, encircling his stomach with both her arms. Grateful, he leaned forward and kissed her hair. She sighed with pleasure.

Only then did Drangar realize they were not alone anymore. Behind them the warriors were still feasting, although now they already were deep in their cups. In the ruckus of songs sung out of tune and slurred conversations he hadn't noticed Upholder Rheanna's approach until she settled down on the bench next to them. Gwen seemed half asleep, her breathing steady and relaxed.

"Upholder," Drangar said in a low voice.

"Ralchanh," Rheanna replied.

"That name has no meaning to me."

"It's a proud name, or was, rather," the priestess said, her eyes boring into him, as if looking for something in his mind. Was she performing the same lie discerning ability that the old coot Coimharrin had done?

He didn't care about his ancestry. Why should he? There wasn't anything he wanted to know. Was there? Much like his resolve to keep his distance from Gwen had evaporated, he wondered if his reluctance to discover whom his mother had been wasn't another mistake. In a way he wanted to get to know the person who had shown him what had really happened three years ago. Finally, he said, "She wasn't a dog, was she?"

The priestess chuckled. "No."

"I had a dog once," Gwen mumbled from under the blanket.

Now Drangar chuckled as well, caressing her hair. "Didn't think she was, but with Dog being all mummified and that I had to ask, didn't I?"

"Dog? You called your dog Dog?" Rheanna asked.

"That's a stupid name for a dog," Gwen yawned.

"Shows you how much I didn't give a shit."

"Well, it's ironic, really. Caitrin's nickname was Cat."

Drangar blinked, shaking his head. "So, what was she like, my mother?"

"I've been trying to remember since I realized there's a connection. I was younger than she. I think the age difference was something like ten years, so I barely spent time with her. She hated needlework, which was the one thing most women at court did." It hadn't escaped him earlier, in Dunthiochagh, when she had mentioned the court of Haldain. His grandda had been Justiciar there.

"What's your connection to the court?"

"My family lived there." Drangar sensed there was more to it so he pressed the point. A freeborn or villein member of a Royal court would not necessarily know members of its elite by name, much less their nicknames. Her gaze was on him before the thought was finished completely. "Coimharrin was right," she said. "You have your grandda's insight."

"What?" he muttered, hoping he had heard wrong. Was she telling him what he thought she was?

"Lliania's smile was on Amhlaidh."

"Bloody Scales," he hissed. At first the buggers spread the rumor he was blessed by Lesganagh and now this! Why could he not be like everyone else? Life would have been so much simpler. "Are you saying the Lawgiver has an eye on me?"

Rheanna scrutinized him, as if searching for something. Back in the Palace's dungeon he hadn't felt Coimharrin's intrusion as the Upholder had searched his words for any falsehood. Was she doing the same now? He knew that Eanaigh's Caretakers could, through the goddess's blessing, treat wounds with dirty instruments that did not inflame the wounds, but he knew too little of Upholders to tell whether she was probing his thoughts.

Finally, she broke the silence. "She never speaks directly. Never reveals her intentions, other than giving us insight into the truth of the matter." Then she hesitated. "Truth is subjective."

"Yeah, I heard that before," he interrupted her. "Bloody brilliant, if you ask me. So, when I lie you can tell, but this isn't a matter of lying, it's a matter of knowing. And you know as little as I do." He paused, stroking Gwen's hair. By now she was curled up against him, her head resting in his lap. How she could find any rest in such an awkward position he didn't know. Her presence was soothing "No matter. Tell me about her."

As she had related to him before there wasn't much to say. Caitrin Ralchanh had been ten years older than Rheanna, and as such their paths had barely crossed, other than formal feasts and such. The Upholder knew more about his grandfather, and before he realized what he was doing he began prodding her for more and more information. The urge to belong had never been this strong, and with every anecdote he felt as if he still had a family, a past that did not solely rest on the tainted experiences of growing up an orphaned bastard at the Eye of Traksor. Curiously, it also explained his sense of justice, something that had tossed him into more trouble and grief than anything else in his life. Little Creek, killing Mireynh's traitor son, even the murder of the fool Haggrainh a few months ago, it all made sense. His grandfather had been a just man. This weighing of facts and ferreting out the truth that Rheanna had spoken of on more than one occasion was something that resonated deep in his soul. This echo of understanding, of kinship, also had another, more direct effect on him.

The Fiend that always seemed to lurk at the fringes of his conscience protested, howled, yet its screams sounded muffled as if thrown at him from a great distance. Maybe, he thought, this was salvation.

# CHAPTER 41

## Twelfth of Thaw, 1475 K.C.

Kildanor watched the road before them. It rose and fell with the hills. Not that it was much of a road. The mud gathered in the depressions, turning them into marshland much like the swamp on each side of the Shadowpeaks. Soon it would all drain away, but for now this was the way it was. Not that the hilltops were in a much better condition. With every rise the mud wading merely turned into a struggling climb, hooves, boots, and wheels held down by sucking, freezing muck. Yeah, the weather was better, but at night the cold returned with a vengeance, making travel even harder. The Chosen elves' magic helped some, but they were no wizards and knew very little. Ealisaid tried and failed as often as not. Sometimes the paths would dry up, but just as many times the soil remained muddy, slushy. She blamed it on the agony still wracking her body, and judging from the way her expression changed from calm to pained in a matter of heartbeats he believed her.

They were only a few hills away from Dragoncrest. A glance at the elves told him they were aware of their brethren's proximity as well. Cadwaer, the older of the two, came to him.

"Efflyn and I will scout ahead; we're faster on foot." The elves waited for his nodded approval, and then hurried off.

At his signal the others stopped, which, given the ox-carts crawling pace, happened quickly enough. A look back told him most of the warriors had already dismounted and were now leading their horses away onto slightly better terrain. Morale was low, and it showed in their expressions; they wouldn't be much of a threat to a shield wall, their only chance lay in surprise. So far no one had spotted them, though more than once since leaving Rainbow Ford the elves had come across enemy corpses. Sometimes the deaths had been recent, as if someone had been waiting for them, trailing them from a distance, or ranging ahead to clear the path. Whoever it was, they had to be very good at stealth and archery. House Grendargh's warband most like, but why they hadn't shown themselves was a mystery. On his orders the elves ignored the tracks they had discovered; if their benefactors chose to reveal themselves, they would.

He spotted Ralgon and his woman. When he had begun thinking of Gwennaith Keelan as the mercenary's woman, he wondered. It was obvious they were a couple. Their longing glances made him wish he could feel the same. But that road only led to pain and sorrow. Chosen were not meant to enjoy life; they had a duty.

A commotion from ahead drew his attention back to the road. Cadwaer and Efflyn were racing toward him, and even though elven expressions were usually unreadable, they seemed distressed. Panting they skidded to a stop next to him.

"Bloody Scales," Efflyn swore in between breaths.

"What?"

"They know we're coming, must have missed a scout," Cadwaer explained, still struggling for air.

"The wall's ready," the other elf added.

"Fuck!" Kildanor growled.

"Indeed. Not a chance to get through. Even if we charge, the horses can't make it." By now Cadwaer looked only slightly flustered. "We would not have the speed to break the wall, even if the ground wasn't this mucky."

He nodded. "Horses will never break a properly formed shield wall." If those Chanastardhians were anything like the ones they had encountered in Ondalan, the bastards who had managed to hold back demon-controlled Ralgon, they would hold their ground and let the Horse charge spend itself on their propped up, interlocked shields.

"What are we waiting on?" Ralgon asked from behind.

"The bastards have already formed a wall."

"Fuck," the mercenary grunted and was about to say more when Ealisaid came rushing toward them.

"Can you feel it? Chosen, can you feel it?" she yelled.

He stared at the Wizardess, wondering if the woman had completely lost her mind. "What the Scales..." He never finished the sentence. Now he felt it, the same distress that had penetrated the air in Cahill manor. Demonology! No, he reminded himself sternly, not that. Forced magic.

With a groan the Wizardess sunk to the ground, and before he was able to act the elves were at her side, helping her to her feet once more. She hung limp between them, moaning incoherently.

So focused was he on both the roar of magic and Ealisaid succumbing to the forces of fact tearing through possibility he almost missed the transformation Ralgon was going through. Rigid, eyes aglow the mercenary stared down the road toward the enemy's camp. No! This intense a glow he had only seen once before, before the Fiend had butchered its way through Ondalan. "Ralgon!" he barked, hoping to draw any reaction.

"He... is..." Drangar's voice was cracking; each word took one wracking breath. "Gaining... the..." He saw the struggle to keep the Fiend, the demon, at bay, leapt off Dawntreader, rushed to Ralgon's side. Gripping him by the shoulders, he tried to shake some sense into the mercenary.

"Let me pass, you landlubbers!" A shout came from down the hill. He didn't have to look to know it was Gwen. The change already affected Ralgon. Gwennaith of House Keelan surged up the hill, shoving so roughly those who didn't steer clear of her that she left a trail of surprised looking warriors lying in the mud. Her voice, it seemed, was the one thing that truly did help Ralgon. He regarded the shaking man. It was as if two equally strong forces were tearing him apart. Did he dare to slip into the spiritworld and observe what was really happening? No, he might lose hold of the mercenary and make Keelan's task even more difficult.

Gwen was at Ralgon's side, holding his hand, leaning close to speak to him when the ground shook. The tremor was followed by a massive boom. A cloud appeared beyond the hill, right where the enemy camp was. His ears rang with the force of the sound that echoed and intensified in his mind. Kildanor stumbled, almost lost hold of Drangar while behind him he heard the Wizardess and the elves scream in agony. In his hands Ralgon convulsed, back arching as if fighting against a great weight. He could almost smell the forces pounding in on the man. Gwen was leaning close, talking, at least her mouth moved. He did not hear a word, could not hear anything other than the roaring in his head. Then, as if a dam had been closed, the onslaught of inhuman noise stopped. Sound reached his conscience once more, and Kildanor realized Gwennaith Keelan was screaming.

"Come on! You can beat it, dear, come on!" She had one of Ralgon's hands in both of hers, clinging to him.

In his grip Ralgon shook, eyes ablaze with white-hot flame. How could he have forgotten that fire? They had shone even stronger in Ondalan, but not by far. Pupils, the only dark still remaining in those fiery orbs, darted from left to right, unaware of either him, or Gwen, or anything else.

Ralgon's mouth moved, unintelligible words spewing from his mouth with the saliva of his mad ravings.

"Drangar, please," young Keelan said, leaning close to him, tears in her eyes. She kissed him, probably hoping it would return the man to his senses. "Please," she whispered again, her red tresses shrouding the seizure-stricken face like a curtain.

He had to do something, anything, but couldn't for the life of him come up with a plan. The Chosen were warriors, first and foremost, not healers.

"The chant!" he heard Ealisaid shout from behind. "You need to get in there and sing the chant!"

He was about to turn around and stare at her when it hit him. Of course! That was it, the same thing they had done a few months ago when they had dragged Ralgon out of the stupor he had been in when returning to life. But he would feel safer if he had a Caretaker to sing with him; aye, he could do it alone, theoretically, but the Hymn to Sun and Health had more meaning when sung by followers of both gods. Where was a Caretaker when he needed one?

"Dragoncrest," he grunted, heaving Ralgon off the ground.

There was bound to be at least one healer in the fortress. If not, he would enter the spiritworld alone and try his best to sever the demonic lines. He glanced at the contorting body in his arms, wondering how much longer the mercenary could fight off the fiendish influence. Last time it had been days; maybe they'd be lucky again. "We need to break the siege!" he shouted. "Cadwaer, go check on the bastards again."

Giving a brief nod, the elf sprinted off. An elven Chosen was something he had never encountered, and two made him wonder just what the Scales was really going on. The Hold was safe, and would remain so until the Chanastardhians figured out how to cross the chasm. And who had forced magic so brutally that even he had been able to feel it?

Kildanor caught Ealisaid's attention. "What was that?"

The sorceress shrugged. "My guess's as good as yours."

He regretted being ignorant of magic. The boom and cloud could only mean one thing, but until Cadwaer returned he did not know for sure. If the enemy had been destroyed, who in this world had the power to do such a thing?

Cadwaer came back into sight, legs a blur of motion. "Gone," the elf panted.

"What do you mean gone?" Chosen and Wizardess echoed.

"There's nothing left in front of the chasm, nothing, no tree, no shrub, no blood, or grass, the entire camp has vanished. See for yourself."

He had watched Ealisaid's reaction to the report. Her face had lost all color, and the constant shaking of her head indicated just how shocked she really was. Not that he could blame her. Such large-scale destruction hadn't happened since the Demon War. Dragonfire was capable of reducing a house to ashes, one had even melted part of Dragoncrest's wall, but to obliterate an entire warband was something he had only seen demons do. It made sense, the feeling of all chance and hope being sucked from the air pressed into a steely coffin of firm control, those things he had felt, later than Ealisaid, granted, but still. And it was this same certainty that had shoved Ralgon over the edge. The decision to move had barely entered his mind when he saw that the Wizardess and his fellow Chosen were already heading for the far side of the hills.

He looked first at Dawntreader then at Ralgon's Hiljarr, and finally at Gwen who was still holding onto the mercenary, urging yet reassuring whispers streaming from her mouth. "We need a cart," he grunted as yet another convulsion tore through Ralgon's body. It felt as if there was even less resistance now. The black dots of the pupils were almost lost in the surge of brightness that was Drangar's eyes.

"On your horses!" someone, Upholder Rheanna he thought, shouted. The priestess rode into view a moment later, looking at them, concern lining her face. "The wagons will be here shortly," she said, turning her mare around and yelled, "Get moving, you lot!"

"Thank you," Kildanor said.

"What for? Doing my duty?" she replied, her lips a grim line. "The demons striking at him again?"

"Aye," he grunted as another seizure made Ralgon rear against his grip. "Whatever caused the Chanastardhians to vanish also battered down his defenses."

"I wish I could help," Rhea said. "Almost makes me wish I knew how to heal."

Gwen must have heard her for she snapped, "His mind's fine! It's the Fiend; no healer can deal with that!" Then, her voice reverting to the soothing tone she had used on Drangar. "Don't let go, dearheart. Please, come back to me."

How was it possible that this butcher could attract such a gentle and beautiful woman? No, that thought was foolish. Ralgon was not the killer, he reminded himself. He was not the creature or creatures trying to gain the upper hand in his mind right now. He had not committed the slaughter in Ondalan. The struggles seemed to have abated for the moment, but he was unwilling to relax his grip even for a heartbeat. The gods only knew what Drangar—no—the demons would do once in charge. Most likely relive the carnage, bring destruction. "Get a move on," he snarled at the riders that passed them slowly, gawking. As if this situation needed an audience.

"You heard the man," Rhea added, her voice so commanding that the horsemen spurred their steeds into a quick canter.

He could almost imagine her in a throne-room as had been her birthright. The aura of authority surrounded her like a beacon, and she knew it, using it to her advantage. Had she been younger he would have suggested her to Cumaill as a wife; she was far better suited for the rough, direct Baron than Neena Cahill. The only thing that spoke favorably for Úistan Cahill's daughter was she could produce heirs. Rheanna and Cumaill were a far better match, personality wise.

"What are you staring at?" the Upholder asked, obviously having noticed his expression.

"Nothing of import," he said.

She nodded then spurred her horse after the warband.

He watched her ride away, and realized that he was dreaming of things that would never come to pass. Houses Duasonh and Cahill would merge, if Sir Úistan had his way, and he had no doubt that Cumaill, once he realized they were serious about making him King, would agree to marry the Cahill heir. At least she was good-looking, and from what he could tell, she would know how to use her brain and command the Palace's servants.

Another spasm shook Ralgon and he turned his full attention back to holding the man. He hoped Dragoncrest's Caretaker knew the Hymn to Sun and Health, not that he was looking forward to tearing away the golden wires. The first time had been painful enough. Killing Ralgon wasn't an option, the bugger would most likely return from the dead anyway, probably with even less control over his body than now. No, the only option was to free him from the demonic influence and pray it would not happen again.

Galen and the other Chosen at Dragoncrest were as surprised by their elven brethren as he had been, and Kildanor would have loved to enjoy the brief reunion, but with Ralgon still shaking and twisting in his grip there was no time. He didn't even have time to inspect the field of dust that had been the Chanastardhian camp. Only the gods knew what had happened there.

The Wizardess had preceded him, and thankfully had talked the Caretaker, an aging man named Conlae, into joining them in the spiritworld. They had managed to tie down Drangar so that he now could slip into spiritform unhindered. It had become easier, and now only a few calming breaths were needed to thrust his mind away from his body.

Immediately he saw Ralgon, solid as always, before him. The golden wires were not only stuck in his limbs but also in his head, and no matter how the mercenary struggled, twisted, and thrashed, he could not shake the demonic bonds.

Kildanor waited. His first sortie into this world of swirling shadows had taken a tad longer also. No doubt Conlae was going through the same doubts he had. He was half tempted to thrust back into his body and see what took him this long. Instead, now that he seemingly had the time, he decided to take a look around. Dragoncrest held many mysteries, and though curious, he decided against exploring the fortress. The sheared off land right in front of the chasm beckoned him, and he didn't resist. Maybe the spot would reveal more of what had happened.

Surprised, he discovered that, unlike any place he had ever walked as a spirit, Dragoncrest was as solid here as in the real world. Which, now that he thought about it, made sense. What the Hold kept imprisoned surely was able to escape through most means known to mortals. The doorways on ground level, however, were as insubstantial as he was used to. Even crossing the gap was easy.

He was halfway across when the swirling mists of the spirit-world coalesced into a solid mass not unlike the fortress's foundations. But instead of walls blocking his path and vision, he saw tents and fire pits. And frozen in midst the unmoving camp, as if a painter had held the likenesses of every Chanastardhian warrior, were men-at-arms. Hundreds of them, some standing in a tight shield wall while others were in mid-stride heading for the line. Nothing and no one moved. How had magic been able to rip an entire warband out of one world and put into the next without killing them?

How long he stood there, Kildanor did not remember. Only when a ghostly hand appeared before his eyes did he tear his sight away from the grotesque likeness of life. Ealisaid looked as stunned as he felt, and the Caretaker who had followed her grimaced as if he was about to vomit. But instead of staring at the still life, the man struggled to avert his eyes from the chasm they were hovering over.

Ealisaid motioned for the castle and drifted off again, Conlae following her. She was right. It was pointless to continue without Ralgon at least being remotely sane once more, and even if they could have tossed the man into the chasm, that would barely solve the problem. He drifted away, steeling himself for the ritual.

It had been harder this time. While in the Palace dungeon he had to only remove one of the godsdamned things, the multitude of lines stuck in Ralgon now resembled the strings of a mad puppeteer. The visions of demons he had seen every time he had torn one out still flickered through his mind. In the end the hymn had almost been too short, and instead of pulling them out one at a time, he had resorted to grasping whole handfuls, yanking out a dozen at once. And on the last syllable of the last word, Conlae had looked up at him and had torn away the one line embedded in Ralgon's stomach. Kildanor had been so focused on the wires stuck in appendages that he had missed the one that, like the golden perversion of an umbilical cord, had pulsed in the mercenary's center. Conlae had done the right thing, but had not been prepared for the blood and the demons. The Caretaker had screamed himself to sleep. He now lay unconscious in his cot. Kildanor knew well the kind of visions the Eanaighist was experiencing; the priest was living through his worst nightmare. If Eanaigh smiled on him, he would wake with nothing but bad memories left of the experience.

Ralgon also slept. The Chanastardhian lass watched over him, as always.

Despite his weariness, Kildanor couldn't find the rest he badly needed. He stood on Dragoncrest's massive battlement and gazed at the even spot of dusty land that had held the enemy warband. How had magic been able to lock all those warriors away? The thought made him sad; dying would have been a better fate for the enemy. He couldn't tell whether they were aware of their situation or not, and prayed they felt nothing.

Stuck in the spiritworld, could there be a worse fate?

Her footsteps were not nearly as light as they had been, but he was still able to tell the Wizardess was coming toward him. He stayed as he was, waited for her to come to a halt. The cowl that now hid her disfigured features most of the time was drawn back. Glancing at her, he saw that, from this side at least, the scarring looked less severe.

"Enjoying the cold?" she asked. If she was joking, he couldn't tell.

"You saw the same thing as I," he said after a moment's hesitation. "How can this be?"

She shuffled to face him, the scarred tissue preventing her from merely turning her head. "I have no idea." Ealisaid looked as if she wanted to say more, so he held her gaze and waited. Finally, she went on. "Forcing magic into certainty isn't really something I know much about. What we do know, however, is that someone made sure we had a clear path." The thought had crossed his mind as well, but he remained silent, encouraging her to speak on. "Whoever or whatever did that is powerful." She shuddered, and added, "Very powerful."

"Who can be this powerful? How much blood did it take?"

Her nod was quick, brief, and a grimace of pain twisted her face. "So, you agree that someone wanted to help us?"

"Aye, just needed confirmation, don't want to go off on any wild theories."

A smile creased her scars. "Still, the question remains. Who was it, and how did they do it?"

He scoffed. "Sometimes I think that the more we live with our companion the more questions are thrown our way."

"I wouldn't want to trade with him. There's bound to be some part of him that just wants it over with, one way or another."

It was as if the fall had changed her even more. "Not much left of the arrogant wench, I see."

"Was that a compliment?" Now her voice had almost returned to the slight teasing it had possessed before. He could imagine the Lady Wizardess standing here instead of this broken shell.

"You've come a long way," he replied, evading the answer.

It was her turn to chuckle. "So have you. Be that as it may, I think we're going to be better off without any more interference. We were able to free Ralgon this time, but we have no Caretaker with us, so the Hymn cannot be properly repeated should this happen again."

"I agree."

"Get some rest, Chosen," Ealisaid said, putting a scarred hand on his. "I'll try to find out something about this." She bobbed her head into the plain's direction.

"You'll be all right?" The smile she gave him, although it almost split her face, was full of broken and missing teeth.

"I'll be fine. Good night."

# CHAPTER 42

## Fifth of Seed, 1476 K.C.

From his room Darlontor watched the procession of refugees enter the courtyard led by Machlon's Knight Protector, Gaedhor. It was a band bereft of vigor; the strain of travel showed. Some of the weak huddled on the two wagons, others rode donkeys, and he even saw a few being carried by younger men. From the leading wagon stumbled a figure of pity. Sword-arm in sling, Lleufor looked about the deserted bailey, scowling. Had the man's face not been in full sight, Darlontor would have missed the Shieldwarden's call in the general commotion. He heaved a sigh and turned to meet the newcomers. The encounter, he knew, would be as bad as the past few times the Council had met.

To his surprise it was Dalgor who intercepted him on the stairs. "Uncle, we need to talk."

"More demands from Arawn?" he asked wearily. In the past months it had been enough of a struggle to maintain order. Gryffor's followers, the fool called them faithful, had gone beyond the demand of sending an envoy to the Chanastardhians in order to secure Dunthiochagh and thus Drangar. Thankfully Arawn had intercepted the messenger they had sent. How the warleader had done so mattered little, by now the ever-increasing brawls between the two factions had become more and more brutal. If Darlontor protested the means that had been employed to stop the envoy, it would only sour his relationship with Arawn.

"No," Dalgor stated. The boy's familiar face had changed

in the Kumeens, and the two attempts on his life—by Gryffor's men, no doubt—had scarred him even further.

"Lleufor and Gaedhor..."

"Can wait," his nephew interrupted, put a firm arm around his shoulders and steered him back to his study. "This talk you have postponed for far too long."

"What about the rest of the council?"

"Kevonna already knows, so do Berleven and Arawn." The door shut behind them. "As for Lesganagh's false prophet, his voice matters not, he is insane." Dalgor guided him to the chairs near the fireplace and pushed him down on one.

"Misguided, perhaps..."

Again, his sister's son interrupted. "If it weren't for the elf, we would already have full-scale skirmishes breaking out." Dalgor positioned himself in front of him and remained standing. "The danger is real, uncle. Not only from that fool Gryffor, but also from Danachamain's disciples." A shudder ran through the younger man. What had he seen in the Kumeens? Was it worse than it had been? He shut down the memories as they rose. "The bloodbeasts are numerous, but you know that. Have you seen how few people survived the winter? None of our messengers reached Ma'tallon or Crossads. We're cut off, and you still deny the facts before you."

"Facts?" Darlontor echoed dully. "What facts?"

"The elf said Danachamain has risen from the dead, a fact that you failed to mention." Dalgor held out an index finger. "Second, bloodbeasts have assaulted every manor, village and town in our fief, herding everyone here. Why? Maybe because it will only take one fell strike to wipe out the entire order." It was pointless to ignore logic and knowledge that had for too long been banished to the deepest recesses of his mind. "Thirdly, the Kumeens are alive, a separate entity, an extension of the fallen Chosen's will." Darlontor stared. Just how far had Dalgor managed to penetrate the enemy stronghold? "Aye, uncle, I saw them in all their terrible glory, more demon than man now, both of them. I saw their..." A booming knock on the door interrupted him.

For a moment Darlontor stared at his nephew, was about to

shout for the new arrival to leave, when the portal swung open. In strode Lleufor, Shieldwarden of the fief. "What the fucking Scales is going on?" the man roared, courtesy and etiquette, usually so important to him, had been worn thin on the road. "Instead of a fortress and the brotherhood ready for war I see three camps of people vying for supremacy! Whilst you fools have been bickering and fighting amongst yourselves, a handful of farmsteads and at least two villages were butchered."

Darlontor opened his mouth to reply, but Lleufor's glare silenced him immediately. "Don't give me that defender litany, old friend. The only thing you are defending now is your cracked honor. Otherwise you would have nailed Gryffor and his staunchest supporters to crosses weeks ago. While you tried to ignore every godsdamned sign, we were holed up in Hlathan a mere twenty fucking miles from here, fighting off wave after wave of those monsters. Twenty fucking miles!"

From the courtyard the sound of Gryffor's voice rose above the din. "Brothers! Sisters! Heed my words!"

"What the Scales is he up to now?" Dalgor grunted, already halfway to the window.

He was a step or two behind Lleufor, and as he reached the glass panes, his nephew had already wrenched the window open. Now Gryffor's voice rang unhindered. For the moment, however, Darlontor was not interested in the man's proclamation; his focus was on the screen of men and women that surrounded the false prophet. All of them bore arms and he even saw the glint of chainmail underneath a few tunics. But what troubled him most was the openly displayed bloodbags hanging from their shoulders.

"Our worst fears have been realized!" Gryffor boomed. "Death is at hand, hunting us, and the only way to prevent what is happening is to march for Dunthiochagh and capture Drangar Ralchanh!"

"Imbecile," muttered Dalgor, shaking his head.

"He worries about Drangar?" Lleufor exclaimed, shocked. "As if the boy controls the bloodbeasts attacking us."

"Gryffor, ever the fool!" Arawn's voice rose above the murmur, shrieks, and wails. "This will not end with Drangar dead, and you know it!"

"Aye, it will not end there, our vigilance is eternal, Lesganagh has given us this duty and we will slay those who stand against us! First Dunthiochagh and then the rest."

Darlontor stopped himself before he could shout out that Drangar had already left Dunthiochagh. That information would have made things worse. The elf remained silent, and the others did not voice their suspicions. "Where is Lloreanthoran?" he asked instead.

"Who?" the Shieldwarden said.

"You think he can calm him?" Dalgor inclined his head toward Gryffor.

"I truly do not know, he might defeat a dozen, maybe more, but there are far too many out there. Close the window nephew, and go to Arawn; he will need your help. Tell him he is right, we need to strike at the Kumeens." It was time to face his demons, figuratively and literally. "Lleufor, get the weak away from the courtyard, I want them nowhere near Gryffor and his ilk."

"What will you do?" Dalgor asked, pulling the window shut. Was there concern in his voice?

"I'll wait for him to make a mistake."

"You think he doesn't know you are watching?"

"Oh, he knows, but he will want to make a spectacle of challenging my authority, what little is left of it. Lleufor, if anyone asks, tell them we will do what is necessary to banish the threat once and for all." Maybe, he hoped, there was a chance of getting the situation under control without having to face all of his nightmares.

The two men hurried out. Now that the glass muffled the sound it was harder to hear what Gryffor had to say. It mattered not. He would draw the line here, now. The Shieldwarden was right, he should have stopped this nonsense months earlier. Kevonna was right; it was time for him to be the leader once more. Arawn's demands were reasonable. He did not need Dalgor's report of the demonologists' stronghold. He had seen the place decades ago... No! That was a bridge he dared not cross.

"Darlontor!" the shout rang through the glass. He waited.

# CHAPTER 43

Despite being a stranger and also the only elf at the Eye of Traksor, Lloreanthoran was the sole person each of the three sides vying for dominance trusted. Or at least they allowed him to relay messages between the different factions. So far it hadn't come to serious open bloodshed. Tempers were rising, knives had already flashed in the night, but no one had been killed yet.

Gryffor's followers were the worst, edged on by their fanatic leader. Now, with winter finally defeated by spring, they clamored for decisive action and favored an alliance with the Chanastardhians to take Dunthiochagh, in addition to Drangar Ralgon. Darlontor, Arawn and excitable Gryffor, while not on speaking terms, only agreed adamantly on one thing: none revealed why Ralgon was so important.

His own research into the matter had already been curtailed, and he was banned from an entire section of the archives. So far, Lloreanthoran had obeyed the decree, but his patience was waning. It would've been easy to slip past the guards posted at the entrance, but he knew the situation was bad already. Any impulsive action could bring the whole of the fortress crashing against each other, using his actions as a focal point.

In the past weeks his knowledge of and capacity for using bloodmagic had grown substantially. The Sons, despite their claim of being a defensive force, had focused on offense; very few chants and spells were directed at protection. The books he had studied were obviously adaptations of other works, that much the text actually revealed. As to how the Sons of Traksor had gained access to the knowledge, he knew the answer to that. The Lightbringer had opened this path for the disowned prince. From where it came from remained a mystery.

"Darlontor!" someone shouted in the courtyard.

His meditation cut short, Lloreanthoran opened his eyes. He stood and walked to the window, pushing the shutters open. The Eye itself was a marvel of architecture, but only a few windows had glass panes to keep the chill out and allow daylight in. His cell was like most others, drafty, bleak, not that any of the other rooms he had seen so far were any different in appearance. Everything here seemed focused on one thing: discipline. Not that the current situation had improved matters. Entire passages were filled with rubbish and rubble, silent memorials to the occasions when hostilities had not remained on the verbal level.

Now the courtyard was packed with humans standing amidst refuse. And there, at its center, surrounded by his followers stood Gryffor. "Darlontor!" the faction leader shouted again.

A quick count told Lloreanthoran that all members of this group of warmongers were assembled, armed and armored, ready for battle. He recognized Gaedhor among the bedraggled creatures trying to push away from Gryffor. The refugees had finally made it. His first impulse was to rejoice, but the situation they now faced was anything but joyful.

"Darlontor!" Gryffor's voice boomed. Surely the erstwhile leader of all the Sons had heard. Was the old man once more underestimating the threat?

In recent weeks the Priest High—a title only few still addressed him with—had retreated further and further from those siding with him. Even he'd had a hard time talking to the man. He was by no means a good judge of human nature and the accompanying expressions, but the images he had gained from delving into the man's mind had clearly shown him how afraid Darlontor was, and how that fear was not focused on the impending doom but on a truth, he tried to hide. Never one to give in to idle speculation, he had left it at that. If he was able to pick up on the duplicity, the few people who still straggled to the aging Priest High's banner knew of it as well. Not that they spoke with him. Most of them were idealists, believing more in the position than the man himself. And as the days passed, more and more people abandoned him. None of them sided with Gryffor; most had changed allegiance to Arawn.

Dalgor, the young man he had rescued in the Kumeen Mountains, was still cryptic about what he had seen in there. But his decisiveness and enthusiasm had fanned the flames of determination within Arawn and his followers. Unlike his uncle, Dalgor knew full well what had to be done and was dead set to see it through. What terrors dwelled in Darlontor's mind, he could only guess. The abominations in the Kumeens were something he knew about first hand. Dalgor's proposal to strike at the mountain area was sensible, and given the fact that he had also fought the bloodbeasts, he was inclined to agree. If asked, he would join the assault, but so far no one had spoken the question. Arawn did not want to charge with only a portion of the Sons, he wanted support of the entire Order. Scales, he was almost ready to come to terms with Darlontor. The only thorn in their sides was Gryffor.

"Darlontor!" the rogue leader's voice echoed up to him once again. "Come on out!"

"He's too frightened, the old man," someone taunted.

"Why should I be afraid of you?" the Priest High's voice sounded stronger than it had in weeks. Had something changed?

"Will you give us your blessing?" Gryffor asked.

"To go north and join forces with Chanastardh? No!"

"We need to end this; we should have ended it years ago!"

"Allying with the Chanastardhians will not help us in any way; they do not concern themselves with us."

"He is in Dunthiochagh!"

Gryffor's statement was met with silence, and though he could not see Darlontor he felt the old man knew something, was aware of something the others were not. "We will get him, with or without you." The last was shouted by another Son, and was met by agreeing murmurs. "We will finish it!"

"And what will you finish, fool?" From the other end of the complex, Arawn had left his part of the fortress and stood atop the stairs leading down to the courtyard. He saw Dalgor pushing through the ranks milling about the bailey, making his way to his superior. "Will you finish the peace between Kalduuhn and Danastaer?"

"Danastaer is dead!" some hollered.

"So, you'll ally yourselves with its conquerors?" Darlontor asked. "Will that change the bloodbeasts prowling our lands? I think not!"

"With Drangar dead the threat will be over." The speaker was cuffed by Gryffor, much to the amusement of his peers.

"Will it now?" Dalgor shouted.

Gryffor turned and looked at the younger man. "Come to pipe the same tune as your mentor?"

Though he couldn't quite see it, Lloreanthoran knew by the sound of his voice that Dalgor was sneering. "You intend to storm Dunthiochagh alongside the Chanastardhians? At least we have a goal better than siding with conquerors! Besides, how would you make it north? The woods are crawling with blood-beasts. Ask them, they know! The danger is greater than just one man! The danger lies west not north, I have seen it, them! We need to sever the adder's head!"

"Only that the head is not where you think it is, nephew." Although calm, Darlontor's voice drowned out the shouts of protest.

"Uncle, I have seen what I have seen, and even if we finish what you messed up long ago, we would still have to deal with the Kumeens!"

"We need to finish him first!" Gryffor shouted. His follow-ers bellowed their agreement. "You've failed us the last time, old man; we'll go to Dunthiochagh and finish him!"

"No!" the word was spoken by both uncle and nephew.

"What? You'll force me to stay?" Gryffor chuckled. "You"— he pointed at a spot above Lloreanthoran—"have maybe a dozen people still standing with you! And you"—his finger wandered over to Arawn and Dalgor—"dare not fight your brothers."

"Don't be so sure of that," Arawn replied.

"What? You're siding with him now?" Gryffor yelled.

"At least he doesn't go about threatening others! At least he does not rattle swords and proclaim the desire to fraternize with a nation bent on subjugation!"

"All we want is to get Ralchanh!"

"I forbid it," Darlontor said, the Priest High's voice sounded unusually calm. Then Lloreanthoran heard him speak once more, but this time only he could hear him. *Elf, wizard, be ready, I fear the worst is only moments away.* Darlontor was using magic to communicate with him. Some part of him wondered if the human had pricked his finger with a pin to draw blood or if he had resources available to him that none of the others had. The elderly man gave him little time to consider, for in the next instant his voice rang across the courtyard once more. "I am the Priest High, Gryffor. I command the Sons of Traksor. Not you, nor anyone else!" Was he provoking his rival intentionally?

"You've lost your way, old man! You had it in your power to kill the Ralchanh bastard years and years ago and did nothing. You failed in your duties!"

"And you?" Arawn countered. "Is your planned invasion of Dunthiochagh not against the mandate set for us when we got this fief? If we so much as lift a single finger against anyone else, we won't have time to pack before the King evicts us! Think, man, think!"

"Look who talks!" Gryffor spat back. "Weren't you the one clamoring for war yourself?"

"Aye, but not against Dunthiochagh, oaf, against the Kumeens. You should bloody well start using your head!"

"Silence!" Darlontor roared, but those allied with Gryffor ignored the Priest High, spitting accusations at Arawn's followers. And still Lloreanthoran had no idea what they were talking about. Why did everything revolve around the Ralchanh person? What was so special about him?

"Cernwyn paid for it, they all paid for it!" amidst the shouted obscenities Gryffor still managed to be louder.

"He should have followed the rules. And so should you!"

"Are you threatening me? Are you aping your uncle now that you're back on his good side?" The question was accompanied by loud jeers. Gobs of spit flew toward Dalgor and Arawn. Alarmed, Lloreanthoran saw that the more hotheaded Sons had readied their swords, hiding them underneath their cloaks. If no one intervened soon, blood would spill. He had no idea how many Sons were as adept at magic as Dalgor, doubted it were many, but still, once the fuel for their magic flowed copiously there was no limit to what they could do.

*They'll come to their senses, trust me!* Darlontor whispered. The statement only roused his ire. How could the idiot calmly watch as his order annihilated itself?

*Why should I?* he hissed back. *In the past month you have given me little enough reason for doing so. I am no further along in my duties than when I came here!* The accumulated frustration of weeks of inactivity finally broke through and he uttered a relieved sigh, glad to have his thoughts finally out in the open. *You used me to get your nephew back, and still you have told me nothing!*

*It will be revealed all too soon, I'm afraid.* He detected sadness in the human's thought, as if Darlontor knew he was facing something he could not escape.

Below, on the courtyard, things were heating up. Arawn managed to keep his followers in check, but Gryffor encouraged his to lob stones at their fellow Sons. One struck a refugee woman on the temple, and under outraged growls she collapsed. This was the drop that broke the dam of patience, and the anger surged outward in the muffled scrapes of blades being drawn. Here and there Lloreanthoran spotted Sons opening their bloodbags, smearing red on their palms and arms, chanting. He was familiar with it, but had not expected to see so many of them actually employing forced magic. What was becoming dreadfully apparent though was that only those of minor status strengthened their body this way. The others, people like Dalgor who possessed a better grasp on this magic, did nothing. Maybe they were coming to their senses, Lloreanthoran hoped. The chanting below stopped.

For a moment it seemed as if the Sons of Traksor were about to abandon this exercise in futility. Then, someone from Gryffor's side hurled a spear at his estranged brethren. Empowered by blood, the missile didn't arc lazily across the courtyard; no, it was like an arrow shot from a longbow. It impaled one man, and drew a short path of destruction through Arawn's ranks.

The following shout of approval was short-lived as the victims' friends retaliated. The responding barrage employed spears, axes, and shields. The shields were as useless against missiles as a dragon swimming in the ocean.

Pandemonium reigned. Now both sides charged one another, the cutting, weeping, sobbing, moaning, the crashing of steel on steel filled the air. Why wasn't Darlontor interfering? Was the old man afraid like Gryffor had claimed? Lloreanthoran wished he were standing with the Priest High, if only to see what kind of battle was fought on the man's face. He was about to turn and head up to the next floor when, all of the sudden, the noise ebbed away. He whirled around, dreading what he would see.

Blood curdled on the dirty cobblestone; torn bodies strewn everywhere, but a great many still stood, were still alive. And every single one of them stared at the gate.

In rode a man on a white horse. Following him were a group of five, but the Sons' attention was focused on the first rider. A collective hiss of surprise ran through the ranks. Then, it felt to Lloreanthoran as if all resentment between one another had been brushed away by the appearance of this single rider, they all faced the gateway, crouching, ready to do battle once more.

The rider, obviously stunned, reeling from what he was seeing, held up his hands, first in a placating gesture; then he hammered his palms against his forehead, screaming.

"Don't! No!" Darlontor shouted from above. "Do not..." he never finished that sentence. As he had feared the spilled blood empowered the surviving Sons, and a score or more charged the seizure-stricken rider, shouting, "Get him!"

Lloreanthoran thought the brotherly bloodshed had been bad, what followed was worse.

# CHAPTER 44

Their trip from Dragoncrest had been uneventful. The group that had seemed to pursue them, a score of Grendargh insurgents as it turned out, caught up with them in the ruins of Dunlan. After their initial disappointment at them not being Chanastardhians, they had agreed to accompany them as far south as Crossads. Courtesy of the rebels' knowledge of the area they had evaded any enemy patrols. From there they had followed the Elven Road west, always staying out of sight. And still Cat Ralchanh's son insisted someone was following. None could verify his claim, and soon they dismissed his suspicion. Even protective Gwen Keelan wondered about her man's sanity.

The Wizardess, Ealisaid, had stopped her jaunts into the spiritworld after Dunlan, stating that she could not unravel the mystery of the Chanastardhian warband that was trapped in the other dimension. Rhea still didn't believe her, but now, with Cat's son suspiciously scanning the area with nervous eyes, she had other things to worry about. Dragoncrest's riddle had to wait.

Now, four days south of Mtain Geer, Drangar Ralgon was getting moodier by the mile, and she was tired of his brooding, his glum outlook on everything and everyone. She had tried to understand the seizures and the visions of demons, which was useless since she could not. They were deep in Gathran Forest on a dirt road that threaded its way through looming trees. The Eye of Traksor had to be close, because as noon approached Drangar became even more withdrawn.

There hadn't been many relationships in her life, but she knew enough of her own heart to realize just how lost Gwen was. Whenever the younger woman reached out to comfort him, he pulled away, and Rhea'd had just about enough of it. It was obvious Gwen cared for him deeply, and the fool was shattering any hope of the two becoming a couple. The noble from Chanastardh had little experience with men, Rhea could tell that much already, and the kiss the pair had shared weeks ago was probably just a memory. Or maybe, she thought, Drangar's mind was so occupied with his own misery that he just had no time for anything else. After all, the kiss had happened right before the seizures.

She saw Gwen scowling in frustration and turning her mare away from Drangar. Her horsemanship had improved, yes, but Rhea could tell the girl wasn't really comfortable in the saddle. Gwen headed her way, and fell in alongside her, looking hurt and confused. It was best to wait, until she was ready to talk. She didn't have to wait long.

"What is the matter with him? I only want to help," the younger woman complained.

"He is in a world of his own, fighting his—" She paused, searching for a more appropriate word. Then, having found none, she continued "—demons. Not only those of his vision. I think he fears hurting you."

"But I love him."

"Maybe, despite his relationship with Hesmera, he has never been in love before."

"But they were to marry."

"Aye, maybe he did love her." She thought a moment then said, "He lived in isolation for two years and struggled with the death he thought he caused, hating himself probably. Now here you are, and he feels drawn to you—never you doubt that! We all saw the looks he gave you. Aside from being drawn to you, you also help him fight off whatever is troubling him. Maybe he thought with you he could control it. Dragoncrest changed all that. And now he fears for himself, and you."

"I don't care, I just want him to know I am there for him," Gwen retorted. "I get the worry and being afraid part. But I don't care. I heard Lord Cahill's men speak of what he did in Ondalan, and I still wanted to know him."

"Maybe he's afraid of that too."

"What do you mean?"

There was a sudden halt in the column as Drangar, who was second in line, reined Hiljarr and scrutinized the eastern woods. Rhea and Gwen didn't even bother looking. If a strange pursuer had been with them since Dragoncrest and hadn't done them any harm so far, what was there to worry about? A moment later their trek continued.

"Maybe he is afraid of who, or rather what, he is."

"He's one of the kindest men I've ever known," Gwen said.

Her look of utter conviction made Rhea smile. Then grim reality reasserted itself. "He doesn't think so."

"What? How can he not?"

"You know what he did as a mercenary?" She recalled, after much prompting from Nerran, that she had seen Ralgon years ago, in one of the border conflicts in Caendeel to the east. War had never been pretty, and even though the lined shield walls had a certain grace to them, the clash of wood, leather and steel always pounded war's harsh reality into the awareness of any observer.

"No, but General Kerral said he was viciously good at what he did," Gwen answered, shaking her head.

"You have practiced in the wall, right?" The younger woman nodded. "Before the walls meet, sometimes, you have idiots brave or foolish enough to try pierce the enemy's wall before they lock." Gwen's eyes widened, as she understood the sheer foolery of such a maneuver.

"It's suicide." The statement was as true as most others Rhea had heard. "Those who do won't last long against a tight wall." Her own charge against the Chanastardhian shield wall atop Dunthiochagh's battlement had been as suicidal as it had been necessary.

"Aye," Rhea said, giving a quick nod of agreement.

"Are you saying he charged the walls?"

Another nod, there wasn't much she could add to the facts. Gwen had only training experience with shield walls, but even that memory of how solid a good formation was sufficed to make her understand what state of madness one had to be in to try to break such a wall. She merely said, "All the time, if the rumors are true. He succeeded as well. No wonder they said he was blessed by Lesganagh."

Gwen considered for a moment then said, "But he isn't."

Rhea shook her head. "No, he isn't. If what Kildanor says is true, he isn't blessed at all." This, she thought, wasn't entirely true. Coimharrin had told her of what had happened at Eanaigh's temple, of how Ralgon had judged the former High Priest. She barely paid attention to the road, and suddenly she found Drangar riding at her left, looking worried and weary as usual.

Gwen muttered something unintelligible, and he said, "Please stay." The first kind words or at least not harsh words he had uttered in days. "I want you to hear this as well." His look turned to Rhea. "You can discern the truth?" It was more statement than question, and she nodded her head, waiting on his next words. "But it is always subjective, right? Upholder Coimharrin said so."

"Yes."

"You pray to Lliania in order to gain this ability."

"Yes." Where was this leading, she wondered?

"I didn't. At Eanaigh's temple I mean. It was easy, with the solid gold cob towering above the altar. But when I heard the session and the lie spewing, I knew I had to do something. I had to stop the bastard from evading justice. Lliania's Curse I always called it, because I could never stand injustice. Pisses me off when liars get away with it."

"You could have killed him," she suggested, aware of Gwen riding next to her, staring at Drangar.

"Yes and no. Yes, I could have killed him, but no because it didn't feel right." He paused, looking at nothing. His face contorted as if in pain then he said, "A few months ago, near the village Carlgh, I killed the lord's nephew. Served the swine right. I'd heard rumors of what he was like, cowardly scum. The villagers didn't stop talking when I was there. If you're silent they just lose interest and go about their business. He was a right bastard. On my last day there, the fool made his entry once more; molested a girl just because he could. Made me angry, and I stopped him. He followed me and tried to attack me. I snapped his neck, thinking it was better to kill him than the villagers. I knew he deserved it and that Her Scales would do the rest." He paused again. "Me and my cursed sense of justice," Drangar muttered.

What was right and what was wrong, the eternal debate, even among Lliania's followers. Ralgon wasn't self-righteous, and in his situation, Rhea might have reacted the same way. Still, those who felt drawn to be judge and jury usually ended up in Lliania's priesthood. Was it possible that...? A fragment of a memory clawed its way to the surface. She remembered the Justiciar having done the same. He had not prayed to Lliania on occasions, had judged by merely listening to people's statements. For her, for Coimharrin, the priesthood, prayer was needed before they could discern lies. But now that she thought of it, she had rarely seen Amhlaidh Ralchanh pray before passing judgment. Had Cat possessed the same gift? And if so, had she passed it on to her son?

"You look concerned." Drangar's voice broke her reverie.

"No... yes... I'm not sure."

"Tell me of my mother, please."

"There's not much more to say than what I've already told you. She was older than me and was off studying with the Librarians most of the time, I think. Though we both lived at Court, her world was separate from mine." It wasn't a satisfying answer, she knew, but it was the only one she could give. There was no point in fabricating something; if Drangar had inherited this trait of his grandfather's, he would have known a lie for what it was.

"What about my grandda?"

"I love you," Gwen suddenly said.

Drangar's gaze drifted away from Rhea. "I know" was all he said. Then he sighed. "Dearheart, I don't want to hurt you." Rhea needed no prayer to tell this was the truth. "It's just that I don't know what the Scales is going on, the seizures frighten me, and I do not want to lose control again. I'm afraid that your presence might not be enough to rein me in. I need to finish this first."

"We need to finish this first," Gwen corrected.

"She's right. We're all in this together." His troubled look loosed a thought she had harbored for a while now but never truly considered. Was it possible? "You never trusted anyone?"

Ralgon's face answered before he said a word. How could this be? How could he claim he had loved Hesmera and felt something for Gwen now when he had never trusted a soul? Had he trusted himself? Did he trust himself? She doubted it. Things weren't bright to begin with where Drangar was concerned, but the pressure of the murder and the raging demons struggling for control would've done sufficient damage to even a strong self-confidence. Now, she realized with a start, the wall-breaking Scythe made sense. It was anger mixed with a tremendous lack of self-preservation that had turned Cat's son into the bane of the battlefields. He most likely had only begun to care about anything after the village, and certainly after he had met Hesmera. Rhea caught Gwen's expression and knew she understood as well.

And still Drangar hadn't voiced what his face was screaming. She wanted to tell him he could trust her, and wondered how. And even if she did, would he believe her? Would he believe Gwen? He barely trusted himself, and with past events, at least those she knew of, she couldn't blame him. Did he even realize what a sad life he led? What she realized though, was that there was precious little time to let trust grow.

It was Gwen who broke the silence. "You have to say it."

"And mean it," Rhea added, nodding her thanks to the woman from Chanastardh.

Like an animal cornered Drangar's eyes darted this way and that. He had to tell them, had to bring it out in the open, otherwise none of them could truly help. And he was smart enough to realize it. After all he'd had two years of introspection. "I trusted this," he finally said, patting his sword. "How sad is that? Not much to show for a life, is it?"

It was out, though now they had to find a way for him to trust in himself. He looked as if he wanted to say more, but something off to the east had caught his attention. Rhea saw him squint, scanning the woods. "Let's finish this!" he growled, spurring his charger toward the trees. "Kildanor, our shadow has shown itself!" Then he was off the road, between the oaks, and gone from her immediate sight.

"He's running away again, right?" Gwen asked with a sigh.

"No, I don't think so."

"But this shadow is a convenient distraction."

"Give him time," Rhea replied, but silently she wondered if Gwen was right.

Kildanor was with them in a moment, followed by Ealisaid, who still struggled on her mare. The Chosen frowned. "Think he's going to catch it today?"

"We won't have many other opportunities," she said. "Once we reach the Eye the journey is over."

"I'll help," the Wizardess said. In an instant her face acquired the blank look they had all come to associate with her entering the spiritworld.

"As if that'll work," Kildanor snorted. He then turned Dawntreader and followed Drangar into the forest.

A resigned sigh escaped Gwen.

# CHAPTER 45

It was out, finally. How many times had he thought about it? He couldn't remember. It had always lingered there, near the surface, but he had always been afraid to actually consider it. With the forest closing in around him, Drangar tried to focus on the task at hand. For not more than an instant had their pursuer shown himself. Was it just another way of avoiding the issue, he wondered? Was he running away from the fact that he had never really trusted anyone, including himself, for most of his life? And who could blame him, shunned as he had been during all of his childhood. Even the adults had avoided his company. Then, after he had run away, life hadn't been much different, really. There were comrades, yes, but his violence had frightened most into keeping their distance. Sure, when he had been drunk his temper had cooled, and there had been Kerral and Hesmera, but had either of them truly helped him gain confidence?

He caught sight of his prey. There! Behind the thornleaf! Now it darted for a thicket. Hiljarr, sensing his confusing thoughts, hesitated. No, Drangar decided firmly, whoever it was that followed them had to be in league with the Sons, had probably been tracking their movements, and now was off to warn them of his coming. If they knew, they would be prepared, and he had a good idea of what his reception would look like. Dalgor's attack had made the situation quite obvious.

The scout had to be taken. There was a time for being introspective and thoughtful, but it was not now. He spurred Hiljarr into a canter, and even that much speed was dangerous, considering the roots and ferns riddling the ground. He was of half a mind to dismount and follow the bastard on foot, but past attempts had already shown how fleet the scout was; their only chance lay in riding him down.

Nothing moved in the thicket. From behind he heard the hoof beat of another horse, Kildanor's Dawntreader most like. The Chosen, the only person who seemingly believed him, was as keen on catching their shadow, but where Drangar merely wanted to eliminate the threat it posed, Kildanor wanted to strangle information out of him. Not such a bad idea, really, but whenever he pondered the issue all he could think of was what Dalgor had done in Cahill Manor, and the poisoning and stabbing in Shadowpass. He still didn't know how he had survived, or how he had been returned to life, and that worried him as well. One always heard about nonsense like that, people returning from the grave to fulfill some duty or another, but those stories were usually bullshit tales made up by a lunatic to gather fools for a cause. No one had ever truly come back from the dead. No one, except him. Drangar banished the thought; the scout had to be taken. That was important, the answers to all the questions were with the Sons of Traksor, only a few miles away now, and if they wandered into an ambush, he would never get them.

"Sure it wasn't a trick of light?"

He turned and saw Kildanor reining his charger to a halt. The Chosen certainly was the better horseman, which suited him fine. On the occasions he had been forced to do battle from horseback he had managed fairly well, though Hiljarr had saved his neck several times. He preferred to fight afoot. "No trick," he said, eyes scanning his surroundings. Asking Kildanor to trust him right after they had established he hardly trusted himself was the pinnacle of stupidity, so he said no more.

There! The budding leaves on one of the shrubs next to a pillar-like steeloak moved. Drangar thought he saw a shadowy outline of a figure crouched behind the twigs. "Let's end this," he growled. His sword was unsheathed before his feet touched the ground. A reassuring pat on Hiljarr's flank, and then he sprinted for the hidden scout. Silent, the figure remained still. Had his eyes betrayed him? No, there the bastard was!

Despite the fact that the Eye was only a few more miles down the road, Drangar felt calm. Nervousness, he knew, should have flooded him. It didn't. Instead he was comforted by the presence of his friends. Yes, they were his friends; only the recent conversation with Eluned, Rheanna, and Gwen had made him realize how foolish he had been. For his sake they all wanted to help him finish this, even Kildanor, although the Chosen had admitted that he was also in it for knowledge about his wayward brothers. He smiled. "Wayward brothers" was a curious way to describe the two fallen Chosen. Of course he knew of Ethain and Ganaedor, there wasn't a single soul in the Sons of Traksor who hadn't heard their tale of woe. He couldn't remember more than a few tidbits, but the pair was known as "the demonic brothers." That they were Kildanor's by blood, however, had been a revelation.

His head throbbed, as if he was hung over.

He looked at Eluned and Gwen riding side by side, talking, grateful the older woman accompanied them. In matters of the heart, it seemed, she knew more than any of the others. Ealisaid, hunched on her horse like a sack of turnips, looked as if her scars were troubling her again. No wonder, and though Eluned had tended to the Wizardess's ailments throughout the journey, he wondered if he was demanding too much of her.

Kildanor, as always, rode point, but now Rhea was with him. Maybe they were discussing his past again. Ralchanh—how he had despised the name, his name, when he had lived in the Eye. "Throw Ralchanh to the falcons" the other children had chanted more than once. Back then, and still today, he did not understand their reasons. He had been the Priest High's child, yes, but despite what the others might have thought, it had never been a privileged position. Far from it, Darlontor had put more pressure on him, demanded more of him than had been expected of anyone. How many times had he stood in the courtyard practicing swordplay? He barely remembered. It wasn't the kind of thing necessarily used in a shield wall, and the Sons had never been a warband. Instead they clung to ideals most people only read about in books.

The headache returned.

He wasn't afraid to face them. Not anymore. With Gwen at his side, Drangar felt as if he could face the world and still walk away from the conflict.

Ralchanh—maybe being a part of that family wasn't such a bad thing. His grandfather had been like Coimharrin, even though the old coot pretended to be absentminded half the time. Amhlaidh Ralchanh, Justiciar at the Royal Court of Haldain, the thought filled him with pride. Rhea and Eluned were right; it was a proud heritage.

Maybe underneath the mountain that weighed on his conscience he was a decent man. Decent, good, both attributes he never would have attached to himself. Scales, he had killed so many people. But so had others, Eluned had told him more than once, always supported by the rest of the group. Even the episode at Dragoncrest hadn't shaken their faith in him. Someone believed in him, as a person. They didn't see the Scythe, the one man insane enough to charge every godsdamned opposing shield wall. Now that he thought of it, Drangar still found it hard to believe he had survived at all. Training with House Cirrain's warband had shown him how effective a wall was. It had made him realize that what he had done time and again was impossible. No single man should have been able to shatter a barrier of shields like he had. Back then he had used bloodmagic without even knowing it.

Gods, he needed to lie down and close his eyes. Maybe then the throbbing would stop.

Ealisaid and Eluned had spoken about it in detail, argued the issue until the solution left was that he was gifted in magic, "innate talent" they had called it. And as angry as he had always been, he had, of course, resorted to forcing reality to alter things to be the way he wanted them to be. Bloodmagic, forced magic, they had flung so many words at him he barely understood what the Scales they were talking about. What all this had to do with the demons was something they would find out at the Eye of Traksor.

He was glad to have met Eluned at Cahill manor. She had nurtured him back to health after Dalgor's attack. Yes, she knew much about magic, but anyone willing to waste their life away in a Library could read up on it. And despite her...

"Bloody headache," he grunted, bunching his lids shut.

The Eye was what mattered, and the answers hidden behind its walls. Friends, the thought made him smile despite his throbbing head. He patted Hiljarr, for a long time the stallion had been his only friend. Now he had five more, and he trusted all of them.

Something white glittered through the trees. Actually, the way he remembered the Eye, its walls glowed white no matter what time of day. Drangar looked up. The days had been getting longer once more, yet his body told him it was time for supper. His stomach grumbled.

The sun was setting, slowly descending in the west. Soon the Kumeens would hide it. How often had he stood on the battlement of the Eye and watched the needle-like spires of those mountains impale Lesganagh's Glowing Orb? If they lived through this, he would have to show the spectacle to Gwen, maybe even Rhea. He doubted Kildanor, or the other two women would enjoy such a sunset. Ealisaid always complained about light hurting her eyes. And Eluned seemed more interested in stories and history than the world around her. No, he decided, it was best just to share it only with Gwen. Once all of this was over.

Gloom had spread over Gathran as they halted one last time. Eluned said it was best to be prepared, and though Drangar was loath to delay their arrival even longer, he agreed. He would have liked a bath, to wash hair and body, and shave the beard that was once more covering half his face. Not that he looked any different from Kildanor, who was just as unkempt. The women weren't much better off, and for that he was grateful. At least he did not stick out as the vagabond amidst those of nobler blood. Not that the grandson of a Justiciar, even a bastard, was anything to be ashamed of. He wondered who his father was. Darlontor had made it quite clear that he wasn't, so who had gotten Caitrin Ralchanh pregnant? Though knowing who it was would change little, nothing at all actually. That his mother was dead was fairly evident. How else could her spirit have taken him to the past, or ask Rhea and Eluned to look after him?

Eluned came toward him as he slipped into his leather tunic. She always seemed to know when his thoughts drifted off into the darkness. He regarded her calm, unblinking face, adjusting the fabric so the chain would fall properly. It was as if she knew what went on in his mind. Gwen still guarded his sleep but had given up her position as the person he confided in most of the time.

"What's bothering you?" Eluned asked. The throbbing, it had almost gone a moment earlier, returned.

Drangar shook his head to clear his thoughts, and then said, "I was wondering who my father was."

In reply she yawned, stretched shoulders tense from the long ride, and answered, "It matters little. The past is the past and cannot be changed." The words sounded familiar, but he couldn't recall where he had heard them and who had said them. "Stay focused, understand? You can beat this thing in your head, I know it." She slapped his shoulder, closed her eyes, and stretched again. "You are strong, otherwise you would never have made it this far. And you have us to watch your back. Don't worry."

He tried to give a courageous nod and must have succeeded for Eluned smiled toothily. "While you're here, will you help me with this?" Drangar unfurled the length of cloth that held his chain armor. A bit of rust had settled on the steel. "Should've paid more attention," he muttered, giving Eluned an apologetic smile.

For a moment it seemed as if she would detest the task, and he was about to withdraw the request when Gwen, already in her leathers and chain, came to a halt beside Eluned. "I'll do it," she said, somewhat distractedly.

"Something wrong?" he asked as he slipped his arms into the chain.

"Nothing, just a headache," Gwen muttered, tightening the straps on his back. "Got some rust here."

"Yeah I know, was too busy not thinking about fighting and

killing." He turned, wanted to thank Eluned for her advice, but she already stood with Rhea and Kildanor who were helping each other with their armor. "Headache, you say? Must've been the food, gone bad I think."

"Yeah, moldy bread's a bitch." He chuckled. A last tug and Gwen let go. "There you go."

"Thank you." He turned around, eyes searching her face. "For everything. I know I'm a mess, but I do care for you, a lot. It's just that I need to sort this out…"

She silenced him with a hand. "You talk too much. I understand, why else would I be here?" Then she proceeded to strap the bracers to his arms. "Just don't do anything stupid, will you?"

"Like what?" he asked, thinking he had a good idea what she meant. They had indeed grown close.

"Oh, the sort of thing that earned you your title," Gwen muttered, retrieving the leg guards from his pack.

"I doubt they will form a shield wall against me." Actually, he wasn't sure how they would greet him. "I just will not let them imprison me again." Ealisaid, he saw, stood apart from the others, holding her head. "What's wrong with her?" he asked, tightening the armor straps.

Gwen glanced over her shoulder the direction he was looking and shrugged. "She says she's feeling dizzy."

"Bloody bread," Drangar grumbled. Finally satisfied with the leg guards, he belted his sword. By now, after the weeks of training in Dunthiochagh, he was once again used to being encased in leather and steel.

"Aye," Gwen said. "What will we do when this is over?"

The matter had crossed his mind almost every time he thought of his upcoming encounter with the Sons of Traksor. He had always refused to consider it, too much depended on what would happen in a little while. "I don't know," Drangar said. "I guess we should go north."

"North?"

"Aye, by now Anne's warband will be back in Chanastardh and Mireynh's messengers will have reached Herascor informing Drammoch of your desertion."

Her face brightened. "You mean we will go help my da?"

"Can't go about with you being gloomy as well, can we?" He wanted to say more, how much he cared for her, how much he wanted her to be happy. He never got the chance, for Gwen jumped him, embraced him, and kissed him long and hard.

"Your beard smells," she remarked a moment later, nose wrinkled, stepping away from him.

He wisely held his tongue.

Something was odd about the Eye. The circular clearing was immense—almost a mile in diameter, but even from five hundred yards off, Drangar could tell something was wrong. He stared at the white wall and the northern gatehouse, trying to decide what he didn't like about it. There was the obvious, of course. The bastards were responsible for Hesmera's death, and that alone was reason enough to despise the inhabitants of the fortress. And it clouded his objectivity. But there was more. Dusk was almost upon them, yet he saw no indication of fires being lit on the battlement and torches mounted in the brackets on each side of the gate.

He found it hard to focus, squinted every few breaths. The throbbing hadn't passed, and it seemed to be getting stronger. Gwen rode beside him. He glanced over to her and saw she was rubbing her temples as well. A quick scan of the others showed him the same. Kildanor was frowning, Rhea also, and Ealisaid had shrunken even deeper into herself, if such a thing were possible. For a moment he wondered if he had missed something, and then remembered Eluned. She looked strained as well. Bloody bread, he thought grimly. Winter had one advantage over the other seasons: food did not spoil as easily, and were it not for the snowstorms and constant gloom everyone seemed to walk in, he would have wished for it still to be the cold season. No. He shook his head, tried to clear it of the annoying pushing and pulsing that went on behind his eyes. "Stay focused," he whispered, and found himself wishing that Dog were still with him. Her stern reminders would have worked wonders.

Now he knew what bothered him about the Eye. Not only was there a lack of illumination, the sentries were missing as well. What the Scales was going on?

The throbbing became a stabbing that drove tears to his eyes. A loud shout echoed over the clearing, and he felt the others' eyes on him. But it wasn't he who had screamed. The voice had sounded from the Eye.

Finish it. He had to finish it now. Already he felt his determination, his resolve wavering. And there was something more. After Cahill Manor and Ondalan and certainly after Dragoncrest he was familiar with the feeling. The Fiend was striking again! It was growling in pleasure.

He spurred Hiljarr on. The others followed immediately. Did they know he was struggling again? Probably not. Whenever he had told them the fiendish presence was still there, Ealisaid and Kildanor had gone into the spiritworld to see for themselves. And every attempt had been futile. They had detected nothing. They were wrong. Why bother telling them he felt the wires reaching for him once more if they could not see? Even Eluned… who? He dared a glance back at his friends… companions. Who was that person riding next to Rhea?

Another boom. It sounded like shields splintering, or wood being torn apart by a slingthrower-stone. Then all air was forced out of his body by a massive punch to the chest. Breathe! He had to breathe! Gasping, Drangar rode on. Hiljarr, ever the stalwart companion, was as surefooted as always, pounding the dirt underneath his hooves. Air streamed back into his lungs. Hooves battering the road thundered behind him. He didn't have to tell them what to do, they knew. Maybe they sensed something was wrong. But there was no time for maybes.

The next sound he was quite familiar with. Screams of the dying issued from the Eye. What the bloody Scales was going on in there? He felt the coils of gold unwinding from the blackness, reaching out for his mind, his body. No, the bastards would not win again. He was master of himself, his body, and his mind. They would not use him again!

He reached the gate. It stood ajar; he could ride through easily. From beyond he heard the sounds of battle, armies clashing, as if shield walls miles long were hammering into each other. The others were behind him now. Hiljarr, so long untried in

battle, danced nervously beneath him. He reached forward, patted his neck, spoke words he hoped sounded soothing. With
all this noise it was impossible to tell the charger anything. At
least he tried, and Hiljarr noticed his touch and calmed. "We've
been through so much, old friend," he said, knowing full well
the animal did not hear. It mattered not. The words were meant
for him as well.

Another wave of anger, rage—something—hit him. Drangar
looked ahead, squeezed his thighs, and let Hiljarr do the rest.
He patted his sword for reassurance. There would be no need
for it, if he could help it.

Hiljarr inched for the gate. The horse, Drangar knew, was
smarter than most, and craftier. Years of sheep herding even
when Drangar had been too beat-down, had taught the charger
a lot, and now he seemed to know it was best if the gate was
wide open so the others had an easier time passing through.
Another push, the steeloak portal swung wide.

Another wave hit him, but now it came not from within but
without. Hiljarr felt it also, shied, and had to be urged on.

The courtyard was a battlefield. The smell of blood was
heavy in the air, he heard the screams of the dying, the grunts
of the combatants. The Sons were fighting each other!

Then they all turned as one. Somebody shouted "No! No!"
but whoever it was, the bloodied masses did not listen. As one
they charged.

Hiljarr, panicked, reared, almost threw him. Someone—
Drangar saw little aside from the teeming mass of armed men
and women—threw a spear. The weapon was a streak in the air,
a blur almost too fast to see. Again, his mind reeled, the golden
coils swarmed.

Hiljarr went to the ground, falling backwards. The wedge-
shaped spearhead sent gushing out of the charger's back, the
bloody fountain drenching him. The roaring inside his head
vanished in an instant. Hiljarr, no! His horse didn't even have
the chance to whinny one last time. Aside from the chanting,
screaming, howling horde charging at him, Drangar heard
nothing. Saw nothing. Hiljarr! No!

The world turned red.

# CHAPTER 46

Something was wrong. Ealisaid was certain. She couldn't tell what it was, but she knew. She glanced about the others munching on dry bread and some apples that had seen better days. They all looked distressed. Nothing new there. They were close to their goal. Of course they were tense.

But that was not what bothered her.

She looked at Gwen and Drangar, smiled. They were closer now, and she was happy for them. Eluned's timely intervention had done them good. Eluned somehow knew what to say and what to do to help others; she was good at tasks such as these. During the trip down from Dunthiochagh Eluned... who?

Who was this person?

The world seemed upside down for a moment then righted itself. And Ealisaid knew she had been thinking about something important. Something she now couldn't remember.

They were back in the saddle sooner than she wanted, and though she understood the urgency, her back, legs, and behind ached so terribly she wondered how the Scales she managed to stay on the horse at all. But she did, and the trek continued.

She turned and looked at the others. Kildanor, Rhea, Gwen and Drangar, they all looked weary—she paused, and then recalled there was one more to their little band: Eluned. It seemed as if she alone did not suffer from fatigue. Instead, she sat boldly upon her gelding, focusing on the road ahead.

She remembered the day they had met in... what was that place again? The more she concentrated on the incident the blurrier it became. Where had they met? Who had they met? Sharp pain lanced through her head. Ealisaid cringed, ground her teeth, and stared at her horse's bobbing head. Why couldn't she remember where they had encountered... It was maddening. The agony behind her eyes increased the harder she tried to recall. A look over hunched shoulders showed Gwen and Drangar looking more asleep than awake.

Ahead were Kildanor and Rhea, both slumping as well.

Where did they come across... her?

Ealisaid prided herself on having a good memory, but the more she rummaged through her mind the less she felt she knew. Something was definitely not right. One moment she saw two companions in front of her, the next there were three. How was that possible?

The stranger... Eluned... turned and looked at her, and for a moment she felt transparent. Eluned squinted, shook her head, her gaze wandering back to the front.

Someone had followed them... and Eluned had taken care of the... Drangar had chased the scout into... spy. He and Kildanor... had been sent by the Sons of Traksor... had cornered their pursuer... to monitor Drangar's advance.

A realization dawned in that part of her mind not occupied with understanding the confusing images: one set of memories was overlapping another, if only she knew which one was real. She went back further, to Dunthiochagh, looking for an anchor that might jolt her brain into its regular patterns.

Eluned had found her lying on the street after... had been brought before the Baron... and taken her to rest... in the dungeons. No! She felt this was wrong. She hadn't rested in the dungeons. She had been miserable in them. They were smelly and loathsome, and... she had seen what terrible things would happen, if she... had seen Drangar on the bier, dead yet alive still. She had... been given a vision by the gods... alerted Kildanor and the Baron to... avoid something... coming alive again. The woman who had screamed and raged... against the demons, and that Drangar was the key.

She squeezed her eyes shut, tried to focus her thoughts. One set of memories was real, the other was not. She remembered waking in her house, alone. Dust had settled on everything. Her attempts at contacting the Citadel had failed. Her garden had been built over. She had destroyed a house or two and killed some people. The pain lessened.

Next thing she remembered was waking up in... a cave—No! It was a damp dungeon, no bloody cave! She had woken with her hands bound tightly and a metal contraption encasing her tongue. No one had served her tea! The taste of iron on her tongue, in her mouth—a gag meant to hold a wizard at bay—triggered other images, feelings, smells. The stench of urine and feces lingering in the corridors initiated an onslaught of other memories. Culain, the illusion, her exploration of the Citadel. They were few at first, but they heralded an avalanche of others.

Like a dream, or nightmare rather, the false memories washed away, and all of the sudden Ealisaid knew there had never been a person called Eluned accompanying them. In fact, until Drangar had charged into Gathran everything had been normal. Now, at least for her, reality had taken its proper place again. Which forced the next question into her mind: Who the Scales was the woman riding with them?

Eluned, or whatever her name was, had already proved capable of using magic well enough to weave an enchantment on everyone. Why it hadn't worked on her was something Ealisaid would ponder once the current problem was dealt with.

But what could she do?

One thing she had learned from Nerran, through all the rudeness the Paladin usually displayed, was that a battle was best fought when the enemy was known. She had to get to know their enemy before taking action.

Replaying the meager facts helped little; all she knew for sure was that this person was a wizard of tremendous power. How else had she managed to weave a web of lies and fabrications around them. Yet, it seemed as if it malfunctioned slightly. The others looked more tired than she remembered, and the way they reacted to low hanging branches, the lack of speed with which they dodged them, indicated that not all was as desired on the enemy's part.

Maybe, she thought, the woman riding before her was an illusion as well. At this point she dismissed no option, no possibility. But mirages only worked in this world. In the spiritworld any such spell was nonexistent.

Ealisaid hesitated, and thought of giving Eluned, who had been such a resourceful ally over the past weeks the benefit of a... No! They had not traveled with that woman. Hunching over, assuming the position the others knew so well, she slipped into the spiritworld, immediately focusing on their new companion.

Perception, she knew from experience, was different in both worlds. While one could observe general events in the bodily world from the realm of spirits, the opposite was impossible. Or so she had always thought. But when the object of her curiosity turned and looked right at her, a moment of panic stopped her momentarily. Could Eluned see into the spiritworld? Concentrating to clear her mind, Ealisaid regarded her target. And still she felt she was being watched.

A smile crept on Eluned's lips and remained there, knowing and mysterious. She appeared the same as Kildanor and the others in the spiritworld. Maybe the tiring journey made her see... She hesitated. Something shifted around Eluned's smile. The smoky skin rippled, moved. The face, so plain and unassuming only moments earlier, changed. It looked as if a waxbust had stood too long in the glaring sun. Terror, a sense of wrongness flooded her as she stared.

The bubbling mass of skin and hair rearranged itself, not according to her expectations, not into a different human face. No, this was something different, alien, frightening. No book she had ever read mentioned a creature such as this. What was that thing? Feline, graceful, deadly, its features the stuff of nightmares, yet there was a keen, knowing intelligence in its predator eyes. The horse it was riding on was a shadow of nothing here in the spiritworld.

"You do know that you're flaunting your presence to any who would have half a mind to look for you, don't you?" the creature asked, its—no, her—voice crisp and clear as if Eluned stood right next to her. And what the Scales was she talking about anyway? She did not signal her presence to anyone! The feline pointed a clawed hand at something beyond and behind her. Ealisaid turned and saw the blazing phoenix hovering above her. Who had put it there?

"I reckon your superiors whilst you were hibernating," the being all of them knew as Eluned said. "Aye, the name, well it will do for now."

Who and what was she? And what was she doing here?

"It'd be much easier if you spoke," Eluned said, waving dismissively at the others. "They can't hear us."

How could one speak in the spiritworld?

A chuckle that sounded more like a cat coughing. "As with everything else, you just have to want it."

It was that simple? The creature remained silent. Ealisaid willed herself, her spiritform, to create sound. To her surprise it worked. It was almost inaudible, but she heard the hum she had been thinking of.

"You don't have to move your lips, little human, will the words into existence."

Involuntarily she thought of a trumpet blast, which, to her shock and delight, issued forth immediately. Eluned nodded approvingly. "What are you?"

"A traveler." If all her questions were to be answered in such a nebulous manner, quitting now would be as good as anything else. Eluned spoke on, obviously reading her mind as well as before. "I'm here to see that your companion Drangar survives the day."

"What is he to you?"

A short pause, and then Eluned said, "A means to an end, my means to end what should have ended millennia ago."

"And what are you?"

"I'm what your kind falsely calls a demon." Ealisaid's instincts screamed at her to run, slide back into her body and warn the others, but something about Eluned made her stay.

"Falsely?" she asked, feeling as ignorant as Ysold, only she was even less clever than the child.

"When Lesganagh brought light and warmth into the world, after the gods had defeated the firelings, he created my ancestors. We call ourselves sunargh, and my kind was long gone before the elves almost repeated our mistake."

"Your mistake?"

"Child, what did those wizards teach you? No history,

obviously, but then why should they? It is long gone, and your short-lived species barely remembers what they had for supper two days past. So why should you recall something that was ancient history when your grandparents were young?"

"And you?" Ealisaid retorted. "Why are you here?"

"I've always been here." Eluned said with an enigmatic smile. "You need my help and I yours."

She almost asked why the sunargh had not shown its true nature immediately, then imagined Kildanor's reaction, and couldn't blame her for deceiving them. Instead, she said, "It was you following us?"

"I had to make sure the foolish heirs to the prince of foolery wouldn't make an even bigger mess than they already had." Eluned paused, her spirit looking at the still-solid figure of Drangar hovering above his horse's shadow. "Curious little man, don't you think? Trying so hard to run away from everything and still being dragged back the way he came."

"What do you know of him and his problems?"

"Unfortunately, not all I wish to know; even the Great Library didn't yield all the information I need."

This surprised her. The Libraries of Traghnalach were repositories of knowledge, and everything worth knowing was stored somewhere in their archives. The mere thought of something not appearing in the records sent a cold shiver down her spine. "How is that possible?" she asked.

"It isn't, and yet it is. Sometimes the gods are struck just as blind as the rest of us."

"How?"

"Magic, child, magic. A determined mind can interfere with even divine perception."

She wanted to ask more, wanted to know who exactly Eluned was, and if she could learn anything from her, but the sunargh cut their conversation short with a swift gesture. "No more time to talk. Can't you feel it? The fools are at it again."

She felt it, the presence of blood that enslaved magic into certainty. Yet it still was not as strong as... "Dragoncrest," she muttered. "That was you?" she asked as inspiration struck her. "You banished those poor souls into the spiritworld."

A very human shrug of the shoulders was all the answer she needed. "I do what's necessary."

"You do know what effect it had on him?" Ealisaid pointed at Drangar. "He had a seizure."

Eluned stopped and whirled around. "He had what?" she snarled, fangs showing behind drawn back lips.

"You don't know?"

"I wouldn't ask if I did, woman, now out with it!"

"Your bloodmagic caused the coils to reattach."

"Coils?"

"Those golden wires that drill into him. We figure it's usually him being angry or... well, bloodmagic that causes this. Both are the... demons' path to dominating him."

"Damnation."

# CHAPTER 47

Even from this distance Kildanor could make out the intricate frescoes that were chiseled into the Eye's white walls. At its center stood a massive plinth that loomed over the battlements, its long shadow stabbing eastward. He couldn't discern what exactly the carved images displayed, but he felt certain they were of a religious nature. If Drangar had been truthful, the Sons of Traksor operated under the guise of a pious order dedicated to executing the will of the gods in their vigil against the demons. They even went so far as to have their own Upholder and Caretaker, even an Orbmaster. Danastaer hadn't had a living priest of Lesganagh for decades, so if the Sons truly counted one of them amongst their numbers, he was anxious to meet him. But unlike the Chosen whose vigil was divinely appointed, the Sons had no such legitimate claim, or so Drangar told them. Subterfuge was a method they had employed long before Drangar's so-called cousin had redecorated Cahill Manor's turret-chamber.

Now, as the distance evaporated under the steady beat of their horses' hooves, he was able to see more of the pictures, all of them commonly known tales of deeds of the gods, nothing special about it. Then he felt it.

The weariness that had until now dragged his senses down vanished instantly. Bloodmagic pulsed within the Eye. He turned and looked at the others. Ealisaid was walking in the spiritworld again, Drangar brooding as always, Rhea talking to Gwen, and Eluned as alert as she had ever been. Didn't they feel it? Given Ralgon's frightening loss of control near Dragoncrest, he had expected the mercenary's reaction more drastic. Here he sat, however, so absorbed in his thoughts that the pull and push of the demonic forces didn't faze him. As long as he behaved no differently everything was fine. If things got out of hand, the matter would become infinitely more complicated.

Suddenly from within the fortress came the clash of weapons, screams of the dying, and what sounded like splintering wood, and off Drangar was, spurring Hiljarr to cover the remaining distance. Surprised, Kildanor motioned the others to follow.

The clash of steel drowned out all other sound, and Ralgon was still riding, unopposed. By now their appearance should have alerted even the most drunken guard, yet their approach met with no resistance. Taking his eyes off the mercenary, Kildanor chanced a scrutinizing look at the battlements and was surprised to see them unoccupied.

No one observed their approach.

Now Drangar was at the gate, and instead of having to bang against the wood, his horse gently pushed one gate aside. Who in their right mind would leave a fortress unguarded and open to everyone?

The answer presented itself the moment Drangar rode through the gatehouse, opening the view for the rest of them. Immediately, Kildanor understood what was going on. It reminded him of the failed rebellion in Dunthiochagh months earlier: The Sons of Traksor were fighting each other!

The moment Ralgon entered the courtyard the hostilities ceased, but only for that single instant. Then, despite the shouted orders of some people, the majority of the still standing Sons unleashed a wave of bloodmagic-propelled steel against Drangar. Hiljarr shied, toppled, a spear piercing his throat. Somehow the other missiles hung in the air, unmoving. The air was so saturated with demonic—no—forced magic the Chosen could almost touch it.

Then he felt as if he had woken from a dream, and a few things happened at the same moment. Red mists rippling off him in a constant stream, Drangar Ralgon shoved the horse's carcass off him and launched himself at the Sons. From the corner of his vision he saw someone coming to a stop next to him.

Panic, fear, hatred surged through Kildanor as he turned to stare at the demon. His sword was already out of its sheath. The demon glanced at him, shook its head as if telling him he had more immediate problems. Somehow the fiend did convince him, and slowly he turned to stare at the charging Drangar, blood still hissing off him.

In Ondalan, he had only seen the results of the carnage, not the origin. Bodies torn in half had sufficed as witnesses to the Fiend that now controlled Ralgon; they had driven home the point that angering Drangar was the height of stupidity. But none of them had seen him rage. Now they did. From behind him he heard a shocked intake of breath, Gwen most like. The lass who had only seen the man she loved suffer some sort of seizure and had been told of the grotesque feats of slaughter from Úistan Cahill's men now saw of what her love was capable of.

At the same moment the weapons, still suspended in the air, clattered to the ground. On both sides of him people shouted, trying to convince the fanatical mob to halt their attack. As if peaceful negotiations were still an option.

Drangar, sword still scabbarded at his side, plunged into the Sons of Traksor like a wedge, his movements reckless, not the controlled motions of the man Kildanor had come to know. This was a completely different person. The Sons surrounded him, swept in behind him like a wave.

What should they do? Help Drangar? Defend this… his line of thought ground to a stop as body parts sprayed out of the roiling, milling throng of armed men. The horrified shrieks were accompanied by the sizzling hiss of evaporating liquid. A red mist rose from the ground, hiding the slaughter behind a veil of crimson.

Drangar hadn't killed that many to justify such a cloud. Where did the blood…? Kildanor paused, taking in the entire scene. Around the edges of the pulsing mass of bodies pushing against Ralgon he saw the remains of a good dozen fresh corpses, their blood staining the ground.

An arm slapped on the ground next to him. He had to do something. Anything.

"Wait, Chosen." He had forgotten the demon! "This is not your battle."

How could it say that? Of course, it was his battle. "I promised I'd help him." Why was he talking so casually to it?

"Look deeper," the demon said.

"Do what she says," Ealisaid added dreamily.

The spiritworld? Did they mean...? Of course they did. He had done it in Ondalan when Drangar had struggled against the possession.

The noise made it hard to concentrate. Shouts urging the combatants to stop rang unheeded through the courtyard, adding to the din. The occasional pained gasp of another Son being rent apart added to the turmoil. He had to focus, find his center, and enter the spiritworld.

Slowly, it seemed, the shrieks and thuds and shouts faded into the background. Then, suddenly, he felt a clawed hand yanking him out of his body. Startled, Kildanor looked at the person, demon, who had managed to pull out his spirit with apparent ease.

"Not me," it said. "Him." It pointed at the shadowy cloud of bodies. He turned and stared, and did not believe his eyes.

There, in midst the shades were two Drangars. One was as solid as the other. Golden cords stuck in one, like strings attached to a doll, pulled by an overzealous puppeteer. Not an inch of body was spared. This Drangar ravaged the shadows about him.

The other, just as furious, hacked at the cords with a sword. The weapon changed shape with every swing, growing, shrinking, coiling, uncoiling. Every pass was a sure cut, the cords it struck snapped back, only to reattach themselves an instant later. The Drangar wielding the blade looked just as mad as his counterpart, shouting, spitting curses, attacking the regenerating strings relentlessly.

"He is fighting it," Ealisaid sounded muffled, unlike the demon whose voice had been as clear here as it had been in the real world.

"Aye, he learned that he could and that he must," it said. "Prepare yourself, Chosen!"

Kildanor didn't even feel the transition. He was back in his body, seeing a group of warriors turn from the carnage to find easier targets. Others were retreated entirely, their superiors' orders finally reaching their minds.

"Rhea, Gwen, to arms!" Normally he would have expected the Rider to make a glib remark, but the only thing he heard from behind was steel sliding across leather. He drew his sword. "Stay in the saddle as long as you can."

As the Sons charged, he saw that the blood spattered on their armor evaporated as well. They hesitated, but only for an instant. Then they charged once more.

Like the missiles of a few moments ago, these ones stopped suddenly, held at bay by an invisible wall. Just how much bloody magic was in this place?

"I have them," a voice spoke into his ear.

"Scales!" Kildanor chanced a look around. Aside from Gwen and Rhea, who kept close to the one horse carrying Ealisaid's limp body, and the demon's shell next to them, he saw no one nearby. He glanced at the Sons as they struggled against their invisible bonds then let his eyes roam the fortress's interior. There! At a window stood... He blinked. Another elf? Here? What the Scales was going on?

"Stand aside!" a voice shouted from up ahead.

"Gryffor don't do this!" another yelled.

"This is what we should have done from the beginning, Dalgor! You were on our side, now you side with him?"

"I know a weapon when I see one, and against the enemy we need every good weapon available!"

"Bullshit! Stand aside, I have him!"

More blood sizzled off the paving stone. The Sons around Drangar parted, revealing the mercenary's raging figure caught inside a glowing cage. From what the Ladies Cahill had told them, Kildanor guessed it was like the one that had imprisoned Drangar in the last year.

"Chosen?"

Irritated he looked about, and saw the demon sway on its feet. "What do you want?"

"To help him." It nodded toward Drangar.

"How?"

"Is there a way to remove the cords?"

Why was he even talking to that thing? He ground his teeth and remained silent.

"Gods, how can you be so selfish? If we don't get rid of those things, he will be gone! Tell me how!"

"The Hymn to Sun and Health, sung by both a Lesganaghist and an Eanaighist while the strings are pulled out," he answered, hating every word exchanged with that thing. "Not that we'll find a Caretaker in this slaughterhouse."

"You'll have to do it alone," it said.

"Right," he replied, snorting in derision.

"Lesganagh made the other gods, foolish human. He is in them all, so one dedicated to him is also dedicated to the others. You have to do it alone, and you can do it alone!" insisted the demon.

All Kildanor could do was stare at the thing.

"You need to sing the Hymn and pull out the cords."

"The last ones almost killed a Caretaker," he retorted.

"I will protect you!"

From up ahead the thing that was inside Drangar shouted in pain. Irritated, Kildanor glanced at the prison's pulsing light. "A demon? Protect me?" He barked a laugh.

"You can trust her," Ealisaid said, sounding as far off as she had in the spiritworld. "Help him."

Once, long ago, during the Demon War, Kildanor had sworn to kill every demon in sight. Now he knew that this oath would not be fulfilled. "Very well," he growled, looking at the mass of body parts around Drangar, the blood steaming away into the air, feeding the cage around his friend. Yes, he considered the brooding man a friend, and he was finally able to admit it to himself.

Whoever shielded them from the missiles did a thorough job. He looked at Gwennaith Keelan; saw the terror in her eyes that mirrored that of Sir Úistan and his retainers in Ondalan. Such carnage wasn't new to him, but he could have done without seeing it again. It wasn't Drangar, he wanted to tell her, reassure her that the man she loved was fighting the demons that held his body in thrall.

"Chosen, now!" the she-demon snapped in a voice that brooked no argument. Not that he was about to question her.

The spiritworld slid into place around him like an almost comfortable glove. Kildanor floated toward Drangar.

# CHAPTER 48

Cat's son was trying, but he had no chance. She knew it, and most likely he did too, but despite this sense of defeat emanating from him, Drangar Ralchanh did not give up. That he had been able to manifest a weapon to use in the spiritworld was no simple feat; Lightbringer gave his will the credit it deserved. Still, they were far from being safe.

None of them, Cat included, had ever relayed to her just what exactly was troubling the man. Yes, there was the bargain, and now that she saw the golden wires attached to almost every inch of his body, she realized what was going on. The final tile to complete the mosaic had been delivered by the Wizardess recalling the seizure that Drangar had suffered near the Hold. Bloodmagic made the barrier brittle. She was almost tempted to venture to the Veil of Shadow to see for herself, but there were other things that needed to be done.

The books she had given Prince Tral had taught him well, and he in turn had passed on some of the knowledge to his followers. Now one of those was trying to destroy her only means to end one threat forever. Had Cat known? Not initially, but her spirit had died and been reborn as a Servant of Lliania. She had to shatter the cage.

Overpowering the human's feeble magic was easy, and the radiant globe disappeared almost instantly. A quick return to her body to see what went on in the courtyard, and then back to the spiritworld. At least that was her plan. The hazy shapes solidified around her.

Lightbringer looked around. The scene was almost the same, but now the Sons of Traksor were being held back by two of their leaders. She remembered one of them from a vision of the past, Cat's past. He stood amidst a whirlwind of crimson mists, holding the others still.

Drangar twitched. The Chosen must have managed the severing quicker than she had...

Drangar charged the one who had imprisoned him. His movements were more graceful than she thought a human capable of. With a start she realized it was not Drangar who was controlling the body. The Chosen was still working.

Cat's son barreled into the older human, wrapped his hands around the man's throat, and pulled off the head. She was back in the spiritworld in that same instant, rushing to help the Chosen remove the coils. There was no time to consider her blunder. She should have waited; she berated herself for but a moment. Then she was at Kildanor's side.

He had done a good job, but a few score lines were still embedded. Drangar, the real one, was swinging his spirit-blade ineffectively at the coils, and Kildanor pulled them out, his singing filled the otherworld's deathly silence. She knew the song, had first heard it sung by the elves after they had won their freedom. Without a moment's hesitation she joined her voice to the Chosen's, singing just as loudly. Then she reached for a handful of strings and pulled. Another followed, and then two more, but there was no time to see what Drangar was doing; she only hoped he would be left intact when she returned to her body. Lightbringer's fingers wrapped around a thicker strand firmly embedded in the stomach.

The vision almost drowned out everything else.

# CHAPTER 49

This was like Ondalan. He was aware of the Fiend moving his body. No nightmares, no flashes of gory details; Drangar was the sole front row spectator for the demon's use of his body. And he had thought watching himself kill Hesmera had been bad. Now he knew better.

As his hands tore out the arms of one of the Sons, he began to struggle against the invisible prison that was his body. There were no walls, no boundaries, but also no escape. It was almost as if he was back in that cold dark place in which he had been trapped after his death. No matter which way he charged he always ended up in front of the windows that were his eyes. What was this place?

His hands were embedded into the stomach of another Son. Drangar turned away in disgust as the body came apart in a spray of blood.

Somehow, he had expected to see the blood-filled pools with the demons once again—yet another image that would never leave him—but there was only darkness. Ealisaid had explained the spiritworld to him, and this was not it. Had it been, he would have seen clouded shapes of his surroundings in the real world. Had the demons locked him away for good within his own mind?

The thought was too terrible to dwell upon. Kildanor was probably already trying to rip the golden coils off his other body, like he had done at Dragoncrest. Another idea rose. If this was his mind, his prison, then he could dictate the rules, change them if necessary.

Drangar tried to concentrate.

He lost focus again and again when his hands tore apart another Son of Traksor. Yes, he had no love for the bastards, but no one deserved to die like this. He wanted to vomit, run once more.

But he had no place to withdraw, and he was tired of running and hiding, fed up with the demons that wanted to dominate him, to possess him.

He remembered what had calmed him before. The one thing that had made him look like a lunatic killer more than anything else: sharpening his sword.

This was his mind; he was a god here, even if someone else pulled his body's strings. Here he could do anything.

The familiar hilt was in his hand the instant he thought of it, in his left the whetstone. Settling in front of his two windows, he began running the stone up and down one side of the blade, his eyes never leaving the slaughter. He had to remember it all, the horrors, and he had to hone his anger as sharply as the edge of his sword.

In this place of silence, he heard the scraping of the whetstone, so familiar now that it lulled him despite the carnage. Ealisaid and Kildanor had said it only took a point one focused on when one wanted to leave the body behind. Drangar concentrated on the without. He wanted to be right outside of his body.

The darkness of his prison was replaced by another. This new one, however, was murky, foggy, and for a moment he felt lost. Then he saw it, his body. It was as expected, like Kildanor had explained: a solid form amidst the shapelessness of smoke. And attached to it were hundreds and hundreds of glowing coils.

To his surprise, the sword had made the transition with him. Did he consider the weapon a part of him? Maybe. It mattered not; all that was important were the steel in his hand and the wires piercing his body.

He swung.

And swung, finally finding an outlet for the pent-up frustration that had lingered within for so long. The threads came apart easily, and for a moment he dared to hope he could actually sever them all. Then, as if a ghastly hand was guiding them, the cut parts reattached to the remains in his spiritbody. Again, he severed the strands, and again they grew back together as if knitted by unseen hands.

What the Scales was this? He howled, screamed in anger, raged like a madman, cutting and cutting, watching the bloody wires heal faster and faster. He noticed someone approaching. In the murk of the spiritworld where shapes bled into each other, identifying whom it was proved difficult, and only when this newcomer was a few yards away did he recognize Kildanor. The Chosen was singing, and in a way he couldn't quite understand Drangar was able to hear the Hymn to Sun and Health. Something dislodged in his mind as he remembered hearing that tune before, though then it had been two voices, as was proper. Now there was only one.

As Kildanor sung, he reached down and plucked dozens of wires from his spiritbody and didn't bother to look up.

Pain hammered into his mind, and instantly Drangar was back in his body. There, through his eyes, he saw a gleaming cage surrounding his possessed flesh. It was like the one the bastard Dalgor had summoned in Dunthiochagh. But this time the summoner wasn't his cousin.

Through the prison's glittering fabric, he saw a man he vaguely remembered. What was his name again? Thoughts racing, retracing his childhood and youth here in the Eye, faces of those he had grown up with rushed by. Dalgor's was the first, immediately followed by Darlontor and a host of others who had tortured him with their cruelty.

Gryffor, yes, it was Gryffor. He couldn't have guessed the older man was so well versed in magic, hadn't known any of the Sons used magic at all.

Another wave of agony engulfed him, tore at him. There was nothing he could do but stare at the spectacle without. Kildanor was doing a far better job at removing the wires than he had. It was useless to return there.

Then, as if struck by a hammer, he realized what the cage was doing! It wasn't meant to merely imprison him. He felt the tugging, pulling, as if his body, mind, and soul were being rent apart. Gryffor's magic, as Dalgor's before, was meant to separate the Fiend from his mind! Whatever Kildanor and others had accomplished before was only temporary at best. Ever since his death and return to life, the wires had returned when he was angry, or when bloodmagic nearby. Gryffor wanted to kill the Fiend, exorcize it.

Gods, he prayed silently, let him succeed. He was tired, ready to give up a life that had only brought him misery.

Gods, he pleaded, let him succeed, even if it means death. Death was preferable to the constant watchfulness. Life without emotions was not preferable to death, Gwen had shown him that already, and Drangar hoped it would be over quickly.

Did Kildanor even realize what the Sons were doing? No. How could he when he himself had only understood it at this moment. He had seen executions. Criminals and traitors quartered by horse. Never had he wondered what the victims felt at the moment their limbs were torn from their body. Now he knew.

Caught in his anticipation, actually wanting Gryffor to end this once and for all, he clung to the sight of the aging Son of Traksor working his magic.

Then, suddenly, the pain was gone. As was the cage. The almost severed fiendish part reasserted control and surged toward Gryffor. No, gods, no! He hoped Kildanor would succeed before his clawing tearing hands reached the sorcerer, before they tore out his... the old man's neck offered little resistance to the demon's strength. Blood gushed, but only for a moment. It turned into crimson mist almost immediately.

Then, accompanied by a twinned scream of rage and frustration and fear, Drangar was in control once more. Only now it was too late.

"Stop!" someone shouted.

For a moment he considered playing dumb, pretending he was waking just now, but only for a moment. He was tired of it all, tired of the lies, the games, tired of knowing nothing.

The ring of blades that surrounded him at a safe distance parted on each side of him. From his left came Darlontor, robes flowing as he rushed toward him. The other man closing in on him was none other than Dalgor. Both looked scared. He didn't blame them. Beneath the anger, he was just as afraid.

"I had nothing to do with this!" he said, raising bloody hands in surrender. A ridiculous statement given that the courtyard was spattered with limbs and guts of those his hands had just torn apart.

The wall of swords closed behind the two people he had, at one time, considered family. "I know," Darlontor said.

Stunned by the reply, he looked about, searching for Gwen's supporting eyes. She was with Ealisaid and Rheanna, supporting both Kildanor and a being he knew well enough from his nightmares. "Godsdamned demon!" he hissed, drawing steel.

In response the Sons around him raised their shields once more. Some turned, looked the way he was staring, suddenly swung away and now faced the demon as well. Even the men who had called for the fighting to end unsheathed their blades.

Swooping down from the sky was a man. The stranger landed beside Drangar's companions and raised his hands. "Don't." The word was spoken softly, yet it rung through the entire courtyard. "She is here to help."

To his surprise the Sons complied. He, however, wasn't as willing to believe the stranger. "Why the fuck should I believe you?"

"Because," the demon answered with shaky voice, "I'm the only chance you truly got, son of Cat."

The reference wasn't lost on him, but he just wanted less riddles. Only moments ago, his agony had almost ended, now he had to live with it once more, and wanted the bastards responsible for Hesmera's death to tell the truth. He turned to Darlontor. "What is wrong with me?" His voice sounded less furious than desperate. "Why did you kill Hesmera? And what the fuck did you do to my mind?"

"Not here, boy," Darlontor said. The bastard Dalgor scoffed. "What?"

His cousin shook his head. "Tell the truth to all of us."

"You can't be serious."

Drangar looked from one to the other, wondering if this was yet another deception. He was surprised to find Dalgor's face lacking the scorn it had held months and years ago. "Yes,

I am, uncle. You have been avoiding the truth like poison, only revealing bits and pieces to us; maybe even lying to yourself. I am with Drangar on this one!" Was that really the same man who had not only threatened to kill him, but also promised to rape the Cahill women?

"So am I," voiced another elderly Son. And another.

The crowd parted for his friends, comrades. And the demon. He was wary of its presence. Kildanor, he saw, was still unconscious, and the wizard who had been protecting the fiend, he realized now, was no man at all, but an elf. "So am I," spoke the demon, its voice sounding stronger now.

"Best to come clean, uncle," Dalgor said soothingly.

In Darlontor's mind a battle was fought. Drangar saw it clearly on his adopted father's face. A twitching eyelid here, deep heavy breaths, and finally the Sons of Traksor's Priest High exhaled almost doubling over.

"Well?" Drangar said, ready for anything, hoping that all this would come to an end now. "What say you?"

"I was wrong about so many things," Darlontor began. "But the gravest mistake I ever made was deceiving you, Drangar." A brief pause, and then he spoke on. "You are Caitrin's and my son. I kept it so well hidden from everyone, even myself. Tried to deny it was true, because your existence is an affront to everything the Sons stand for. When you ran away, we had to act."

"Why?" Drangar asked, feeling cold all of the sudden. "Why did you try to kill me?"

Darlontor took a deep breath and with a blank face, looked at him. "Because on your thirtieth birthday you will become the vessel for the prince of demons, Turuuk."

To be continued in:

# SHATTERED WALLS
## Light in the Dark, Book 4

# About the Author

Ulff Lehmann has spent quite a while waiting on his Midlife Crisis, and decided he won't go there. For the past two decades he has been developing the stories he is now publishing. Born and bred in Germany, Ulff chose to write in English when he realized he had spent most of his adult life reading English instead of his mother tongue, and brings with him the oftentimes Grimm outlook of his country's fairy tales to his stories. A wordsmith with a poet's heart, Ulff's goal is to create a world filled with believable people.

According to his friends, his place is utter chaos and filled to the brim with books, CDs, and DVDs. In an earlier part of his life, Ulff turned his love for music outward, singing in two bands. Nowadays the only singing he does is in concert with his shower, and it thinks his voice is still acceptable. His passion for movies led him to begin Movie and TV studies at university, begin being the operative word. He didn't finish. Instead life pulled him this way and that until he finally understood he was a storyteller.

www.ingramcontent.com/pod-product-compliance
Lightning Source LLC
Chambersburg PA
CBHW072334020726
47506CB00004B/880